Boscombe

Moss Croft

Copyright © Moss Croft 2023

The moral right of Moss Croft to be identified as the author of this work has been asserted by him in accordance with the Copyright, Designs and Patents Act of 1988.

All rights reserved. No part of this publication may be reproduced, transmitted or stored in a retrieval system, in any form or by any means, without permission in writing from Moss Croft, nor be otherwise circulated in any form of binding or cover other than that in which it is published and without a similar condition being imposed on the subsequent purchaser.

ISBN: 9798378951468

The Novels of Moss Croft

Boscombe

Stickerhand

Ghost in the Stables

Crack Up or Play It Cool

The Flophouse Years

Rucksack Jumper

God Help the Connipians

Raspberry Jam

About the Author

Moss Croft is a pen name. Could be the chap who works nights at the petrol station, always wears a cap. Never seen that fella with a book in his hands, so I guess it's a longshot.

Contents

Chapter One:
A Week Without Children   Page   7

Chapter Two:
In the Lord's Knowing Gaze   Page 71

Chapter Three:
Punching a Boy in Sittingbourne   Page 121

Chapter Four:
A Halo is not a Cooking Pot   Page 177

Chapter Five:
The Changing Room   Page 231

Chapter Six:
Thrice Crowed the Cockerel   Page 289

Disclaimer

This is a work of fiction and resemblance to real persons or events is the result of unforeseen coincidence. Swear to God.

Chapter One:

A Week Without Children

Friday, 27 May 2016

'Capaldi-Clarke, how may I help you.' Lily doesn't think about the words as she says them. Could be a computerised answering service, so little attention is she lending to her job. The gentleman calling states his purpose, she has heard it before. The blah blah blah. Being a solicitor's receptionist isn't to do brain surgery. She probably passes muster even when her thoughts are a mile away. At the school gate. She guesses her children will be excited, looking forward to a week with their father. Even the drive to London might be a thrill. Lily has no car. Uses trains and buses pretty sparingly, seldom strays far from home.

It's only for the Whitsun holidays; they'll be back. She should relish the chance to be herself. Enjoy some downtime. It's hard for her—not that young anymore—eight years a mother, partner to Trent for three years before that. Home alone is the strangest feeling. On the other end of the telephone, the elderly gentleman tells her of the alterations he wishes to make to his will. She gives it half an ear.

'I can make you an appointment to come in. I can't change it. I'm not the solicitor.'

Pretty brusque; she registers her own tone of voice too late to do anything about it. The gentleman continues to ramble, telling her the value of his piano, his book collection. Lily pictures none of these, imagines only her children's journey: A35 out to the M27. She thinks it runs past the garden centre Alice took her to just over a week back. Nice place. Not that Lily has a garden to speak of, Alice bought a patio rose. The children's father never had a car when she and he shared bed and bills. Their London life. He's new to the game in her mind—hopes he drives safely—had a license back then, simply no car. Trent does some kind of delivery job these days. Should know what he's doing if he drives for a living. She glances at the clock on the wall. He's been holding the same job down for two years, that's longer than he ever managed in the days of Trent and Lily.

'You'll need to sign it too. Are you free to come in one day next week?' The gentleman had paused in his unattended monologue, so she jumped in. He confirms that he is available—she hopes she didn't cut him off, that her timing wasn't rude—they agree upon a day. Lily records it in the electronic calendar of Sharon Prior, the youngest solicitor in the firm. The greatest availability. While she logs it, Lily thinks of her own sparse plans for the week ahead. Bank holiday Monday and a couple of days annual leave which sounded good when she booked them. No idea what to do with them now. Meeting Alice tomorrow, and that's it. No plans. Nada. Mustn't sit and stew on what her children are doing in Shoreditch, they'll be back in Boscombe soon enough. It isn't a competition with Trent. And if it was, she'd win hands down; they love her like she does them. And Trent pulling his weight is a good thing. It's the change to her routine that bugs her. Not having them around, her Jo-jo and Ami.

'I'm sorry. Thank you,' she stares at the handset. 'Yes, goodbye Mr Lawton.' Is she fumbling her lines? Didn't listen to very much that the gentleman said to her. He could complain but the old ones seldom do. Never about her, it's one or two solicitors that worry about that stuff. Ruminating on her idling life would be a poor excuse if he did. Became the first. Lily glances across her desk, sees young Mr Clarke—Simon, the son of the company's founder—standing in the doorway. She fears he has appraised her inattention on the call, found her wanting in this role without which she would struggle to pay life's bills.

'Everything all right, Lily?'

There is nothing unkind or accusatory in his tone, perhaps he didn't spot how offhand she was. He could have been daydreaming himself for all Lily knows. 'Yes.' She smiles to herself as she sees, clutched in Mr Clarke's right hand, a green bikini. Shiny fabric within clipped cardboard packaging. 'Have you developed a daring dress sense, sir?' She seldom talks this way at work. Office decorum can be inhibiting.

'This,' he says, and laughs as he raises it up for Lily to see more clearly. 'Well, I suppose it's an explanation. Cindy asked me to pick it up at lunchtime. It's my belief that she will be the one wearing the darned thing.'

'It's lovely, sir,' Lily states. She feels relieved that he has not thought the comment an impertinence. Would never have made a joke if Gillian Garrett, the po-faced office manager, had been at her desk.

'Simon, please. Call me Simon, I have no expectations of a knighthood. Slimy solicitors don't merit them generally speaking.'

Lily's eyes return to her screen, she wonders if she should contradict his self-deprecation, while broadly agreeing with it. Slimy Simon.

'Enjoy the bank holiday, Lily,' he continues although her face is no longer in his gaze. 'Go to the beach. Get yourself one of these.'

Lily keeps looking at the computer screen. From the corner of her eye, she sees that he holds the green bikini aloft. 'Thank you, sir,' she intones. She doesn't jump to his orders outside of office duties, wishes she'd never made the facetious comment.

* * *

The ping of the microwave advises Lily that a plastic tray of once-frozen lasagne is ready to eat. She slides it from tray to plate, takes it across to the lounge to eat in front of Shoes and Slippers, the long-running soap opera she has never bothered to keep up with. It crosses her mind to be different, to utilise the time her children are with their father more constructively. The thread is lost and television no solution.

As she arrives at her seat, she hears the four musical notes which signify an incoming text. Hurriedly she places the plate on the arm of the sofa and steps back into the kitchen, picks up her wafer-thin phone from the worktop. The text is from Trent, confirming the safe arrival of Jo-jo and Ami in Shoreditch.

Traffic good, Ami sick once

Trent will have coped. The poor kid is no traveller, can go weeks without entering a car. Motion sickness was Lily's fate too, back when she was five. Ami's current age.

As she forks food into her mouth—television on but unattended—the landline rings. It is the rarest thing. Lily again puts the plate aside and steps into the hallway.

'Stephens,' she answers.

'Good evening, Lily. I hope you are well?'

'Mummy, yes. Hi.' She tenses ever so slightly; this is an unexpected call.

'And the two little ones?'

'With Trent from tonight. For a week. Whitsun holidays.'

'Oh heavens. Well, I suppose he is their father.'

Lily frowns at her mother's comment. 'He is Mummy, and he's doing his bit.'

'Yes.'

For a moment neither speaks.

'...and you have phoned because...?'

'...to talk to you, Lily. Why else? And you are right there is some news. Your father has a minor operation next Tuesday, at St Catherine's. Nasal polyps. They need removing, you see. Nothing for you to worry about, thankfully. It's a regular procedure, that's what the consultant said.'

'Good,' replies the daughter. 'Good that there's nothing to worry about.'

A further short silence sits between mother and daughter, an echo of the weeks that pass without word from one to another.

'Why does he need them taken out, Mummy?'

'Before they turn cancerous, I think. They aren't cancerous yet, so nothing to worry about.'

Lily murmurs assent, pleased that she is not required to worry. Uncertain if she really could, were the situation more serious. Her parents are not her children.

'When he's out and recovered, might you be able to bring the grandchildren up to see him, dear? To see us?'

'How long will Daddy be in hospital for?'

'Only the day, dear. Day surgery. You know how much we like to see them.'

'I don't know when, Mummy. We'll speak about it again. This week they're with Trent, back in Shoreditch.'

'Yes, you said.'

* * *

The television is on most of the evening but she pays it little more attention than she did Mr Lawton on the other end of the telephone call at work. Drinks a glass of supermarket wine, chooses not to pour herself a second. Impresses herself with her restraint. Thirds and fourths have been known to pass her lips on the night her children first take their leave. Lily won't get maudlin this time. By ten o'clock she takes herself and the novel she is reading to the bedroom.

The maisonette feels empty to her although it is not. Lily is in it still.

Saturday, 28 May 2016

Bowl of cereal and a shower, Lily pulls the front door closed behind her. Goes up Cooper Road feeling refreshed from a longer sleep than usual. Jo-jo likes to lie in but Ami never does. She wonders if she might have left home without a needed item, or maybe left an electrical appliance switched on that should be off. Thinking harder she knows nothing is amiss, these few days without children can be disorienting. Not a care in the world, and it is not her way of being. There was such a time a hefty eight years since, its abeyance changes a person.

The sun is bright, dazzling. Misleading too, a chilly sea breeze catches Lily by surprise. She should have brought a coat, not just a thin cardigan. Or maybe if you dress for spring, it will come!

Her friend, Alice, lives on the far side of the high street, further from the sea than Lily. They each have a daughter in reception class. Girls who shared playgroups when Lily first moved to Boscombe. That took time getting used to. Moving away from the louder mums of London to homespun Alice. Lily fluctuated between loving and hating her new life, unkindly thought her new friend boring in the early weeks. She's turned full circle, won't be going back to London, and young Alice—ten fewer years on this Earth—is a true friend. She doesn't envy her the nice house or the reliable husband, trappings Lily must live without. Pleased for Alice.

As she rings the doorbell, Lily lets a smile crease her face. The deep timbre of its sound, two sustaining notes, bring to mind old films set in fifties America. A nice prospect, she and Alice will spend the morning together: girls about town.

* * *

Boscombe

They take the pretty route down to the sea. Alice wears shorts and T-shirt; the sun may warm the day later, right now she has goosebumps. 'I'm getting a tan,' she says and Lily laughs. 'You'll always be white, dressed in jeans.'

Lily nods, agrees. Always has been, always will be.

The sea is limbering up for the bank holiday weekend. Every fourth or fifth person they pass seems to be jogging, running. Taking a dose of exercise. In the distance Lily sees an impromptu fitness class, women mostly, limbering up on the sand. Stretching muscles and holding poses which she doubts she could match. As they draw near to Boscombe pier, they pass fixed exercise apparatus. 'Should we try it, Alice?' She points at a man and woman beginning to grapple with the equipment.

'Bloody bonkers,' says her friend.

Lily chooses not to contradict her. Sees an appeal in it. These fitness buffs look pretty warm, and they do it without coats.

They walk between the piers. If the day warms it is by the tiniest fraction. At Bournemouth pier they go up the stairs to the café bar. Lily orders two coffees and takes out her purse. Alice pushes her hand down, insists that she will pay.

'Which table are you girls sitting at?' asks the barman. Dark-haired, tattooed; he looks them up and down.

'We can carry them across,' Lily tells him.

'No, it'll be a few minutes. Just point.'

Alice jumps in. 'Out on the terrace, that side.'

'Are you sure?' asks Lily when they are going through the door to the colder outside.

The terrace is busy with coffee drinkers. Lovely views, looking west across occupied sand. Families starting to plant themselves upon it. A few children and water-sports enthusiasts in wet suits, the rest keeping coats on. The sun dazzles, promises a warmth they have yet to feel. 'Love it,' she replies, and Alice hoists up her T-shirt, sunning her midriff. An old man and woman at a table seem to point at her. Old people in coats. 'It's summer,' she says, in their direction. They return her assertion with a smile.

'You're mad, daft-mad,' Lily tells her.

As the two girls sit at the only vacant table, Alice rearranges her clothing, lets the T-shirt fall back down. It really isn't warm yet. As she is smoothing her ruffled clothing, Lily catches Alice looking at two young men in cycling Lycra who have just stepped out on to the terrace.

'Do you mind if we join you?' asks the taller of the men. No other table is vacant, and the girls sit beside empty chairs.

'Please do,' gushes Alice, patting the seat to her right. Her enthusiasm prompts Lily to nudge her shoulder, snort a laugh into her ear.

The two men put small packs on their chairs, the taller—unshaven, his clothing exposing muscular arms and legs—murmurs a thank you. 'Yeah, very good of you,' says the other, whose attire covers him more fully. 'It's sixteen,' he says to his friend, referring to the table number. 'We're just ordering food.' He nods at the belongings, implicitly requesting that Lily and Alice mind them. Do not concede the seats to others.

'We can watch your stuff for you. No problem.'

'Jesus, Alice,' says Lily when the boys have gone back inside, 'you sound like you're gagging for cyclists. And you were so happily married the last time I looked.'

'I'm not gagging for anyone, and it's you who isn't married, petal. A little male company will do you good.'

'Cyclists are too skinny,' says Lily.

'And so are you. Which one do you want?'

Lily looks blankly back at her.

'I'll talk to the other; it's all the same to me. I'm not on the market.'
'And I'm not a side of beef.'

'Go tall,' Alice instructs her friend as she sees the two men heading back towards them. The one allotted to Lily moves a pair of sunglasses from one hand to the other. Momentarily puts the temple tip of the glasses' arm between his lips.

'I've got ten years on him,' whispers Lily.

* * *

The two men sit on the vacant chairs, both glance at the girls. The one in the short Lycra pants, the taller, rubs the back of his calf. Lily thinks it a nervous tic, or he is absent-mindedly reminiscing about an old injury. Ridiculous! There is no way on Earth that Alice is setting her up on a date. Not with a young lad who intends only to drink coffee on Bournemouth pier.

'Anything good on the menu.' Alice breaks the silence.

'What?' The man leans forward, stops rubbing. 'Yes. It's eggs for me.'

'I'm Alice,' she says, thrusting a hand towards the shorter, more decently clothed, of the two men.

'Bernard,' he tells her. 'And this is Johnny.'

'Yes, I'm Jonathan. Johnny.' He too shakes Alice's hand.

Lily is grinning now. Recalibrated her thinking, reckons these young men are barely in their twenties. She has fifteen years on them minimum. They may be within five or six of young Alice. Shaking her head, she stretches out a hand. Does as her friend has done.

'This is Lily,' Alice tells the group. 'My best friend, Lily.'

'Are you waiting for food?' says Johnny.

'No, just coffees for us,' answers Lily. 'Have you cycled from far away?'

'Barely started.' Johnny again takes the sunglasses from his nose, looks intently at Bernard as if seeking permission to talk. 'I cycled from Littledown; Bernie lives in town anyway. The big plan was to do a round of Purbeck but matey here is a wee bit hungover.'

Bernard laughs at this, no denial. 'Eggs and coffee, eggs and coffee,' he says under his breath, Johnny smiling back at the phrase.

Lily glances at Alice, her facial expression enquiring what she is making of these immature non-contenders. 'And your plan B?'

'Eggs and coffee,' says Bernard at greater volume.

'Maybe cycle off alone,' says Jonathan.

'Is this your regular weekend thing?' asks Alice.

'Yeah, he's always hungover.'

'I am not. We ran up to Romsey last Saturday.'

'Ran?' says Lily.

'On the bikes, cycled.'

'You must be very fit.'

'Super-fit,' says Alice. 'Look at them!'

Lily tries a subtle shake of her head when Alice catches her eye. Tone down the pointless flirting, she hopes to communicate. 'What do you get up to when you're not cycling?'

'Or drinking?' adds Alice.

Jonathan strokes his two- or three-day stubble. 'Looking,' he replies. 'Bernard is the smart one. He's doing his finals in a couple of weeks. At the university here.'

'You're a student!' Alice sounds ridiculously enthusiastic to Lily's thinking. 'What's the course?'

'Business.' He is suddenly shy, says the word as if it is shameful. 'Just business.'

'Good stuff, good prospects.'

The boy nods at Alice's endorsement.

The other man, the one Alice has designated as Lily's prey, looks out across the sand. His head moves fractionally up and down, eyes following a paddleboarder on the waves.

'And what do lookers do?' Lily asks of Johnny. Wishes to hear him explain his cryptic assertion.

'I've done this and that, I'm looking for work.'

Lily nods, tries to look as sympathetic as she can.

'I do some delivery stuff but it's zero hours. Bicycle courier. I like it well enough, just the money's crap.'

'Johnny was working at a carpet place in Southbourne. He's a skilled fitter and everything, it's just the company folded six months back,' says Bernard.

'Too bad,' says Alice. 'Can I say, you're not from round here.' She puts a West Country burr into her voice as she says it. Not always there but a speech pattern she easily falls into. Dorset born and bred. 'Lily isn't either, it's okay and everything.'

Bernard nods, no argument with her central point. They both have West Midland accents. 'Our families are in Bromsgrove, I'm here to study and my mate followed.'

'Good on you. It's the best place, isn't it?' Both men smile concurrence with Alice. Sitting on a veranda overlooking sea and sand: everyone loves Bournemouth.

The barman comes across, coffees for the girls. 'Ladies,' he says, placing the drinks in front of them. He glances quickly at the young cyclists, eyes straight back to Alice and Lily, smile tumbled away. 'Can I fetch you anything else?' he asks, pointedly avoiding eye contact with the boys. Both girls shake their heads. As he leaves, Lily catches her friend's eye and stifles a giggle.

Before either has taken a sip of their drink, a young waitress in an old-fashioned black pinafore dress places a tray containing two plates of egg on toast and two large coffees in front of the cyclists. 'Are you waiting for food?' she asks the girls and, again, they shake their heads.

The boys tell the girls about growing up on the edge of Birmingham. They've known each other since they were toddlers. Their parents are friends, neighbours, live just a few houses apart. The taller boy, Jonathan, is a year older than Bernard. Teachers held him back a year in secondary school. 'I might have felt stupid, not being good enough for the next year, but I thought I was dead clever, finally sharing a class with Bernie here.' The pattern has continued: they went drinking together so often in Bernie's first year here at university that Johnny lost the job he'd secured to support the move. Bernie tells the girls that drinking heavily had little impact on his academic performance. 'Universities factor it in for first years.' Lily laughs and Alice just looks puzzled.

Losing his job was a wake-up call for Johnny. Within months he good as quit alcohol. Drinks only rarely and very little. Bernard wears a grin while his friend explains the merits of sobriety.

'That's really good,' Alice tells Jonathan.

'She can't talk,' says Lily. 'Really, she can't.'

Johnny's love of cycling has come to dominate his decisions. 'My bike is at the centre of my heart.' Lily thinks it the strangest expression, wonders if she could be similarly enthusiastic about cycling or running. Declaring such a love to near strangers sounds a bit terminal.

Bernie has a job lined up, starts in August. He will work in recruitment at a small agency in Poole. When Lily tells him that it proves the course has been advantageous—worth the debt—he shakes his head. 'My dad is mates with one of the partners.'

Alice comes clean. 'I'm married, boys,' she says, showing her wedding ring. They smile; Lily imagines that they spotted it from the off. 'Lily, on the other hand...' and as Alice speaks the older girl laughs, makes a gesture with a finger across her mouth. Zip it.

'Are we going to Purbeck or not?' the taller boy asks the shorter.

'I'm egged up, I'll give it a go,' says the hungover one.

A Week Without Children

'Brilliant sharing a table with you,' says Jonathan.

'Brilliant,' his friend confirms.

They pick up their belongings and leave. Gone without an exchange of phone numbers; no planned reconvening of the foursome or any bi-gendered subset derived from it.

'They were very nice, you've really got to flirt more, Lily-petal,' says Alice when the boys are out of earshot.

She lets out a splutter of pent-up laughter. 'Alice, you're bonkers. I felt like their mother. And they are gay ...' She looks closely at her friend, her smiling friend. '...you saw it too, right?'

'Johnny was well into you. Not gay, petal. Loved your whole pale-skinned goddess look.'

Lily laughs at Alice. 'You have got to be kidding. He follows a friend to university just to work as a carpet fitter...' They both leave the thought hanging a moment. '...if he's lucky. In and out of work. Do you think they've had a tiff?'

'Lily, what do you mean? They're off cycling together.'

'They are but think about it. His bike is the love of his life now. How anyone knows what the love of their life is when they still suck their thumb is beyond me.'

'He never sucks...'

'Metaphorically. He's a baby boy. I've got too many years on him, and a mild interest in the opposite sex. And I own a bicycle—got to tell the truth about this—there is no love between us. I keep it in a shed.' Lily giggles as she speaks. 'Johnny is an out-of-work sunglasses-sucking egg eater, I'm afraid. Not really boyfriend material. Not for a mother of two.'

'Metaphorically indeed. You talk like you should be the one at university.'

The two girls leave the café, head up through the park towards the town. This day is a treat for both. They don't argue over boys. Alice loves Martin, and Lily—like Johnny vocationally—is looking. Doing it without expectation. She has children, responsibilities, no longer the dissolute girl of her teenage years. Boscombe is not Sittingbourne.

* * *

As they walk, Alice asks Lily, 'Do you miss him?' She does not say his name aloud but the object of the question is certainly Trent.

Boscombe

Lily reflects upon it before answering. She thinks Alice perceptive, caught her mood. Her ex is only an occasional subject for them to speak of. Lily even thinks that Alice talks less of Martin than she might, for fear of striking an unintended note of glee. Life's lucky dip has favoured Alice. Love—such as it was for Lily—is a distant memory and she worries that she has become hardened by its absence. Since living in Boscombe she has poured maternal love upon her children, received its asymmetrical return. Lily shares more with this friend than she does with another living soul; she is not a natural sharer. Some days, parting from Trent feels like escaping the asylum, no longer living poor and frantic in East London. Conversely, she also thinks her better destiny—an equal with whom to share this life—has slipped from view. No longer possible. 'I'm good at living alone. Still to decide if I like it, mind you.'

Alice queries how alone she is, then acknowledges that Jo-jo and Ami are dependents, not intimates.

'I don't miss Trent,' Lily clarifies, 'I made my mind up and I don't change it. But I didn't decide to be alone; it was just a consequence. So, I must be missing something, mustn't I?' They walk through a stretch of the lower gardens in silence, until Lily smiles at Alice, indicates she did not intend to dampen spirits.

'You should have flirted with the cyclists more,' her friend chips in.

'I said I'm missing something. Didn't say I'd lie down naked on Boscombe Beach until I get it!'

'Ha!' laughs Alice. 'That would definitely work.'

* * *

In the town's bookshop, Alice sticks to the children's section. She chooses a book for Bryony, her three-year-old. Crocodile related. Seeks out Lily's advice on suitable reading for Wendy. Her older daughter is Ami's age. Lily answers, and then she enters a private world searching and choosing reading matter for herself. Hands clutching two, three and then four books at a time.

'You must have loved school,' whispers Alice.

'You know I hated it. I'm learning what I never did then.'

They pay at the counter, the avid reader refusing all offers by Alice to contribute to her purchase. A fat Barbara Kingsolver novel set in Africa, Lily's treat to herself.

A Week Without Children

* * *

It is seven-thirty on Saturday evening with no Ami to bathe and no Jo-jo chattering away. Lily idles in front of television programmes that hold no interest for her. The screaming pop music fare served on the airwaves belongs to a generation which has come after her. To Alice, Jonathan and Bernie. Lily looks questioningly at the wine bottle opened yesterday, then takes it up into her hands. Before she has poured a drop, the phone rings. The unlikely landline once more. She takes bottle and glass with her into the hallway.

'Stephens.' She recognises the returned voice. Feels disorientation in it. 'Mr Clarke,' she says, 'am I needed at work?' Solicitors don't have emergencies, less so the kind requiring the assistance of a receptionist. This Saturday-night call from a partner is unprecedented.

'No' he replies, 'I'm not ringing you about work.'

This is odd, work is all that he and she have to speak of, and that only sporadically. Dictation, audio tapes, that is the extent of their relationship. She wonders momentarily if he has news of her children in Shoreditch but that makes even less sense.

'What is it, sir?' she asks with bewildered urgency.

'Lily, Lily,' Simon Clarke says in a gentler tone than she is used to hearing him deploy. 'I know your situation, sympathise a great deal. I understand that your children are...' He intonates this statement into the question it answers. '...with their father?' Lily acknowledges that this is true. 'I heard it in the office, and thought you might like some company on a Saturday night. It sounds like you're all on your own.'

Lily slides onto the floor beside the telephone. Wine bottle unopened, a clean glass on the carpet beside her. Takes a breath before replying to this unexpected advance. 'How did you get my phone number?'

'Contact numbers are on employee home screens, Lily. I'm a senior manager. Have access. Would you like me to come over? You're such a bright girl, I'd like to keep you company... I'd love it.'

'Sir, I don't think...'

'It's Simon, Lily. Please call me Simon.'

'I don't think it is best to mix business and...' She pauses, unsure that she should even be debating this point. '...not best, sir.'

'Business and pleasure, Lily, we all need pleasure. It would be mine, my pleasure, to come to see you...' He pauses as if expecting her rejoinder. '...if you're alone. It is not my wish to intrude or to interrupt. You are alone?'

Lily doesn't answer. The silence across the open airwaves exerts a pressure within her head. She feels the slow drumming of the pulse in her temple.

'I'm in the neighbourhood, Lily, calling from the car. It would be no trouble. I'd love us to meet up this evening.'

She feels a surge of anger. Lily has always kept a distance from this charmless man. Why the hell she made the bikini comment on Friday, she'll never know. She rises up from her cross-legged posture, stretches the cord of the phone as she walks three paces to her front door. Slots the privacy chain into its small metal rail, pushes across a high bolt which she last touched during her first week in this maisonette. Must've been three years ago. 'Where is Cindy tonight, sir?' she asks, grateful to have trawled up his wife's name from within her churning brain.

'M-my wife is at her sisters,' he says slowly, then laughs, 'I have the night off. Shall we make a date of it? I can take you somewhere if you'd prefer.'

'No, sir.'

'Not tonight?'

'No, sir, not...'

'Look, it's Simon. You can call me that at work, you know? I gather...' Simon Clarke pauses, hesitates before the drone of his voice resurges. '...Mrs Garrett has outlined your situation. Gillian Garrett. I understand you have no man in your life at present; I think I could be the one to fill that void.'

'Simon, sir...' She feels the beating of her angry heart. Wants to swear at him, resists only because he is a partner in the firm she works for. He is her employer, he and three others. '...have you discussed the matter with your wife? Is Cindy also keen that you should *fill* my void?'

There is a brief silence and then she hears the click which tells her that Simon Clarke has ended the call. Lily remains standing in the hallway, looks at the telephone handset. Peers into its earpiece from where this extraordinary conversation invaded her maisonette.

A Week Without Children

Briefly speculates that she has gone mad, imagined the whole thing, then the sound of his voice is back inside her head. His plummy, ingratiating, wheedling little cocksure voice. She feels a hatred for him as she never has at work. Raising herself up from the hallway carpet, neck of wine bottle and stem of glass held in her left hand, Lily mouths the word, shit. Says it out loud, quietly but audibly. 'Shit.' She calculates that this unsolicited call may cost her a needed job. She cannot picture working in proximity to him. Not now. Simon Clarke holds all the aces; could deal her a P.45. 'I'm in the neighbourhood,' he told her. What kind of creep drives around the corner before making an unsolicited call like that? His wife at her sister's.

At the kitchen table, Lily picks up her mobile, texts a quick, ***Can I call you,*** to Alice. She finally starts to pour wine into her glass — wonders if it is wise to drink it, what if that pompous piece of shit actually comes around — and as if by magic, her mobile is ringing.

'Alice,' says Lily into her phone, 'Alice.'

'What is it, petal?'

Inexplicably, Lily is crying, sobbing, weeping. She did not know that she felt this fraught, this upset by a stupid phone call. Tears say it landed on some nerve or other.

* * *

Alice sits on the lounge floor opposite Lily, holding a half-drunk glass of wine. She has heard the full story, understands the dilemma. Spat a bit of sympathy bile out herself. Vitriol about the sinister Simon Clarke whom she has never met.

Lily is starting to laugh again. 'I'm sorry to have made you come over; Martin will be wanting you back.'

'He's not been zoned in on by a horrible boss; he can manage without me for an hour, Lily-petal.'

'Yes, but I'm fine. Really.'

Alice slaps Lily's knee lightly. 'I was thinking,' she says, 'Martin's boss is actually a woman. He answers to an Angie. Angela Keeley. Do you think all bosses prey on their underlings?'

'I'm an independent woman, Alice, if Clarke thinks of me as an underling, it's his bloody problem. I'll never be under him. Never ever.'

Alice laughs throatily. 'Got that. But Martin might like it, being subservient to Angie. She's attractive with it, wears suits like a man, fitted for her figure. She's a lot older than me...'

'I'm a lot older than you, it means nothing. Martin loves you, Alice, surely you know that?'

'Yes, but it's different for men. Bloody Simon Clarke probably tells his wife he loves her, it didn't stop him phoning you, did it?'

'Martin is a better class of person, all round. Don't you be worrying about Martin.'

'I'm not. I was just thinking...' She laughs self-consciously. '...how would you be, Lily, if you were the boss? A few pretty boys in the workplace. Would you look up their numbers, addresses, call them. Stalk them?'

'I would not! And I'm not cut out to be a boss. I hate being told what to do, and I don't like telling others either. I'm not a hypocrite.'

'Oh, I think I'd call them all, if I was the boss. Call the good-looking ones. I wouldn't now, of course, I've got Martin and he is brilliant, like you say. But if I was alone, sex-starved, and could just call up one from a list. Worth a try, wouldn't you say?'

'Power corrupts,' Lily scolds Alice. 'And I hope you don't mean I should have given that sod Clarke a try. Me being alone and sex starved...'

'God, no! Not you, not with him. You're nothing like that, Lily. I know you're not alone by choice but you're not one to just run with anybody. I would be, I need Martin to hold me in place.'

Lily laughs openly, puts a hand upon her friend's arm. 'Alice, Alice, you told me...' She regroups her thoughts. '...married at twenty-one, Martin was only the second fella you even went with. You're imagining yourself to be some kind of slapper, and you really aren't.' She hugs her friend while continuing to laugh at her.

'Married because I was preggers,' Alice says pensively. 'Hey-ho, it all worked out fine,' she adds in a brighter register. 'Lucky me.'

'You are lucky.'

'You can't have him.'

'Of course, I can't,' says Lily, 'he has you and Angie to take care of.'

Before long, Alice is away to her husband. Lily, alone in the maisonette as before, feeling like her old self, her true self. A thunderclap stronger than whatever it was that undid her. Drew out the tears she never knew were there to be cried.

A Week Without Children

Sunday, 29 May 2016

Everybody does it, she could be one of them. Lily laces up her trainers at nine forty-five in the morning. Wearing black shorts and a Bournemouth AFC football shirt. It was a free gift at a promotion party that Martin, Alice's husband, insisted they all attend a year ago. The local club getting into the premiership. She doesn't care for football, spotted that it was a big deal for a town like this. Went along. Thinks she looks okay in the kit. Not too masculine, she hopes. She wears her hair in a single ponytail, the black sheaf splays a little. A roving black stripe amid the fixed ones on the shirt. It flops across the tiny children's rucksack that she wears.

She opens her front door, smiling quietly at the freedom her children's absence is affording her. Door closed, and off she runs. Alice will think her crazy but a hell of a lot of people do it every day.

Her pace is okay. Lily is reasonably fit, walks everywhere, cycles a little. Swims in the sea come summertime. May have her first splash of the year later today. The beach was a big attraction for her when choosing Boscombe three years ago. Never went when she was growing up, hardly at all. Her mother hated it, grumbled that the sand got everywhere. Now, Lily takes Jo-jo and Ami down to it throughout summer, on weekends or after school. Six hundred yards from home, beach is a must.

As she comes towards the cliff top, she turns for the ornamental gardens. Seeing the tall trees in view, she ups her pace, finds the energy to race a little, padding down her trainers with the certainty that she is indeed a runner. She notices the older dog walkers, a pair of young cyclists. For a second, she imagines it will be Johnny and Bernie, but it isn't. Johnny's lack of interest in her was a good thing. A kid. And she wishes the young cyclists well—ever polite, no creepy phone calls—why Alice blinked her eyelashes at them, she'll never know.

Down the hill Lily jogs; the air is not yet warm, and the running, the adrenaline, the raised heartbeat, gives her a feeling of invigoration. Should have done it sooner. She realises that her pace will take her past another jogger. The back of the girl's golden legs, the matching mauve shorts and tank top, suggest an outdoor fiend. Is this allowed? Is it discourteous? She can't resist it, increasing her pace ever so slightly—not wishing to run alongside or engage with this meticulously dressed athlete—Lily feels a thrill as she passes. She turns her head for the quickest of glances, tries not to look smug.

'Hi,' says the jogger.

She is young—younger than Alice—slim, fit. Perhaps she's already run a hundred miles and Lily is misguided to imagine it a competition. 'Hi,' she answers. 'Great morning.' Although she is ahead, she eases her pace, regrets trying to show off. Lily is new to jogging. Barely half a mile in.

The other girl finds her pace, they are beside each other, she turns her fine-boned face towards Lily. 'How far do you go?'

'When I'm out of juice, I stop.'

'Do you do all the stretches?'

Lily is not certain what this means. She recalls the fixed apparatus close to the pier, imagines the girl is referring to some limbering up or winding down. 'Mostly just run,' she replies, a truth this morning and she has not so much as suggested that it is a long-standing routine.

'Do you want to try?' asks the young girl.

Lily nods as she runs. 'Show me.'

* * *

Boscombe beach glistens the palest yellow beneath the early morning sun. The tiny waves lapping up the sand make only the faintest sound. Lily sees a dispersed squadron of young men and women, the occasional old one in their number, using the late spring morning to exercise. Tone their bodies. She is on the verge of joining their ranks.

Caroline—the name the girl has shared—is standing on the sand. Hands on hips. She wears better than a football shirt, has a sweatband coloured the exact same shade of mauve as her T-shirt and shorts. It doesn't keep her luscious fair hair from her face, provides a fashionable accompaniment. Lily sees the men on the promenade looking at the pair of them. Guesses that few rest on her, the young girl who knows all the stretches must catch every eye.

'Sit-ups first,' says Caroline.

Lily nods sagely as if she knows this is the correct way to start

A Week Without Children

exercising on a beach, and Caroline drops to the sand, initially hugs her knees up to her body then begins to stretch her sunned legs out to the front of her. Lily follows suit—smiles—not played any such physical copycatting since primary school.

The younger girl has her hands behind her head, legs bent a little, she leans back to the sand, and then pulls herself up by her stomach muscles. Lily does likewise. Quite easy, she finds.

'Keep it up,' says the girl as she does the manoeuvre for the seventh and eighth time. Her tone of voice is all encouragement. Lily started to struggle at three; she sees that her initial thought—stretches are a doddle—was premature. 'It's all stomach muscles. If we didn't, we wouldn't use them much,' says Caroline.

'Oh, I think I used them for giving birth; suppose it was years ago.'

'No!' says Caroline. 'You don't look like you have children.'

'I do. Plenty of mothers look like me.'

'Maybe, but surely not years ago. Are you really any older than me?'

'Sweet little liar,' says Lily. The kid is as young as the boys yesterday, the cyclists. She's easier company to Lily's mind.

Caroline is back on her feet. 'Can you do this?' she asks, bending down and placing both palms on the sand while keeping her legs straight.

'Probably not,' answers Lily. She stands and dips. Touches the sand but not flat-palmed, not with the posture and poise that Caroline manages.

'I'm twenty-four, Lily,' she tells her between dips. 'You're what? Twenty-five? Twenty-six?'

'You're my new bestie,' she laughs. 'I couldn't fool a blind man I was that. Add ten, Caroline.'

'No!' An astonished look crosses her face, and Lily wonders if the girl is acting. 'I'm not killing you with this routine, am I?'

'Makes no difference; I'm close to the dead place, being the age I am, aren't I?'

Caroline laughs, sits down on the sand. 'Let's talk.'

'Where did you run from?' asks Lily as she drops beside her, accidentally sliding with the curvature of the sand so their buttocks touch. Extracts herself a few decent inches.

'Christchurch,' answers Caroline.

'Oh hell, you must be ever so fit. I only live a half mile up the road.'
'Not to worry, Lily, you can jog back to mine.'
'I bloody can't!' she laughs. 'This is my first day doing this...'
'No!' Caroline again expresses surprise. Lily is pretty certain it is genuine this time. 'You must work out, look at you.'
'Fetching and carrying for two little ones—well, Jo-jo is eight now—it's a physical life, it really is.'

Caroline asks one or two questions. She learns that Trent is no longer 'on the scene.' Then she asks Lily if she has a boyfriend.

'It's not that simple,' she says, thinking what she always thinks. Men don't want a girlfriend with two kids. 'Actually, it's dead simple. A straight no. How about you?'

'I do and I don't.'

Lily looks directly into the pretty face of the fair-haired girl, awaiting an explanation for her oscillating state.

'I did but now I don't. I keep dumping him. Really, I do it quite often.'

'Keep dumping him,' Lily echoes. 'Do you do it like a Friday night treat?'

Caroline grimaces. 'I think I love him but he's not much good. My parents hate him, he's not reliable. He was a boxer for a time. Glad to say he's stopped all that. Frightening to watch him at it.'

'Whoa, whoa,' Lily interrupts. 'I have you down as a bit...' She takes her eyes, looks straight at her green irises. '...middle class, no offence...'

'None taken.'

'...aren't boxers all thugs. You can do better...'

'Don't talk like my mother. They're not all thugs although Clive just might be one. I'm a hopeless judge when it comes to him. And I did dump him a week ago. I've not given in to his texting and calling yet.'

Lily, with mock sincerity, gives Caroline a lecture, the central tenet of which is that dumped doesn't mean see you later. 'That's the point of dumping. No more. Don't pull old pizza out of the food waste, Caroline. You put it in there for a reason. I got shot of Trent, and I had to extract myself and the two kids. And he never even boxed.'

Caroline stops smiling. 'I don't know what I should do,' she says plaintively. 'Connections, we make them and can't shake them, don't you think?'

A Week Without Children

'You love him, Caroline, foolishly perhaps but there it is. I can't make connections, that seems to be my trouble.' At this point it crosses Lily's mind to tell the girl about Mr Clarke. The swine who ruined last night for her. Doing it with a five-minute phone call.

'What are you thinking?' asks Caroline.

Perceptive young girl, and so Lily tells the story, admits the shock—the sheer imposition of it—made her cry. Not on the phone, only afterwards. She runs her through it all, word by word near as she can remember. Even the call to Alice after the bastard had hung up.

'I'm sorry, but...' Caroline is starting to smile as she says this, although she has attended the story closely, seriously.

'What's funny, Caroline?'

'...I'm sorry that you cried, that you were upset but you were brilliant. Told the dirty sod to consult his wife before harassing you again. Take a bow, Lily.'

She likes the reply: this girl really gets her.

Caroline rummages in the small rucksack Lily has laid on the sand. It's a bit overfamiliar, going through her stuff, she says nothing. Shares a similar intimacy with Alice, although they've known each other for more than thirty minutes. The new friend pulls out Lily's red bikini top, nods approval, then seems to have found what she needed, swipes the screen of her smartphone.

'Hey,' says Lily.

'I'm punching my number in. I'm your new bestie, remember.'

Lily laughs. 'You don't look like a phone thief.'

There is no breach of etiquette beyond the speed with which this girl and Lily have arrived at a point of understanding. Lily picks the bikini top from the bag, 'Are you coming in, Caroline?' she asks.

'Not really equipped. You should have told me it was a swim party before I set off.'

'I can't resist it; I can swim more when my little ones are away.' When Caroline says nothing, Lily adds, 'I'd rather they were home, of course.'

They talk on a little, Caroline glancing at her watch a couple of times. Then she gets up to jog the miles back to Christchurch. 'Sunday lunch awaits.' Her parents are taking her to a hotel by the riverside. They sound affluent to Lily. The two girls exchange a hug. Lily has enjoyed meeting her, however little they have in common. She is in a different league at jogging and push-ups, and her running clothes were no freebie from a corporate party. Still lives with her parents.

* * *

After the sweet girl has left, Lily takes herself to a small showering cubicle on the promenade, enters and pulls the door to. Changes into her swimwear. Just the top—vermilion red—she will swim in the black shorts. It's long been a habit of hers. When she's ready, she opens the door a fraction, sees there are few people swimming this far up the beach. It is early and most are closer to the pier and coffee shops. She steps away from the cubicle, walks with head raised. She thinks she looks okay, slim. That girl—Caroline—admired the top, although she didn't see it on Lily. Wouldn't guess her twenty-six if she did. Lily closes her bag and carries it back out, onto the promenade and down the beach. Swimming's fun; if there are eyes upon her—a handsome fella who likes what he sees—it could cap a nice morning. Slim chance but it must happen to someone. To Caroline every time she steps into the eyeline of men.

* * *

The shock of the cold takes the breath from her lungs. Quickly, she finds her rhythm. Forward crawls into the oncoming waves. The only other swimmer close by is a man who might be her own age. He wears little goggles. Makes his face look as if he is repairing a watch, not undertaking an athletic activity. The pair swim out and back, as if in synchronisation, although neither knows the other. Lily finds herself holding her shorts, ensuring they are not drooping as she stands at the end of her swim. Waterlogged but she is decent. 'Flipping cold,' she tells her erstwhile companion who stands some fifteen feet away.

'Not if you swim every day.'

She tries not to be obvious as she looks at him; the man is as white as she, muscular. Hair in a tiny ponytail, a tattoo on one arm, another on a leg. Words written upon his body which she cannot read from where she stands. The man walks out of the shallows, strides up the beach. Lily thought he looked okay, sensed no return of interest although they spent ten- or fifteen-minutes splashing in close proximity.

A Week Without Children

Back on the beach, she has no towel. Shivers, shrugs. Well under a mile from home. She pulls the Bournemouth AFC shirt from her small rucksack, pulls it on, knowing that the bikini top will dampen it in seconds. She sets off for home at the slowest of paces. A running motion while barely running at all, thoughts of the warm shower on Cooper Road.

* * *

Early evening, and the cheapest main course on the Indian takeaway menu is only half-eaten. It tasted good. Lily affords herself a treat like this when the children are away. Microwave the remainder tomorrow lunchtime. It's a consolation prize; she misses them, little Ami and growing Jo-jo. Jogging felt good, being alone, not so much. She wanted Trent to share parenting during that first year of separation when he was too angry to try. She doesn't wish the standoff back, much better the children see their father. Jo-jo hated it that year, poor kid. Never ever falling out like that again. Long stopped loving him but Trent always loved the kids.

She has not brought out the wine bottle this evening. Thought about it, the conclusion was no. Clarke won't call, that's not the worry. She gave him short enough shrift. How to behave around him in the future troubles her. He might prove vindictive. Subtly so. She has contemplated making a noise, telling the other partners. Shaming the slime-ball. The snag is that her office is not a Saturday morning stroll with Alice. She can't imagine talking about it with anyone in there. At work, she is the unassuming receptionist, treated well enough most of the time. It can be patronising. She's a 'star' and a 'trouper,' and those who say it drive Audi's and BMW's while Lily budgets for bus tickets. Stars and troupers must put up with a lot of shit.

She seldom drinks at all when the children are home. A single glass after Jo-jo settles, weekends only. She's noticed herself drinking more when they are away. Can't bear the idea of being the boozy woman, that isn't her. Not the twenty-sixteen model, anyhow. Alice drinks like a fish, Lily did the same at her age. Times change. She's long stopped letting her hair down, and she used to be really good at it.

Weekend gone, bank holiday tomorrow. The boys in the café were Alice's thing, funny but pointless. The call from Simon Clarke is best forgotten; she should never have cried. Alice was a treasure, dropping everything, coming around. She remembers he—the unwanted caller—quoted Mrs Garrett, who she has occasionally trusted with personal information. Whatever figment the old cow told Simon Clarke she will have embellished it with her own bitterness.

Lily liked the girl, Caroline, fit young thing whose number is now sitting in her phone's contact list. She thinks she'll text her, knows she will need to do so soon or it'll never happen. Her stomach was something else. Toned. She had encouraged Lily to touch it, feel the firmness. Muscles on her and still a petite girl. Running and getting fit looks like the way to go.

* * *

Later in the evening, Lily succumbs. Her old laptop open on the dining table, her profile has been on Date Local for fully eighteen months. Very seldom looks at it. It only happened against her better— and Alice's most insistent—judgement. Even the profile picture, showing Lily standing with one hand on her hip in front of her own sofa, is daft. She thinks it suggestive of the world's least inspiring furniture showroom. It is why she is messaged by cranks and only cranks. Alice once told her not to judge those she had not yet met. Good advice in the wider world although Alice met Martin through the friend of a cousin. Never tried any of the sad cases who post their overblown profiles on Date Local.

'Love your goth look. I'm free Tuesdays and Thursdays.' This is a message from Guy, a local boy, man really, whose own profile picture shows him with a pint of beer in hand and another on the bar beside him. She contemplates replying, correcting his assertion that she is a goth. Black hair and pale skin can be the most natural thing. Could add that goth music is shit; thing is, she never actually replies to any messages on this site. Replied only once, fella called Ben.

That was some strange date. It happened between Christmas and New Year which she now considers an absurd time to go on a first date with anyone. First after Trent whom she took up with nearly a dozen years ago. Trent collected the children on Boxing Day lunchtime; two nights later she was in Pascale's, the Mexican place on Southbourne Grove, with Ben of Date Local. The culmination of a month of poorly executed Facebook flirting.

Online, Ben had complimented the appearance of the furniture showroom woman, and told her he was a music producer. He sent sound files attached to emails. Well-trained school choirs and solid local rock bands. When they met, he was older than his photo—she guesses they all are—fully a decade older. He was still complimentary, confident eye contact, good table manners. Even surprised her by paying for the food. She thinks she would not have gone around for coffee after if he had been drinking, Ben never touched a drop. She never said it in the restaurant, the date was a lukewarm get-to-know-you affair. No chemistry.

His place, one road behind Pascale's, turned out to be his mother's place too. Her name on the deeds: he never said it was hers but his music job turned out to be crummy. No professional acts on his cv. Being told to shush—by a man approaching fifty because his mother was asleep upstairs—was not much of a date. When she decided to make this clear, leave with her instant coffee undrunk the man became an arse. He took hold of her wrist, saying 'Stay. Lily, stay!'

If she knows anything, it is that she is not a dog. 'You're hurting me,' she said in an assertive voice intended to clear up the misunderstanding.

The bugger shushed her again and again. Insufficiently thoughtful of her assailant's mother's need for sleep. That was his gripe.

'Ben! Ben!' she shouted, even louder, 'the answers are all no. I'm gone. Don't see me out!'

He released his grip; she was able to walk away. Lily never learnt if she woke the old lady; on the front step Ben asked—implored her—'Shall we do this again?' and Lily heard no trace of humour in his ignorant question. There was desperation in his voice, enough of the stuff for them both. Why had she even gone to Pascale's? Not ready, and her kids don't need another man. Trent is in their lives if not hers. As she reflects upon it this evening, she wonders what made her go back to his house, his mother's house; she didn't take to him in the restaurant. Alice can line up all the gay cyclists she likes, Lily won't be putting herself in any compromising situations ever again.

On New Year's Eve, she messaged the Date Local administrator, reported Ben's uninvited grappling. They removed his profile.

And now a man called Guy—if that really is his name—wants to see her goth look on Tuesday's and Thursdays. Lily guesses these are the nights his wife's badminton group or art class meets. There are some creeps in Boscombe just as there were in London. Sittingbourne worse still. And she is not a goth. Lily pushes the lid down. Why does she even check the messages?

She'll go back to the beach in the morning. A swimmer may pay her more attention than tattooed Charlie managed today.

Monday, 30 May 2016

For Lily the morning begins with a bowl of the kids' chocolate cereal. Never consumes the like in front of them. Tells them it's too sweet; imagines if she says it often enough, they'll think it's important. Today, she is a jogger, one who slept only sporadically. A little sugar could be just the fuel she needs.

She's decided not to run quite so early. Dressed for it though, it will happen. The same black shorts, this time matched with a simple black T-shirt. Her goth look! For the first time since they left, she takes herself into Jo-jo's and Ami's bedrooms. Pretty clean, Lily runs a tight ship, believes there is more love in a well-kept home. Tidying Ami's room is the simpler task. Not the doing but retaining the lightness of mood. Ami never objects and if Lily sings the tasks—'Clothes on their hangers, toys in their boxes,'—Ami will sing along and pick up and put away as the song dictates. Jo-jo has become a contrarian. 'I like them there, Mum,' he will answer back when she is picking clothes, toys, spare bedding from his floor. He even argued that she must tidy Ami's room more because it's smaller. 'Big rooms can cope with mess,' he declared. The boy is clever, finding ways to direct it constructively is the puzzle. She went a bit off the rails for a time in her teens, hates the thought of either child veering that way.

'Why can't I have food in my room?' he asked with indignation only last Sunday.

'You know my rules, Jo-jo, so you mustn't sneak it in.'

'A snack, it's a little snack.'

It was half a loaf of bread and a pot of marmalade they were talking about. 'I don't want crumbs and smears and smells in your bedrooms. I give you snacks.'

'But why do you have to decide what? I wouldn't bring food in here

A Week Without Children

if I had my own kitchen.'

Lily had found his line of argument amusing: a prospective lawyer should the world really need another. When she opens the bedside table next to her son's bed, she sees an empty biscuit wrapper on the bottom shelf. She's no idea when Jo-jo filched them from the kitchen cupboard. Running. When they are back, she must take him running, that's the headline in her mind. He has a little weight which he probably shouldn't have. He's active enough, podgy not wobbly. If she takes him running every day, he'll burn off every jammy dodger and marmalade butty he furtively consumes. Of course, there is Ami, five-year-olds can't really go jogging. Then she rethinks it. Perhaps they can? Start young and the gold medals will follow. It's nice to picture her sports-mad family of the future, shouldn't forget it's only her own second day. Could all prove a fad.

After cleaning, Lily lies down on Jo-jo's bed, hopes that this is a form of limbering up, readying herself for the big run, although everything she is doing delays its start. She rubs the backs of both her calves with each hand, squeezes her thigh muscles. It might not be preparation for anything. Caroline would know, Lily could ask her.

* * *

She cannot understand where this sleep came from. Being a mother has never exhausted her. Well, more than never but not much. And she is on a short break anyway. Being a receptionist is not tiring. Piss-easy aside from maintaining office decorum. The effort required to look busy. She's slept on her son's bed for close to three hours, not jogged at all this morning and now it's past midday.

There can be no better way to greet her wakened state. She puts her training shoes on, glances in the hall mirror. She can carry it off, reckons herself a decent-looking runner. Puts a few bits and bobs into the tiny rucksack she runs with. The hand-towel she wished she'd packed yesterday, a bottle of sun lotion, bikini top. Wonders who she might meet on the beach today.

* * *

Out of the door with a grin on her face. The old lady opposite lifts the Venetian blind to watch her go. Not who Lily is hoping to attract but it's a start. She follows the same route as yesterday, quickens her pace.

Boscombe

Might run far up the promenade. Swim at Southbourne rather than Boscombe. Yesterday's decision to work out on the sand was Caroline's choice. Lily fell in with her, not something she typically does. A likeable girl, uncomplicated. Or maybe just complicated enough with all that boxer-boyfriend business. Lily won't repeat yesterday's routine, not at this time of day. Won't be doing sit ups for tourists to gawk at.

In Boscombe Cliff Gardens a pair of joggers running in the opposite direction pass her; the man flashes a smile. 'Good pace,' says his female partner. Lily wonders if it's a platitude. 'Thank you,' she shouts over her shoulder. Stays appreciative. This holiday—this very short break from her children—is a chance to connect with herself physically, be fitter, run and swim. She should have done this in twenty-fourteen, in twenty-fifteen. Living by the sea demands it of her. The sea air feels curative upon her bared flesh.

Running down the hill, towards pier and beach, she finds herself mesmerised by her own stride. She wonders if she is bouncing along with too great a kick in her step: does flinging each foot high in the air behind her make the running quicker, or does it slow her down, almost jumping into the air resistance of each successive bound? It feels funny to be discovering the joy in athleticism. It comes to her that she never spoke to Alice yesterday, never told her what she'd done. Running, push-ups and stretches. Coming across Caroline.

When they first met—just three years ago—Alice was almost as slim as Lily remains. She makes jokes about filling out. Her love of ice cream, evening comfort eating. Lily hopes that Alice gets along with Caroline. Or maybe Lily shouldn't call the interloper. She doesn't want to lose favour with her closest ally in this life.

On arriving at the pier, Lily comes almost to a stop. The promenade is heaving. On the beach, volleyballers play on roped-off courts; families spread themselves across the sand; floats and boards and swimmers and paddlers have invaded the water. It is a glorious afternoon beneath the spring sun. She jogs on the spot, feels the exhilaration of still running while the idle tourists dither. She decides she is in the mood to run on. All the way to Hengistbury Head if the going is good. Beach looks a bit crowded for swimming.

The dense throng around the coffee shops and burger bars impedes her jog. Once beyond them, she is able to resume a little of the gazelle-like gait that brought her down the hill. She becomes aware of the bounce of the small rucksack on her shoulder blades. It is not unpleasant; only the tiny bottle of lotion is angular, everything else in there is soft. Her phone wrapped up in the towel. The crowd thins out, becomes thick again, thins out. She runs towards a family pushing a toddler in a buggy; as she is about to pass the mother swings the pushchair into her path, unaware of her imminent arrival. Lily is agile, she makes a hurried sidestep, bounces herself to the left. No collision with the chair, the child. 'No!' shouts a male voice. It rings in her ears as she feels something sharp hack at her calf. Clattered from behind, Lily tumbles forward. She hits the hard tarmac, pain shooting up her left leg. The discomfort of her fall turns to agony as the cyclist and his offending bike, spill upon her. She reaches a hand to her aching leg, cannot move at all for the man on top of her.

'Fuck,' she shouts out. 'Sorry.' Lily shouldn't speak that way in the presence of a family, a small child.

An older man—grandfather of the toddler, she imagines—has crouched down to her. Kneels on the promenade. 'Stay still,' he instructs.

'I am so sorry,' says the cyclist extracting himself from above her. 'So, so sorry.'

'An accident,' Lily states, adding 'Careful,' as the man begins to lift his bike from on top of her.

She puts her hand on her calf, draws it back. Blood thick on her fingers.

'Oh, goodness,' says the cyclist. 'I am so sorry.'

Lily glances at herself. Legs sprawled out. Feels badly injured, her head swims. The cut looks awful, feels it too.

The bike removed, Lily pulls herself into a sitting position, says to the two men attending her, 'Look in my backpack. There's a towel.'

The older man glances at the young one.

'I'll do it,' says the cyclist. 'I have first aid.'

Lily sits in the middle of the promenade; people step around her. The bike and buggy are to one side, the mother and child now down on the sand, waiting for the older man to return to them. Lily is in agony, it must show upon her face.

Boscombe

The young man holds the yellow hand towel to the back of Lily's calf. It turns crimson in no time. 'I need to get you to the hospital,' he tells her. 'It doesn't look good.'

Lily's jog is over. This young man—errant cyclist in a checked shirt and brown chinos—certainly isn't taking her to hospital on his crossbar, and perhaps she really needs to go. He'll be long gone before an ambulance gets here, that's what she thinks.

A lifeguard has appeared and he exchanges words with the cyclist. Lily feels a small fury. Is the man who felled her deciding the course of events? Even as she thinks it, she knows it was a fifty-fifty. She stepped away from the pushchair, he failed to change course. No intent. The victim of an accident, not an assault. Maybe the young mum should have looked around but Lily has probably guided a child's buggy as haphazardly herself. May have done so on this very spot, back when Ami still travelled that way. She feels the heat of tears welling behind her eyes—not of anger, or even for the day's disruption—something is hurting and hurting.

'Can you get me out of here?' she asks, voice breaking as she says it.

The lifeguard looks her over quickly while nodding assent. He can help her. He gesticulates grandly to colleagues a hundred yards away, back at the lifeguard station. They wave back, semaphore understood. 'There's a buggy, a wheelie-thing. I'll get you off the prom.' Then he steps from her vision and she hears him whispering to the cyclist. It annoys her. What's he got to do with it?

'Ow,' shouts Lily.

'Sorry,' says the old man. 'I need to go. I hope you're okay. Patched up quickly.' He gestures towards the little one on the sand, his grandchild, she thinks, who is crying now. Those tears are not in response to anything Lily has done. She never clattered into the pushchair. She nods, says nothing, wonders why the old man has to tap her leg—her bare leg—to say goodbye. Does her injury turn her into public property? It was the right leg he touched, not the one bearing the principal wound, and she notices how grazed that one is too as she looks it over. The bicycle pedal tore into her left calf but right leg took the brunt of the fall. As she turns on her side she feels bruising to her hips. The lifeguard has turned her legs an inch this way and that, advised her that nothing appears broken. A relief but far short of the fitter, springier Lily which she imagined herself to be when setting off for this run. A little over fifteen minutes ago.

'What are you doing?' Lily asks the cyclist. He has picked his bike up from the ground and seems to be walking away. She is seldom this assertive with unknown men. It's not as if they met on Date Local.

'I'm locking it up,' he shouts across the promenade. 'I'm taking you to hospital. I am so, so sorry.'

Lily reappraises him. Not giving up on her is good, and she is mostly shouting and crying.

A man and girl from the lifeguard station have arrived pulling a very basic contraption. An orange trailer on which she may lie if she can comfortably get upon it. It's unappealing; she wonders if she shouldn't just walk it. The vehicle is befitting sacks of potatoes. What a sight she has become. Hospital by plastic cart.

She starts to rise and then exhales another pained sound.

'No,' says the first lifeguard, 'we need to keep the leg elevated. You're still losing blood.'

The cyclist assists the three lifeguards as they raise her onto the potato cart. She feels acutely conscious of the men handling her, the way they put hands under her thighs. The girl lifeguard has an arm around her back. 'You'll be all right, sweetie,' she says as she steps back. Something about her reminds Lily of Caroline. And yet all thoughts are a blur, she could be imagining it.

The two male lifeguards pull the trolley. 'Coming through,' they shout. 'Coming through.'

Lily finds herself at the familiar roundabout by the pier. 'I'll get you a taxi,' the cyclist tells her. She thought there might be an ambulance, now it seems the journey will cost.

'My bag,' she shouts, suddenly aware that she has left the scene of the fall without it. Where are her phone and purse? The phone was inside the towel that has now absorbed so much of her blood.

'Here,' the cyclist shows her. He clutches it in the hand by his side.

The towel itself is still around her leg, a record of her plight. The once yellow flannelling has turned red. She gestures for the bag and dips a hand in, feels the sun lotion and then the purse. Rummages frantically.

'I put your phone in the front pocket,' the young man tells Lily. Has he punched in his number, as Caroline did the day before? She cannot imagine calling the man who has ruined her bank holiday.

A taxi pulls up, it has been called earlier she realises. Done, perhaps, by the young man who directs his bike so poorly. Only the first lifeguard remains. He and the cyclist help her into the vehicle. The taxi driver is old, he has a ruddy face. 'You can't bleed on my backseat,' he says. She bloody can, thinks Lily. But she is feeling too woozy to argue, to voice the thought.

'I'll pay if it needs cleaning,' says the cyclist. She feels confused about him. A good Samaritan, or is it his own mess he's cleaning up? Most of all, she dislikes being the mess. Cut and bruised, unable to walk a short way or look after her own phone. Needs an unfashionably dressed stranger to keep her on track. This isn't her in regular time.

* * *

In the taxi, the young man sits next to Lily. Closer than necessary in her opinion. The heat is overpowering, sweat amassed upon her brow, her clothing only T-shirt and shorts. A bloodied towel around her left calf. As if sensing her discomfort, the young man scrolls down the passenger window, lets in the air. Very considerate, she grants that.

'No,' says the old taxi driver. 'Windows up, I've got air-conditioning.'

'Then set it properly, please,' says the young man. 'It's like a sauna in here.'

The driver grunts, while his left-hand goes to the panel, makes some adjustments. 'I don't seem to feel it,' he says.

'I'll see that you're all right,' says the young man. Holding her gaze, speaking earnestly. 'Would you tell me your name, please?'

Lily tells him. Thinks what a caring soul this boy is proving himself to be; the accident was only that. And he never quite stops apologising.

'I'm called Garth,' he says. 'Garth Addicks.' He speaks quietly about himself. Lives a few miles away, in Northbourne; likes to cycle on the promenade as often as he can before the high season, while it's still open to bikes. 'I've never hit anyone before,' he declares.

Lily finds herself laughing so much that tears track down her cheeks. She waves a hand, trying to dismiss the look of alarm on the boy's face. 'It was a funny way of saying you're not a complete idiot.'

A Week Without Children

The taxi is stuck in traffic, they continue to talk in low voices. The lad isn't obvious but Lily feels him appraising her, exposed in shorts and a tight, sweat-drenched T-shirt. Blood and tears too. She must look a state. 'Have you spare clothing in there?' he asks, pointing at her tiny rucksack. 'Jogging bottoms, perhaps?'

'I can't remember what I packed.'

He—Garth—starts to root once more in her backpack, pulls out the small red bikini top, quickly pushes it back in again and Lily thinks that he looks more embarrassed than it justifies. Face went bright pink. 'I expect I haven't anything,' she tells him.

'I'm so sorry I've done this to you.'

Lily shakes her head; accidents happen. Tries to weigh him up—Garth, assailant and rescuer—she's unsure if he is super-confident or awkward-incompetent. Her judgement has gone awry, found her indecisive. He's taller than she is by some inches, and then meek with it. A funny quality in a grown man. Today hasn't gone to plan, perhaps the morning sleep was the problem. Nobody plans on getting themselves a few hours in casualty. Not on a busy bank holiday. This rumination brings her tears back over the brim. What is wrong with her? She's not a cry-baby, didn't shed them in Sittingbourne and she lived through some shit there. Once or twice in London, mostly over break-ups, two big ones and a couple less seismic. Never cried in Boscombe until the insufferable Simon Clarke phoned on Saturday night. Made her feel stalked. And now this, about three bouts already today. Pain is the primary source and she feels sorry for herself—curtain briskly drawn on her running career—she doesn't do self-pity. Mustn't start now.

Garth has a hold of her hand. 'I'm sorry. If I'd spotted you and braked quicker, we wouldn't be here.'

She dries the tears with the back of the hand she extracts from him. Leans to adjust the towel, the bloodied weight around her elevated calf.

'And I really should have spotted you...' He looks in distress as he pauses before completing the thought. '...you look lovely.'

'I doubt that,' she splutters out. Uses the heel of her hand to push the tears back. And these are the result of laughter at his poorly timed chat-up line. 'I think you're stuck with me for an hour or two more if you really want to see me back out of the hospital.'

'I couldn't rest until you are home,' answers Garth. 'If I wasn't with you, I'd only be praying for you.'

Lily turns to look out of the window, it might be a sweet thing to say, she isn't sure. Not a line any man has tried on her before. Looking lovely trumps being prayed for. And he said it while she looks like roadkill.

* * *

When they arrive at the casualty department, they learn that waiting times are running at one and a half hours. Neither Lily nor Garth knows if this is good or bad. Longer than they would have liked, shorter than they feared. Garth drags a footstool across the waiting room, and then the triage nurse trumps it, brings Lily a shaped leg elevator with a thin plastic sheet upon it. 'I'll come back and clean you up,' she says.

Lily has already told Garth she is single, said it in answer to his question about who to call, not as a way of short-circuiting Date Local, the website she has vowed never to use again. Now, in their passing-the-time chat, she tells him she has two children.

'At home?'

His tone sounds like a panicking social worker. It does to her. 'They're with their father...' Garth looks at her through narrowed eyes. '...we were never married.' And now he looks utterly perplexed. She had earlier said that she 'never married,' in reply to his question about phoning a husband. Garth must have taken it to mean always single. She and Trent used to live as married couples do, short on the paperwork but who needs it. She sees him mouth the word, children, to himself. Stupid lad, younger than her by miles and he could be tutting like her mother. No audible sound, just a po-faced expression, disapproval of kids outside wedlock. Unless she's reading him wrong but that's how it looks and she thought her grandparents' generation were the last to have that shit ingrained into them. Lily looks away from prissy Garth, tries to read the hospital posters from a distance. There is one about inoculations she hasn't read before. Her parenting is fine; who gives tuppence what a lad in a checked shirt thinks about anything? When the silence has dragged along for too long, Lily says, 'We were together for eight years.' Garth smiles, she is not at all sure what it signifies. 'We tried hard, just weren't quite suited.' He continues to smile, doesn't look into her eyes as he had earlier. 'We were so ill-suited that I could no longer stand the sight of him,' she says quietly. Hoping to make something clear to her maybe-judgemental hospital companion, without wishing to draw the many strangers within earshot into dramas past.

'I'm sorry to hear it,' he finally concedes.

* * *

The nurse is as good as her word, returns to clean Lily's wound before the doctor arrives. As she pulls the curtain around the cubicle, she asks Garth, 'Do you want to hold her hand?'

'No,' says Lily.

'I'll be waiting,' says Garth.

Can't make head nor tail of him.

* * *

At five forty-five in the evening the taxi pulls up at Lily's front door.

'Thank you for staying with me,' she says. It's been a marathon, waiting on a doctor for twice as long as they were advised on arrival.

'The least I could do.'

Garth pays for the taxi; Lily offers but he turns it down. Does he owe her? Everything is accidental today. With his bicycle, he gashed her calf so badly it needed twelve stitches, not something he's ever done before. He made that very clear. And the doctor advised that there is tissue damage to the muscle. 'It'll heal; I'm afraid you're going to feel throbs and pangs and twitches for several days.' He prescribed painkillers, stronger ones than the over-the-counter jobbies. When he was preparing to stitch, disinfecting the area deeper than the nurse had done, the doctor asked her if the bike was clean. She shrugged, unsure. An improbable source of HIV but she recalled nothing pristine about Garth's bicycle. Then she yelled louder than she has since childbirth such was the invasion of his acidic cleaning agent into that deep wound. 'Stings a bit,' observed the young doctor, while Garth, quite literally, pushed his head through the curtain. She waved him away, felt touched by his concern.

Garth places Lily's left arm over his shoulders in order to walk her to the door. The taxi driver offers to help, shows far greater sympathy than the first cabbie could muster. A woman driver, of course; it's men who are insensitive to suffering, Lily's long known that. As she thinks it, she wonders if Garth is an improvement on her mental archetype of his gender. He is odd, wears the shirt of a man thirty years his senior, at least he's a gentleman.

As they enter the maisonette, and Garth helps her rise over the lip of the UPV doorframe, he hugs her more tightly around the waist than she thinks strictly necessary. Can't decide if she likes it or not.

'I'm so pleased I've got you home.'

For the umpteenth ruddy time, she can feel tears welling inside her. It might be his kindness, and if he is taking liberties with the squeeze, crying is the wrong response.

'I'm starving hungry,' she says, hoping to distract herself, talk nonsense to avoid another flood of the damned tears.

'What can I fix you?'

This man is a puppy dog. 'Garth, what do you want from me?'

He returns her gaze, seems to think hard before speaking. 'I'd like to talk to you, tell you a little more about myself. Only if you're happy to hear it. I've been imposing on you ever since I collided with you. I know you must have had the most horrible day.'

'Talking's good, Garth, right now I'm quite literally starving. Do you want to fetch us chips, or Chinese or something? I'll pay, mind. I need to clean myself up, then we'll eat, and you'll talk.'

'I would like that very much, Lily. Truly, there is nothing I'd rather do.'

* * *

When Garth is out in search of food, Lily phones Alice. 'Will you call me in exactly one hour?' she asks. 'I'm about to eat a Chinese with a strange man. I'm not sure I should even be doing this.'

Alice fluctuates between alarm and laughter—and sympathy, of course, when she learns of Lily's accident—she is amused by the idea of jogging, can't quite see the point. 'I can come over, petal, pretend it's by chance.'

'No, just phone. If I say the word cheeseboard, call the cops.'

Alice laughs while agreeing to do as asked. 'I've got your back,' she says.

By the time she hears her the buzzer—Garth Addicks, returning

A Week Without Children

with fried rice, pork and chicken—Lily has dressed again following a quick almost-shower. By sitting on the bath side, she has successfully used the showerhead to clean those parts of her body the doctor didn't bandage. Managed to accidentally dampen the dressing on her left calf. Before putting on her tracksuit bottoms, she saw that the wound has bled again. May have done more harm than good. She feels better for being clean anyhow.

She lets Garth back inside, and he insists that she sits down. He takes the thick brown bag into the kitchen to decant onto two plates. When he brings it to her on the sofa, he starts fussing over her like an old woman. 'Do you want a cushion to rest your food on?'

'You did my leg; I can still hold a plate.'

Garth takes the old armchair; they sit across from each other and begin to eat in silence. Lily thinks the stranger in the house looks sheepish now. She knows a little about him already, they talked in the hospital. The lengthy waiting time gave them no alternative. He has neither wife nor girlfriend; he left school for a college course in two thousand and two which—she has estimated—makes him six years her junior. Works with children but he never explained what he does. When he finally starts talking, Garth looks only at his plate of food. Not at her at all.

'I think I ran into you by chance, Lily. It hurt you, not something I would ever plan to do. I am not that kind of person, I promise you.' Lily listens up, the way he speaks is faintly amusing. 'And I also think it was not chance, could not have been chance. Because there is no chance.'

'So, you did plan it?' says Lily, a wry smile on her face. This is one weird boy, repeats on a loop in her mind. Is he too clever by half, talking about fate and chance, or might he be simple-minded? She has not figured him out despite the hours in his company.

'It's not in my power to plan such a thing, you see. I've met you now, and take it as my duty to care for you. Being largely responsible for your injury. It wasn't something I could just walk away from.'

'I'm glad you didn't Garth. You could have though, many others would...'

He cuts her off: 'I cannot guess why the good Lord would choose an unpleasant accident to put the two of us together. However, it's what He's done, and He always has His reasons.'

The edging pieces are all connected, Lily sees the emerging picture with surprising clarity. 'I think you believe all that, Garth—Jesus and God—I respect it, I really do. I must add, it's not my thing. Never gone in for that stuff.'

'Lily, I've spent hours with you already. I've figured it isn't your thing, I even think you blasphemed when the doctor disinfected your wound...' He smiles while he says it, explaining not admonishing. '...and I'm not telling you this to try and convert you to my religion, I'm telling you about myself.'

They sit in silence again before Garth finds more of himself to reveal. A suddenly crestfallen face. 'Do you think I might be a bad person, Lily?'

She sits a little more upright. 'I don't really know you, Garth, so I can't discount it. But you've been brilliant to me all day. If I leave out gashing my leg open, that is.'

'And that was a horrible accident, one I need to atone for. I am so sorry. I knew I had to see you to hospital and then back home. I think of it as a duty, having brought you to this juncture. What seems unfair, oddly unfair, not unhappily, I enjoyed it, Lily...' He glances away from her gaze as if embarrassed by his thoughts. '...no, let me rephrase that. I didn't enjoy hearing you scream; I'm not that bad. I loved your company, I...' Lily thinks she sees him redden as he prepares to say what is on his mind. '...I have loved looking at you all day. Is that self-indulgent of me?'

'We look like what we look like, Garth.' Inwardly she finds it funny and a little comforting, to see how embarrassed he is saying all this. The Christian boy seems to have a little crush; very nice that she can still do that to a fella. 'Do you mean that you wouldn't have helped me if I was cross-eyed with a face full of warts?'

'No, I'd have helped you. I understand where my duties lie. It's more confusing because you're beautiful, I wonder if the Lord is testing me or treating me?'

Lily can't help him with his dilemma. Knows she is many notches short of beautiful, enjoys hearing his contrary assertion. Thinking any of it to be the Lord's business is pretty insane. 'In my book, it was chance, Garth, and I got the wrong end of it. You look okay yourself,

A Week Without Children

apart from the checked shirt. Looking at you is not worth the stitches. Does that sound rude? I didn't intend it to—you look quite nice actually—pain, hospitals: I'm not a fan ...'

'I don't think I've explained myself well,' he interrupts. 'When I told you that it was nice to be in your company, I really wasn't looking for you to say it back. You will think it was chance, Lily, because without God everything is chance. I already told you that I've never done this before.' He looks a bit rueful, his head down, and eyes looking up. Directly at her. 'I would never attack a girl with a bicycle as a way to meet her. It's not a sound approach. And I didn't really know what you looked like when I saw you from behind, so it was the same as chance to me. To God, not so. Everything that happens is part of His wider plan.'

Lily is quietly laughing at this, enjoying the ridiculous philosophising. At least some good has come of her day: a funny story to regale Alice and Martin with. They'll want to hear this one again and again.

* * *

As Garth is washing the plates, spoons and forks, in her small kitchen—tasks he has insisted he complete—Lily shakes her head for thinking about him. One minute she gets him, and the next she doesn't. Easy company but for God on his shoulder. He is more than harmless: a truly well-meaning man. Her leg sports twelve stitches that may refute it, she has long put aside blaming him. Christians never wilfully ram their bikes into running girls. Not as Lily has heard. And then Garth believes it is part of the Lord's wider plan—gets very serious about it—and God's purpose he does not profess to know. Whacky but there's no harm in it, she supposes. And what of her? A non-believer on the wrong path, Garth had the cheek to say it. He said it nicely, inoffensively. And she's no intention of joining up.

Lily wants to ask more about his work. He described the residential school he works at—tricky kids who have been thrown out of mainstream—Baxter's School. She's heard the name; it's miles away from here. That stuff interests her more than his funny religion. Lily has thought a time or two that working with children would be a good move for her. Give her more purpose than Capaldi-Clarke's ever has. Saturday night's telephone call from Simon Clarke stirred the idea again; she is not a good fit in a staid office. Straightlaced, stiff as boards—or philanderers casting their nets—the lot of them. She is worried that she couldn't manage Garth's type of work, might not have what it takes. His opinion could help her to decide either way. He might be an expert in the field, a recruiter even. He has seen her cry about a hundred times today which must be the opposite of the strength of mind needed.

Singing comes from the adjacent kitchen and Lily bursts into giggles. He's acting the idiot, singing a rendition of Onward Christian Soldiers in a warbling falsetto voice. Sending himself up. 'Garth, quiet! My phone's ringing.'

'Sorry,' he calls, putting his head into the lounge in which she sits, leg elevated. A big grin on his face, pleased to have entertained. She waves him away with a hand and a smile as she swipes the tiny screen.

'I am worried, Lily. Is it cheeseboard?'

'Alice, no worries. What do you mean, cheeseboard?'

'Right, keep talking...' Alice's voice goes faint, not speaking directly into her phone. Lily hears her shout, 'Martin, call the cops. Now! Nine, nine, nine, send them to number eleven, Cooper Road.'

As Lily starts to say, 'No, no, no,' she hears Martin saying something to Alice. Thinks he might be offering to come and fight the man.

'Are you hurt? Just say yes or no.'

Lily is laughing, worries that she is about to waste police time. 'Alice,' she shouts over her friend's frantic questioning, 'no police, no cheeseboard, no panic. He's called Garth; he's a lovely boy.' She looks up from her phone. The subject of her compliment is standing in the doorway, looking both puzzled and pleased. Lily had to say something to stop her, Alice was going a bit crazy.

'Now you've said cheeseboard again, petal. I'm confused as hell.' Then she lowers her tone, 'If you want us to call the police end the call immediately.'

'Then we must talk some more, Alice. I am not going into detail now but we've had a nice meal, and I'm being well taken care of...'

'Oh,' interjects Alice, sweetness entering her voice for the first time this call. 'You deserve a bit of that. How's your leg?'

'I think it will look ghastly for a few weeks but that's about it.'

'Not in pain?'

A Week Without Children

'Only when I think about it.' Lily finds herself wincing. The pain is always there, Garth has distracted her well. 'Bugger running,' she says.

'Hear, hear,' Alice chimes in; Lily feels fractionally deflated. A brief foray yesterday and today's interrupted jog is all she managed. Felt good before the calamity.

* * *

Lily has stretched out on the sofa, Garth sitting opposite. Each has a glass of wine in hand. When Lily questioned if Christians drank, Garth said that he first had to bless it, call it communion. Must have been a joke because he hasn't.

'Tell me again where the cheeseboard comes into it.'

'No. I've told you once, pay attention. Why do you think I would be good at the work? Children's homes, that type of stuff.'

'You're a natural. Just be yourself, Lily. What you did, asking your friend to call you, that was the right way to play it. I never thought about it because I'm police checked...' Garth looks squarely at Lily, raises his broad shoulders. '...in my job we all are. Obviously, you couldn't verify this. Very sensible to phone your friend; don't be embarrassed...' Lily likes his face, he's a good-looking boy. Weird, or maybe he just seems that way because she hasn't any Christian friends. Nice to look at is good. The upset of Boscombe promenade has long departed. She can focus on him properly now. '...cheeseboard, why cheeseboard? Not the simplest word to drop into a conversation.'

'Oh God, Garth, I wonder...' Lily pushes her hand through her hair, worries how she looks in a cream sweatshirt and navy jogging bottoms. Stops worrying as she peruses Garth's old-man shirt. '...will I see you again, after tonight?'

He draws himself up straight. 'Lily, I believe it's for me to ask you that.'

That's mad too, she thinks, mad in a sweet and old-fashioned way.

'I'd love to see you again, properly.' Lily looks directly at him as he speaks. 'You and I, without doctors and nurses.' That hangs in the room for a little while as they look into each other's eyes.

'Your church,' she asks, 'is it Catholic or something different.'

'Something different, very different. It's called The Church of the Men of Judea.'

Boscombe

'The Men of Judea?' The words sound like an affront. 'What do the women do, Garth? Bake cakes.'

'No, the name comes from the Acts of the Apostles. From the Bible. Women are more than welcome in our church. They are the equal of men; our pastor is a woman.'

Lily feels reassured. Never heard of the church—doesn't sound as backward as the Catholics—shame the women don't get a mention in the credits.

'I'd rather tell you about my church another time.' Garth looks pensive. 'You're looking tired, Lily, I'll tell you another time.'

'I'm whacked with nowhere to be but this sofa. Do you live alone in Northbourne, Garth? Where's family?'

He tells her all he can. Candidly, happy to share personal information with her. Lives in a flat above a shop, began paying a mortgage on it five years ago, job changes and low pay have kept him in it. He says he has 'paid nothing but interest.' Makes a joke about the flat roof. 'It rained in, so I got a second mortgage to buy a bucket.'

Lily can't work out how poor he really is: a homeowner and he paid the taxi to and from the hospital.

'My parents live in Ferndown,' he tells her. 'It's a little bit annoying. It feels like they're following me around.' Garth explains that he was brought up on a Dorset farm, his father a tenant farmer, paying rent for two hundred acres. No real riches, the owner of nothing. 'We were The Borrowers: borrowing to pay rent to a landed family who never came near.'

'Did you want to farm yourself, Garth?'

'It's a mug's game. Tough if you own the place, slavery if you don't.'

'I don't know it,' says Lily, giggling. 'You made it up.'

He looks blankly at her.

'Threepenny Ha'penny: there's no such place. That's what you said the village was called.'

He laughs with her. 'There is so! And it's called Sixpenny Handley. That was what I said.'

'Threepenny Ha'penny, that's what you said first time round.'

'Stop devaluing it. It was all I had as a kid. Sixpenny Handley. Terrific name, looks like a Constable painting. I won't be going back.'

'So, it was all grouse shooting and pushing girls into haystacks in

A Week Without Children

your youth, was it Garth?'

'Pretty much but we were only tenant farmers. The poor beaters.'

'What does that mean?' Lily is from Sittingbourne, not familiar with rural ways. 'What's a poor beater.'

'Beaters. We had to bash the moorland heather, beat it with sticks to make the grouse fly up from the undergrowth so that the rich landowners could shoot them back down again. I was shot in the rump once and Sir Humphrey gave me an extra shilling for my trouble.'

'No!' Lily looks shocked.

'Of course not, Lily! I've never been to a grouse shoot in my life. You brought it up, romanticising about rural life.'

Lily shrieks. Throws a cushion at him. Feels like a schoolgirl for doing so.

'They're retired now—my parents—that's why they moved to Ferndown. Two years ago, they moved out. A tiny two-bedroomed place after close to forty years of saving every penny.'

Lily thinks he looks serious again, wonders if the pillow was too much.

'I bought my own place before they ever did, if my little flat counts.'

'Garth, I left Sittingbourne, where I was raised, a long time ago. I hated it. If my parents moved into the next town along from Boscombe, I'd be off. Scotland probably.'

Garth nods. 'They don't get my beliefs. Don't like me belonging to the church. Can you imagine that?'

'Must have been tough,' she says, not that she really gets it either.

'I think they'd rather that I'd knocked up a girl from the village or become a hitman. Honestly, they are that anti-religious.' Garth watches as Lily laughs at his funny line, and then his eyes enlarge. 'Sorry, no, that came out all wrong.' The boy is blushing. 'The knocked-up thing, I didn't mean it. I can be such a fool.' Garth is on his feet, going towards Lily who has tears in her eyes. 'Are you alright?'

'Fine,' she says when she can breathe again. 'That's so bloody funny.'

'I thought I'd offended you, made you cry.'

'No. Your face was a sight. Don't pussyfoot on my account. Say it how you see it, Garth. And I don't think I was, by the way. We don't get on anymore but Trent and I both love the kids, wanted them more than we wanted each other in the end. That's just the way of it.'

They share a few more small and easy intimacies. He has a sister he speaks fondly of, then sounds bitter when explaining that she came to church for 'many, many weeks' after the family moved to Ferndown, briefly joining the choir he organises, then suddenly gave it up. He believes his parents turned her against it.

Lily explains who's who in her family, no detail beyond the dislike she feels for her mother. Says only the name of her brother. Gary. A brother two years younger. That she often goes six months without speaking to him doesn't enter the conversation. Gary has kids of his own; however, he's not a father in any meaningful sense. Two boys she considers shining examples of neglect. He sees them in Maidstone, not that access visits count as parenting in her book. She heard that the parents of the youngster who more recently bore him a daughter—the Margate girl who Lily has never even set eyes on—have frozen him out. Try to prevent Gary from seeing his baby girl at all. The court has agreed supervised access. She catches herself in thought, sharing none of this. Garth is childless, probably oblivious to the feelings having one's own children arouse.

'I need to be going, I've taken up your whole day,' he says.

'You have,' she replies, 'and for that reason you cannot go without giving me a big hug first.'

She remains on the sofa while Garth kneels and hugs, an awkwardness to his posture and uncertainty in his proximity. Chest on chest but without any pressure exerted. And Lily wouldn't have minded, she's come to trust him in no time at all. Perhaps Christians can't squeeze a girl until a vicar's cleared it. Blessed the breasts or whatever nonsense his sect go in for.

'I've got your number,' he tells her, rising. 'I will...' No more words come. The thought remains unexpressed.

Lily reaches out a hand for him to lower his head again, Garth does as beckoned, and she puts it behind his head, pulls him forward and kisses him quickly on the lips. 'Nicest day in a while, apart from the stitches and the moronic taxi driver.'

He blinks long and hard. 'I think I'm meant to make the running here. I was trying to say, when I call you, it will be to ask you on a date.'

She smiles as he says it, feels like something has come of her jog.

'Give me a few days for the leg to get better.' He nods. 'And I'm fetching the kids on Saturday...'

'I'm calling sooner than that,' he blurts out.

'Call any time, sunshine.'

Then Garth is away, back to the beach, the scene of the accident, where he has locked his bicycle. He has told Lily that he will have to ride home without any lights. Never expected to be away from Northbourne for so long.

Tuesday, 31 May 2016

Alice and her children are spending the afternoon in the maisonette. Lily would have gone to her house but Alice told her not to walk on it. The wounded leg. The children are a little fractious, inhibit conversation. Alice is excited that Lily has met someone. The older friend says, 'Shut up,' every time she raises it.

'I think he's only seeing me to assuage his guilt. I was just avoiding running into a kiddie's buggy, stepped aside a pace. He was cycling far too fast.'

'You're mad with him for colliding with you, and then going out with him anyway?'

'No, it came out wrong. He didn't mean to do it, couldn't have known that I was going to change direction.'

'Chinese on the first date, Lily. That was how Martin and I began, you know?'

'No, I didn't know. And last night was not a date. He was just being a nice Christian boy. Did I tell you he works with children? From broken homes. Works in a special school.'

'Yeah, you'd love that.'

'I'm interested in his work; it's something I could do in the future. I might be good with the kinds of kids he works with. Garth said that I'm a natural.'

'Oh, he's buttering you up big time, petal.'

'Shut up! I want a different job, get out of Capaldi-Clarke's. Garth is a bit young actually.'

'Lucky Lily!' Are you sure he wasn't the tall cyclist from Saturday, come back for a second look?'

'Fool! He wasn't like him at all. I told you that boy was gay, certainly never looked at me for more than two seconds.'

Wendy and Bryony, Alice's two small children have torn a magazine, a television guide, Lily waves a hand, indicates it doesn't matter.

'While Garth was keen as mustard,' Alice concludes. 'He looked at you and you at him, both liked what you saw. He's going to call you on a date...'

Lily interrupts her, can't be listening to such a babble of nonsense. 'I don't think he will. He was being nice after the accident but in the cold light of day...'

'He will. He's bound to,' says Alice, 'and you would be bloody good working with children, Lily. Children who've had it tough. You'd be a natural.'

* * *

When she is alone, that evening, Lily decides that she will text Caroline. She never mentioned her to Alice. Told her of 'limbering up on the beach,' without a word about the pretty young friend she made along the way. No reason, just never got round to it.

> *Hi there, Caroline. I ran a little faster on Monday, thanks for the encouragement. A cyclist still ran me down and I have a dozen stitches in my leg. No running until July is my best guess. I will return! Lily.*

She lies back on the sofa, picks up a library book she's been reading for over a week. Raises her aching leg, stretches it out across the cushions. While she is still flicking her eyes back and forth over the page, trying to remember what was last going on in the story, her smartphone makes its robotic musical announcement.

She grabs it, hoping Garth may have texted, made good on his promise of a date. She sees an icon of a doe-eyed young girl on her phone, doesn't understand how it has arrived there. It's new. She clicks on the in-come text and finds it is an instant reply from Caroline. The crafty girl must have done some digital ploy unknown to Lily when she held her smartphone, conjured this Disney-like image onto the screen when it receives a text from that particular phone. The name in the directory is simply Caroline Y. Lily moves from screen to screen, tries to work out how she has linked the image to her contact, cannot fathom it, nor recall what the Y stands for.

Aw, that's gruesome. Don't be down, see you soon, Caz
xx

Wednesday, 1 June 2016

On Wednesday, Lily finishes her library book, watches a studio audience debate the referendum on television, and hobbles up to the shops on Boscombe High Street. The stitches are only a minor discomfort, she will be able to return to work in the morning, as planned. It feels like she has wasted her annual leave. Invalided out of a decent break, denied the joys of jogging. Not that Alice would see it that way.

The evening is a dismal one, torn between the thought of seeing 'young Mr Clarke' at work—he is at least ten years older than her, the word 'young' attributed to him only because of his father's occasional involvement in the company—and her diminishing hope that Garth might call. Confirm the reality of their hypothetical date. When she can bear it no longer, Lily phones Alice.

'I'm dreading looking at fuck-face tomorrow.' Alice is silent, may not have grasped the context of her dramatic introductory line. 'Bloody Simon who tried to come around my house on Saturday.'

'Oh, poor you,' replies Alice, once she's tuned in.

Lily says that she decided to look for other work. Can't do it right away, not after the accident on the bank holiday. She is stuck at the solicitors for a while longer. 'I can't go limping into job interviews but one day I'll work with children in care. They're always looking for residential staff in the Advertiser.'

'Yes, they are. Do you think Garth might help you? Advise you how to go about...'

'Fuck him! I can do it on my own; I'm a natural.'

'Has something happened?'

'Yes, zilch.'

'I see. Well don't get so despondent yet, Lily...'

'I wouldn't leave him hanging on like this if I'd promised to phone,' she says sharply, the promptly returned text from Caroline in her mind. The boy was adamant that it was his role—the man—to make the running, and then he doesn't get off the starting blocks. That's what she was thinking before this call. Holds in as much as she can. No intention of sounding self-pitying. 'He's not interested in an old one with two kids already.'

Alice doesn't argue the point this time.

Thursday, 2 June 2016

Lily is never in the office at eight-thirty. Not when she has to drop off the children at school. This and the next day are rare exceptions.

'Everything alright?' asks Mrs Garrett, watching her intently as Lily limps to her desk, the bandage visible beneath the yellow-print summer dress she wears.

'Not much,' Lily answers, feeling strong and righteous, knowing this old gossip blabs about her to all and sundry. To the odious Simon Clarke. 'I'm missing the kids, and I was attacked by a cyclist. An accident with his bike that is.' Her colleague gives her a concerned look. 'Blood, stitches, X-rated stuff.'

'Oh, Lily, and you all alone. Have family been looking after you?' says Mrs Garrett.

Lily shakes her head. If the woman knew an iota about her, she would know the question is a stupid one. Gary cannot look after his own fly buttons, and she will drink hemlock before submitting again to her mother's care.

The work is not taxing, Lily's on top of it, focussed. She devours task after task. As she types, files, prepares invoices, answers the telephone, she thinks only that her job is nonsense. That she should be helping wayward children, goes round and round her mind like a never-forgotten tune. By ten o'clock in the morning, Lily is surprised to note that Simon Clarke has still not arrived at the office. Sharon Prior, a solicitor who is younger than Lily, is making herself a coffee in the corner of the office.

'Is young Mr Clarke in court today?'

Sharon gives her a funny look before answering. 'Did you not hear? He fell off his bike on the bank holiday. Out on a New Forest track. They had to get the air ambulance to him. Broken collarbone, ribs too,

A Week Without Children

poor chap.'

Nobody told Lily. They could have called her at home—broadcast the big news—she never shared her accident either, not until Garrett asked this morning. No air ambulance for her, just a plastic cart. 'I hadn't heard.'

'Gosh, and you came off a bike too, I gather. Nasty. Thankfully yours was minor.'

Lily nods as if in agreement, not minded to correct her. Lily wasn't cycling but a bicycle wrought the injury. Simon Clarke's hospitalisation is the rough justice God metes out to stalkers, and hers a benevolent mishap. Unlikely, although Garth Addicks might agree. Not that he's ever going to call.

At lunchtime, Lily checks her phone, something she cannot do in working time—Capaldi-Clarke operates a no-private-calls policy that reflects the worldview of the now-retired senior partners—she sees a text from pretty-smiley-face, Caroline.

Can I run your way this evening? Caz xx.

She replies with quick thumbs.

Please do. I'm at 11A Cooper Road. Lily S.

Why can't Garth be a bit more like Caroline? Communicate yay or nay. The silence is the killer.

* * *

After work, back in the maisonette, legs up on the sofa, as much from habit as need—left calf still wincingly tender to the touch—Lily decides to call her mother. She wonders if she can bear to take the children to see her parents on a forthcoming weekend. It's a horrible chore.

'Stephens,' says the parent upon picking up her phone.

'It's Lily, Mummy.'

'Oh, and we were just talking about you. What a coincidence.'

'Really,' she says, pulling in her lip. She is their only daughter of whom to speak; one of just two children the woman bore. Perhaps her parents talk about her very rarely. Lily requires at least two glasses of wine before she will speak earnestly of her mother with another soul.

'Yes, yes, we were…'

Lily cuts her off, worries that she won't like what she hears. 'I was thinking of bringing the children one weekend. Saturday is better for the trains; the Sunday service is a bit useless.'

'Not to bother, dear, they were just here. You cut me off, we were talking about you with Trent. He only left an hour ago. He brought the grandchildren to see us.'

'What happened?' she asks, feeling flustered by this turn of events. 'Trent brought Ami and Jo-jo to see you. How come?'

'They are our grandchildren, Lily, dear. And Trent is almost family. I know you never quite did things properly.'

'Mother!' she feels her face flush, swings her legs around to sit upright for what is now a million miles from the casual conversation she'd unrealistically hoped for. 'Since when do you and Trent even speak? How did you contact him?'

'We've always had his number, dear. For emergencies.'

'Emergencies! He didn't come to put out a fire, did he?'

'I don't know what you're upsetting yourself about, Lily. I told you when we spoke on Friday last that your father was having an operation. It can be an emotional time, and he wanted to see his grandchildren.'

'You told me not to worry. Is Daddy all right?'

'Yes, on the mend.'

'Did he...' Lily cannot frame the question; her skin feels cold as she asks it. '...has Daddy got cancer?'

'No dear, they removed the thingummies. He's all right.'

'He was a day patient?'

'Lily, yes, that's how they do it these days.'

'He couldn't wait until I could bring them. Jo-jo and Ami?'

'Lily, it's been a most emotional time and seeing the little ones...'

'Did Gary bring his tribe too, the boys...?'

'We see them...'

'Was he around, seeing as how Daddy is needing to gather his grandchildren? And little Emma. Do you have an emergency number for Emma's mum too?'

'Now you're just being cruel, Lily. Poor Gary barely gets to see Emma. I'm afraid we're all biding our time with...'

'But his boys were around?'

A Week Without Children

'No, we've not seen Gary for a little time...'

'What did he say? Trent. What did you all say?' Lily is snapping now, no longer attending to her mother's replies. She feels tears in her eyes, she shouldn't be speaking like this. 'You and Daddy and Trent were all talking about me, with my children listening. Can you inform me what you were saying?'

'Well, I think everyone of us loves you, dear, so it was nothing bad. Trent misses you ...'

'I doubt that. Is it really what he said?'

'Not in so many words, dear...'

'So, you are not actually going to tell me what was said?'

'It's quite hard to recall when you keep interrupting.'

'I'm sorry. I'm pleased you saw them. Are my children well?'

'Yes, they are...'

'Thank you, Mummy, goodbye.' Lily hangs up. It has been unbearable contemplating her children spending time in hated Sittingbourne without her there to navigate its pitfalls. She is their protector from Esme Stephens. Trent never could smell the poison; his own mother, his dad too, were pleasant people through and through. Poor but well-meaning. He has no defence against a virus like her mother. Lily swings her legs back up onto the sofa, pulls her knees up. She feels tears coming back, tries to drive them away. She's missing Jo-jo, his cheeky games, the laughs and hugs they have together. She hates it when Ami is not with her; only five years old that lovely girl, and it is Lily's job to cherish and protect her. Not the little girl's fault that Trent didn't make the grade. Oh God, it's complicated. Her tears have abated. She never cries, she thinks to herself, while recalling blubbing a whole damned river since Saturday night, Clarke and pain and ignorant taxi drivers. The mother from hell, Hades, purgatory, the underworld. Sittingbourne.

Her smartphone vibrates against her thigh and then its feigned musicality begins, she reaches between her legs, where it fell when she let it go after abruptly finishing the last call. She looks at the screen, will not answer if it is the woman in hell trying to clamber back into Lily's realm.

'Hello,' she says tentatively, no caller name appearing on the screen.

'Lily, it's me, Garth. Do you remember me?'

Boscombe

Her anger dies away. 'Yes, I do remember you, the nutter with the bike.'

'Half a bike, Lily, but that's another story. I said that I'd call you, and this is it.'

Lily waits.

'Call you to ask you out on a date.'

'Oh that...'

'Is it too forward? I hope you're not...' His voice has just gone up an octave, he brings it quickly down. '...have I misread the situation, Lily? I wasn't trying to be presumptuous.'

'A date, Garth. You're not backing down now you've said it are you?'

'I'm not but if you want a little longer to consider it, I shall be waiting and praying...'

'Garth...' Lily is giggling again, '...we're on. A date without doctors, please.' She wonders what to make of him. Was he even trying to be funny?

'I have ideas where to take you. How's the leg, Lily? Can you walk at all? I know a place or two towards Southbourne which we might go to but...'

'It's improving, sunshine. I've been to work today; you may remember I was off for the first two days after regardless...'

'I didn't make you miss work, did I?'

'No, pre-booked holiday. And I wish you had really, I'm sick of it. Garth...' Lily has suddenly drawn a serious tone from within herself. '...it'll be a proper date but I want you to tell me honestly about your work, your job. I'm hoping to try it, something in that general area.'

Garth agrees to do it. He jokes about making notes, doing research on any other topics of conversation Lily would like him to raise. They find some of the rapport from Monday. Not bad on a phone call, and she liked looking at him; high time she went on a date. Garth tells Lily the half-bike story, and she is shocked. When he got to the promenade on Monday night, where he'd locked it against a railing, it was without its front wheel. She sympathises, even suggesting that it is her fault in a roundabout way. He will have none of it. 'I lost a front wheel; you had a dozen stitches: I got off lightly, Lily.'

She wonders whether to tell the boy about the phone conversation with her mother. It remains complicated, she is not sure if a childless man will get it, although she remembers that he has some gripe or other with his own parents. On balance, she chooses to keep this one to herself. Lily is never at her coolest on the topic of her mother. Not by a long chalk. 'When will the date be, Garth?'

'I've a church thing tomorrow, I sort of run the youth group. Saturday night would be perfect for me.'

'Oh, sorry, sunshine, picking my kids up from London on Saturday. Whatever time I'm back it's a staying-in night. First with them for eight days, life's purgatory without them.'

'I see...and I understand.'

Lily wonders if he does—if any childless man could come close— at least this one's trying.

'I don't really do Sunday nights, Lily, church can go on until nine...'

'You go morning and evening?'

'Yes. I'm a bit of a fixture actually, I strum guitar for the hymns...'

'Oh, this I must see.'

'Yes. Come to church, Lily, I'd love that.'

She doesn't answer, no wish to sound dismissive.

'Not the date, Lily, we'll still do that.'

'Not on Sunday. I'm sorry, my kids don't stay out that late.'

'Bring them to the morning service. You'll still get to hear me play guitar.'

'Sorry, Garth, I don't think it's my thing. Please don't be offended.'

'You're right, I shouldn't be pressing you. I'm an enthusiast, I know. Can't help how I am about it. Listen, is Wednesday evening next week a possibility for our date?'

Lily agrees, confirms no taxi will be needed by that time. She will be able to walk to Southbourne, if that is where he is to take her.

When the call is over, she texts Alice.

> ***That sweet boy, Garth, phoned. Could you babysit on Wednesday, pretty please? First date in a hundred and fifty years.***

A reply appears within a minute.

> ***I knew he couldn't resist you. Yes, I can. You are a liar: about six months by my reckoning.***

Lily thinks about this cheeky reply before texting more.

Boscombe

My first date in Dorset!

Seconds later a further text comes in.

First? What about the dating-site chappie?

Lily has shared most experiences she has had in Boscombe with Alice. Her recent meeting with Caroline is the exception.

He was an arsehole and I never date them. Love Lily.

* * *

After these contrasting calls and messages, Lily again has an awkward shower. A war wound to keep dry. She is at the stage of choosing clothes to wear when the doorbell rings. Puts a dressing gown on over her underwear, and goes to the front door. Uses the chain, feeling underdressed, then through the open slither she sees her young friend, the same smart running clothes upon her tanned body.

'Caroline, come in, I was just getting dressed.'

'No need, Lily, I'm not really,' she says, gesturing down at her own exposed skin.

Her friend has been running energetically, she is glowing, sweating in truth. Caroline must always look terrific, not an ounce of fat, well-toned, her face is a little redder than Lily recalls from Sunday, and she has a dampness on the small of her back, the light mauve T-shirt far darker between her shoulder blades.

'I'd offer you a shower but I've used all the hot water.'

'Whatever for? I'll be running back. This is a pitstop.'

Lily takes Caroline into the lounge. Explains a little about the situation: her children will be back tomorrow.

'I was worried when I heard you'd had an accident. Show me.'

Lily turns her left leg, points at where the dressing gown ends. The site where dressing and bandage cover her calf.

'Poor thing,' says Caroline. 'Did they give you tetanus?'

'I was in such a daze I don't know what they did. A nurse cleaned it, then the doctor did the same again. It hurt like fury when he poured something over it. But the jab? Maybe. I wasn't myself.'

'Did you have family with you, a boyfriend?'

'I don't have a boyfriend,' she replies, before wondering if she sort of does.

'Oh sorry, I remember now. You did say when we met.'

A Week Without Children

'The boy who ran into me came though, he paid for a taxi and stayed with me in and out of casualty.'

'Oh Lily, isn't that creepy-weird? The guy runs you off the road and then pretends he's your friend.'

She starts to laugh, wants to explain that she's going to see him again. Doesn't do it having heard the girl's initial judgement. 'It was an accident, Caroline. The guy was all right, caring.'

'Good for him, I think family can be better than strangers.'

'Most can. My family's the exception. Thankfully they live a hundred and fifty miles away...'

'Oh golly, are they that bad?'

'Do I shock you?'

'No, just... Lily, I live with my mum and dad, they mean the world to me.'

'I left for London in my teens. Avoid Sittingbourne to this day. My parents really aren't my sort of people.'

'Golly,' says Caroline, 'it's probably time I moved out, not that I've any plans to do it. I love them to bits. They let me be me, look after me if I'm poorly. I think that's what proper parents do, or am I just lucky?'

'You're lucky and I'm pleased, Caz. It's what I hope to be for Ami and Jo-jo. My own just didn't come up to the measure...'

Lily feels calm, likes this all-round happy girl. Thinks she might be educating her. To her surprise, Caroline gets up and pulls Lily to her feet, puts arms around her and says, 'I'm sure you are everything to those children that your mother should have been to you.' As she is enjoying the moment, the sentiment, although she'd not felt any expectation of such physical comfort, the girl rolls her arms inside Lily's dressing gown, hugging her ever so closely, although the girl's chin is over Lily's shoulder.

'I've got to go now, sweetie,' says the young comforter.

Lily is taken aback by the girl's confidence; calls out, 'Thanks for coming,' as Caroline is once again on the pavement and running back to Christchurch. Lily shuts the door, opens her dressing gown, wondering if she can smell the girl's perspiration on herself, following the unexpected and intimate hug. She's certainly not showering again. Too much of a faff. And Caroline was sweet, sympathetic; boys probably line themselves up for her. Can't expect a girl like that to fathom her own connection with Garth. Not that Lily has any idea how it will turn out; she's trying the guy for lack of an alternative.

Friday, 3 June 2016

Friday in the office is a better day than Thursday. Lily knew in advance that Simon Clarke would not be there and it lightened her mood. The forthcoming date with Garth is the topping. Lily decides very definitely to tell no one at work about this planned outing. It's her business, not Gillian Garrett's. And the prospects aren't good. Garth is too young; he has family baggage that might be as bad as her own. Born-again Christians are an odd lot, won't say it to his face, but she can't think otherwise. She'd like him to hold her, hug her, as Caroline had the night before. There are certain feelings she's lived too long without.

Late morning, Mr and Mrs Clarke come around the office. Gregory Clarke—old Mr Clarke as he has only been styled since his retirement—his son still laid up in the hospital. To the best of Lily's knowledge, his wife has no first name, certainly not one spoken in her presence. This is an unexpected visit and she briefly thinks they've come to announce Simon's death. She has mixed feelings about that. In fact, they are collecting signatures for a get-well-soon card, surprising that both come into the office for it. Gregory's status is principally a retired partner, name on the door but he doesn't have office or chair, and his wife was never employed here. Lily has seen her precisely twice before today. She guesses they have tasked themselves with this chore because the presence of kindly Gregory Clarke will garner more signatures than would arise if left to Mrs Garrett.

After a lengthy rumination in front of the old couple, she writes her piece.

Mr Clarke, all the best, Lily Stephens

It earns her a perplexed look from the man's mother while saying more than enough in her own estimation. Lily spends the rest of the morning completing the half-sentence in her head. All the best...pain killers are being given to the worthier patients. Others along those lines.

A Week Without Children

When the working day is over, Lily starts to saunter towards the childminder's house, after a hundred yards she checks herself, gets back on track. She misses them that much. Ami and Jo-jo.

Saturday, 4 June 2016

The train up to London is very crowded. Lily couldn't find a seat when she got on at Pokesdown. Standing up was horrible. The shooting pains in her calf.

She got lucky at Christchurch, a teenage girl vacated a seat close by and Lily took it before anyone else could. She takes out a book to read then finds she's not in the mood for it. At Brockenhurst station, out of Dorset but barely, she pushes the novel aside. Is she really going through with this date? An evening with Garth Addicks. After a week without children, the responsibility is about to land back on her plate. Jo-jo is a treasure but, at eight years of age, he needs her guiding hand. He's independently minded, a bit of reigning in required. Ami is the best of her. She has no available time, no headspace, for a boyfriend. He's a guitar-strumming holy roller. Can't see where he's going on a bike, and she certainly isn't going to his funnily named church. The Men of Judas except that isn't quite it. All religion is pie in the sky. The kids love Trent whatever she thinks of him, might struggle if she brought another man into their lives.

Her thoughts shift to the office: she's never liked it there. The fashion store in Bournemouth—her first job in the area—was a poorer wage. Required her to find more childcare; every working Saturday was a nightmare. Young Mr Clarke's collarbone won't keep him away forever. Whatever else it was, Garth's phone call feels like the antidote to Clarke's Saturday night stunt. Perhaps she remains desirable. To married men and the God squad.

After initially meeting Caroline on Sunday, Lily had mentally vowed to run and swim on the beach each day until the kids returned. Find a way after that if she could. Fit Lily didn't quite materialise, not that she's a quitter. She meant it when she told the girl she'd be back. Her ruminations make her conscious of the injury. Lily accidentally nudges the man in the seat beside her as she fiddles down below to feel around the dressing on her left leg. It hasn't moved; she thinks it may have bled. She cannot put her leg up here, cramped together in the train seats.

'What are ye doing down there?' The nudged man has a harsh Scot's lilt to his voice.

'I'm sorry, I felt uncomfortable.'

'Well don't spill ma drink...' He points a finger at his Red Bull, 'or I'll spill you!'

She turns away, looks down the train carriage. Miles and miles to roll with him by her side. Standing in the aisle is not an alternative. She closes her eyes. 'I'm going to try to sleep.' She hopes it will discourage further outbursts of unfocussed aggression.

The man burps, momentarily sounding like her teenage friends of long-ago Sittingbourne. The corners of her mouth turn upwards. That was a grim time, and she was once every bit as vulgar as the stranger in the seat beside her.

* * *

Waterloo Station is noisy, vibrant, alive; Lily has always liked it. The queue to get through the barrier, from platform to concourse, is a latent pop festival. People of every hue, income and culture. She keeps stooping to feel the bandage through her torn jeans. Thinks them a poorer clothing choice than crossed her mind early morning, revealing a little flesh and, to the observant eye, evidence of her injury. The white of the bandage. She notices how multifarious the dress is here, the contrast from Bournemouth. Two Nigerians—or Ghanaians perhaps—in florid African dress. And there is much flesh on display, London in the early summer. A girl no older than Caroline wears ripped jeans with more holes than actual denim. A black girl wears a miniskirt of dazzling silver. Lily wouldn't dare to wear something so eye-catching. There was a time. The girl looks amazing.

When she left Kent, came to London, age nineteen, Lily dressed in whatever she felt like. Worked in fashion stores; bought great stuff at discount prices, lifted a thing or two from under their corporate noses. She did bar work too because shop assistant pay wasn't great. Working in the nightspots was a smart move, good times but not drunken times on her part. Not when she was working. The days off were the blur. She met Carlo in one of those clubs. She thought he was the love of her life for about six weeks; a wife in the suburbs he never once mentioned.

Later, Trent offered real love; he was a serious young man, if not a reliable one. When she brought Jo-jo home from the hospital it felt like the culmination of their great romance. They loved him, loved each other. Not much money but lots of something good. Each relished their parental duties. Looking back, she knows that this was when they lost their focus, their earlier warm relationship turned into battles won and lost. Neither of them was so much as a pinch selfish; each tried to prove themselves the more loving of their little boy.

When Lily asked Trent to stay home one night so she could go out with a couple of girls from work—shop workers—he had laughed at her. 'I'm looking after my boy every night. I've not been out this month. You have a princess of a time. I'll always be here for Joey, and you know it.' Why that fair-enough summary had turned into a blazing row remains a mystery to her. Lily recalls disliking his tone, feeling it was accusatory. She wasn't his princess, never had been, never wanted to be. The pair of them were city rats, making a home in the shabby side of town. Raising a treasured child in a bed-sitting room. A child who was starting to speak, talk, need his own space.

And this may have been the nub of it: Trent was better with the children than he ever was at any kind of work. He would turn his hand to anything: removals; the meat market. He worked as a security guard in Harrods for a time. His give-it-a-go approach was not a qualification, didn't make him good at it. He briefly did a lot of things; nothing stuck. He made her laugh when he told her how the manager had prepared him for the Harrods job. 'Pay extra attention to the black boys,' the head of security told him without a hint of self-consciousness. Lily smiles remembering Trent saying, 'If I nick stuff and then hand myself in, I reckon they'll give me a raise.'

They stretched to get the rented place in Shoreditch, got the keys about one month before baby was due. The lovely bundle of Ami. Arguing about money had long been a fixture. Lily recalls expressing milk so that Trent could bottle-feed six-week-old Ami while she pulled pints in a club on Appold Street. Worked until three in the morning, four or five nights a week. The money needed to stave off an eviction notice. Arguments, arguments. She really had loved that man, perhaps for two years, almost three years, before the children were born. And in some echoey way for a good while longer.

She is on the tube now, heading again for Shoreditch. Different address, same in every other way. She never blames Jo-jo or Ami, never for a second. She and Trent failed to keep what they once had. She and Trent. Lily never shirks responsibility, even wonders if she should have looked over her shoulder before stepping into the line of Garth's bicycle.

* * *

'Hi, Lily,' says her former lover as he opens the exterior door of the flat block. Their son is by his side and Ami hangs onto a rail halfway up the stone staircase. He leans in to peck her on the cheek. Done for their children, the need to appear civil in front of them. She allows it, reciprocates nothing. 'Come in for a cup of tea. If I can find any.' He smiles apologetically.

'Are they packed? I need to get them back home.'

'Come in and I'll get the bags.'

'They aren't, are they?' she whispers, hoping her criticism doesn't reach young ears.

'All packed.' He says it with a grin. White teeth illuminate the shadowy hallway.

Lily nods, studies the lines on his cheeks. Trent is only a couple of years older than she. He has aged since they separated, the seaside air is her elixir. 'I'll wait here.'

Trent puts a hand on her shoulder, squeezes it so lightly it is barely discernible. 'Is it your mother?'

'No, it's not my bloody mother,' Lily hisses. 'She didn't steal the children. You took them to Sittingbourne. You did that.'

'Lily-petal...'

'Just Lily, please.' She's grown to like Alice calling her by it. Trent got there first but it's inappropriate now. An ex is no part of a flower.

'Lily, when she phoned me, she made out it was Gordon's last chance to see them before departin' this life. Then, when I got the real story off him, it sounds like he's healthier than what I am.'

'You're a fool then, Trent. You could have phoned me. Don't go poking around Sittingbourne without consulting me. Rules.'

Jo-jo has drifted up the stairs to stand with Ami and watch their parents' incomprehensible dust-up from there. He even puts an arm

A Week Without Children

around his little sister.

'I can't phone, you don't pick me up.'

'Text first, Trent. Text me what you want to speak about. Rules.'

* * *

Back on the concourse at Waterloo, Lily takes her little ones into the coffee shop. She has hugged Ami close all the way from Shoreditch High Street to here. Hugged Jo-jo when he let her. She hasn't cried but having them back is a joy that brings her close. Now, in the balcony cafe, she shows them her bandage. Ami tugs at the jeans like she should take them down, show her properly. 'Boscombe,' says Lily. No stripping off in a public place.

She was gagging for a cup of tea at Trent's, couldn't bear to be with him for a minute. Taking the children to Sittingbourne! They can talk nothing through nowadays, and it's true she never answers his calls. Separations must be shit for kids, she thinks, not that any harm would have followed if soft-in-the-head Gordon had left her mother. Lily might have made more of an effort for the silly old duffer if he'd done that. The children choose pastries, unaffordable pastries that she pays for anyway, little change left from twenty pounds after buying three drinks to go with them. She loves these children.

* * *

When the designated platform number appears on the overhead screens, she rushes them to number nine, through the barrier and they dash to get the seats with a table. Journeys are easier when they have space to spread out all their snacks and puzzle books. Today is a lucky day.

The train rattles its way back home. A better one than Sittingbourne or Shoreditch ever were. There is security in not requiring anything to be different. She pulls Ami into yet another hug; 'Hey,' says the girl, the unexpected embrace drawing a line across a face in her colouring book.

Lily muzzles a kiss onto the top of her head. 'Back to Boscombe,' she says.

'Back to Boscombe,' parrots Ami.

Jo-jo says nothing, embarrassed by displays of affection in public. The age he has arrived at.

Boscombe

* * *

The train sets down at Clapham Junction and then starts up again in no time.

'I thought it was you,' says a familiar voice. Caroline is standing in the aisle before her. Lily smiles back at her, surprised they are sharing a train. 'Are these your little ones? Aren't they adorable?' She nods concurrence. 'We've been to London to see a show.' She glances over her shoulder. Diagonally opposite, and halfway up the carriage, an older couple wave at her. 'Mummy and Daddy,' Caroline explains.

'Was the show good?' asks Lily, as her young friend slides into the seat next to Jo-jo.

'It bored me but they loved it. A morning on Oxford Street was rather nice.'

Lily appraises Caroline. She looks stunning as only money can buy. Her hair is neater than when running, precise, her clothing is of exceptional quality, contoured as if for her alone. A summer dress that modestly exposes a little tanned shoulder, a far cry from the fleshy display on Boscombe beach. She really is a princess.

'What's your name, sweetie?' she enquires of Lily's son.

'Jo-jo,' he tells her, looking momentarily at Caroline and then staring back at the comic on the table.

'Do you mind me sitting beside you?' She says to his frowning face. 'Can I be your girlfriend for the journey?'

Jo-jo laughs, Ami immediately laughs along.

'What did you buy?' asks Lily.

'Clothes, clothes, clothes. I'm just a spoilt brat. Did I say that I work in a private gym, just part-time; the money is hopeless. How can I move out when Daddy keeps buying me all the things I don't deserve?'

Lily laughs. Loves how Caroline talks about herself, and her easy charm with the children. Lily glances down the carriage at the man with the chequebook. He can't hear her, would surely only shrug if he could. Caroline is the most delectable girl.

* * *

'Not far,' Lily repeats many times as she walks her moaning children from Pokesdown Station to Cooper Road. She never relents in her own optimistic chatter although, in truth, her leg is hurting like crazy. It's been a long day. Caroline, who got off the stop before them, was good company. Occupied the children like a nursery teacher. Helped make the journey go smoothly.

When she has opened the door and they are safely home, she feels a self-satisfied hurrah, wants to hole up for the rest of the weekend. She probably will. It's not so late, all went smoothly, on balance, and she picks fish fingers from the ice box while the children re-enter their bedrooms as if they have returned to Earth from space. 'You tidied, Mummy!' they shout, and she cannot tell from the kitchen if it is praise or annoyance. One of each, her best guess.

'If you keep messing, then that's what mummies have to do.'

'Daddy doesn't. He's as messy as me,' says her son.

'Yes, and he loves you. In my house, we keep to my rules. Got that?'

* * *

And in the late evening, when Lily has been in and out of their rooms, seen that both children are truly sleeping, lost in a dream world that she hopes is as beautiful as their faces, Lily sinks into the sofa. Stretches out her tired legs, feels the sore calf. She determines that she will go on the date with Garth; Alice has agreed to sit in the maisonette for the evening, mind her sleeping youngsters. She'll learn about working with troubled teenagers from him; work out if it's for her or not. Young Caroline must have been a pleasure to be with at that age but when she—Lily Stephens—was thirteen, fourteen, fifteen, she was an obnoxious run-around. She isn't sure if she would have the patience to work with a kid anything like she used to be.

Three musical notes sound in her jeans pocket. She pulls it out, takes a look.

Are you back safely?

The text is from Alice, and as she is replying, her smartphone again emits its brief musical announcement, a smiley face on the screen.

Lovely to bump into you today. Your kids are the sweetest, Caz xx

She thinks Garth should text now; three welcome-home texts would be perfect. Despite pangs, pains and twitches, she falls asleep on the sofa, still waiting for it. No recognition from Garth that she has

Boscombe

journeyed to the capital and back to collect these precious children.

Chapter Two:

In the Lord's Knowing Gaze

Sunday, 5 June 2016

He puts sufficient enthusiasm into the strumming, and most of the eighty-strong congregation are clapping along; however, Lord of the Dance is not a hymn Garth cares for. The words do not have the gravity of the hymns he cherishes. It's a crowd-pleaser, not a discourse worthy of significant meditation. Next to him, three teenage girls—who form the choir at The Church of the Men of Judea, Northbourne—are belting it out. Their voices are high, clear and strong, and they sing this one with an excitement Garth would relish were he less critical of the hymn's worth.

> *They whipped and they stripped and they hung me on high*
> *And they left me there on a cross to die*

The girls' singing is unnecessarily joyful. Shouldn't really celebrate a whipping. It is eternal remorse we must feel for Christ's sacrifice. The fact that He has subsequently forgiven us is another of His miracles, the most remarkable of them all. While Garth strums, he wonders if he's wrong. Pastor Margery would say it's not a crime to enjoy a song. A fair point but for the weight of our Lord's suffering. As he puts down his guitar, Julie, the girl on the end, gives him a thumbs up. Praise for his playing, he assumes. Jesus is the one to praise, not him. He makes a displeased face: there are no thumbs-ups in the Bible.

When the congregation is seated, Margery pulls herself up from her high-backed chair, two hands move to her wheeled Zimmer frame and with it she guides her overweight body the few steps to the church's low-standing pulpit. Garth admires her—the lady is still in her forties—she will battle through the sermon, her arthritis seeming of no concern. He doesn't know her opinion of the unfortunate physical state with which God has burdened her. They enjoy lively conversations of which her disability has been the subject of none. 'Beautiful singing everyone, prayer time now.' She gives the congregation the warmest of smiles, squeezing her eyes briefly together and then allowing her head to bow. Garth considers her frightfully informal. Her style may be a factor in the swelling number of congregants this spring. To his knowledge, he and Peter Carter alone regard it as slightly irreverent. The Church of the Men of Judea is not an old denomination but its members hope to live with the fervour of first-century Christians, certain of Christ's imminent return. Sobriety looks like the safe bet. He may have been a bit frivolous on the bank holiday with Lily. Not at the hospital but when they were back in her flat. It's the same for him at work, to win over non-believers you have to behave far more like one than comes naturally.

'There are some sick for us to remember in our prayers. Mrs Dunn is once more in the hospital. Dear Lord, thank you for the time you have given Mrs Dunn on this Earth. Ninety-four years and counting, and we pray for her return home from hospital. We love her so. We hope you do not need her yet, Lord.' Garth sits facing the congregation, guitar on a metal stand by his side; he glances across, head bowed only a few degrees. 'Lord, we think also of Simon Clarke, husband of Cindy Clarke, who we understand you are caring for with the help of our own Southampton General Hospital. Simon is not a member of our church while Cindy, of course, is here today. And we extend our love and prayers to them both, wish him a speedy recovery from a particularly unpleasant accident that befell him Monday last.' The pastor looks up from the small lectern before her. 'We are here for you, Cindy.'

Garth feels the warmth within the small church. Everyone responds well to Margery's mother-hen schtick. She is selfless in her delivery, more overtly humble than he can muster, try as he does. He even wonders if the dismissive glance with which he met young Julie's raised thumb was an act of rudeness. The girl might construe it as arrogance, and that was far from his intention. He could learn a thing or two from Margery. Her relentless good humour might be another way of preparing for Christ's return.

In the Lord's Knowing Gaze

'We thank you for your continued mercy, Lord, Amen.'

'Amen,' they echo back. Eighty strong voices, there is no half-hearted mumbling in The Church of the Men of Judea. They are truly thankful and equally certain that his mercy will not end.

'Today, everybody, I'd like to talk about the importance of keeping our faith and the pressures that pull the best of us away from His Word. Things which may give rise to doubt or cause us to stray, renounce or deviate from the true path.' She pauses and looks up towards the low ceiling of their church, premises adapted, not built, for this pious purpose. No frescos in The Church of the Men of Judea, she stares upon fading white emulsion. 'Oh Lord, let your wisdom be within my words.'

'Amen,' say the congregants, more quietly this time. An insistent hum.

'For those of you who wish to read it directly, this is drawn from Ephesians, twelve to fifteen, just twelve to fifteen,' says Margery. 'Saint Paul—my favourite saint, truly, he has bequeathed us so much wisdom—he said, and I quote: "*Those who want to impress people by means of the flesh are trying to compel you to be circumcised. The only reason they do this is to avoid being persecuted for the cross of Christ.*" What did he mean? Well, I'm going to try and tell you.' Garth looks across at Julie, and at her two friends, Samantha and the new addition whose name he forgets. They are unwavering in their attention. She has young and old eating out of her hand—St Paul is serious stuff—the entire room contemplates the epistle to the Ephesians. 'We should regard circumcision as a metaphor here; it may be the whole story in some parts of the world, I think it was when Paul wrote the letter. It works just as well as a metaphor. When it is easier for you to deny, renounce, or ignore your faith, to nod along with the ungodly crowd, of whom there are very many in the world today—in Bournemouth today—what do you do? Well, I think the phrase "*impress by means of the flesh,*" is the important one in this verse.' Margery pauses, takes her hand off the lectern. Just standing without her frame or other aid seems like a miracle for this physically debilitated woman. 'You all know the phrase, "temptations of the flesh," some of you may be stirred by them every now and again...' A ripple of quiet giggling flickers across the until-now silent hall. Garth allows his own lips to upturn, pictures Lily in her black running shorts, the excessive amount of her flesh he saw on Monday last. 'We are impressed by means of flesh, are we not? We are tempted but also beguiled. We like to see others. Youthful boys enjoy gazing upon young girls, and fellas, the girls like looking in the opposite direction. Some of you have a little something.' Garth hears a giggle from Julie and her friends, thinks Margery may have strayed into crowd-pleasing. 'Like the sign says, "You can look but you cannot touch." Remember our teaching, young ones. We may feel tempted but we are resolute in our Christian faith. And that's why we must consider the very next thing that Paul wrote: "*Not even those who are circumcised keep the law, yet they want you to be circumcised that they may boast about your circumcision in the flesh.*" Let me pause here so that you may think over what it is that's bugging our St Paul.'

This is a favourite device of Margery's, asking those gathered to contemplate how they would interpret scripture. She may ask church members their views on the crux of her sermons many days after their delivery. Peter Carter, who styles himself as the youngest church elder, told Garth that he has started making notes. Garth assumed it was a joke although Peter is a dry fellow, didn't crack a smile whether it was or wasn't.

'Now everyone, when St Paul says, "*not even those who are circumcised keep the law,*" it clearly behoves us to think, not twice but two thousand times, before allowing ourselves an ignorant interpretation of his words. He is writing about the struggling faithful, not exclusively about people who are Jewish. Today we might substitute the word, baptised, in place of his word, circumcised. When Paul was writing, and with great awareness of, and even reverence for, the power and standing of the elders of the Hebrew synagogues, he was really speaking to power. If we are to do this now, it might be politicians, popes, priests and—yes, you've guessed it—pastors like me, whose hypocrisy could draw the ire of an aspiring epistle writer. Let us not rest on our laurels or gloat over yesterday's clever victories, let us be vigilant. I think this is Paul's message, coming to us through time. I hear that today. Do you?' Garth sees it, she has brought relevance to a passage he has read many times but not before felt this certain of its meaning. Margery does this

In the Lord's Knowing Gaze

remarkably well, sees afresh what is within the Bible. He watches as she pulls her reading glasses from the lip of her lectern, pushes them into her puffed cheeks, reads on: "*May I never boast except in the cross of our Lord Jesus Christ, through which the world has been crucified to me, and I to the world.*" Do you see what he's done here?' Again, she pauses, lets the congregation reflect. 'I wonder, I really wonder, do any of us care to boast that we, in our devotion to Jesus, feel we have been crucified, perhaps metaphorically so, crucified, nailed on to wood, as He was.' The church is hushed as she pauses. Garth feels the pain of those nails. 'I hope not children—and we are all children in contemplation of this fraught suggestion—we have nothing to boast about. We must feel only humility in the light of the wonderful gift God has given us: His Son. We know this because Paul completes this passage saying: "*Neither circumcision nor uncircumcision means anything; what counts is the new creation.*" Let us again give pause to contemplate these words.' The broadest smile crosses her face. Garth's too as he dwells on that special beginning. The reboot, as Peter, who works in computing, calls the second coming they all wait impatiently for.

Margery bows her head, takes the Zimmer-frame in her hands and, as the church is thinking about her words and those of Saint Paul before her, shuffles again to her seat. Garth is in awe of Margery's ability to breathe new life into the beautiful thoughts within the only book that matters. He finds it an invigorating experience, hearing the pastor's daring interpretations of verses he knows well. It jolts him into thinking more deeply about God's love. The Words and thoughts of the messengers He sent in those momentous times.

* * *

'What you said on Friday,' says the girl, 'it really stayed with me.' Garth nods, he is pleased if a youngster pays attention to the short talks which he gives at Friday youth group. 'I tried it that night and ever since,' she continues.

He wishes he could recall the girl's name. The talk she liked was about prayer. She is in his small choir; awkward that her name has slipped his mind. She's only been in church a couple of months, fourth week singing out front. And he's really itching to speak to Peter and Margery, who are drinking coffee together in the corner. He could take his leave of her less rudely were he to use her name. Make the apology personal. Marooned, Garth nods politely. 'I'm so pleased this has helped you get closer to Jesus.'

As he steps away, he hears Julie and Samantha giggling. They are the other choristers. And the core of Friday youth group; he sometimes gets a dozen to attend. A few seem to like ping-pong more than religion. The lads turn up because the girls are there, pretty Julie Rivington more popular than the ping-pong table.

'...it is by far the best way to engage them. Be engaging!' says Margery to Peter as Garth sidles up. He quickly gathers that Peter, the youngest elder who has championed Garth's wider involvement in church leadership—helping him become deputy leader of the youth group, and Elspeth Dunn has been the leader in name only for two decades, it's Garth's project—is praising the pastor for her skills of captivation, her positive effect on attendance at The Church of the Men of Judea, Northbourne. Garth wonders what to think of this. He and Peter have spoken about her style, speculated whether, in the long term, it could prove to be taking them in the wrong direction.

'Margery,' says Garth, 'Ephesians was a truly excellent choice. Your analysis blew me away.' There is no arguing with the Bible, and she spreads the Word thoughtfully.

Slowly congregants drift homewards. Peter and Garth both live alone; they will stay longest, wash coffee cups, do their bit to help the service run smoothly.

He walks briskly up to the exit door, tells Cindy Clarke, as she is leaving, that he is praying for her husband. When she asks, he confirms that her son told him of the accident on Friday. Young Ronnie attends youth group. 'Yes, he enjoys your club,' says Cindy. 'He wouldn't come this morning, you'll have noticed. Unlikely to be at evening service but I'll try.'

Garth nods. Ronnie Clarke is one of the boys who spends youth group pestering Julie. Or pleasing Julie? Garth isn't sure how girls with looks like hers feel about their admirers. They're both fourteen years old; Garth runs a tight youth group, ensures everything is above board. Tells them about Jesus whenever there's an opening.

* * *

They said they would see each other again at evening service; however,

In the Lord's Knowing Gaze

on Sunday afternoon Garth walks around to his house. Peter, both church elder and man of means, has long been his mentor, his unofficial spiritual guide. On arrival, Peter welcomes Garth into his bungalow, ushers him straight through into the well-tended rear garden. He has set out a table and chair to enjoy the afternoon sun. The smell of freshly cut grass—a task which Garth assumes Peter completed on Saturday, can't picture him toiling on the Sabbath—mingles with the scent from his well-tended rose bed.

While his host goes to the garden shed to fetch a second folding chair, Garth looks at the books his friend has beside him. A copy of Lord of the Flies sitting on a garden table atop his friend's study Bible. A curious juxtaposition. He read it in school, enjoyed it, Garth recalls. The Golding, that is; the Bible he completely ignored in his school years. Only in adulthood has it become his constant companion.

'Can I get you a cold drink, my friend?'

Garth shakes his head as Peter sits down on the newly unfolded chair. 'I just want to say...' He states it as matter-of-factly as he is able. '...I met someone.' He sees no discernible surprise on his friend's face, ploughs on. 'It's a...the person who I've met...it's...' At the door of his mouth, this word seems surprisingly shy. '...well, in fact, actually...it's a lady. I've met a lady, Peter.'

His friend's face is unchanged, the look of a thoughtful man. He says nothing for some fifteen or twenty seconds. 'I am pleased,' Peter's considered reply.

'I think I am....' Garth stumbles on the words, indecision about quite how much of his inner thinking to reveal. 'She is...' He regroups his thoughts, stomach turning, although the absence of food since eating a little breakfast cereal may be the major cause. '...beguiling. I have enjoyed her company, only once but truly enjoyed it. Peter...' He feels a tug of trepidation as to how the church elder may react. '...the lady in question is not yet a Christian.'

'Garth, my friend, therein lies the answer you seek.'

'It does?' Garth finds himself smiling; Peter has teased him with a riddle he cannot unscramble. Hadn't even asked a question.

'Yet. Your choice of the word, yet, Garth. It spoke most clearly to me. You have certainty in her destiny, and therefore the path is a righteous one. I am pleased for your friendship, and an imminent conversion will be the still greater joy to our Lord...'

'I'm not quite as optimistic as you, Peter. Early days, shall we say? She is...the lady in question...' It is not like him to be this hesitant. '...well, she's a single parent. A mother to two children.'

His mentor's face takes on a sterner look. 'What is the nature of your relationship to date, Garth? And the young lady's expectations...'

'Peter,' he says, 'by my calculation, she's not as young as all that...' He finds himself revealing one awkward fact after another, cheeks reddening. '...she is a few years older than I.'

'Garth, we should not talk of your friend in so abstract a manner. Pray tell me the name of...' He turns his head toward his open patio doors—a telephone's trill emitting from inside the bungalow—Peter rises from his garden chair. '...your sweetheart,' he says before disappearing through the patio doors.

Garth glances once more at the books beside his chair, he hears Peter's mellow voice, engaging some other seeker of guidance on the telephone. Garth doesn't listen. His reason for coming today is solely to be sure of the path he has chosen, his wish to act upon God's unspoken instruction in setting Lily in front of him on Monday last. As the minutes tick by, he starts to wish he had accepted a drink. It is a warm afternoon and apart from a morning coffee and a second at church, he has drunk nothing all day. He often forgoes his lunchtime meal on a Sunday but he is flagging, parched. Hungry.

'Lily,' he states when Peter finally returns.

This extracts a quizzical look from the householder. '...of the valley?' offers Peter in rejoinder.

'You've forgotten,' says Garth, a catch of laughter in his voice. 'Forgotten what we were talking about. Was your phone call so enthralling?' Peter doesn't answer; Garth thinks Peter has a razor-sharp mind, and this lapse most amusing. 'MI6 stuff, was it?'

Peter smiles back at him. 'You think I was hauling one back in from the cold? You read too many potboilers, Garth. Or perhaps my software firm should diversify, run a few spies. We could infiltrate the Church of England. Turn them!' Garth's laughter gives him a dry cough; Peter stands. 'Come,' he says, 'you must have a drink on this hot afternoon.' They both walk through the patio doors. A smart modern kitchen of dark grey worktops, Peter draws a large carton of melon juice from his tall upright fridge, shows it to Garth with a gesture of encouragement, and pours two tumblers full. 'It's lovely stuff,' he says, and they chink glasses as Russian vodka drinkers might. 'Your lady-friend's name is Lily,' Peter finally states, drawing on the mental prowess that has served him so well in the computer business. Garth nods. 'Is she divorced?'

'Long separated from the father of the children. He lives in London, and she in...'

'But she hasn't divorced him yet? This is most serious, Garth. It is a sin to break asunder a marriage. Their temporary unhappiness requires resolution, it is not an opportunity for you to usurp the husband's rightful position, however well—or poorly—he is currently fulfilling his role. You know that in our church...'

Garth shakes his head throughout Peter's soliloquy, finally interrupts. 'They never married. Lily is as divorced as she could ever be.'

'Are you confident that you are taking righteous steps, my friend?'

Garth gulps a little air before answering, drinks some melon juice with which to wash down the air. 'I think I am,' he replies. He feels frustrated—Peter sees only obstacles—not yet given the chance to explain how the Lord brought them together. He and Lily.

'I hope you are. Of course, the lady would be most welcome in our congregation, an opportunity for her to let in the light. I have reservations, Garth, about the wisdom of pursuing a relationship in the hope that she later follows this course. Pursues a Christian life. She has twice born children outside of wedlock; not once, Garth, two times. It is not for me to stand in the way of your happiness. I do think the path ahead looks most uncertain.'

'I don't know yet if she will make me happy. Hope it, don't know it. Even our meeting was the strangest thing.'

'It was? How so, Garth?'

'I can't really explain it, expect only the Lord could do that. I accidently knocked her down with my bicycle...'

Garth relates the events of Monday last. Her scant clothing and their parting hug, he chooses not to share. Garth knows that he has counselled youngsters at youth group with every bit as much caution as Peter is advising him to adopt. Doubt is the immediate outcome.

In his heart, Garth has long feared there is room only for our Lord, Jesus Christ. Alongside this, he has the nagging feeling that Peter cannot empathise with the joy which Lily's company brought him. He wonders if the man has ever had a similar experience. Felt a connection with a woman. It seems improbable as he listens to Peter's uninspiring advice.

* * *

The evening service has drawn a good congregation, over sixty people, he thinks. Margery's sermon is equally inspiring to that preached this morning. She draws on their doctrine of acts of goodness, the importance of doing as many as we can in our time on God's Earth. It is a central tenet of The Church of the Men of Judea. Garth makes a deliberate effort to be encouraging to the three girls who comprise his choir. 'You were terrific tonight,' he tells them when the service comes to an end. Girls enjoying their singing is a good thing he has decided. It might be Lily's view, that's his sense of her. People are starting to drift away; the evening sunlight tempts those who wish to chat out into the rear courtyard. It's a simple space, soft red tarmac laid down in the building's former life as a day nursery. Highly practical for the mother and toddler group that Cindy Clarke and a couple of other congregants run. In April, Pastor Margery donated a small olive tree, one she had initially bought for the garden of her tied house. Garth carried it here from two roads away, it remains in its black plastic bucket, garden-centre logo running round the rim. An olive tree sounds biblical but this one still looks as it might if it was on sale at the nearby superstore.

Garth stands beside the tree watching Julie Rivington, resplendent in a yellow frock. He wonders if it is his place to advise her to wear longer skirts to church. There is a click of fingers to his right. He turns his head; Margery has a wicked glint in her eye. It feels as if she has caught him eyeing a girl half his age, when in fact he was simultaneously picturing Lily. Not that he wishes to explain this thought to Margery.

'A word,' she says quietly in his ear. Then she pushes her frame past him, nods her head indicating that he should follow.

The young man enjoys a good relationship with his pastor despite his misgivings about her style. She is a novel mix: fun and devout. He

In the Lord's Knowing Gaze

understands that her life has been one of suffering. Before she came to know Christ, she was the victim of an abusive relationship. Peter has shared this with him; Garth hasn't spoken of it directly with Margery. He cannot picture how she conducted herself at that time. No victimhood evident today. Arthritis has crippled her and still she is on top of life, at ease with how she navigates the world. An inspiration, if a little too modern for his liking. Maybe she will prove just right for the new, broad-minded Garth. Since his talk with Peter this afternoon, he has determined that he should keep his eyes wide open while not giving up Lily at all. Peter failed to grasp the big point: the Lord made him collide with her and, therefore, Garth must embrace the consequence. Follow whatever path He has set before him.

The wheels of her Zimmer frame click across the wooden bricks of the short aisle, up to the church's front door, they step out onto Paisley Street. It is a quiet mid-evening; a family browse an estate agents window.

'Tourists,' the pastor states, then she steadies herself, releases her grip on the frame and puts a sisterly hand upon Garth's shoulder. 'Peter telephoned me before the service. I imagine you can guess what he wished to talk about.' Garth nods, wasn't expecting it and nor does he find it surprising. 'I think you have gathered already, Garth, that I am more progressive in my outlook than Mr Carter.' He nods, feels buoyed by this introductory comment. 'I actually had you down as more like Peter than me but I am most certain we are all rooting for Jesus Christ. Deep down we must be.'

'Yes, Pastor, and Peter and I adore what you have done for our church. If we are surprised by your tone, some of your more light-hearted comments...'

'Yes, yes, Garth. We shall have other times to discuss the merits of my steady-as-she-goes approach versus Peter's sackcloth and ashes.' She lets her quickly formed grin dissolve. 'My concern this evening is the state of play inside your head. Do you have strong feelings for this young lady, who I understand has already born two children to another man? A man whom you have yet to meet.'

'I believe my head is clear. It is my wider feelings which are unfamiliar. A new venture for me, Margery. I have chosen to meet the lady—Lily—again, may choose to continue to do so. That cannot be wrong, I am a man of proper self-control; however, never have I thought I must stay single for a lifetime.' Garth feels exceptionally pleased with himself. He had not anticipated having this conversation, pleased he has expressed himself better than he managed in Peter's garden.

'As I said, Garth, my outlook is more progressive than Peter's. His reservations, however, are not unfounded. I fear that a lady of this much experience—he said she is older than you, and in possession of no known faith—may have her own expectations and offer you temptations that will be a challenge for you to decline.' Garth feels himself redden while inadvertently picturing Lily in the black running shorts, the matching T-shirt, in which she endured the casualty department. Margery's devilish reference brought this about, he hadn't thought of her appearance since he last looked at Julie Rivington. 'I would suggest to you that it may be an unnecessary challenge, Garth. Consider carefully if you really wish to put yourself in this much jeopardy. We, in this church, know how devout you are.' She pauses, seems to think for a moment before continuing. 'You know the story of Gandhi, no doubt. I don't want you to think we...'

'Gandhi?' Garth has a puzzled look on his face.

'...very devout, very devout. Chaste. Not one of ours, obviously: a devout Hindu, and chaste to a fault. That was Gandhi. He would sleep alongside naked ladies, very young ladies, girls really. And he did this when he was an old man. Mr Gandhi did it just to test himself, make sure he could still keep to the path. To be certain that he would always resist temptation.'

Garth raises an eyebrow. 'Very strange, and I feel a little offended by your point. I won't be sharing a bedroom with anyone; surely you know that much about me? To hold a hand, to give warmth is not...' Garth pauses, hopes not to blush as he says the words that have come to him. '...of itself a harbinger of libidinous behaviour.'

Margery holds his eye as if calculating whether to trust this explanation. As his point drifts away with the ensuing silence, the pastor smiles. 'So that's not your bag?' Garth nods back at her. 'You're not in it just to resist the temptations but resist them you will, along the way?'

In the Lord's Knowing Gaze

'I'm just getting to know her. We may have stopped seeing each other altogether in a week or two. I'm probably a bit eccentric from Lily's viewpoint. She hasn't any Christian friends to my knowledge. And I think it unlikely that she has people from her agnostic friendships lining up to counsel her against seeing me...'

'Now, now, Garth, don't take my counsel as criticism...'

'I'm not. I was just saying...' He lets the thought, the comparison between his and Lily's circles of friendship stay unexplored. He knows nothing of her friends, hopes they do not censor him for his belief, although such persecution happens to a believer in the modern world. Not all the time but often. Ridicule can rain down like missiles on good and caring Christians, so sinful is the wider world.

The pastor takes a hold of the walking frame, grips it tightly. 'I've known other men like you, Garth. Admired them—each and every one—but I haven't often found them to be of the happy sort. Serving Jesus is a responsibility, I don't think He intended it to be a burden, it simply turns out that way.' Once more, she pauses; Garth keeps his eyes firmly upon her, wishes to hear her out. He should contemplate closely all that she says. 'I have worried that you were not happy, Garth. I've prayed for you, for greater happiness to come into your life. You explained to Mr Carter that you believe God has already interceded in bringing yourself and this lady—your Lily—together. Into a hospital emergency room, curiously. I suspect you are right. It might be my prayers He has answered not just your own, do you see? In his wisdom, He has surprised me, and if I do not look quite as delighted as I should it is simply because this type of relationship, between one so devout and one who has not yet heard a squeak from our Lord Jesus Christ, can easily go awry. That is my experience.'

Garth coughs, involuntarily but it stops the conversation, and when his throat is sufficiently clear he says, 'I will dwell closely on what you have said. The Lord set Lily before me and it is my dearest wish to learn from it as He intended.'

'Yes, yes,' Margery Cox nods, 'and bring the girl to church. And if she doesn't know a word of the Lord's prayer, I shan't bite her for it.'

'You never bite, Margery.'

'...and my sermon this morning, you were listening weren't you, Garth?'

'I loved it, Margery. It's everything we live and breathe.'

Monday, 6 June 2016

Garth catches the early bus, takes it to a stop the far side of Ringwood. From there he walks to Gerry's house. Two hundred yards—no more—and soon after eight o'clock, they are chuntering out of town in her old Ford Fiesta. Both work at Baxter's School, a dozen miles away in the New Forest. Their shared shift pattern helps Garth to make the journey.

'Did you have a good week off?' asks Geraldine. The school was closed for Whitsun week, the residential pupils back with their families or foster families. A children's home for Declan Keane.

'Mustn't grumble,' says Garth. He seldom does and the issues on his mind—his imminent date with Lily—make him unusually ebullient. He will not disclose it to Gerry. Doubts if she would keep it to herself. He can picture the suggestive winks that would follow from certain ribald staff members. If the children got wind of it, his abasement would be complete. Only last term he elected to deliver the inspirational talk, the part where a sermon would sit if their school assembly was a proper service. Before giving the quasi-sermon, he discussed his topic with Mr Lorimer, the head teacher. They considered whether it was wise or foolish, Garth asked the question while hoping for the endorsement which Lorimer supplied. He gave a ten-minute talk—practised in front of his bathroom mirror two nights before and gone over in his head on the morning of its delivery—Garth explained to the boys the concept of celibate choice. He advocated with a degree of passion uncommon in that forum. The simple goodness in it, the lack of complication. He advised that it was the only permitted pre-marital state for practising Christians worldwide. Held true for most other faiths. The school celebrates diversity and Garth tried to climb on board. The Christian minority. He suspects every boy in school said, shouted or whispered, 'Can't get any?' or some similarly crude phrase, in the week that followed. It did not inspire as he had hoped. Staff members said, 'Good on you, mate,' and 'Nice spin on it,' a few other insincere compliments too. The job's great but Baxter's can be a challenging place to bear witness.

In the Lord's Knowing Gaze

* * *

Garth's duties are light throughout the school day. In the early afternoon, he supervises Damian Taylor. Not for the first time, the boy has earned himself an exclusion from his planned lesson. A fight in which he split Paul Frost's lip was sufficient. Garth applies discipline calmly. The boy will go through four pages of his maths workbook; he may ask Garth questions but Garth will only suggest how to proceed, Damian is to complete his own work. He must. This should take forty of the fifty allotted minutes; for the final ten, Garth will take Damian to see the two donkeys which live on-site. It is the one activity this otherwise-hardened boy enjoys more than fighting.

Garth understands, through discussion with the school's visiting psychologist, the justification for this reward. Damian is having a forty-minute redress for the classroom spat. His brain has a short attention span—better than a goldfish but not yet a hedgehog, is how the psychologist put it—he will link donkey petting with the task which has earned it. The splitting of Paul Frost's lip long past. If Damian does his schoolwork without fuss there will be every reason to introduce positive stimuli, the donkey reward. The boy seldom conforms. Forty minutes of it is worth making a song and dance over. As sinners in the wider world declare their transgressions to be unexceptional—greed, intimate relations outside of wedlock—so boys at Baxter's may have concluded that smashing property and fighting are simply their ways of being. Rewarding them for seeing it differently will shift their perspective, extended punishment for being who they are would only increase their frustration.

Garth enjoys doing this. Many of his colleagues can't attend to the detail of it as ably as he. Others might talk about the donkeys when Damian should be doing maths, the comical beasts holding more interest for them than the manipulation of numbers. They don't see as precisely the need to make the bargain both clear and non-negotiable. Garth has made similar deals within his own life, even though the precursor to his repentance never included violence and might have appeared obscure to those for whom right and wrong are mere words. Not opening and closing of the gateway to heaven itself.

Damian asks a question or two of Garth. His worksheets are all about money: he must calculate what combinations of groceries are available to one with a limited budget. This may give him needed life skills, no one expects him to be especially flush in the future. With Garth's prompting, he sticks to the task, and after the allotted time they walk together to the field behind the football pitch. 'Good work, Taylor. You've turned it around today, given yourself a lot to be proud of. Do you see that?'

'I can do the work, just can't stand doing it with all them others, Mr Addicks. I prefer doing it with you.'

'Taylor, you know I'm not even a teacher. Use your class time, succeed on your own merits. Hard work is what's got you petting the donkeys today. It's the only way to get a decent footing in this world.'

'Yeah, it's just the way the other kids look at me—not Declan, the rest of them—I don't think you would like it. Not if you had to put up with it every day.'

'Will you just consider what you've said, Taylor? Do I down tools with other children? Do they put me off work? No, I do not. Just like today, with you, they are my work. We can't choose when to turn it off or on in ordinary life. We must apply ourselves then reap the benefits. Remember that. Now go and give out carrots.'

Garth smiles to himself as the boy breaks into a trot, runs towards the donkeys who do not judge him.

* * *

After school Garth sits in the lounge of Stone, one of the four houses which comprise the residential estate. Rihanna is on shift with him: a good worker, she involves herself tirelessly with the boys. She challenges Garth now and again, queries if his Christianity is a perverse motivation. Does he do the work for Jesus and not for these downtrodden boys? Doing what the boys need to get them on track is the purpose of Baxter's School, she says. God doesn't come into it. Garth prefers the intellectual stimulation of an argumentative atheist like Rihanna to the sentimental smiles of the many pluralists, the live-and-let-live brigade. He hopes to have a productive afternoon and evening with the boys, and maybe a civilised debate once he and she are alone. The boys in bed. At ten forty-five, an hour and a quarter after lights out, Rihanna will go to Rowan Unit where she is rostered for night cover. An hour and a quarter without disturbance is not a given. Some evenings are sheer bedlam.

In the Lord's Knowing Gaze

When they come into the house from school, the boys are excited. It's the way of Mondays, and particularly those first Mondays after a holiday break. Both Garth and Rihanna monitor the children, learn what has changed over the last nine days in the homes and families of the boys. Garth advised Rihanna that he will talk with Paul Frost, discreetly supervise him bathing. There have been concerns about his stepdad; they must report every scratch and bruise. His split lip is the work of Damian Taylor.

When the group divides into those who wish to play football and those who will cash in the first of their week's gaming time, Rihanna grabs the football, flashes Garth a smile that decides which of them will supervise which cohort. It seems right, Paul is a gamer. Rihanna Williams has dressed for football, for the sun. She wears shorts and a T-shirt, which contrast with the chinos and lumberjack shirt on Garth. He knows he will not raise the matter, is apprehensive of criticising a girl for dressing in a particular way, suspects he is not the only one to notice her figure. The brown of her thighs. In an excessively male environment and with boys exclusively aged thirteen to sixteen, he considers her clothing unwise. She doesn't breach Baxter's dress code: a discreet earring her only visible piercing and her short trousers are of the safari type, not as short as Lily wore all the while they were in the hospital. Garth knows how boys think, wonders if Rihanna is naïve. She is liberal with her hugs when boys are unduly upset. Garth is too but he reckons that there is a difference between a comforting arm from him or from her. They may infer a meaning from young Rihanna's hugs that she does not intend. An availability. Garth knows she means well, works tirelessly for the boys.

He observes three boys each at a different computer station in Stone's second lounge, a room euphemistically known as the library. Games on screens—usually involving shooting guns and beams at incoming attackers—has become its focal activity. The small bookcase serves only to maintain a pretence. Just glancing at the small display brings Lily to his mind; she enjoys reading, told him as much. Something they have in common. As he watches the boys, Garth feels his trousers vibrate. He dips a hand into his pocket, turns aside as he glances at his pulsating mobile. It is not Rihanna; staff at Baxter's carry mobiles that, in work time, serve to communicate across the site. Lily is calling him and he feels as if his thoughts have summonsed her. He must not pick up, no personal calls allowed. Presses the X, cuts her off. With his back to the room, he texts her with quick thumbs.

Working. Will call you at end of shift - Garth

He turns back to the room. Two of the boys are laughing, and Garth momentarily worries that he is the joke, the Christian who finally has a girlfriend. He dismisses the thought. They cannot have guessed what he was up to, must imagine he was responding to another worker here at Baxter's. Nine out of ten times it would be. Paul has moved the angle of his chair, hunched over the screen, a barrier between him and the world. It is not the first time and nor is it a good sign.

'Do you want to help me do the cooking, Paul?' With his back still to the room the boy shakes his head. 'You can choose the veggies.' The boy does not so much as turn around. Garth places a hand on Paul's shoulder, 'Truth is, I need the company in there. I'd love you to peel a few carrots for me.' Paul stands, says nothing as he heads for the kitchen. Garth smiles to himself. Rihanna says he is too formal, 'stiff,' she calls it; on the other hand, Barry Rogers calls him 'boundaried' and Barry's view matters. He is the deputy head of school, lead responsibility for residential. Years and years of experience. 'I can trust you boys,' Garth tells the two he leaves in the library. They scarcely glance up. Garth knows he cannot, it is just the most positive message he can leave them with. The best chance he's got and someone must prepare the evening meal.

* * *

While Paul is peeling potatoes, smiling more than he ever does during his obsessive game station time, Garth hears him starting to hum. Not much of a melody but it is happy humming. A turn-up.

'Would you believe this,' says Garth, 'on bank holiday Monday, some toerag stole the front wheel from my bike?' Paul stops humming and lets out a nervous laugh. 'Really, they plumb took it.'

'From your house?' he asks.

'Boscombe seafront.'

'Well, I've never been there, so it wasn't me, Mr Addicks.'

Paul's denial sounds sincere, brings a smile to Garth's lips. 'I know it wasn't you; I never said that it was, I just wondered what you thought about people who do that? My bike locked up, so they just flip the wheel off. That was all they took. Front-wheel, the frame was still locked to the railing.'

'Do you think the thief's collecting the parts to make one for himself?'

Garth chuckles heartily at this. 'Now that would be a clever ruse. No, I don't think they were doing any more than having a laugh at my expense.'

'Wasn't it crowded at the seafront?'

'It was evening, after dark, so probably not.'

'Was it a daft place to put your bike, Mr Addicks?'

Garth laughs again, hopes Paul does not feel it is at his expense. 'Perhaps it was. There was an accident on the promenade, so I took...' He stops speaking for two seconds, checks his phrasing to ensure Lily's name—even her gender— doesn't slip into the conversation. '...the unfortunate victim to hospital. It took a while and when I got back, my front wheel was missing. Stolen. Dumped somewhere further along the coast, I expect.'

'That's harsh, sir. You do a bloke a good turn and someone else robs you. The accident wasn't a set-up, was it?'

Now Garth's laughter is a little uncontrolled. 'It really wasn't,' is all he can add. He sees Paul looking at him strangely. It might be a rare sight: this most serious of residential care workers taking life so lightly. He laughs and jokes with the boys only infrequently, speculates inwardly whether an imminent conversation with Lily is making him light-headed. This thought leads him back to his doubt: that she is ringing to say he is too young—too Christian—for her to associate with. He is certain that Jesus put Lily in his path for a purpose; Peter and Margery—church members for whom he has the greatest respect—don't seem so convinced. Not that it is Jesus's plan, or even a good one. If she were to discard him now, it might be simpler all round; he wishes for the exact opposite. Enjoyed her company one week ago; Lily looks gorgeous. When she goes to church on his arm it will be a fine day. He worries that he has dwelled upon how she looks a little too much. Won't get into any compromising situations like Gandhi. He has mixed only with the like-minded for too long. He recalls the words of Margery's sermon, the words of Saint Paul, New Testament truth: *Neither circumcision nor uncircumcision means anything; what counts is the new creation.*

* * *

When Rihanna and the boys return from football, they all eat the meal together.

'You cook okay for a guy,' she tells Garth.

'Better than you, Ri-ri.'

'It's not "okay," it's dead good.'

'Because he doesn't have a wife.'

The boys all have an opinion about him, and it crosses his mind that he could prove their last point wrong. Not quickly, can't happen until Lily converts. Doesn't say it or anything like it, far too much to explain.

The mood is calm throughout the meal and the early evening. The boys tease Rihanna, without ever overstepping her rather loose definition of acceptable behaviour. Try no such nonsense with Garth.

* * *

At half-past nine the boys have settled, one or two are sleeping. It's an excellent end to a first evening back. 'Rihanna,' asks Garth, 'can you listen out while I make a quick personal call?'

'Sure thing, bro,' she says.

Garth returns her smile. The term, brother, has purchase as a greeting at church; Peter is a frequent user. It is Christian if antiquated, and Garth has often thought that the street talk, which Rihanna is apt to adopt, might be biblical in origin. He is also aware— following her exposition during an Afro-Caribbean-themed culture night—that Rihanna's Trinidadian parents settled in Winchester before her birth. She has known only Hampshire, not the East End of London or Kingston, Jamaica. And he understands also—a point she made very clearly—that there is racism, even here. Rihanna can feel alienated from white men because of how too many have spoken to her. He is grateful that she never tarnishes him with that brush. They debate their contrasting passions for this work but always get along. Biblical language and modern black speech: well, surely the disciples of Jesus were a gang, and one antithetical to the order of their day.

In the Lord's Knowing Gaze

Such are words.

In the small sleeping-in room, in which Garth has placed his overnight bag, and has yet to make up the bed, he sits on the bare mattress. Handles his phone like it is a precious metal, scrolls the contact list. He finds his latest entry: Lily. Presses green and immediately hits red before a ring has rung. He tries to think what to say to her, then remembers that it is she who initially called him. Their first date is two days away. Monday last was an odd thing: a nightmare for her and a dream for him, he fears. Gently he taps the green key once more.

'Stephens,' she says.

'Hi,' he is already unsure whether he should make this short, business-like—technically, he is still at work—or whether to try and engage her in the kind of meandering talk that swallowed so much of their bank holiday. 'It's Garth, returning your call.'

'...and you're still on for Wednesday?'

'I think so.'

'Think so? Having doubts...'

'No, I'm not, are you?'

'Oh Garth, let's not squabble like my children. I think...'

'Sorry, I was calling you back. I've worried you were calling it off, that's all.'

'I can't hear you properly,' says Lily.

'I'll try to speak clearly but I have to keep my voice down. I'm at work.'

'At this time?'

'Residential work, it goes on round the clock.'

'Gosh. Do you have any children with you?'

'All in bed.'

'Like me. Kids asleep, so I've taken myself to bed. Reading. A little chat is nicer if you're able.'

'Sure,' he says, finding himself picturing her lying in a bed like his, in a room like this. Then tries to erase the thought. Not get ahead of himself. 'And the call was just for a chat?'

'Yeah, and I was worried.'

'I don't want that. I'm always good to my word, Lily.'

'I was worried that it was an act.' A short silence oscillates between them. 'I was well out of it last week. My leg hurt like buggery. You were good to me—Christian—you work with children. I even saw you were young and handsome. Late at night when I can't sleep, I think you cycled into me with a pre-planned backstory...'

'What!' If she's making a joke, he doesn't get it. At church everyone trusts him. At work too. He wants to tell her this, fears he would only sound boastful.

'Tell me truthfully that I'm the first girl you've picked up in casualty.'

'Lily, yes. I don't date. Well, I'm going to, aren't I?'

'No! We didn't talk about this. You must have had proper girlfriends before. Garth. You must have!'

'Ha! The last time was years back, two dates with a girl from church who used the meetings to explore her doubts. I counselled her, it wasn't romance. I felt like she wanted me to deliver a sermon.'

'And before that, a proper girl?'

'In my teens, a little. Not any like that since finding my faith. Not at all.'

For fully thirty seconds silence pings back and forth between them.

'Are you sure you want to do this?' she asks.

'I do. I really do. I hope there's something in it for you.'

'Yeah, I bloody hope so,' she says with a laugh.

Something too particular to discuss without once more seeing each other's faces is lingering in between the words they speak. They natter a little. Lily tells him that work is more tolerable because the creepiest man in the office is in hospital and cannot bother her from there. Garth asks about him, what makes him creepy. Finds Lily has no wish to expand the initial comment.

'I can handle him,' she says, and it comes to him that she will have handled a great deal in her life. When the phone call ends—Garth confirming that, on his once-again-two-wheeled bike, he will cycle to see her by seven-fifteen on Wednesday—he looks at the screen, and sees that thirty-five minutes have elapsed.

* * *

When he returns to the kitchen where Rihanna sits at the table, she pushes a cold mug of coffee at him. 'Better microwave it.' Garth knows that he was off the floor for an inordinately long time. He keeps his

In the Lord's Knowing Gaze

eyes down. 'Paul was crying.' He frowns now, hates letting down a colleague. A child. 'You should have been here, Garth. That's why they pay us. To look after the kids. I gave him a hug and it shut 'im up, but he talks better to you. You know that.'

Garth looks into her face. 'I'm sorry. Look, I'll be writing up until midnight, so I'll put in the time. If you want to knock off early, Rihanna, that's okay with me. I left you alone for quite a while. Shouldn't have.'

She looks at him intently, he doesn't know if she is cross or sad. She might have missed the repartee, the debate. They only get to share a late evening once in the three-week rota, Rihanna always seems to enjoy their free-ranging discussions. And Garth believes her simple dictum—we should love any kid who has been dealt a crap hand in life—is in every way as Christian as his own outlook. What she lacks is the framework with which to implement it. She says he looks into the Bible instead of his heart and he agrees with the narrow point. Considers it is the wisest, most reliable course known to man.

'I'm sorry, Garth,' she says finally. 'I'm being harsh. You always cover for me if I've got shit going on. What was the call? Not family problems, I hope.'

He finds himself smiling as he shakes his head, wonders if he should trust this girl with the truth. Cannot. Won't let his fledgling attachment become known in this unforgiving environment. 'Just some things to arrange,' he says. 'Sorry.'

She looks at him as if he might be her adversary. 'What like repairing-the-cooker things?'

'A bit like but not quite that. Do you mind if I keep this one to myself?'

His colleague shrugs.

* * *

She, Rihanna, has long gone across to Rowan Unit. Her sleep-in room, on-call to the four boys living over there. The corridor of Stone, this unit, is utterly silent.

'Will you take me dancing, Garth?' It is not only the words of the question which Lily asked that run around inside his head, it's the tone. The anticipation. He thinks his new friend—his secular friend, as Peter styled her—has had a tough life. Alone with two young children. She sounded sweet, plaintive, on several occasions on the previous Monday, mostly when she was at her most vulnerable. The barely clothed woman on the bed in the casualty department taking refuge from her pain through conversation with sympathetic Garth. Even in her home, where she curled herself up into a ball on the sofa opposite him, he felt her femininity most present when she was closest to tears. Tonight, she asked him this question: 'Will you take me dancing, Garth?' A tug of longing in her voice. And he had already said that Wednesday was to be a meal out; she was referring to the days and weeks ahead. Asking what else they might do. She also said she can't dance until her wound has healed. The damage his bike ravaged upon her.

As he dwells on her words, he likes her optimism. Her certainty they will continue to date. Garth worries that his reply was terse. He didn't mean it to be, went for funny and missed. 'I'm shit at dancing.' He who never swears had become infected with the vernacular of his lady-friend, his girlfriend as he has determined he should think her. She'd sparred, verbally sparred, and that has probably been the way of most of their intimacy. In the way of his work with recalcitrant children, he struck a bargain, made a pact. 'When you come to church, Lily, I'll have to go dancing. See what my feet can do then.' She laughed but he wonders if he had already lost the moment. His phrase, 'I'm shit at dancing,' is unlikely to be running around inside her head at one-thirty in the morning as 'Will you take me dancing, Garth?' does in his.

Wednesday, 8 June 2016

On the bus home from Ringwood, he feels washed out, thinks he may need a daytime sleep before going on the date. His working hours are gruelling: all day Monday and Tuesday, sleeping on the unit both nights, and then rising to see the boys get to morning classes before taking the rest of the day off. And he will be back again for Thursday lunchtime through until the boys leave school at three-thirty on Friday. This long shift, since Monday morning, was an unpleasant one. Not every minute but the restraint on Tuesday evening was awful. Physical intervention, Garth hates it. He's completed all the training, couldn't be better prepared. At least he works in a school where it occurs infrequently, where other methods—distraction and room management—keep the peace for the bulk of the time. On training days, Garth has met staff from other settings who told him they have to hold boys—even out-of-control girls, although Baxter's School has none—on a near-daily basis. Rihanna says they can't be managing them properly.

Damian Taylor was visiting Stone—not the house he resides in—following a conciliation meeting between him and Paul Frost. After the meeting, Paul and one other boy went on a trip—ten-pin bowling—with Rihanna. Damian and a boy named Kai were messing about in the lounge. Garth had an uneasy feeling and texted for support. Before the supporting staff had come over, Damian had broken a window, done it wilfully, no accident about it. And nor was it really vandalism. He'd flipped, found a mood darker than any Garth has before seen in Damian Taylor. The boy had a shard of glass in his hand, picked it from the mess he made of the window. Then he acted as if to cut his own leg, placed a corner of the glass onto his jeans while his eyes challenged Garth to stop him. He has dealt with many tricky situations in the last three years but this seemed worse than most. He feared where it would end. When Garth felt a vibration in his leg, he hoped the incoming text was confirmation that the support would be immediate. It's what he'd requested. Damian was shouting out, shouting to be left alone.

Garth had the presence of mind to reach out, not threateningly, offer a helping hand. Damian Taylor began crying and Garth tried to take the large shard of glass from him. It slipped to the floor—tentative baton exchange that it was—and shattered. Surprisingly noisy. At the very moment it dropped, two male staff from Red House, the largest residential unit on site, entered the lounge. They must have heard the breaking glass though they had yet to hear a word about how it arose.

'What the fuck is he doing!' shouted Ryan. Big stupid Ryan, a staff member whose value to Baxter's is less than zero in Garth's estimation. Why would anyone in their right mind swear at a troubled and traumatised boy. A poor kid who had, in the moment before, already dissolved into tears. A kid from the house in which Ryan works most of his shifts, and then that was the nearest thing to any sort of rapport he could manage. Swearing at the poor boy.

Garth was holding Damian's wrists, ensuring he couldn't pick the glass back up. He had hoped to try a consoling hug just as the support arrived. After Ryan's idiotic raising of the temperature, Damian shouted, 'Fuck you!' All Ryan's fault; it had been going as well as it could before he showed up. Damian rolled his head into Garth, butting him in the chest.

'No, mate. It's all right. Just calm it.' Garth tried to restore the order achieved before Ryan Short pressed all the wrong buttons.

'Fucking queer! You're not bumming me!' The boy shouted unfounded accusations at Garth as he tried not to let go, to use the wrap hold taught in training. The floor was awash with broken glass; Damian was not right, his upset foretold of some trauma removed from anything occurring in the room at that time. Garth has no illusions about the pasts which haunt these children.

Ash, who came in with Ryan, took control well, signalled for Ryan not to touch the boy. In the end, Ash and Garth took Damian to the floor, did so gently, no bump or bruise, they were exceptionally careful and avoided anyone of them being cut by the broken glass. Not a scratch.

Ryan began the task of talking the boy down. 'Sorry mate,' his first words. 'I needed to understand what was going on.'

This might have been a loose but improved translation of the inflammatory way he began his short time in the room. His petrol on the fire already smouldering inside this boy. Damian gave Ryan no quarter for absolution. 'Fuck off! Fuck off! Fuck off!'

'You better had,' Ash said quietly.

Garth and Ash held the boy for twenty minutes, initially Garth had to exert a great deal of force to keep both legs from kicking out while Ash held the torso, talked softly to the boy. In time, they were able to ease off a little but still held him down. Damian seemed to need the security the hold gave. He resisted even when his face was no longer angry, punched out once or twice when they tried to release him before he was ready. Didn't trust himself free of the hold. It was all timed and recorded, it is what staff do. The boy cried off and on but he no longer directed his ire at them. Once Ryan was out of the room,

In the Lord's Knowing Gaze

Damian turned all his anger upon himself. 'I'm a dickhead,' he repeated. It meant nothing to Garth, and nor did it sound good.

Garth asked Ash, the shift leader across the site, if he could swap with Ryan and work through the evening with Damian. He did not want to push the boy away in his hour of need. 'Good thinking, Addicks. I'd have you over Shorty any day of the week.' It was indiscreet talk from a supervisor. Everyone at Baxter's must know it by now, Ryan Short isn't cut out to be a residential care worker.

That's the main event that has drained Garth, worrying about it robbed him of sleep last night, as picturing Lily had the preceding one. Now, after alighting from the bus and walking around the back of the shops above which his flat is situated, Garth notices a familiar car parked in the nearest bay. A familiar figure in the driver's seat. He goes to the window; feelings of apprehension. This is an unprecedented visit.

'Hi Mum. Is everything all right?' he says, as she winds the window down.

'I thought I'd catch you. I was in town.'

In other circumstances, Garth might smile at this lie. Northbourne offers nothing that his mother cannot secure in Ferndown, she is here to seek him out. He might laugh about it in retrospect, in the interim he feels only unease. Tries to calculate the possible motivation for the unlikely event. He goes to the family home reasonably often but neither his father nor mother have been at his in four years. They offer the excuse that they don't like the steps. He thinks their bungalow is the size of their comfort zone. The extent of it.

'I want you to talk to Claire.'

'You'd better come in,' he says.

* * *

Over a cup of weak tea, he hears his mother's concerns.

'She's taken to her bed.' This is said without a second's eye contact. 'Gets to work late now. That's unheard of for our Claire. You know that.' This second point seems to contradict the first, Garth doesn't point it out. Allows his mother time to say all she needs. 'I think there might be a boy involved.' This one he adjudges to be pure speculation, he knows that Claire shares little, if any, of her personal life with their parents. 'She's close to you; you can put her straight.'

No longer. Garth's counsel suits those in The Church of the Men of Judea, those who appreciate the source on which it is based. Acts of goodness are the route through difficulty; the New Testament contains the answers to every question a soul can raise. His sister has rejected it all, she is beyond his reach. And Garth once had higher hopes for Claire than he did for himself. The cleverer of the pair in childhood, she spent three years obtaining an art degree then, upon its completion, moved straight back to the farm in Sixpenny Handley. Wrote away for jobs but nothing of worth came her way. Earned a little money working with toddlers in a local playgroup. Barely pocket money. When Wilfred and Penelope Addicks—the latter of whom now sits across from him in his spartan flat—moved to Ferndown, retired from the labours of modern agriculture, Claire came too. Like an old sideboard. She picked up further work with pre-school children, this time at a private day nursery. Acquired the job easily enough. It is not what the family had anticipated when she left for her course in Leicestershire at eighteen, six years ago. She has idled as an adult.

'Do you think she's depressed, Mum?'

'Pills? She doesn't need pills. Not Claire.'

'I don't think I have any special powers to talk her round.' As he says the words, Garth realises that he is closer than any other in the family. He can pray. Prayer works, not that his mother is likely to acknowledge this truth. And Claire would be equally dismissive, her attitude might even inhibit any intervention the Lord chooses to bestow.

'I'm making roast chicken. You need proper feeding too. Just come around and try, like old times. Cheer her up or at least find out what's got into her...'

'When, Mum? Which day?'

'Tonight, Garth. It's the only chance this week. You know your own shift pattern, I take it.'

He pictures the grubby paper on their bungalow's kitchen wall, his three-week rotating shift pattern. His parents have had it hanging there since he began working at Baxter's, keener to know where he is than to actually spend time with him, Garth often thinks. It was Claire who shared their major gripe, one his parents have never voiced directly. 'He's too full of God for our liking,' his mother had said and

In the Lord's Knowing Gaze

Claire confided. He thinks it a meaningless construction. God is within us all; the real error is that too many also flood themselves with a corresponding volume of denial.

'It'll have to be Friday,' he tells his mother. 'No, Saturday,' he corrects himself, remembering the church youth group of which he is a lynchpin.

'Today, please, Garth. It's your sister we're talking about here.'

Garth doesn't want to let his sister down but must. The alternative is to let Lily down. And he cannot. He has felt excited for more than a week at the prospect of seeing her again. Not a predicament he can explain to his mother, will not speak to her of Lily yet. 'I've another church thing,' he says. It isn't true but it's credible. He won't be eating chicken in Ferndown tonight.

'Garth, we raised you, I'll have you know, not the ruddy church.'

When she leaves—shortly after that coarse pronouncement—he decides he has been lucky. If the two of them had come together to persuade him, his father, Wilfred, alongside Penelope, the swearing would have taken the roof off. All farmers swear, Wilfred Addicks could win prizes for it.

* * *

For Garth, sitting across from her in the beer garden of the Perkin Inn, this is a new life. He finds so much simple goodness in Lily, the thin lines on her face when she smiles at him are a joyous sight. Her hair is immaculate. He enjoyed its slightly wild quality on bank holiday Monday—a chaotic day—hospital and tears. Today, in his eyes, she looks like a film star. Her black hair is straight but for the slightest curve as it passes her shoulder. Eyes of the richest blue. He sees both action and serenity in them: a capable girl, she has raised children in London, decamped to Bournemouth single-handedly. Tonight—and his presence just might be the elixir—she relaxes. He wonders if he should have joined her, had a glass of wine. There are two snags: he's overly conscious that tomorrow is a working day, an early bus; and Margery's comment about Gandhi has stuck in his head. Resisting beautiful women is easier when one doesn't meet any. And Garth has no need for wine, he is drunk on Lily.

He tries to recall their names, Joseph and Amy. Lily always calls the boy by a nickname and pronounces the girl's name with a flat first vowel: Army. He didn't meet them tonight; they were in bed. He briefly saw Lily's friend, a girl called Alice. She's back in the flat—babysitting—while he and Lily eat. Seemed nice, a lot younger than Lily. Shook his hand on arrival, after giving Lily a greeting hug, a contact he envied. Garth has not touched Lily this evening, he'd like to but it might not be very Gandhi. Lily is telling Garth about a lady called Gillian who works in the solicitors' office. Her line manager. She's laughing about it but there's an edge to the story. Lily doesn't like her and she lets it show.

'Is there a little schadenfreude in what you're saying?' he asks.

'Don't be a bitch, said in German. You make your point politely, Garth.'

He laughs, still finding their feet but it feels comfortable between them. How he might secure this lovely girl's attendance at The Church of the Men of Judea nags him. And raising the subject could kill the mood.

Lily puts a finger on her plate, runs it along a smear of mustard sauce that accompanied her dish. 'How do you feel about pudding, Garth?'

He has budgeted for this. 'I feel very good about pudding,' he says, then finds himself blushing, imagining that there is a meaning implicit in the question which he has not properly understood.

Garth stands and fetches a menu from a neighbouring table; they confer briefly and then he goes to the bar to place the order. Puddings turn out to be less risqué than he feared. When he returns, Lily is on her feet. 'I need the bathroom,' she says.

While she is away, he closes his eyes. He can still picture her, see the rise of her breast with each breath taken. The top she is wearing, a simple cream-coloured blouse, is low cut, or she has left an extra button open—he has no eye for fashion—she simply looks superb. The sound of the sea carries. Not visible from his seat, he knows it is just over the hedge and across the road. The clifftop is there from which a path leads down to the beach and, when silence briefly prevails in this beer garden, the wash of the water, the sound of waves rolling towards the unseen beach, comes to him. A mesmerising accompaniment to the look of Lily. When she returns, his date arrives so softly on her feet that he fails to turn his head, unaware of her presence until she places her hands on his face, covers his eyes. He is not good at such horseplay. Asks if she is wearing perfume, the scent on her hands pleasantly assaulting his nose.

'It's just the soap from the ladies.'

As they wait for pudding, Lily asks him to talk through his working week: what he did; the challenges faced; to explain why the children are at Baxter's in the first place. When he first told her his job role, she declared that she would like to do similar. She's too full of life for a dull office job, he can see that. Garth speaks in a low voice, his work a confidential matter.

'What do you mean restraint?' she asks as he tells her about the events of the evening before.

'Hold him, Lily. We had to hold him on the floor for a long time.' She looks shocked, Garth wonders if she is reappraising whether such work is for her at all. 'I hate it too, Lily, hate having to do that to them but he was going crazy. Might have cut his own leg with the glass. We couldn't tell what he would do next.'

'Will they sack the dickhead? Ryan, wasn't it?'

Garth signals for Lily to lower her voice, wonders if the wine has disinhibited her. He enjoys the close attention she pays him. Work dominates his thoughts second only to Jesus Christ. 'It was unprofessional and I don't like working with him because he keeps doing that stuff. But the thing is, Ryan was scared. He heard the glass break, maybe he thought Damian was attacking me. His idea of how to take control was to start shouting, even swearing. All wrong...' Garth pauses, thinks through how to make his next point clearly. '...the thing is, Lily, he was scared, and it is my best guess that Ryan's dad was a swearer. It was what he did when things went wrong. So that's how Ryan's autopilot works. We're all products of our upbringings.' Lily nods, listening intently. He loves seeing her blue eyes resting upon him alone. Her intelligent and enquiring gaze. This girl has had it tough, it might be why she can relate to the Baxter's boys. 'Can I tell you some personal stuff, Lily?'

She leans in, places a hand upon his. 'Please, Garth. I want to hear everything about you.'

'My dad was a shouter, a swearer, a bit of a whacker with a slipper when I was young.' He leans back in his seat. 'Don't look like that, Lily.

I'm thirty. I'm telling you what happened not looking for sympathy. The reason I say it is because I could have become like Ryan, or even Damian. But I'm not. It's difficult to pin down when I made the decision to make a step change, not to be a watered-down version of my own dad like most people end up being. But it doesn't matter...'

'It must matter.' His friend—his girlfriend—is very animated. 'I don't get you. It must matter, not turning out like your horrible dad?'

'Yes, but the decision to change isn't the key. All kids whose parents fall short of the mark say that they want to be different. It doesn't often work out, doesn't change the auto-pilot. How can we really change the way we're wired?'

Lily nods her head. 'I made that decision,' she reminds him.

'For me, the difference is the church. I am new in Christ, a different man than the child my father raised. Born again, the Lord forever showing me the way.'

Lily leans back in her seat. Looks at him over her raised dessert spoon. 'Good for you,' she says.

They eat their respective puddings.

* * *

The temperature in the beer garden has dropped, both put on their jackets. Lily has three glasses of wine inside her, Garth none. 'Are you sure?' he asked before buying her the third, tap water drinker that he is. They arise from the table and cross the road to the cliff top, drift down the sloping path to the seafront promenade. They are no more than a mile east of the site of the accident nine days ago.

'On the sand,' declares Lily. She takes him by the hand, and they start to go down the four broad steps that drop from path to beach. She stops, stoops, takes off her sandals. Garth is in trainers and socks, thinks it is too late in the evening to be messing about. He looks closely through the fading light as she spreads her toes into the sand. Will do as she asks. As they walk, she removes her hand from his, brushes her own down the back of her lower leg.

'Careful,' says Garth. He guesses that she is itching beneath the bandage, where the scar rakes down her calf, stitches still in place. Another week and a nurse at the doctor's surgery will remove them, she has told him. As Lily pulls herself up, he places a hand across her shoulder, feels it is a wanted comfort when Lily's arm traverses his waist. She leans into him on her tiptoes, kisses his lips. There is a slim crescent moon, offering insufficient light to illuminate the way in front of them. Beneath it the water glistens, pretends itself a box of jewels.

Saturday, 11 June 2016

On Saturday night, at the cinema complex, Garth is having a minor but very visible, meltdown. Lily tells him so. His weekend has not been as simple as he hoped. He spoke to Claire at length in the afternoon but again declined the evening meal with family, giving an excuse which—in common with the one he told to his mother the previous Wednesday—was far from the whole truth. Quite fictitious. Before leaving the bungalow in Ferndown, he gave his mother his considered opinion: Claire is okay. It's normal for young people to avoid spending all their time with their parents. 'She needs a place of her own,' he said. Not that it can happen while she works short hours at the nursery.

He kept from his mother—as a safeguard to prevent it from entering his father's two red ears—Claire's confession of furtive and excessive drinking. She even showed him the hip flask she has taken to carrying wherever she goes. Neat vodka sipped at all times of day and night. He told Claire that she will jeopardise her job—lose it—if they learn that she consumes alcohol on the premises. Can't be under the influence when in charge of minors.

'They can't count toddlers in that place. Won't notice if I'm a little tiddly. I've got a degree and that turns me into gold dust on their books.'

Garth didn't argue the point but worries that tiddly doesn't come close to describing the state she gets in. She has hidden it from their parents while he brought it out with a simple show of concern. A couple of open questions. No one sees the deer in the thicket but it shows itself at dusk, again at first light.

He is grateful that Lily has volunteered to pay half, to split the bill, on this their second date. She said she understands his stretched finances, budgets her own life with the utmost care. On Wednesday, she said, 'This is for paying for everything, Garth,' as she kissed him on her doorstep. Held his face in her hands as his own held the handlebars of his bicycle. Pushed her tongue into his mouth. He was surprised by the intimacy—on a first date!—but most of all wanted to argue, make her rethink the point. The kiss had nothing to do with his parting with money, that would be akin to prostitution. He held his tongue only for fear of spoiling the evening. And now, looking at the poster for the film that Lily has suggested they watch together, reading details he never thought to check when she said the name of the proposed movie, he is once more fearful of quite how debauched his secular friend is proving herself to be.

'It's a comedy, Garth. Or a comedy thriller. Something like that. We're only going to see it for a laugh.'

'Sorry.' He doesn't want to argue with her, not about this, 'I think the classification means it's an eighteen. It's X-rated stuff, Lily.'

'It's all right, Garth...' The corners of her eyes have creased, smile lines. He is again mesmerised by the vitality in her face. '...I turned eighteen a little time back.'

He takes her hand in his, hopes this denotes the importance of the matter to him. 'I can't go into a porn movie, Lily. I simply can't do it.'

'It's not a porn movie! It's a comedy. For making you laugh, not getting horny. He...' She points at an actor's face on the poster. '...plays a fading porn star.' These words come from the leaflet in her hand. 'It's the set-up, to make it funny. It's not a porn film. What do you take me for?'

'But you can't be certain. You said that you never really go to the cinema these days. And I can't watch this. I pray for people who go to porn films, Lily. I don't muck in.'

'I should have brought you to watch the bloody cartoons with my kids.' Lily has dropped his hand, taken a step back from him.

'I'd have loved that.'

She is looking at him strangely and he means only to imply that he would like to meet her children; he said the same on Wednesday and again earlier today. Lily lets out a little snort of a laugh. Less than lady-like, he thinks.

'Please?' he says, 'I can't watch this...this smut.'

'All right Garth, we'll not watch it. But they don't show the dirty movies you're thinking about at the fucking Odeon. And don't be thinking I go to watch them. It's men who watch porn. Your lot, matey, not us girls.'

'I'm sorry, I'm sorry, I'm sorry.' She says she doesn't watch them, so he should believe her. Couldn't bear to sit through a film he could never admit to having seen when back at church. Boys at Baxter's swear on every shift, still it shocks him hearing Lily use the f-word. 'We're a funny lot, Christians. All my fault. You might get used to me.'

'I might Garth, and I don't mind cartoons, just not tonight. What's your plan B, sunshine?'

He treasured it when she first called him by this bright name. It comes to mind now that she might use it on her other boy, her eight-year-old son, and he hopes to lodge in a different part of her mind than young Joseph. Or Jo-jo as she always calls him. He was a fool to have sounded so keen on cartoons. 'Should we walk to the pier?'

Lily assents.

* * *

As they leave the cinema complex, she asks him questions about his beliefs, his religion. Gently probing, respectful questions. He thinks she looks at him admiringly when he tries to enunciate the importance of the youth group. 'The kids at your work need it more,' she throws into the mix. 'They have it harder, so isn't that better? More Christian?'

'I don't think Baxter's is Christian at all. I follow the working practices. The psychology we use makes a lot of sense. The Bible is off the premises. Nobody there reads it but me.'

'Is that what you think? If the boss isn't Christian, the work must be satanic or something?'

'No. Actions are everything. I do the work because it's an act of goodness, and I bring something into the world of non-believers...' Garth sees that Lily is openly laughing at this phrase, and he was trying to be very specific. It is a central belief of his church that all its adherents should undertake acts of goodness. Do them as frequently as they can. It is the action, the good they do, which pleases God. He tells Lily about Peter Carter. 'He's a computer genius—can't help making pots of money—he dedicates all his time to online protection. How to keep children safe when they use the internet. Peter believes making money alone is no reason to get out of bed in the morning.

Boscombe

He's a selfless man.'

Lily repeats back the pots-of-money phrase, says it as if she doesn't quite believe him. Garth thinks she is still cross he wouldn't watch the dirty film. 'You call it the world of non-believers, Garth, but all of us believe something. Getting onto each other's wavelengths is the problem. You've got your head, I've got mine: different crap inside. Isn't the world of non-believers just a made-up place, no more real than heaven? You imagine a comedy film is pornography, sunshine. I think you're making the world scarier than it is, frightening the faithful into sitting tight in their pews.'

Garth feels conflicted. He dislikes what she says, it is only how those off the path see it. She looks gorgeous, animated as she debates. 'It is complicated. All sorts of people do good, not only Christians.' Saying this brings Rihanna to his mind and he knows that talking about work has been more agreeable to Lily. 'Have I told you about the girl I work...' He stops mid-sentence. Speaking about another—younger—girl with whom he also enjoys lively conversations is a wrong turn on a second date. Clever of Garth to spot it in the circumstances.

* * *

Before they reach the pier, they stop and sit together on a bench in the Lower Gardens. The air is still warm; a busker plays saxophone a little further along the path.

'She's good,' says Garth.

'Do you vote?' asks Lily.

It is a question from nowhere, he gives her only a puzzled look.

'Are the men of Judea allowed to vote, Garth?'

'It's just the name of the church. We don't call ourselves the men of Judea.'

'Sorry, I didn't mean any disrespect. Do church members vote, you're not like the Amish, are you?'

Garth finally laughs, the first of a tense early evening. 'You think we farm with donkeys in the village of Thre'penny Ha'penny.'

'Oh God, I've offended you. Sorry, Garth.'

'No, you want to know about voting. What especially?'

'Does your church have a take on this Brexit vote, Garth?'

The referendum is a fraught subject at Friday youth group—

arguments—young people have asked his opinion on the matter. Garth's instincts lie with Peter, the possibility of taking back control is attractive. 'The church doesn't tell people how to vote, Lily. I think everybody can see that the European Union is not a godly one. Bureaucratic where a little dogma might make all the diff...' He pauses, Lily's jaw is hanging open. '...we don't tell people how to vote.'

'No, but you clearly have a view. What were you saying?'

'Peter said it really, made a good point. In the first century, Christians lived in the certainty that miracles could happen in their midst. They listened to God who whispered instruction to them. Or to the most devout of them at the very least. We don't think He has gone away but very few pay that voice attention. We've let money become our goal.'

'Garth, the vote is to leave or remain. What are you going on about?'

'I know it's not a straight line, Lily. But leaving looks far more likely to lead to evangelism's triumph than the status quo. We can't simply keep everything as it is.'

He sees her duck her head into her open palms as if he has told a hilarious joke when he has not. Then, at a stroke, her face changes, darkens. Jaw clenched. 'I talk to Marta. You won't know her, she works in the late stores on the main road, at the top of my road. Every time I go in, we chat. It's the Polish shop, you know...' Garth wonders why she is looking so cross, she isn't making any point at all. '...the fucking bullshit that lady has had to put up with. Egging the window, the nasty graffiti. It was nothing like this before Cameron called the stupid referendum. I'm remain, Garth, pretty sickened by the racism of it all. I thought your church would be.'

'We don't advocate racism, it's just that the EU doesn't make miracles happen...'

'What! What the fuck are you on about? Are you with the racists, Garth?'

'No. We abhor racism. I abhor it.' Garth starts to wonder if he understands politics at all. He hadn't known that women like Marta— there is a similar shop in Northbourne, in the parade below his flat— are having it rough.

'I don't think the crackpots leading the vote are on board with your evangelism, Garth. If you vote to stay in, you make a stand against that nonsense. The fucking racism. Anything else is just supporting it.'

'Yes, well...' He recalls how Pastor Margery voiced caution about raising the matter in youth group. She may be on Lily's side for all he knows. '...I'm still listening to the debate.' Lily rolls her eyes, turns her head towards the saxophonist. He might talk to Peter again, suggest he rethink. The resumption of miracles is not on the ballot paper; Lily makes an intelligent point. Really shouldn't have sworn while making it.

* * *

When they reach the sea, Lily decides the water trumps the pier. 'Socks off this time,' she says, and Garth does as she asks, eager to hold on to any connection that may remain. He feels like he has loved and lost; however, it could be that he has no experience to draw upon. The brief girlfriends of his long-gone teenage years were flightier than Lily, less anchored in their lives. She didn't walk away and he thinks they had a row. Two. Perhaps if he had gone into the cinema she would have agreed to come to his church. A two-way street is not even that without traffic. 'It's all right,' she tells him as they leave two pairs of shoes behind on the sand.

Lily stoops down and folds up his left trouser leg and then his right. He suppresses a giggle; it feels as if she is tickling him. After this intimacy, he again takes her hand and they walk into the waves.

'What about your stitches?'

'Fuck 'em,' she laughs.

He likes her carefree attitude, dare not pull her up on the language. A date is not a shift at Baxter's School, not youth group. And the F-word is the rarest thing at the latter. The teenagers who attend The Church of the Men of Judea have, without exception, enjoyed more measured parenting than he did, and judging by her language, than Lily also. She is a little like him, an upbringing that did not guide her well. He has found the true path and she is still searching. Garth would like to be her guide. 'Tell me about growing up,' he says.

'All of it?' Lily sounds light-hearted, all disagreement left with their shoes and their socks.

'Just as much as you want to say.'

'Shit, Garth, none of it but I expect I should. You being a bit of a boyfriend and all.'

In the Lord's Knowing Gaze

He feels warmed by her words. 'Your father, for example, I expect he swore a lot?'

Lily stumbles in the waves, laughter making her double forward. 'I never heard the fucker swear once. The effing and blinding is all me, I'm afraid. Do you want me to tone it down?'

'I'm sorry, Lily. I'm not telling you how to speak. If you want to work with children...'

'I get it. I sound like Ryan, the stupid one. I don't swear with my kids, Garth. Never. But we're adults, aren't we?'

'We are children before God.' He says it like a reflex, smiles apologetically when Lily snorts out a laugh. 'It's not how you see it, I know.'

The water is exceptionally gentle, the waves mere ripples. Lily has led him out to knee-depth, her dress raised. It is still light, although no one else is on this part of the beach. He keeps glancing down at her slender legs, cannot help himself. She is his girlfriend. The Lily-fashioned turn-ups of his second-best pair of trousers have become saturated with seawater, while she simply lifts her dress a little higher. Shows him a little more. He wishes he could push it entirely from his mind—the despoiling of his clothing—be as easy-going as Lily. He wonders if she wishes to go skinny-dipping—he has heard of that—she wanted to go to an X-rated movie earlier. He can imagine Lily raising the dress right off her body. Might have to turn down another suggestion, resolved as he is to be as good as Gandhi.

'I'll not swear then, Garth, your quite right. If I can describe my parents without, it will be a first. I'll try. Good for you, wanting a true picture, not just my bitterest feelings.'

She puts an arm around his waist, he feels like she is his guide now. They have turned back towards their shoes but after walking two paces, she pauses. Stock-still in the shallow water. 'Daddy is a wet lettuce, nothing but a limp thing who has never asserted himself for ten minutes in this life. His opinions are just my stupid mother's opinions gone stale. Only my mother can pull them from the ground, sharp and crisp and pungent. Daddy only cares about being in her good books. He doesn't think anything really. Not about me; not about the world. When I was a kid, she, my horrible mother, was the most controlling—I want to say bitch but that might be swearing, so

I'd best avoid it—the most controlling lady-dog imaginable. She lived my life for me. Stupid ballet lessons, stupid piano lessons. I know I should be grateful, lots of kids like that stuff, but little Gary—he's my brother you might remember—he was just larking about from the age of nothing. I had to be something, had to be it for Mummy. I was not a free agent; do you get me?'

'But kids aren't really free, they need to be shown how to live.'

'Mine are! My kids are free. You had weird parents too, Garth. Thre'penny Ha'penny sounds like it was stuck in the dark ages. We're kindred spirits, survivors. And I'm not inflicting any of that on my own children. Set the next generation free! That's what I say.'

Garth finds himself full of questions. Children should be shown a path, not left to fend for themselves. Loves that he and Lily are kindred spirits. Her beliefs—the nameless, nebulous uncertainty within which she has chiselled a path—may have some thought behind it. That doesn't make it right. He must steer Lily in the direction of Christ. The redeemer.

'I don't think I want to talk about being a kid, Garth. I was an awkward little so-and-so, gave my parents a hell of a run-around. My best excuse is that Gary was worse. Did I tell you that he was sent to young offenders?'

'No.' Garth is surprised to hear it.

'Robbing shops with a gang in town. He was no bloody good at it. Sorry, I swore then. Caught, caught again, caught a couple more times, three months inside. I couldn't stand it, couldn't stand him by then. I only visited twice, both times with Daddy. Guess what?' Garth stands on the lip of the water's edge. He can guess nothing. Gary might be back in prison or he could have become a born-again Christian. He looks at her face as they stand in lapping water. 'Mummy didn't go once. Not once, not ever. Her boy was only fourteen years old when he was in there, baby prison or whatever they call those places. She just ran her stupid florist's shop. Wednesday evening, she went to choir. Do you know, Garth, our house—every window ledge—was always crammed with blooming flowers. Whatever hadn't sold, the last of the flowering stuff from Mummy's shop. Crammed full most of the year. All year long it seemed. It looked like...I don't know what it looked like. Pretty. Such a pretty house, it

In the Lord's Knowing Gaze

can mask a hell of a lot. That was my childhood, Garth. Mummy pretended. Pretended the interior matched what you saw from the road. She pretended I could play the piano when I never got the knack. I left home first chance I could, went to London. Seldom went back. And then when I did, when I took Trent to meet my parents, well...'

They have walked back to their shoes; Garth sits in the sand and Lily follows. It's dry, will not spoil their Saturday night clothes. As they are sitting, she places a hand on the top of Garth's knee, keeps hers drawn up high. 'Can't let sand at my stitches,' she explains. '...you see, Mummy never said it but she could never stand the fact that Trent is black.' This is news to Garth; he hopes he has not let his surprise show. He abhors racism as he has already said. We are all God's children; they've had a couple of black congregants at The Church of the Men of Judea but they never stayed. This is the first he has heard of her former partner's skin colour. He erases the thoughts he has earlier put in his mind of Lily's children. Had imagined their skin to be as white as her own. Must picture them afresh. 'They didn't bring us up racist, they weren't BNP or any of that shit. Sorry about the swearing, it's spot on for that shower. It was the same principle as the ballet and the piano, Mummy is a snob and Trent was a London lad trying to keep his head above water. He came from a council estate. I often think he was a better bloke than I was a partner to him, not in terms of what we did, we loved each other for a time. But he had it hard. Honestly, strangers picked fights with him because of the colour of his skin. When he fought back—the one time he fought back—the police arrested him, gave him a community order or some crap like that. GBH, they called it. That's not justice, Garth. Trent was the victim every time. And me, I could pick up bar work with a blink of my eyelashes, I looked a bit better back then. I wanted to work in fashion, sort of did but it was a crummy job. Mummy sold the florists, made a packet. She was...' Garth belatedly recognises that he has missed an opportunity to tell her she is beautiful. So wrapped up in her story. '...good at all the businesswoman stuff. She could have helped Trent and me out a bit, I reckon but no, that wasn't her way. She told me after we separated that she didn't dare give us money because he would have taken half when we split up. Two-faced nonsense! Money was our problem, not each other. Her grandchildren were on the poverty line while she squirreled away more than a quarter of a million. And I'm still waiting for the first instalment with Trent three years gone.' Garth feels Lily's gaze on his face. 'I don't want the money, Garth. Everything's great in Boscombe, I'm happy in our little maisonette...'

Garth puts an arm around her shoulder, he cannot understand why she has begun to cry. He turns into her, tries to make eye contact. She puts her face into his shoulder. Then Lily places a hand on his midriff, his shirt not tucked in. A hand upon his waist, on his flesh just above the hipbone.

'I'm lonely, Garth,' she whispers in his ear.

He hugs her tighter.

'Lonely,' she repeats.

'I've got you,' he says. Wonders after he has made the utterance whether his phrase means anything. The English Channel is calm, and he feels the rhythmic wash on the sands mirrored in his stomach, a gentle churning that frightens Garth. I love you, would have been braver reassurance to give to lonely Lily. And he thinks he really does love her. He isn't sure if she reciprocates it. Is she hugging him because of who he is, or simply because he is there? Better than no one.

'I've got Alice, I love Alice but she's got Martin. Did I tell you that I met a girl on the beach the day before you ran me down? Crocked me. I made a new friend on the Sunday, then you on Monday.' He shakes his head. 'Caroline is the sweetest. She came around when she heard I was moping at home, no kids and only one leg to walk on. And I bumped into her on the train back from London. I don't make friends that easily, Garth, I can be headstrong, I know. You're not like me...'

'I do! I love you.'

Lily laughs. A joyous sound, worlds away from her tears. 'I said, "You are not like me." I think you misheard?'

He smiles sheepishly as she probes what he thought she'd said. 'You'd not like me,' he admits.

'Love's a big word, Garth, sunshine. I don't know if me and Jesus can both fit in your heart...'

'So far, so good,' he offers.

Lily kisses him on the lips. 'Buy me a drink. Feed my heathen soul.' Garth agrees. And he hopes she is not seeking solace from her loneliness, the misery of her upbringing, in the bottle. It is mortifying to him that his sister steers such a course.

* * *

In the bar, Saturday night is in full swing. It's an alien world for Garth. Although the music is loud, they have sought out the quietest corner. Garth feels self-conscious about his trousers: soaking wet from the knee down. 'I look like I've peed myself.'

'You're having a proper Saturday night then, sunshine.'

Garth tells Lily that she is the prettiest girl in the pub. Says it earnestly, unlikely beauty-pageant judge that he is.

Lily smiles and nods, seems to accept the compliment 'Not really,' she says when she has bathed in the comment long enough. 'I've seen a couple of girls in here who'd give Caroline a run for her money. And she's a marvel.'

Comparing girls was not on Garth's mind. 'Who's Caroline?'

'The girl on the beach. I told you about her a few minutes back.'

'And you're telling me she looks gorgeous?'

'She does.'

'Has Caroline got a boyfriend?'

Lily shakes her head slowly. 'I don't think so.'

'No worries, I'm sticking with you.' Lily laughs and Garth feels pleased with himself. He has made a secular joke. They are finding each other's wavelengths. Garth repeats to Lily how odd this feels for him; he never goes into pubs. Pleasant and unusual.

She tells him she used to work in them—pubs and clubs—years ago. Pulling pints and measuring spirits. Refusing to do so for the drunkest, those who were too far gone. He asks her how she managed that. Did she feel threatened? 'The more pissed a man is, the easier it is to find his obedience button.' Garth doesn't understand her surprising answer, asks her to explain it. 'If I flirted with a drunk, they would do anything I told them. I'd book a taxi home, kick 'em out. I swear most of them thought I was going to climb in the back of the taxi with them. That it was their lucky night.'

Garth feels saddened by her answer, that Lily had to come so close to offering herself to men, simply to keep order. Her London life was a world away from his small Dorset village. He didn't find Christianity until he left Sixpenny Handley, led a life of few temptations before renouncing them completely.

'I had a fling,' Lily pauses and Garth nods his head for her to continue. Needs to know who he is dating. 'I thought Carlo was the love of my life; he had the fling, for me it was pure heartbreak.' Garth looks ashen-faced on her behalf, takes hold of Lily's hand. 'Daft bugger,' she says. 'This was when you were still playing with matchbox cars or Scalextric. That long ago.' He tries to laugh; wants to tell her he never had a Scalextric but knows it is not having a love of his life—certainly not until Lily Stephens stepped in front of his bicycle—that is on his mind. 'He was as old as I am now—Carlo—or maybe older. He turned out to be such a two-faced liar. He was convincing, I fell for him like an idiot. The first three or four times we went out, he took me dancing. Late night places, after my evening shift ended. He was a customer in the fancy club I worked in. He took me to upmarket ones, danced well, and not a lot of fellas really do that. Carlo behaved like a gentleman on the first few dates. When he took me back to his hotel room, I really can't remember if it was his idea or mine. Why wouldn't I go? Love of my life and all that.'

Garth tries to hide his embarrassment, the image of a younger Lily giving herself to a man is not one he wishes to picture.

'He was a good lover, Garth.' She turns her face right into his, must see his reddened cheeks. 'Don't look so worried about it. I reckon they're the most selfish, the confident lovers. Biggest bloody dicks every way up, but I'd only just turned twenty, what did I know? He asked me to move in; told me he lived there. In the Metropole Hotel: how impressive is that? For about six weeks I did exactly that, quit the bar work. He was an odd partner. With me for about three days solid, then he'd tell me he had to go to Italy or New York and he'd be gone for about the same length of time. When we were out, he paid for stuff I didn't need alongside anything I did. Showered me with gifts, honestly. When he was away, he never left me anything. I still had my own money, just running a bit thin. He hardly had anything in the hotel, one or two clothes, not much. I couldn't believe that he went on business trips with so little. He'd often arrive back wearing suits or jackets I'd not seen before. When I couldn't trust him any longer, I followed him. One evening, he left the hotel for the airport...' Lily makes inverted commas with her fingers as she says those last three

In the Lord's Knowing Gaze

words. '...and I did it like in the movies. He caught a bus out to the suburbs like a regular person, not an international businessman. I flagged a cab, told the driver to follow it. The cabbie looked doubtful but I told him I was tracking a lover. Blokes will always do that kind of shit for a pretty girl. And I was quite pretty back then, that was what Carlo saw in me, I suppose...'

'You're beautiful, Lily,' he butts in. 'I'm sure you were then, as you are now. But it's a gift, not a currency to use for the persuasion of men. Julie Rivington at church...'

'Wrong, Garth. It's for leading men by the nose—or the dick—always has been. Redress the power balance a titchy bit. Anyhow, the taxi driver stopped a short way behind the bus at every stop. It felt exciting but not in a great way. I knew it would come to a shitty end. About five miles from the centre of town, Carlo finally left the bus. I paid the driver as quickly as I could, I remember he passed me back the second fiver, that's how cheap fares were back then, and he said, "Be careful," as if I was chasing down a hitman, not an oversexed Italian. I stayed back a distance, watched which house Carlo went inside. A decent-looking semi. I waited a short time, just thinking, but I really needed to find out what was going on. So eventually I went up to the door and rang the bell.'

Garth sits shoulder to shoulder with Lily in the alcove of the busy pub. Attending her words closely, wishing to be her belated rescuer.

'A woman answered the door, quite old, not forty, near it maybe. She looked at me, a hard face like I shouldn't be there. Which is fair enough looking back. "Who are you? What do you want?" I'd stood on the step not speaking. That's not like me but I'd already guessed who she was. Then I asked to speak to Mr Fasoli. To Carlo.'

Lily sits back and takes a long drink of her wine. Garth cannot say a word. Doesn't wish to condemn her but it is a shocking tale. If he could absolve her for her sins, he would, yet it is only the intercession of our Lord that can do that. He won't bring it up just yet.

'She narrowed her eyes. She might have guessed what was going on before I did. "I'm Mrs Fasoli," she said, "what's my husband got to do with you?" I felt like a burst balloon just hearing the words. Fears confirmed. I could have just turned away. I think, Garth, at that moment I wanted to hear it from him. To thump him most likely. Only after that could I properly walk out of his life. I thought of myself as free and easy, Garth, living with a lover in a hotel. Never pictured myself as his bit on the side, there's nothing free about that. I told Mrs Fasoli—who was as English as me, could've been from Sittingbourne judging by her accent—"I'm his lover." I think I said it stupidly because she slapped me across the face. A sudden swipe like we were in the nineteen fifties. I stood my ground, didn't hit back. I said, "You probably needed to know, but you can keep the bastard." Turned and walked away. She shouted after me, questions like, how do I know you're not lying? Well, I wasn't trying to prove it in court. I'd heard the toad was married. I caught a bus, got my stuff from the hotel. I still had a room in Bethnal Green. I didn't try to get my old bar job back. I wasn't going to let Carlo come looking for me. I was heartbroken but the ending was dignified if you think about it. I even turned the other cheek.'

He nods, trying to keep his face as expressionless as he's able; Garth didn't hear any dignity in the last ten minutes although he hates being so judgemental about a girl who was clearly tricked by an older man. Charm and deceit, qualities Garth couldn't use in pursuit of Lily even if he wished to. They sit in silence, and he wonders if he is meant to be telling her his own sexual experiences. He is doing it. Silence, that's the whole story.

Lily asks a couple more questions about Baxter's School. It is as if she sees he has struggled to assimilate all she has told him. An Italian lover before living in sin with Trent. After another silence, she raises what he never would. 'Garth,' she whispers, close to his ear, 'as a Christian, do you not do sex? I'm just asking, not trying to be funny or anything.'

He feels himself redden. He is thirty years old; this doesn't happen when he counsels the youngsters on a Friday night, and seldom when boys at Baxter's ask their ill-worded questions. It feels different with Lily, she has an agenda. He turns towards her, talks directly into her closest ear, hopes she does not see how uncomfortable the topic makes him. 'We do sex,' he tells her. 'We don't do it until we're married. That's the big one. The correct order. It's all pretty clear in the Bible, Lily.'

She nods, pulls him into an embrace, kisses him quickly on the lips.

'Damn. You don't fancy a quick marriage, do you?'

Sunday, 12 June 2016

Garth plays with Jo-jo and Ami. He is good with them, attends their words, looks interested as they show him drawings and toys. Concurrently he feels apprehension about what those at church—Peter and Margery particularly—may be thinking about his unexplained absence. He never advised that it would happen, couldn't think of the words. The church service in Northbourne will be missing his guitar playing but the girls can hold the tune without him. And Samantha Smith plays guitar passably herself; might give it a go. Never tried outside of Friday youth group before now.

He feels fit from cycling. Garth took the children's mother home from the pub the night before, after explaining that he couldn't break the chastity he is committed to until marriage. 'If I could, it would be with you,' he declared. It put Lily in stitches. He never came inside the house yesterday evening, agreed then to come back this morning. He cycled to his flat in Northbourne, slept fleetingly, woke, ate a small bowl of cereal, prayed alone, failed to phone Peter as he'd intended, and then cycled back to Lily's. Meeting her children is important; he hopes to be a part of her life. He is not a Don Juan who woos girls in clubs and pubs. Could be he's the antidote.

And he is grateful that Lily has explained the children's mixed-race parentage to him in advance. These are fantastic children. Jo-jo is a handful, clever, asks Garth if the cross he wears is for Jesus. Lily looks startled when he says it, she may not have noticed it upon him. It is small and he has not worn such a thing on the Wednesday or Saturday dates. Today is the Sabbath.

'Jesus is my best friend,' he tells Jo-jo. 'I hope you can meet him one day.'

'Ami wants me to talk to her imaginary friend too.'

In the corner of his eye, Garth sees Lily flinch. He pats Jo-jo kindly, 'He's not imaginary whether everyone sees him or not.' He has borne witness before far more effrontery at Baxter's School.

The morning goes well; he is confident that there can be no sex talk around the children. Overnight he has contemplated the Brexit vote, come to think Lily could be right. Politics was never his thing: the connection between our Lord's return and the referendum is tenuous, Peter might have overthought it. Garth got it right about the porn film. Defo, as Lily would say.

He crawls along the floor, Ami on his back, calling him Pony Paloney. Jo-jo re-enters the lounge with two pairs of boxing gloves, and offers him one. 'Just play fighting.'

'Fighting's really not my idea of a game, Jo-jo.' He glances up at Lily.

'Trent bought them,' she mutters. 'No boxing today, sweet pea.'

The bacon and the waffles, the opportunity to meet her children, the time spent observing Lily again in summer shorts and T-shirt, make a heady mix for Garth. He doesn't dare to voice it, not even to himself, but the joy and the unpredictability outshine the Sunday service. When he is preparing to leave, after three hours, to cycle once more to Northbourne, Lily protests. 'Come to the beach with us.' He tears himself away only because he feels the temptation that Lily put his way the night before. Seeing her in a swimming costume might break his resolve completely.

* * *

'Where were you?' Julie Rivington is the first to ask when Garth arrives at church five minutes before the evening service.

'Commitments,' he says. It is none of this young girl's business, but he worries that having a girlfriend is making a liar of him. He has kept it from his mother and from Claire; shared only limited information with Peter and Margery. He will not tell them all he and Lily spoke about. He fears that they will assume he has been lovemaking all night with his single-parent girlfriend. He did nothing of the sort. Well, he thought about it off and on, kept trying to push it from his mind. Spent the night four miles away. Four miles from the arms of Lily. Didn't chance it like Gandhi. Some Christians view the work of the devil quite literally, Garth is one of them. He is racing against time. He would like to do all that the devil tempts—do it with beautiful Lily—before anything of that sort can happen, she must come to church, accept Christ into her life. A marriage ceremony. He absolves her of all blame: God had His reasons for making her beautiful. Garth is holding his own in this Mephistophelian tussle.

In the Lord's Knowing Gaze

* * *

'A word,' says Margery Cox when the service is over. Garth dutifully follows his Pastor out onto the street in front of their beloved church. He braces himself for some barbed comments. 'How many times have you seen your lady-friend since last we spoke?'

He thinks her tone accusatory, as though once is forgivable but the three, which he answers for honesty's sake, may require significant atonement.

'You've got the bug,' she says. Pastor Margery sounds less wise to him now than she ever has before. Her dismissal of his love for Lily as a bug—like influenza or an enthusiasm for surfboarding—gives him reason to suspect that she never found such a love herself.

'I've made a friend, Margery, it's to be celebrated, not remedied with medicine. That's my opinion.'

'Now, now. I was observing not criticising, Mr Addicks. It is your life, and I am interested in it, in you, not trying to change your mind.'

Garth wants to trust Margery while suspecting that she may seek to influence. It is what he does at Youth Group, cautions Julie Rivington from attaching herself to any boy at so young an age. And Margery's comment about Gandhi the week before has lodged itself in his mind. Last night felt exactly like he was sleeping with a naked girl although technically he was alone in his flat. When Lily flippantly asked him to marry her, the answer yes was dancing on his lips. It would solve everything for him—guessed it might have had her laughing again—elected not to answer.

'Does she tempt you, Garth?' asks the crippled lady before him. Clutching her frame, smiling steadily.

'She's beautiful, Margery, but I know who I am. Where my duties lie.'

'I believe you are her junior by some years.'

'Not so many.' He doesn't understand her line of enquiry.

'Lasting partnerships are not built on beauty, Garth, for it is not a durable quality.'

'I think it may be.' He feels himself on uncertain ground, no biblical foundation to his reply. 'Lily is beautiful inside.' Ad-libbing.

'And yet God has not touched her. She has still to experience the inner peace that only forming a relationship with Him can bring. Be very careful of illusion. I trust you, Mr Addicks, I do not doubt that you have attached yourself to a good soul. The concern is that worldly temptations can distort our vision. Don't build a house in the sand, build it beside our church, Garth.'

He agrees. Basically, he agrees and wonders if Lily would listen to Pastor Margery more than she does to him. The woman-to-woman thing.

'Bring her, Garth, bring Lily to this place. I would love to meet her.'

Chapter Three:

Punching a Boy in Sittingbourne

Monday, 13 June 2016

'You know he didn't stay over on Saturday night. You were there, you saw him leave, Alice.'

'Seeing is not always believing, Lily-petal. Did he cycle round the block and then sneak back in?'

Lily outstares her friend, hopes that her wide-eyed look explains her relationship with Garth Addicks.

'You said he was playing with the kids on Sunday morning...'

'Shush it.' She glances at Jo-jo who seems occupied with Ami and Wendy. Fears that he listens to adult talk, and may understand its implications. Or misunderstand it which could be worse. Three-year-old Bryony nestles in her mother's arms; these two women have talked over her head for all of her young life.

They are in Lily's maisonette, toys and games strewn across the living room floor as they have been since Garth came to play on Sunday. Lily, Alice and the youngsters walked back together after collecting the three older children from school.

'I think I implied he could stay,' Lily tells her friend quietly, 'but I shouldn't have said it. Not done in Christian circles and he wasn't for hopping over the line. Not for one second. He's a stickler for doing whatever Jesus says.'

Alice puts a hand on Lily's. 'That sounds a bit weird to me. Are you okay with him?'

'He's great, he really is. I've no idea why he believes in all that—the God stuff—still a great lad.'

Alice's eyes narrow.

'Not a lad, a man.'

She nudges Lily, shoulder to shoulder. 'A great man? Sounds like Nelson Mandela which isn't sexy at all, Lily-petal.'

'No, I said it wrong. He explains working with kids well; he's doing something worthwhile there. Really, he is. Working in a residential school, truants and kids with rubbish families. He does youth work at church too but the kids who go to that one sound dead easy. I could do that if I knew where to begin a prayer. And didn't swear so much...'

'Will you be going? Popping along to try out his church. Find out what it's all about.'

'You sound like Garth. He says that I should but I know I'd only laugh if I had to sit through a service. I don't say it to him, the funny church sounds like a load of nonsense. Forced happiness with a tambourine.'

Wendy has approached her mum holding a buckle in one hand and the shoe to which it belongs in the other. Lily notices that the child is close to tears. 'Hey, what's the matter, sunshine?'

'Broken,' is all Wendy says to her, before burying her face in her mother's thin clothing. Lily glances at Ami, she is still crayoning, and Jo-jo seems to be doing the same. She doesn't think her own children are responsible. Saw neither troubling the girl's feet.

'Oh dear,' says Alice, 'I think you can walk home with it like that. You've a pair of sandals that will do nicely for school in the morning. We can drive into Bourno after school tomorrow, buy you another pair.' She places a forefinger on little Wendy's chin.

Then her daughter starts to cry outright. 'I pulled it and it came off,' she says through her tears. Confesses to her mother.

Alice puts Bryony down beside her on the sofa and pulls Wendy into a hug. 'Well, you won't be doing that again, will you?'

'No, I won't,' says Wendy, her voice suddenly resolute. Sounding older than her years.

Not a problem to Alice, while Lily wonders if she would have forgiven her own children so quickly: shoes are not cheap and the lesson needs learning. As the child returns to crayoning and Bryony puts a thumb in her mouth, she whispers to Alice, 'Simon Clarke phoned me at work today.'

Alice takes a moment to recall who's who in Lily's life, then the penny drops through the slot. 'Not another proposition! I thought he was on his deathbed. Or somewhere close to it.'

'He only came out of hospital on Friday, not in work yet. So many broken bits that he's been plastered head to toe.'

'Serves him right; I'd never heard you cry before that Saturday night.'

Lily falls silent for a second, Alice doesn't press, both are wary of children listening in to their adult talk. Lily reflects upon Alice's observation. She never used to cry; even the break-up with Trent was tear-free. Things have got on top of her lately; she isn't sure why Simon Clarke's call upset her as much as it did. The pain of her leg injury was the cause when she first cried with Garth; then she did it again Saturday last, told him she was lonely. Didn't even know it was true before saying it out loud; always thought she had the patience to wait forever. Putting her children first, not running after blokes. That's what she told herself when she first came to Boscombe. The Date Local webpage was Alice's idea, Lily thought it daft from the word go.

'Crying's normal sometimes, Alice.'

'Tell me about it. I cry when Martin says I can't have a new dress this month.'

'That's blackmail, Alice. It doesn't really count...'

'So, no proposition from the creep this time?'

'An apology while requesting that I swear a vow of silence about his earlier call.'

'Bloody hell,' mouths Alice silently. 'What do you think it means?'

'It means he's as thick as a plank of wood. I was never going to tell anyone at work. If I had blagged, said that a partner asked me on a date, they wouldn't know if I was complaining or showing off. Finally letting it be known that I have a love life. I could have told his wife but I don't know her, no idea what she's like. It might be their favourite pastime, swingers or something.'

'What did he say?'

'He said...' Lily deepens her voice. '...Miss Stephens, I'm ashamed to say I was a little brandied up.'

'Stick with Garth, it sounds like he loves you without the sauce.'

Lily flinches at her comment.

'What is it?' says Alice.

She enjoys the confidences they share but cannot think what her friend might make of Garth's many declarations of love. She calculates that her boyfriend has less experience of relationships than she had attained at sixteen, twenty long years ago. It's amateur versus pro, and she thought her own love life to be fairly standard until this mismatch shed new light on it.

'What?' Alice tries again. 'Is he okay with you?'

'He's brilliant, Alice. A sweet, harmless Christian. You've helped me out twice now, just so I can date him...'

'The kids can stay at mine if you need peace and quiet.' Alice gives Lily a suggestive wink, it draws a laugh and a frown. A guffaw through Lily's suddenly pinched face.

'Alice, seriously, we're not there yet. A million miles from it...' Lily smiles back at the concerned look on her friend's face. '...honestly, he's an uncorruptible Christian...'

'You can do it, Lily, look at you!' Alice puts a finger and thumb on the side of her friend's skinny midriff.

Lily only shakes her head, tells her that Garth is coming around the following evening, probably after her children are in bed. 'It'll be talking, Alice, just talking. I'm cool with that, I like talking.'

Alice shows her a pair of raised eyebrows. 'If he treats you right, I'll like him too.'

Alice has been Lily's mainstay in Boscombe, her antidote to the loneliness she inadvertently confessed to Garth. As good a friend as she has ever known, although there are limits to how that can play out with a young married woman. Lily knows that she is pinning a lot of hopes on Garth: the believer in what cannot be seen, who only met her because the good Lord rolled the dice that way. Sweet, funny and the word Alice said earlier: weird.

Tuesday, 14 June 2016

She seldom sings this kind of nonsense to Ami.

The animals went in two by two. Hurrah! Hurrah!

Lily catches herself; Garth is coming around shortly, it could explain it. His faith sounds more austere by a long chalk. Songs about Jesus's bespoke film classifications might make his top ten. Or the Bible's blanket ban on bonking. She can't imagine them singing this twee stuff in The Church of the Men of Judea. Ami likes it—big grin on her face—knows all the words from her play-group days. Sings

Punching a Boy in Sittingbourne

along, splashes away in the bath.

'I'll get it,' Jo-jo shouts from the lounge when they hear the buzz that is their home's doorbell.

'No, wait!' She has told her son many times that he is too young to answer the door alone. And Lily is not dressed yet, wears a dressing gown over underwear after taking a short bath, before she put Ami into the same water. Keeping down the bills. She can't greet Garth looking like this, the temptress in her undies. He's early, maybe forty minutes early. 'Tell him to wait!' shouts Lily 'He's got to stay out on the step, please!' She can hear her son at the door, hopes he's put the chain on as she taught him. Jo-jo is headstrong, might let him straight in. They got along okay on Sunday.

The dressing gown is a flimsy silky affair, fine in summer, in the privacy of her own home, when there are no celibate Christians looking on. Garth will be torn between lust and disgust: those irreconcilable cousins. She has seen him look at her keenly, carnality is within him but Lily assumes puritanical God would be the knockout winner at this stage in their odd courtship. She could try and smuggle half a bottle of wine down his gullet, it might work. And might not. She has thought, since Saturday last, that it would be wiser if she didn't drink in his company. Not unless Garth does likewise. She doesn't regret much in her relationship with this new and unusual boyfriend. Her unsubtle sexual overtures—that he, as an adherent to a belief system which baffles her, felt obliged to reject—are the sum total. She's finding her way with him, not trying to convert him to her looser morals. To normality, goddammit. As she slips into the corridor, she hears her son speaking in a low voice to the caller. By her bedroom door, Lily turns; he should let no one into the maisonette unvetted by her. 'Garth! Wait outside, please!' she shouts. Her son giggles. Garth wouldn't stay on Saturday night but he turns up when she's near naked, it's as if he is trying to catch her out. 'Back outside! I'm not properly dressed.'

'Oh, nor am I, sweetie,' says the well-spoken Caroline.

'You!'

'Just dropping in. Is it a bad time?'

Jo-jo is laughing, couldn't stick to the rules about the door with this one, the girl who sat next to him on the train. Pretty and bubbly, she's already got him laughing uncontrollably. 'She's scared of my pyjamas,' he tells his mother.

Caroline looks at Lily's son and makes a terrified face, Jo-jo gets the giggles again. 'It's arachnophobia,' she says in a quavering voice. 'Two legs, four legs, even six, they're all okay. The eight-legged ones just freak me out. Horrible, horrible.' She points at his cotton trousers and jacket, her face aghast.

Lily steps forward, in only her dressing gown she is every bit as covered as her friend, perhaps more so. Caroline has called in while running—taking a break—she wears white shorts and a green halter top, shows more midriff than Lily ever would away from the beach. Her blond hair tied back tightly—a few strands left to splay this way and that—a girl who knows how to be looked at. 'I thought you were Garth, didn't want him to see me undressed.'

Caroline pulls Lily into a greeting hug. 'Keeping his hand out of the cookie jar?'

She doesn't understand the phrase for a moment, realises she has explained nothing of Garth to this friend beyond the bare bones of his existence. 'Can I just check back on Ami.' Caroline follows her down the short passageway and waits as Lily enters the bathroom. 'I need to dry her, get myself dressed, and put them both to bed before this fella comes.'

'I've come at a busy time, let me help.' Caroline slides into the bathroom. Ami is standing, the towel in her hands as she gawps at the unexpected guest.

'Get yourself ready for your guy,' Caroline instructs Lily, 'but I can't put spider boy to bed. I'm really scared of those things.'

'Daft bugger, they're only pyjamas.'

Outside the door, Jo-jo sings in a deeper voice than he really has, directing the incy wincy spider song Caroline's way. Last Christmas he chose his own present: simple black cobwebs scaffolded across otherwise cream pyjamas, a spider or two playing tiggy-off-ground. The visitor starts to dry Ami.

'You're a treasure, you are,' says Lily. 'I always wanted a nanny.'

'Hey, even I never had one of those.'

Lily goes into the bedroom, only to find Caroline following behind, little Ami accompanying her all the way. Enjoying a vigorous

Punching a Boy in Sittingbourne

towelling. Jo-jo loiters in the doorway, looks at the girl in shorts as boys are apt to.

'Stop,' says Caroline.

'What is it?' Lily sees the look of concern on her friend's face.

'Oh God, let me see.' Caroline signals for her to turn around.

Lily does as the gesture indicates without really understanding what has prompted it. She fears she has a spider on the back of her leg or similar. An unlikely coincidence, nothing else comes to mind.

'It looks a bit nasty, Lily.' Caroline is kneeling down, lightly touching the damaged calf. A nurse attached to her GP practice removed the stitches yesterday morning, it subsequently bled at work. This evening, Lily again bathed with one leg over the side of the bath.

Ami and Jo-jo are laughing at Caroline. 'You're not a nurse,' says the boy.

Caroline kisses the palm of her own hand, then places it on the long scar. 'Beautiful in no time,' she tells the assembled family.

Lily laughs, thinks what a screwball nanny this one is turning out to be. At least she's nice with it. She likes seeing her this way, dressed down for running, dressed only a little but she has the physique to carry it off. On the train—over a week ago—she was taken with Caroline's sophisticated dress sense, her deportment, this earthiness is less alien to Lily. More common ground with the ever-helpful jogger than with the spoilt child Caroline also admits to being.

'Do you need to dress to impress?' Both are perched on the edge of Lily's double bed when the question is asked. Lily having slipped out of the bathrobe.

'We're only having a night in...'

Caroline leans forward, whispers with a grin, 'Then you already look about perfect.'

Her comment sets Lily off laughing. Caroline really doesn't know anything about Garth Addicks. Nothing whatsoever. 'Kids, can you go through, please. You can find your jim-jams can't you, Ami?'

'Jim-jams, top drawer,' sings her daughter. It's a line in their room tidying song.

* * *

'Tell me again how you met,' says Caroline.

Lily is sitting on the bed in her underwear. Caroline is in her element, painting her friend's toenails. From fitness instructor to beautician. 'I've told you already, he was the boy with the bike. The accident.'

'Again?' asks Caroline. Lily gives her a puzzled look. 'Tell me again how you met your boyfriend but say something that isn't completely mad this time around. Can't you sue him? The scar on the back of your leg doesn't look great and my magic kiss is a long shot.'

Lily's smile gives way at this comment. She is conscious that she is no longer young, thinks that Garth's youth may be part of his attraction to her. And now beautiful Caroline is implying she is damaged.

'You're sensitive,' says the jogger, again kissing the palm of her own hand and gently rubbing it upon that left calf. 'It'll heal up, I know it will. And he's your choice, Lily...' Caroline runs her eyes over the simple black bra, the non-matching white knickers in which Lily sits. '...do you not have something racier for a night in?'

Lily bashes her gently with the pillow closest to hand. 'I do not. Never did have. Anyway, Garth isn't that sort of guy.'

'Oh, they're all that sort of guy, Lily. The question is whether they act that way from the get-go, or wait for you to flick the switch.'

'Caroline!'

'I'm just saying how it is.'

'Really...' Lily feels unsure quite how much to reveal about her boyfriend to this cheeky upstart. '...Garth is different.' As they talk, her friend is all jokes and innuendo; when she tells of his allegiance to Jesus Christ, Caroline nods more solemnly. Desists. 'We both had to put up with tricky parents when we were growing up, it's a big thing in common,' says Lily, and Caroline takes hold of her hand, face completely wiped of its smile. Shitty families might be beyond her comprehension, her father takes her shopping on Oxford Street. Lily talks on and on, Caroline is easy company. She tells her that Garth wouldn't watch a film because a character played a porn star, 'This was mainstream, a comedy about those sorts of people. Not a blue one, I don't watch filth.' She uses the phrase about him that Garth coined when they talked in the beer garden of the Perkin Inn: 'He's boundaried.' Caroline doesn't understand it at first. 'In his job he has to be very strict, show the boys at Baxter's School that they can't beat

Punching a Boy in Sittingbourne

the rules. I think it just about sums him up.'

'I get you,' says the jogger. 'He's drawn lines around what he will and won't do. It sounds a lot more sense than fun.'

Lily likes having a friend to confide in. Caroline has picked out a dress for her; she's good at it. Navy blue, long enough, summery. Soft on her skin.

As they are leaving the bedroom, Caroline turns to her, face suddenly frowning at the dress Lily wears. 'Nuh-no, just the underwear alone. Works every time.'

* * *

'Had I best go now?' asks Caroline.

'Stay a little, it'll be twenty minutes or more before he arrives. Always bang on time is Garth.' Caroline sits down on the old sofa. Lily guesses her friend is curious to meet him, hopes she's not over-judgemental. Lily needs no further confirmation of the strange choice she has made. Doubts it herself without need of third-party assistance. 'Can I get you a glass of wine?'

Caroline shakes her head, 'You'll be needing that. Or drip-feeding it to the boy. Do you have orange juice?'

Lily says 'Yes' then as she walks to the kitchen, realises she doesn't. Did she say it only to avoid sounding uncultured in front of the well-to-do girl? 'I'm out, will squash do?' she calls.

'Perfect,' replies Caroline.

She takes two glasses back to the lounge, sits beside her, takes in Caroline's unexpected presence once more. 'Are you cold?'

Caroline runs a hand over her bare legs. Goosebumps, dressed for running as she is. The steam of the bathroom will have kept her warm; choosing Lily's clothes, less so.

'I'll take myself off before your guy arrives. I must.'

'And you'll run all the way...'

'Can I get you back running?' she interrupts. 'Tell the Garth boy not to shunt up your rear this time.' Lily laughs at her way of speaking, so well enunciated the crudity sounds incidental. 'Were all your boyfriends Christians?'

'No, they were not. And what about your boxer, Caroline? Off, on? On, off?'

'Did you have to ask?' She casts her eyes down to the rug by her feet.

Lily leans forward. 'Sorry sweetie,' she says, conscious she is using Caroline's own word of endearment. 'Tell me?'

'He's...' She leans back against the sofa, runs a hand as if drying tears although Lily can see none. '...not right. My parents always knew it. Clive's not right for me.'

Lily gives her a searching look. 'Tell me?'

'We had to ban him from the gym where I work. He's always trained there. In fact, I met him in the gym, we've both been fixtures since two thousand and eleven, him before that, I expect...'

Lily stops her flow. 'Your private gym isn't a boxing gym, is it?'

Caroline's lips turn into the first smile since the conversation rested on Clive, she pushes a forefinger into her own nose and squashes it as flat as it will easily go. 'I'm letting no one do that to me.'

Lily laughs, likes seeing normal service resume on the pretty face when finger releases nose.

'I think it's ten years since Clive really boxed, he lined up a couple of fights about two years ago, to show off to me. I couldn't watch, sat at the ringside but I couldn't watch. Men punching each other, that stuff is even worse than spider pyjamas.' As Caroline tells her very particular hierarchy of dislike, there is a giggle from outside the lounge, the scampering of feet.

'Sorry,' says Lily, embarrassed that Jo-jo—and little Ami if her ears have calculated the footfall correctly—have been listening in.

'Don't be. I was like your boy at that age.'

Lily thinks about that. It seems unlikely, yet this girl always says it how it is. After Lily has received two affirmative answers to her shout of 'Are you in bed now?' they resume the conversation, whispering, keeping the children from listening in.

'Ten years, he must be tonnes older than you.'

'A bit, I think he first quit boxing at twenty-one.'

Lily puzzles over that: never a proper boxer by the sound of it.

'He does...' Caroline pauses. '...took to body-building.' She glances up at Lily. 'Your face!'

'Phew, they look like inflated men. Rolled in Vaseline, blown up like balloons.'

'Yep, that's my Clive... No, really, he was all right, for a long time.'

Punching a Boy in Sittingbourne

'Did he do the contests? Ripple his back and everything.'

'Your face! They're normal people, Lily. I've known loads. I work in a gym full of them. And he won, Clive won quite a lot of contests. Or rather...' The girl again looks down, avoids Lily's eye for a moment. '...they're not all normal people. He was for a time but I really think it's steroids that does a lot of them in.'

'Jesus, Caroline. What...?'

'They take them because of the muscle growth but—some of them overdo it—it messes with their minds. Clive got paranoid. I dumped him because he was acting weird. I think it's the funny pills, really. A lot of paranoid and crazy thinking. He smashed up the ladies changing room, did it because I wasn't in when he thought I should have been. He went in there looking for me, then kicked off like he was hunting me down. They called the police. Roger—my manager—says Clive will be in court over it.'

'That's awful.' Lily dwells on what she has said. 'Might he come round your house in that mood?'

'The police have simply warned him off; my dad wants me to get a restraining order. I guess I shouldn't nag you about the Christian boy; well done on that front.'

A text comes into Lily's phone, makes it short buzz. She glances quickly at it.

Late setting off from Ferndown, with you in forty minutes

Lily goes through to the kitchen, pours two glasses of white wine, and returns to the lounge.

'Stay a while,' she tells Caroline. Hands her a glass.

As the younger girl takes the drink, Lily notices her shiver slightly. Already on her feet, she places her own glass on the coffee table, paces quickly to her bedroom. Returns with the flower-print dressing gown in her hands. 'Keep yourself warm before the bout,' she says, and Caroline rises, slips the proffered garment over her scant running clothes. When they are again sharing the sofa, Lily asks Caroline, 'Can I tell you something?'

'Sure,' says the younger girl.

'It's something that happened a long time ago, twenty years. When you were aged nothing.'

Boscombe

'When I was as innocent as your Ami,' says Caroline. Doing the maths.

As Lily contemplates the story she has in mind, she wonders what exactly has brought it up. The need to unburden herself; the girl's admission about Clive could have prompted it but the connection is minimal. Lily has never recounted this tale to Alice; Trent was the last to hear it, and that before Jo-jo was born. She lowers her head to take a sip of wine. There is silence in the maisonette. Asked to be heard and then she's not said a word in thirty seconds. This sorry episode has festered unexamined inside her for long enough. Caroline holds Lily's eye while again putting her own glass to her lips.

* * *

'I was a pretty difficult kid at sixteen. This thing happened after I broke-up with my first proper boyfriend but I'd done half the stuff you're not supposed to do...' Lily looks squarely at her friend before clarifying. '...done a bit with boys long before I got a true boyfriend.'

Caroline listens with intent, lips stilled, face rigid with concentration.

'Before we broke up, he told me that one of our teachers told him not to date a tearaway. Probably right and the boy pretty much dumped me on her say so. I wasn't thick at school, just never did any work.' Lily runs a hand over her forehead, through her loose-hanging hair. 'My problem back then was alcohol; I drank all I could and there were plenty of older lads who'd ply a young girl in Sittingbourne. I was trouble.'

Caroline's eyes are fixed on her, they sit adjacent on the sofa. Lily scarcely gives her eye contact. The younger girl pulls her feet up onto the cushion, drawing her legs up and putting her arms around her knees, holding the dressing gown in place. She nods her head calmly. Silently she mouths, 'Tell me.'

'The lad was known as Muzzle, a daft name, horrible name, he'd bitten other kids in fights but I didn't know him when he did that. Earned his horrible nickname...'

'Lily,' says Caroline, concern in her careful voice, 'you had a boyfriend called Muzzle?'

'No, I've confused you. My boyfriend was Aaron—had been Aaron but we'd broken up—a decent kid, better off without me.' She

Punching a Boy in Sittingbourne

smooths down the navy-blue dress which Caroline chose for her earlier. 'He was the first boy that I properly...' Her two hands gesture towards her own most private area. '...you know?' Caroline signals understanding; Lily wonders if she's shocked her; hopes not, their lives are too dissimilar for to be sure. 'I know I was only sixteen, did it with him at fifteen the first few times but this was Sittingbourne, twenty years ago.'

Her friend gestures with an open palm for Lily to continue the story. No need to excuse herself.

'Muzzle was a friend of Aaron's, a dodgy friend really. A neighbour. He was only a year older but he was a much harder kid. Already into drugs. A few of us had tried them—spliffs mostly—he was nutty with it. A real headcase. Out of it half the time. Kids like me, who couldn't get served in pubs, would meet up in a park, a playground. White cider, a spliff if we could get our hands on one. That's what took up our evenings; beat doing homework or watching tele with parents. I'd gone there on a Monday. This was just after Easter break, first day back to school, not even warm evenings that time of year. I was always out, couldn't stand being at home, couldn't stand my mum. There were a few kids there early on, mostly younger ones, children really, hanging on the coattails of the likes of me and Aaron. Not that Aaron was there that night, we'd split up about a week before, like I said. We older girls—boys too I suspect—loved it, pretty cool having young ones look up to us but we always acted the opposite. A girl called Courtney shared her vodka with me, I don't know where she got it. She was about twelve, so I drank the lot, pretty much, and told her to stop moaning or I'd call the police. She left soon after that and so did most of the other hang-out kids, it was probably pushing ten o'clock and they all had anxious parents to get back to. My mum and dad were the same, anxious as hell but that was what I wanted. The only control I had. I'd spend the evening hoping they were worried, pleased if I was making Mummy a little less smug.'

Caroline leans into her friend, shuffles herself on the sofa, thigh to thigh. Gives her a quick hug, says only, 'Tough times.'

Lily feels moved. This girl has worried her parents with a boyfriend she has chosen as an adult, Lily can picture no such rebellion in her when she was still a schoolgirl. Even now, Caroline has settled for her parents' wisdom. Chosen them over the boxer. She doesn't look to be judging Lily harshly so far, and she wants to get this off her chest. Share a rancid slice of her shocking youth. 'I don't really know how it happened, only Muzzle and me were left in the park. I was...' She glances quickly at lounge door. '...fucked-up on vodka. I'd done it a few times before, you see. I had no control whatsoever; I was a mess. And, of course, this Muzzle guy turned out to be a right bastard. He started talking about Aaron, basically telling me what a wimp his friend was. I think he said...' Lily lowers her voice considerably, hopes Jo-jo has remained in bed. '...prick and dickhead, all the nasties for his supposed friend. But really, he was saying, I shouldn't have done it with him. Had sex. He knew all about it, Aaron must have told him loads. He knew what I liked, thought he did. Muzzle said I should do it with him because he was irresistible. His opinion, not mine. That was more than a thousand miles from my opinion. I tried to put him straight but we were in a barely lit park and I was drunk. He kept trying to do stuff to me, just holding my wrists initially. He thought he could persuade me to do it with him. Either that or wait until I passed out from all the vodka. He was a determined bastard but I was on to him by this point. For all my bad-girl ways, I had a clear idea of who I was and what I'd do. What I wouldn't do. Aaron had been a real boyfriend—a stupid one looking back—we'd hung out as real mates for months before we split. When I let him do what he did, it was a decision I'd thought about—a shit one, I'll die if I can't stop Ami from being as stupid as I was at fifteen—but I knew my own mind. I think we all wanted to lose our cherry then: I did, and so did the girls I hung out with. I'm sure you were nothing like that, Caz. But you lived here, didn't have to grow up in stinking Sittingbourne.' Her friend gives her hand a squeeze, lips slightly upturned at the last comment. Probably never been there, doesn't know how pernicious it is. And even Lily thinks she might blame the place more than the shitty town deserves. 'I didn't want Muzzle, never ever, never would have. Even drunk I knew that much. I let him kiss me—which was probably the worst thing I could do—just buying time. Let him kiss me because it was better than the violence he was threatening if I didn't go along with him. He was a nasty bit of work, was Muzzle.'

'Oh, God,' murmurs Caroline.

Punching a Boy in Sittingbourne

'He didn't just kiss me, of course, his hands were everywhere. It wasn't close to warm enough for it but I was only wearing something like you are now, shorts and T-shirt, I think. He had his hands down my pants, I couldn't keep him off. He was an animal. There was no easy way. He tried to push my clothes down. Hurt me, he was rough, hurt me where he should never have fucking touched me. I was panicking—pretty scared of him—and then saw my chance. I heard voices and he was easing off, just trying to kiss me on the mouth to keep me quiet. When I knew the voices were close, could see them despite the gloom, a man and a woman, both calling a dog's name, I knew it was my chance. I pushed him back a short way, Muzzle laughed, didn't want the older couple to pick up that we weren't in agreement about what he was doing, or where his hands had been. "Give me your face," I said. I think it confused him; he thought I was going to kiss him again. I punched him as hard as I fucking could with my right hand. He made no noise but I did the same with the left and heard him exhale. A bit stunned. I think there was a shout from the man in the park but I just shouted, "Help me." Then I hit again with my right, and this was something else. I heard a crack when I did it; I told you I was a wild kid. Muzzle started to holler after that punch. Top of his lungs, hollering like hell. In so much pain it was lovely to see. I'm not being mean in saying it, not after everything he'd done. Loved seeing tears welling in the hard bastard's eyes. And Caz, what happened next was all nonsense. The dog walker—a man of my dad's age—ran over and grabbed hold of me like I was a mugger. He didn't do anything but grab a-hold of me and start shouting himself. I was out of it, really drunk, began crying and heaving. Miles out of it. Muzzle was sitting on the soft ground, groaning very strangely. He looked to have aged twenty years on account of the last whack I'd given him. I think the man's shouting brought other people over. Not the woman—the old man's wife—she stayed back as if I might punch her, and I really wouldn't. Still, I felt relieved; that's what my tears were. Pure relief. I never told the old guy who was holding me why I'd hit the lad, smacked Muzzle. You'd think he could have guessed. The sex things were nothing Aaron hadn't done before—I was game for it with him—but this was Muzzle and I always hated him. Even when I took his weed. I think I'd made it clear enough that I didn't want him, even if the kissing thing was confusing. Maybe not been as clear as I should have.'

'It was him, not you, Lily. You did nothing wrong.' Caroline's brow is creased in a seldom-seen frown.

'Not how everyone else saw it. The police came and...' Lily draws herself up on the sofa before continuing. '...get this, Caz, I was arrested. I'd done Muzzle a broken jaw.'

Caroline hugs Lily again, mutters, 'He deserved it, didn't he? The bastard deserved worse.'

Lily feels on edge from the tale's telling but smiles quickly at her friend's obscenity. 'Said like a Kentish girl.' She runs the back of her hand over her moistening eyes. 'The police had the nerve to charge me. I couldn't bring myself to say any of what Muzzle had done to me, all I told the policeman was "He tried to kiss me." It was a bloke questioning me; I was never even offered a policewoman. Muzzle was carted off to hospital, kept in. His jaw wired up. There would have been more justice if they had left him in the park. More justice in my book. May be slugged him a few more times; I'd have done it for them but that wasn't the way it panned out. Instead, the police took a statement from him about what I'd done. Punching him in the face. Took it from his hospital bed. The idiot old man with the dog told the police it was all me. He'd only seen me fighting, not spotted Muzzle doing anything wrong. I don't think they spoke to his wife and it wouldn't have made a difference if they had. They breathalysed me at the station—the blow into a bag test—not that I drove a car or anything, just busted a horny fucker's jaw. Apparently, I was over the limit for it. My mother turned up at the police station, they called her my "appropriate adult." Wouldn't interview me without one. It was bloody ridiculous; she wasn't even an appropriate mother. She was the cause of all my problems. Truly.'

Caroline says a quiet, 'aw,' then puts a comforting arm around Lily's shoulder.

'Don't touch me!' Lily feels only the bristling anger of twenty years earlier. Puts a hand carefully on her friend's knee. 'Sorry. I'm not telling you because I want to cry about it.'

Caroline inches away on the sofa, takes her eye. 'You broke his jaw. Good shot.'

Punching a Boy in Sittingbourne

Lily finds she is crying as she'd hoped not to. No blame attached to Caroline. She likes the comment that set her off. She really hurt him. 'My fucking mother...' Lily has forgotten Saturday night's resolution to describe her parents without profanity. '...never asked why I had done it, not once. She took it for granted that getting drunk and fighting was simply what I did. She hadn't known where I'd been most nights for about a year and took the phone call from the police as explanation. I'd clearly been out punching boys, that was as much as she thought about it. I couldn't put her right, couldn't talk about where Muzzle had touched and groped me; never had so much as a conversation about the monthlies with her. I'd long been a hooligan in my mother's eyes. She liked having proof. If I'd told her what he did, that he forced himself on me, she would have only thought me a whore as well. I wasn't going to tell her anything, I was through with her disapproval.' Caroline tries to say something, puts a gentle hand on her forearm as she leans forward to speak. Lily will not cede the floor. 'I was charged, they had a witness and I'd sort of admitted it too. Said I whacked him one. More than one. That followed my mother's—my appropriate adult's—best advice. They told me I'd get hauled before the court in a few weeks. I've since thought that maybe my dad went and talked to Muzzle's dad, not that I know it for a fact. I had to go to the police station about two weeks later; Dad accompanied me this time and some sergeant—or whatever pompous rank the snot-nosed git called himself by—gave me a caution. On the night when it happened, I thought it was going to be worse. Young offenders, you know: the detention centre shit. The police said it on the night and my mother said it for days after. And Caroline, whenever I hear about some kid in trouble, or learn that someone went down for something when they were a youngster, I think to myself, that's got to be trumped-up charges; I could lay a bet that they're as innocent as I was. Kids can't talk to police; police know sod all about kids. It's a zero-sum, rough justice. No justice at all in my experience.'

Caroline hugs Lily again, holds her for fully a minute. 'Oh God, Lily.'

'Long time past; thanks for listening,' she whispers. Eyes moist, not really crying. It's been an ordeal to tell the tale.

Finally, they pick up their undrunk wines from the coffee table. 'Your mum was crap,' says Caroline, 'and you couldn't trust her. Are you so sure now, sure that she would have been as heartless as that if she'd somehow learnt you were the victim? The punch was you fighting back.'

'One hundred percent. One hundred fucking percent.' Not a second's hesitation in her reply.

As Caroline looks searchingly at her, Lily realises that Jo-jo is answering the front door again. She must have missed the buzzer, she and her visitor so wrapped up in her story. 'Mum, he's here.'

Both girls stand. 'Coming,' says Lily.

'Wait!' commands Caroline in a sharp whisper. She takes a handkerchief from her shorts pocket, uses a corner to dab her friend's eyes, remove all evidence of Lily's fallen tears. 'You're amazing,' she tells her.

* * *

The entrance door of the maisonette leads on to a short corridor giving access to the other rooms. As Garth gives Lily the awkward hug that is the only greeting their barely physical relationship can muster, she notices that he is looking over her shoulder, taking in the behind of the younger girl, who in turn glances back and catches his eye before turning away. Kissing her palm and waving it in goodnight to Jo-jo as she ushers him back into his bedroom.

'Who is that?' he whispers in Lily's ear.

In a firm voice she says, 'Garth, meet Inger, she is our Swedish nanny.'

Caroline, who is again seriously underdressed—the robe she borrowed from Lily no longer upon her—pulls the boy's bedroom door shut and turns to the two adults. 'Are my duties complete, mistress?'

'No, Inger, there are potatoes to peel and scones to bake for the morning.'

Garth has a bemused smile on his face as Caroline pushes an overwrought hand up her forehead, and declares in an accent from no-known place, 'Always a thousand potatoes. I shall give up this job and return to my reindeer herd in the arctic!'

Lily laughs, never good at keeping up a pretence. 'Garth, meet Caroline.'

The younger girl steps forward, pointing a finger at her breastbone,

Punching a Boy in Sittingbourne

the centre of her crop-top above her exposed and well-toned midriff. 'Me,' she says 'I am Inger. You sacked Caroline, mistress Lily. Not enough potatoes peeled.'

Lily finds herself torn. Caroline is funny but she thinks Garth—her tentative beau, they are not quite there yet—is looking too keenly at her young friend. Lily knows she cannot compete with this girl on looks, although she could never imagine Caroline showing any interest in a boy like him. No need of a tentative beau when the boxers and bodybuilders are lining themselves up. 'Do you need to run, Caz?'

'I think I do.'

As Caroline steps past the couple to reach the front door, Garth puts a hand out; the girl instinctively takes it, shakes it. 'Pleased to meet you, Inger-Caroline,' he says.

She leans towards him and he flinches, perhaps thinking she might kiss him; Lily has already figured he is forever unprepared for such intimacies. Caroline simply whispers something quietly in his ear. Lily cannot hear the words spoken.

Garth nods as the younger girl leans away from him, the pair of them make eye contact, serious faces. Then Caroline step into Lily, gives her a hug of real warmth. Garth watches the two women entwine, Caroline's embrace prompting a broader smile in his girlfriend than his own limp greeting managed to raise.

From the open door—Lily now holding Garth's hand in hers—they watch Caroline begin to run down Cooper Street, in the direction of the clifftop.

'Catch those reindeer,' shouts Garth.

The runner does not turn but as she runs her right arm extends, a single middle finger raised defiantly, rudely, in response.

Garth turns to his girlfriend, a look of surprise on his face.

'She likes you,' says Lily.

'Are you sure?'

'She was just being funny, and...' Lily places her flattened palms on each of Garth's ears, turns his face from the retreating Caroline. '...you've got me to look at now.'

'Sorry,' he says, 'I was thinking she must be cold dressed like that.'

Lily ignores his interest in the girl's attire, opens the lounge door, enters and he follows her through. 'We started on the wine.'

'Who is she?'

'I told you about her.' Lily tries to think whether she actually did or didn't. She has still to mention Caroline to Alice, that fact has popped into her head a few times in the past week. Lily absentmindedly pours white wine into Caroline's empty glass, half fills it, and hands it to him. His face registers surprise but she thinks only of the alcohol, not her failure to wash the flute the girl has used. Garth shrugs and puts it cautiously to his lips. She pours from bottle into her own glass, up to the very top. Why did she tell the horrible story about Muzzle, Lily wonders to herself. Solidarity with Caroline's own struggles with a thuggish ex. That must be it. Was she anticipating a reciprocal story of how damaged her friend felt by Clive? The bonkers boxer, high on steroids. No, it would be unthinkable, her friend is not embittered as Lily fears she has become. Caroline will unleash a dirty laugh now and then but she looks unblemished, virginal. Not that she is, and Lily has no time for them anyway: the never-lived.

'Is she the girl from the beach?' asks Garth.

Lily is so lost in her thoughts that she takes a moment to answer. 'I think so. I know I've told you about her.'

'She doesn't hold a candle to you.'

The comment brings Lily back into the moment. She laughs, snorts one out. 'Caroline could be a model if she was a few inches taller.'

'But you're there already, Lily. Really. Much better looking. Taller.'

Lily doesn't argue and nor does she believe a word. She saw his Christian eye looking appreciatively upon underdressed Caroline. He lets his eyes linger on her now and then, she has spotted that too. She was out of it on their first meeting, promenade, hospital, home; remembers him staring at her legs. She thinks he has looked upon her lustfully once or twice since but she is long out of the game. And she can't trust herself to read this particular boy at all.

'I thought you only just met her?'

'Yep. She comes around when she jogs. I'm a pitstop.'

'You seem incredibly close.'

'We've clicked, that's all.'

Garth leans back into the sofa, folds the discarded dressing gown and places it on the seat beside him, picks up the glass, sips further on his unrequested wine, then puts it back down on the small coffee

Punching a Boy in Sittingbourne

table. 'Do you mind if I bring my bike round the back?'

'Yes, for sure. I never thought.' It is where he stored it the other times he came round. 'Don't want you having a wheel stolen again.'

'What is it?' he asks.

She wears a grin; her shoulders even shake a little. Lily doesn't answer him; she had thought to say, unless such a ruse gets him to stay the night. Alice or Caroline would be more likely to think it funny than this boy ever will. 'Let's sort out your bike.'

Garth leaves by the front door, Lily goes through to the kitchen and out into her small rear yard, thinking she could pour more wine down his throat, see which way that tips him. As she unbolts the back gate, Garth, who had exited the front door, is already waiting with his bicycle. The evening is still light but feels cool in the shadows at the backs of the houses. Garth brings his bike into her yard, leans it against the kitchen wall, then stoops to pick up a child's skipping rope that lies across the paving slabs. 'Nice,' he says, gesturing towards a pot of petunias that Lily has placed on the low inner dwarf wall. Her garden, the little square, was once open behind this wall but a six-foot vertically slatted wooden fence now encloses the tiny, tarmacked space.

'It's crap. I have to take the kids to the park if they're to play outdoors.' Garth bolts the gate shut, puts up no argument in its favour. They re-enter the kitchen and straight through to the lounge. 'You liked her, didn't you?' says Lily as they sit down on the sofa. He is silent. 'I saw how closely you looked at young Caroline. Anyway, I don't think she goes for men in checked shirts. You're no boxer.'

'I don't like her. I don't know her. I came to see you. I'm sure she's all right but I'm glad she's gone.'

'Caroline's a good friend to me but it was a bit rich watching you looking her up and down.'

'I...' Garth stumbles over his words. '...she shouldn't dress like...there are only so many places to look in a small flat.'

'It's a maisonette, Garth—not a bad size—and that's a feeble excuse. I'm here!'

'Lily, I'm sorry, I don't know what I did. I wondered who she was, that's all.' He takes hold of Lily's limp hand. She pulls it back from him. 'Can we start again?' he asks.

'Oh God, yes. I don't know what's wrong with me. I talked to Caz and it dragged some shit up for me, stuff from the past you don't need to know about. I'm...' Lily pushes her hands down her sides keeping going until she has reached the bottom of her dress. '...start again. You've got the best idea's, sunshine.'

'You can talk to me. I...' Garth swallows twice before completing his thought. '...I care about you. Love you.'

'Yes, you said. I'm still going through the workbook on love, Garth. I've never loved someone without...' She listens to the silence in her maisonette, hopes the children are not at the door. '...making love to them at the getting-to-know-you stage.'

Garth nods but his mouth turns into a small smile; Lily thinks he has prepared a defence for this gambit. Has no idea what it will be. Christian nonsense is her best bet but at least his face didn't turn pink this time. 'This is only our third date.'

'If you're saying I'm slutty, Garth, it doesn't bother me. I've met men since Trent and not gone with one of them, I'm pretty choosy actually. But after fifty dates where will you and I be?'

* * *

Lily has drunk a couple more glasses of wine, Garth just a half. Civility was restored when Garth offered to talk about his work, the shift he did on Monday into this morning. She's fascinated by the tales of the Baxter's boys, their sudden mood swings. Once more, Garth had to spend an inordinate amount of time with Damian Taylor. 'I shouldn't have told you the name,' he said, after letting it slip but Lily shook her head. She gets the point of confidentiality, needs a little for her own past. She doesn't tell Garth because he'd only ask for the full story or worry over what she might have said, but Lily is starting to regret telling so much to Caroline. Thinks the girl might stop dropping by.

'So, what makes you think I'm suited to your work?' she asks. 'It sounds way more interesting than typing up audio tapes but what if I'm crap at it.'

'Lily, I think I told you before that you and I are spirit brother and sister...'

'Kindred spirits, that was the wording I agreed on. We're not brother and sister, Garth, you're not having a free pass on the sex that easily.'

Punching a Boy in Sittingbourne

Garth laughs nervously and Lily cannot read what it means; he might like the sex talk, might hate it. '...kindred, kith and kin. Of course, we're not brother and sister, and I do have unbrotherly thoughts about you.' He dips his eyes down with the confession; it brings a schoolgirl grin to her face. 'The work thing: we've both seen beyond the way we were brought up; we're already on board with the idea that many parents aren't good enough. You and I try to see the world through the eyes of the child, the victim in every messed-up family. Sympathise even when they're making the very worst of all choices before them. Help them to choose better; don't ever blame them.'

'Sorry,' Lily mouths as she takes his hand, and slides ever so slightly closer to him on the sofa. He sounds like he would understand her own childhood although he has heard only the barest outline; he must be a real asset to a school like Baxter's. Not many adults really get it; everyone blames the kids unless they've stood in their shoes. Everyone except Garth, it seems. 'I shouldn't go on about sex. It's wrong of me, Garth.'

'You're a natural, Lily. You say what's on your mind and that means you never duck the question. You're a better person than I am.'

She hugs him around the neck, a simple peck upon his lips, to which he responds but Lily pulls quickly away. 'Bollocks!' Garth's eyes enlarge at her language but he must see she's smiling, his arm around her all the while. 'You can't believe I'm better than you. I'm trying not to talk about sex here, Garth; you have so much self-control, you put me to shame. I can picture you handling that Damian boy fine, even when he's trying to punch your lights out. I might be more like that stupid staff member, the one who swore at him, made things worse. I say what I feel but it's a shitty quality. You don't like it. You don't even like me saying shitty!'

'I love you, Lily, I truly do. When I said you were a natural, I never said skip the training. There's quite a lot to it, a need to be consistent—Ryan's a total loose cannon because he isn't—but the work needs people like you. People who care.'

'Yeah, halfway there but you even said I was a better person than you, Garth. I'm miles behind.' She smiles at him. 'I suppose I can swear better than you ever bloody will?'

'You're a great person, Lily. You just don't have a map of where you're going.'

'No one has one of them. Not a real one.'

This sits in the room for a moment. They hold hands across the chasm. The Bible or make it up as you go along.

'You think that there is no answer to the most important question,' says Garth, 'and it makes you a bit dismissive of what I think...' Lily stares at him with renewed mistrust in her eyes. How does he know what she thinks? '...but without any guidance at all you follow a righteous path. That's what makes you a better person than me.'

'I'm not sure that you really know what I'm like, Garth. And I don't know anything about righteous except that it's a pompous word.'

Garth takes a little time to explain his thoughts. She finds him insightful, whether his ideas stem from good sense or an ill-fated infatuation. He tells her that she runs herself down, has had a life of low self-esteem in Sittingbourne, poverty in London, and selfless duty in Boscombe. It makes her discount the good she has done because she doesn't feel in control. She loves her children too much to even think what a brilliant mum she is, sees it simply as doing her best for them. 'You say you were a run-around in your teens, I'm sure you were better than your mother deserved.' Lily enjoys hearing it, thinks Garth might have actually hit the nail on the head. Not that it makes her better than anyone except the puffed-up Esme Stephens. 'Tell me about Trent,' says Garth. 'If you wish. I don't mean to pry; I'm interested.'

Lily's feels calm; she doesn't know if she can love this unpredictable celibate, he is like no boyfriend she has ever envisaged. No dress sense and his religion floats about him like he's stepped off a time machine, fresh from a more Puritan age. Trusting him, on the other hand, is not difficult at all; she has talked to him pretty freely since shortly after he ran her down with his bike. Alice is the only other adult she currently trusts. And perhaps Caroline but she worries the Sittingbourne story was too much. Might have put her off. And here's Garth, a good man, telling her she's the better of the pair. They should get to the bottom of it. 'I only went to London to get away from my bitch of a mother. I didn't have a plan, no bigger goal than being rid of her. Being there at all was a success from my very narrow viewpoint. When I was young,

Punching a Boy in Sittingbourne

I could pick up jobs like no one's business. Crappy fashion-store jobs, all I needed to do was make sure I looked like the girl who wore the clothing. That meant having the clothing, so I'd buy what they sold or nick it if I was out of pocket. I think I've punctured your good-girl pronouncement already, Garth. All true, I'm afraid.' He simply looks back at her with open hands, seems to take her as he finds her. 'I rented a room in Bethnal Green, it was cheap, shabby actually but I was pleased with it. Not twenty yet and I had my own place. I did a lot of stupid things, being a bit of a kid still, and all on my own in London but I could always hold a job down. Paid my bills. I think I'd been at it a couple of years when I met Carlo, the guy I told you about on Saturday night. Before I met him, I was certain that I'd cope alone. Never thought of relying on a man, never thought there would be anyone else looking out for me but me. Then, with Carlo for a short time—sleeping in a fancy hotel might have helped—I started to think I could really be someone, not just a shadow buried in the city. It was a crazy time, did my head in really, because it was over before it began. There never was an us, just a hopeful notion that there might be. I learnt something important, insightful: I couldn't rely on what I thought I knew about myself; I could flip over like a light going on and off. I was genuinely independent one minute, then turned on a pinhead, gave myself to Carlo as if he owned me. I worried that I'd been kidding myself—on the independence front, I mean—and if I wasn't careful, I'd be fooled again and again.' Taking a breath, Lily looks momentarily at Garth. Concentrating as he must on his beloved pastor's Sunday sermons. He smiles back and she can't interpret it. Doesn't want to miss out on the dating game, while his ideas—courtship through to marriage, or more probably the pair enduring some feeble bust-up way before then—belong to a different age. Holding his attention feels good, and they are kindred spirits apparently. The truth according to Church-pants. A bit weird but Garth is all she has. 'What do you want to know about Trent? He was a good guy. Treated me well. He got me past Carlo and out the other side. I wasn't depending on a man, not on Trent; we were leaning on each other. That's how it's meant to work.'

Garth nods, 'I'm sorry, I'm prying, I know. I just want to know you better, what you've been through. Life hasn't been easy for you; I can see that.'

'Trent was a good part of my life, Garth, I wouldn't change much even if I could. My kids...'

'...you must be very proud of them. You do fantastic by them, Lily.'

She shrugs, he's only spent a morning with them. Jo-jo can be a handful. 'I love them to bits but maybe I didn't manage to love Trent and my kids at the same time. Before they came along, Trent and I were thick, you know, close. Proper lovers.' She thinks this might sting but he asked the question and this is the answer. 'We had years where I can't remember thinking of another feller, not fancying or any of that. I'm sure he was the same with me. Can't prove it but we never fell out about that stuff. We neither of us strayed, not while we were making a go of it. He was a reliable lover, Garth, just not so reliable at getting on in life. I was the coper. Holding down a job, paying the rent. After having children together—wanted, planned, loved—he started to seem like a liability. What we argued about was always money. Money and Trent losing his job. And leaving all the housework to me. And money again. I would work and come home to a mess even when he had all day to clean it up. I hated arguing over that kind of petty nonsense. Him out for a burger when there was plenty of food in the fridge, that sort of money row. It shouldn't have to happen but it does. At first, I could love him with a hole in my shoe, if you see what I mean. Then it started to feel like he was making the holes. That was what I couldn't take.' Garth nods once more and Lily prepares to say, here endeth today's sermon, checks herself, won't be flippant. She could say a lot about Trent, how much she misses feeling his body upon hers. Naked in bed. She won't do it; this is one stinking mood she's in but Garth doesn't deserve the brunt of it.

'His mother was a character but no support whatsoever. She played the piano in three or four East End pubs. Got paid a few pounds for it; did I tell you that?' Garth shakes his head. 'She did it all the while Trent was growing up in Canning Town. He reckoned he learnt never to drink very much after seeing too many falling-down drunks in his younger years, in the pubs where she played piano. When I met her, she'd mostly stopped. Living out at Barking by this time, with a different feller. Trent's dad was with a different woman too, he saw us occasionally.'

Punching a Boy in Sittingbourne

'That's brilliant though,' says Garth. 'I always pictured cockney types playing in the East End pubs and then you said his parents were from Ghana. And she played pub piano. Brilliant.'

'No, only his dad is Ghanaian, his mum is a proper cockney. She was shorter than me but other than that I worried that Trent was mum-fixated when he fell for me. She had black hair and the whitest skin but I think that stuff is unconscious. And I think his mum was a million times nicer than mine. Dirt poor though.'

'I see,' says Garth. 'I couldn't tell.'

Lily narrows her eyes at Garth. 'What couldn't you tell, sunshine?'

'I hadn't realised your children are only a quarter black.'

'For fucks sake, Garth,' she spits out 'we're all the same, no sugar and spice and puppy dogs' tails shit in this life. There really isn't. I hate it, all that counting, calculating crap. Look at me, Garth...' Lily lifts her dress a short way, slides it up as she sits on the sofa, reveals more of herself than has so far been visible to him beneath her navy-blue summer dress. '...I'm as white as they come, and I feel ashamed of it every day. Everybody thinks my kids look all black, they're pretty dark-skinned, quite a contrast from me. I'm so okay with how they look, I love every millimetre of them. Tell me, Garth, why it is on this tiny fucking planet that other people can't accept it—the colour of two little children—it hurts the hell out of me. I don't celebrate ten percent or ninety percent, how much of what colour, and I never deny them their ethnicity. Ghana is probably just like England but without the racists. I can't believe you said that.' Lily is shaking her head—an admonishment—even her hands shake a little. 'For fuck's sake!'

'I didn't,' he protests. 'I shouldn't have, didn't think about...' Garth holds up both palms, says nothing for a few seconds. Lily is livid; she doesn't know if he understood the point at all. Racists don't get it: that's her enduring experience. '...I said it without thinking, I haven't really thought about it before. Trent's their father and he sounds to be a...' He looks at the ceiling like it might advise him of the most appropriate words. '...decent role model. You couldn't be a better mother. And you don't need to be ashamed of your colour. We are what we are.'

'I am, Garth. I am ashamed of it. Ashamed of the associations my kids will make when they're old enough to know. A few months back—true story, Garth—I was at Poole train station. Jo-jo had been to an appointment, the dyslexia assessment I told you about. I was getting myself a coffee while waiting for the train back here. The kids were sitting at the far end of the room, away from the counter. Little Ami had climbed onto the table, just larking around not doing anything wrong. Bored. She'd been waiting in an office for over an hour, playing quietly while the education woman, psychologist or dyslexia sniffer-out, whatever they're called, assessed my Jo-jo. This old woman—not that old mind—serving me the coffee, pointed at my children, my beautiful children, Garth, and she said, "That's what they're like." I looked at her, I didn't know what was coming next but I guessed it wasn't going to be good. "Parents of those sorts of kiddie just dump them. It's what they do; they don't supervise them." I think she saw that I looked shocked but she carried right on. Nasty self-righteous git. "It's neglect," she said, "it wouldn't surprise me if they've boarded a train to London and left them here. Dumped them." What do you think about that, Garth?'

'It's offensive, Lily but she was making a misconnection, wasn't she? Didn't realise you were their mother at all.'

'Misconnection! She was hating my children for their skin colour, Garth. Assumed I was another complicit dickhead, happy to hate for no bloody reason whatsoever. I told her to shove her coffee up her arse. Took them straight out, waited on the platform away from that bitch. I should have complained but I don't think you can get a café woman struck off, there's not much further to fall.'

'I think you've had to put up with a few things like that, Lily. I'm sorry, I didn't know, didn't really think through what I said. One race isn't better than another. Not at all. I never meant anything different to that.'

* * *

This evening is a gorse bush. Lily comes back into the lounge from the kitchen. 'Only red wine left,' she says.

Garth shrugs, he has drunk two half glasses of the white, never asked for more. Lily is slurring her words, a little redder in the face than she has previously let herself become in Garth's presence. 'No need to open it on my account,' he says.

'It might be a selfish need.' Lily unscrews the cap regardless.

Punching a Boy in Sittingbourne

'Are you testing me?'

She answers his question with a splutter of laughter. 'I'm getting pissed, Garth.'

'But is it wise? Work tomorrow and what if the children need you in the night?'

'Stay and look after them for me,' she says softly.

Garth puts an arm across Lily's shoulder. 'I can't. I love you. This is not putting me off...'

Lily interrupts his pronouncement, places her mouth over his. As they kiss her hand strays to his groin; Garth lifts it away before she is able to gauge if the talk has stirred him.

'Please, Lily,' he says, 'or I shall have to go, and I will be back. I am pursuing you in my own way.'

Lily lifts her head to look at him directly, feels a little sick in her mouth, and swallows it down. This could get embarrassing. She wonders why she is being so forward when she has been correspondingly worried that he might not be so good after all. He finally said he's going to vote remain, and then he gets overly interested in the precise lineage of her children. And she's too drunk to think through anything tonight, will have to work it all out in the morning. 'Don't go, Garth. Stay and tell me how you know her?'

'What?'

'Have you always known her, been pals before you met me? Did she set you up to do it, the accident?'

'What!'

'What did Caroline say to you? I saw it—the pair of you—as she was leaving. She whispered something to you. Then you watched her running back to Christchurch like she was your lover or something.'

She watches as he struggles to say a damned thing; Garth's face disfigured by the mental anguish of it, lower lip between teeth. Then he looks at her directly. 'She said, "Look after Lily." That was it. She's your friend, not mine. Never clapped eyes on her until today.'

Lily likes the phrase, look after Lily. Maybe Caroline would demand it of him, say it although they are strangers. Sounds plausible; she and Caz have clicked. Caz and Jo-jo as well; two of a kind she said, something like that. Then Lily went and told her all that shit about Muzzle, made herself sound as rough as a sewer rat. Hopes she hasn't lost Caroline as she might Garth if she keeps guzzling down the wine.

'Is that really all she whispered to you?'

'She's a weird girl, Lily. Runs by and makes herself at home. She's staked a claim on you and you say you only met her the day before you did me.'

Lily laughs caustically. 'Caz, you, everyone wants to pop round to mine. She looks out for my kids without ruddy blood samples, the what-percentage-is-white shit?'

'I'm sorry, Lily, and I was hasty saying that about Caroline. I don't know her, nor what made her whisper to me, but I think she's right.'

'She is?'

'I've got to look after you. I probably shouldn't have let you drink so much. You've been in a funny mood all evening. And I don't think alcohol helps when you're feeling blue.'

'Ha! You might be right and you might be wrong. I don't drink a lot, Garth, but then again, I'm not an easy girl to prise a bottle off. I don't really think you can look after me; I'm too awkward, that's the long and the short of it. Never do what the other buggers want you to do, that's my motto. Tough to live with, I suppose.'

'Let me try. It might be satisfying to go along with others—with me—once in a while.'

'Put me to bed.'

'Lily!'

'No funny business, just see me in, see yourself out.'

'Look, I don't know...'

Lily rises, and Garth follows sheepishly as she goes from the lounge, down the short corridor. Opening her bedroom door, she reaches down to the hem of her dress, pulls it up over her head in a single motion. Garth is close, puts a hand on the small of her back, below her bra strap, she feels its warmth but no pressure.

'I can't stay,' he tells her. 'I'll call you.'

He goes back down the corridor, doesn't spend a second longer in her room although she is not indecent. Not as uncovered as she would have let him see if he were game for it. Normal. Lily hears the front door click. Sits down on the bed, hiccoughs. Surprises should cure them, not start them, fancy getting them now. And what the hell is wrong with her? Drunken thoughts oscillate between worry that her looks arouse nothing—she knows she can't compete with Caroline—and her stupidity in trying to goad this honourable man into her bed. He's already made his order of play very, very clear, not that she is a fan of his abstemiousness. It's fun-lover against killjoy; nice talking to him and then he ducks the main event. She strips and puts herself under the covers, then hears a small sound outside her door, a footstep in the hall perhaps.

Lily rises, moves gingerly into the corridor, wearing nothing, sees nobody there, switches on the light. There is a tiny card by the door, it must have fallen through the letterbox, she surmises. Picking it up she sees it is a coffee shop loyalty card, a single stamp upon it, turns it over to see words written in biro.

Will collect the bike tomorrow, you need to sleep.
Love Garth

Lily walks back into the bedroom, puts the card on the pillow next to her head, a token from this dumb, daft boy. God alone knows how he's getting home. Walking! Is he looking after her or frightened that she might bite his head off? For most of this evening, she's behaved like she wanted to do the latter. Not a smart play on her part. He isn't Muzzle, nothing like that bastard. She wouldn't have made a bee-line for his dick if he was. She picks up the card again, lets a few tears come. And they do, little rivulets turn to rivers on her cheeks. Salt in the mouth. It's as good a feeling as she's come across all evening.

Saturday, 18 June 2016

When the phone rings, Lily and Jo-jo are washing dishes, Ami in the lounge where television holds her attention. All are digesting pizza, having a proper family day together.

'I guessed it would be you,' she says on hearing Garth's voice. He hasn't collected his bike yet although they have spoken by phone and texted many times since the debacle of Tuesday night. His shifts, youth group and a family commitment have been the barriers. In a good-humoured call, Lily said to him, 'I'm holding it as surety until you finally stay the night.' She was laughing and when she added, 'Just kidding,' he did too.

They have already agreed that he will visit after church tomorrow, this phone call is just Garth keeping in touch. He's phoned daily since their fall out—from which they easily fell back in—four days ago. The volcano sleeps. Lily doesn't think he's a racist, he just said something dumb; conversely, she drank more than she can handle and acted like a nymphomaniac. He must like those qualities, she told him, in the same delicate conversation in which she joked about the asymmetrical bargain with his bike.

Lily tells him about swimming in the sea with the children. 'Ami has ditched her arm bands,' she says, and while they are talking, her daughter goes to the holdall still in the corridor near the phone, roots out the two bright orange swimming aids and says the word, 'Dustbin,' as loudly as she is able. Walks passed her mother to the kitchen where the receptacle lives. 'Did you hear that?' asks Lily. Garth didn't, so she tells him what Ami has just said. So proud of her little girl.

'I'm whacked after a busy week,' he tells her. 'I'll be seeing Peter for an hour or so this evening and then I'll turn in early.' In a conversation on Thursday night, Garth was at such pains to go back over his non-association with Caroline that it almost made Lily think the reverse. Luckily, she had consumed no wine on that day and her responses were rational, she accepted what he said. The girl has not come back but she will, Lily is sure of it. They've a bond. Caroline sent a text on Wednesday, very sweet, a thanks-for-sharing message.

This need of Garth's to tell her where he is sleeping, his single bed or a similar one in the staff sleeping-in room at Baxter's, is a quirk which afflicted no previous boyfriend. Early under the covers every night this week except Friday. He texted her after his youth group that night to say his head was buzzing, so he was staying up to watch a late-night sci-fi film. Very odd if he thinks she needs the reassurance. She is the one who indicated dissatisfaction with sleeping alone. Lily cannot work out exactly what she sees in him, or him in her. Saying she has a boyfriend feels good, it's been too long. She's only said it to Alice, of course, and Jo-jo seems to be cottoning on.

'I've been thinking,' says Garth, 'I'd like you to meet Peter. You don't fancy coming to church tomorrow, do you?'

'Oh, sunshine, I'm really looking forward to the afternoon with you. And Alice is taking the kids again. You know I don't really get God. I expect I'll come somewhere down the line but I'm not ready yet.'

'I think Jesus is.'

Lily lets her silence be the answer, doesn't want to get into an argument. This stuff is important to him, she can give him space for that. Can't see herself falling in with the demands of any man; Garth needs to figure that one out for himself. To start jumping this way and that at the behest of one who's been dead for a couple of thousand years sounds plain stupid.

'Another time,' Garth murmurs.

'Don't be cross.' She has worried since Tuesday that he will tire of her if she makes no compromises, gives no quarter. 'I promise to steer clear of alcohol tomorrow. Guides honour and all that shit.' Now it is Garth's turn to extend only silence in reply. Lily is unsure if he dislikes the further reference to her state on Tuesday last or if her sign off on it was in some way irreverent. 'And I shouldn't have sworn,' she tries, 'Jo-jo heard it. I'm a bad mummy.'

'You're not that, Lily. Never that. At youth group we used to have a swear jar. Only got it out because this funny lad was coming, by name of Sandy. He was the only reason we needed one. One or two others said the odd word but Sandy was prolific. He had to put ten pence in each time he swore. He asked what we did with the money. When I told him that we gave it to a homeless charity, he went, "Eff, eff, eff, eff," saying that word out in full. When he got to ten, he gave me a pound, said they needed it more than him. We decided to give up on the jar.'

'That's so funny. What happened with him after? Did you figure a different way to get him to stop?'

'No. You win some you lose some. The last I heard he'd changed church. Taken to swearing at the Baptists.'

* * *

They are watching an old film which is showing on a free-view station, it was just starting when she was channel-hopping. Ami is fast asleep, laid out on the floor in the lounge. She watched the first forty minutes or so but it's not five-year-olds' fare. Lily will carry her to bed in a few minutes, she enjoys watching the little girl's chest rise and fall. Loves being close to her children.

Jo-jo watches the television. Transfixed. Lily is unsure if he has laughed at this film once although it is a comedy. Comedy drama. The lead character is the father of a small boy but he's a busy lawyer, never has any time for his son. Lily wonders if it goes over Jo-jo's head but it seems to have a decent sentiment. He will get from it what he will. As the film is drawing to a conclusion, it's obvious to Lily that the man is finally going to treat his son right, put him before his over-paid sell-out of a job. She sees tears welling up in Jo-jo's eyes.

'Are you okay, sweetie?' she asks. It's Caroline's word but she doesn't have a patent. 'Want to talk?'

'No,' he says, eyes still religiously watching the screen. 'I like it, it's meant to make you cry.'

She leans across and places her head on his chest, hugs her son without crossing his line of vision. 'You are one perfect boy, Jo-jo. You really are.'

Sunday, 19 June 2016

A text arrives on Lily's phone at one-fifteen in the afternoon. It is from Garth:

Bus didn't show, so I'm running it

Reading it makes her feel curiously light-headed. This prim and proper young man—whose bike she has hostage for no greater reason than his wish to let her sleep off too much wine—is running four or five miles to be in her company. Garth is not Caroline; the run will exhaust him. Doesn't do it for fun, it is exclusively for her. She wears a yellow-print summer dress, reaches down to feel her scarred left calf. Lily will run again; the wound is still tender but she no longer limps. They could run together in the coming weeks.

She speculates whether to put her tracksuit on, match his likely attire. She stood in front of the mirror while dressing, liked how she looks in the yellow dress; it's pretty, not seductive, she's getting his measure. The contrasting clothing might sum them up.

'Isn't he here yet?' asks her clock-watching son.

'On his way. The trouble is we've got his bike.'

Jo-jo smiles at this. Lily has told him that she only kept it to make sure he comes back. He knows she is making a joke; Jo-jo likes to go over and over anything that is funny, to understand how the levity

Punching a Boy in Sittingbourne

arises. It has also reassured him, she thinks. Before school on Wednesday, when her head was still thumping a little from mixing white and red, he kept asking what they had argued about. 'Is Garf a racist?' Must have heard more of their talk than she ever intended. And the boy still struggles to get his mouth and tongue around certain words.

'God, no!' Lily put him straight. 'Mummy had more wine than she should have. Sorry if I was loud. We were just saying how awful that stuff is, Jo-jo. Garth is with us.'

'Good,' he answered, Jo-jo's most serious face looking into hers, searching for certainty. Lily often asks if other children tease him at school. Fears that the sons of the men who verbally abuse Marta in the Polish stores will be as unkind to her son as their fathers are to that harmless woman. She never told her mother a nanosecond of what went on at school in Sittingbourne. Scary as hell having her own kids out in the thick of it five days a week.

* * *

When he finally arrives, his appearance is a minor shock. Beetroot-faced and utterly exhausted. Poor physical shape for a supposed thirty-year-old. She ushers him in, offers him water. As the facts emerge, it is clear he is just a bit of a klutz. She often thinks his religious beliefs are nuts, then admonishes herself for the narrow-mindedness of thinking it. Today her criticism is a practical one: it is scorching outside and Garth has run from Northbourne wearing black jeans and one of his many checked shirts, sleeves still buttoned down at the cuff. Damp with sweat on front and back, near fungal at the armpits. His brow has developed its own clammy micro-climate.

Jo-jo answered the door, with Lily one step behind. 'Who's chasing you, Garf?' her son asked, but the boyfriend was panting too much to take it on, unable to offer an answer. Now, on the sofa, second glass of water in hand having dispatched the first in the blink of an eye, she teases him with it. 'The atheists, the Catholics, not the Buddhists, surely. Who was it, Garth? Jo-jo and I want to put a stop to it. It's religious persecution.'

'Me, me,' adds Ami, holding Garth's knee as he pants in their lounge. 'I fight dem.' Then she poses with two clenched fists.

'No, Ami-pie,' says Lily. 'We don't fight.'

'Lily,' he manages between gasps, 'I need to take this up a bit more. Get fitter.'

'You don't have any lighter clothes than these, do you, sunshine?'

When he explains that he actually does, Lily finds it sweet: he chose her company—her perfect children's company—over returning to dress properly for a run, or just waiting for the later bus. 'I have some at home,' he pants, 'but I came straight from church.'

'You've not eaten?'

'I usually only have one meal on a Sunday.'

Lily is sitting beside her smelly boyfriend on the sofa, she pats his stomach. 'Not good enough. It isn't a religious fast, is it?'

'Low pay survival guide, more like,' replies Garth, and Lily knows a little on the same subject. Thinks her slim waistline is the result of modest portion sizes more than any exercise regime.

Jo-jo glances between the couple, he even looks a little alarmed to Lily's eye. Her boy has often asked questions about their time in London, recalls—or imagines that he recalls—the single room, before Ami was born. He endured plenty of pitiful meals in Shoreditch. The wage from Capaldi-Clarke is nothing special but she manages, gets a few pounds from Trent most months. 'I'm flush enough to make you a cheese-toastie, lover-boy,' she tells Garth.

'Really?'

'Of course, but you really need to shower. If you had a spare set of clothing here...' She doesn't complete the thought. 'Are you okay wearing my joggers? They'll fit you, they're elasticated but I don't think they'll flatter you. Peachy pink.'

'A dress,' says Ami, 'Joey wears a dress.'

The boy punches his little sister on the arm. Quite hard, and it starts her crying. Lily gathers Ami up in her arms. 'What was that about, Jo-jo?' she asks while seeing he has tears in his eyes. She cannot recall the last time he hit his sister.

The boy gives a heady sob, 'She shouldn't say it. I don't like it; we were playing a game.'

Garth puts a hand on Jo-jo's head. 'It's okay, big feller. Games are just fun. Ami was remembering the fun.' The boy still cries. 'Some men wear dresses but not you. Is that right?'

Jo-jo nods, accepts a short, loosely clasped hug. Garth whispers in his ear, and the boy pulls in his breath, stops crying. 'Sorry Ami,' he announces.

'And how about you, sunshine,' says Lily, turning again to Garth. 'Jogging bottoms or a dress after your shower.'

The man puts a hand over his smile. Ami shouts it again. 'A dress! A dress!'

* * *

Lily thinks Garth can be a bit stiff, it makes her lips upturn as she sits across the kitchen table from him. Both children come and go between lounge and kitchen. They are fascinated by this new man in their lives and correspondingly surprised that their mother has let them spread out every Lego piece they own in the next room. Scattered across the lounge floor. 'Look, Garf,' says Ami, for the umpteenth time, showing off a different assemblage of tiny bricks for him to praise.

He is self-consciously eating a hard-boiled egg, having already devoured the toasted sandwich Lily fixed for him. A drink of orange squash awaits him on the table: Garth lives like a king in this maisonette. True, the food is modest; the borrowed attire—ladies' jogging bottoms and the plainest of her two dressing gowns—are barely princely. Dresses were all flatly refused. 'Not really my scene,' he advised Lily with an eye to Jo-jo. At one point—kids in the lounge—she had told him she was okay with nudity on private property. 'Not I,' his clipped reply.

The decision to actually take a shower was the result of painstaking negotiation. Lily was torn between amusement and frustration while persuading him to do the obvious. Abate his sweaty stench. The sweetener that finally persuaded him was an offer to put his noxious clothing through a wash cycle, twenty minutes in the drier too. Lily had said of the latter, 'It's unnecessary. They'll dry in an hour or two on the line,' but Garth was worried about wearing even this cautiously chosen lady's attire for too long. He offered to pay for the electric, even fetched a fiver from his pocket but Lily cut him off. 'Nonsense, Garth. We're mates.' She looks at his boyish face glugging down the squash; 'lover boy' and 'mate' she has tried, not baiting, just being familiar. Maybe one day.

'Church was bloody good this morning,' beams Garth and it makes

Lily snort. Not unkindly but he even mistimes his swear words.

'What did I miss?'

'When I saw Peter yesterday evening it was mostly to be his sounding board. He gave the sermon today. Pastor Margery has gone to Wales for a few days; her mother is in hospital. Peter took a leaf out of Margery's book. Talked with her on the phone, apparently.' Lily smiles; this boy's pulse rises at stuff she doesn't give two hoots for. 'I think I've said that Margery thinks Peter and I are a bit old-fashioned in our approach. "Preach and pray," she calls it. Says we should relax more. Peter has fantastic ideas when he lets himself go. I'd practiced the chords and things on Friday with the girls, you know, my church choir. Before the sermon started, me and the girls sang that song, you must know it, by John Tungsten. I don't know much about him myself but I know the name. "In the Mood for Magic." It was in the charts a year or more ago.' To her surprise, he starts singing.

Once I walked a mile, a country mile
Towards a copse of trees beside a beck
Imagine my surprise, when I came to realise
The scene was tattooed on the back of my fellow walker's neck

'Ha. Of course I know it, Garth. Me and the kids love that song. Good voice by the way. I didn't expect you to play that kind of stuff, it's scarcely a hymn.'

'I didn't know it, not really, I recognised the tune—the radio's always playing at Baxter's—I don't follow pop music. Peter asked me to learn it last Sunday, the girls were great. My choir. They danced a little too well for my liking. And then, when we finished singing, Peter picked apart the text. You think it's not a hymn but it turns out it is. God is everywhere, Lily, it's all a matter of looking. I think you would have loved it. I wanted it to be a surprise when I asked you to come along but I know you're not ready for church yet.'

Ami dances across the kitchen, singing 'Moo magic. In the moo magic.' It cracks up both adults, and the little girl looks cross.

The doorbell gives its unwavering buzz. 'That'll be Alice,' says Lily. 'She's here early.'

Garth glances at the odd clothing he wears. 'When does the wash cycle finish?'

Punching a Boy in Sittingbourne

'It's all right, Alice will understand why I don't want to date a smelly man; I know you don't quite get it yet.'

Jo-jo is at the door again, letting in the caller, then rushes ahead of her back into the kitchen. 'It isn't Auntie Alice.'

'Here again,' says Caroline, one pace behind him. Garth's face turns a deeper shade of red than the salmon of the borrowed dressing gown he wears. Caroline looks a picture. She wears a short red skirt and a brilliant white blouse above it, gold buttons down the centre line open above her breast line, the very top of a black brazier visible. Intentionally so, too perfectly exposed to be otherwise. 'I'm meeting some friends in Bournemouth,' she tells Lily. 'I wanted to invite you along but it's all girls.' She glances at Garth as she makes her last point.

He shrugs.

'Aw, that's sweet,' says Lily. 'You should have texted.'

'You would have said no; I was planning to charm you into it.'

'I'm going to stick with Garth, Caz. But how did you know I had a babysitter planned?'

'I didn't, you could have brought them with. We're beer gardening; two of my friends will have their children with them this evening.'

'Oh, you're so sweet to think of me. I'm not sure I'd fit in...'

'Rubbish. If I do, you do.'

Lily makes Caroline a drink of tea and explains Garth's washing to her. His odd attire.

'You're a runner,' says the glamorous girl, finally warming to Lily's boyfriend.

'No,' the couple answer in unison.

'He's a sweater and a stinker,' Jo-jo tells Caroline.

'Oh dear, oh dear.' She wags her forefinger at Garth. 'Shape up, mister. Lily can do a lot better than a stinker.'

'Leave him be, Caz,' says Lily. 'Maybe I'm not so choosy as you.' She kisses the top of his head. Poor boy, his inhibitions are an assault course.

Jo-jo and Ami are both back at the front door. Lily never heard the buzzer and it might be that they saw the shadow in the frosted glass. Jo-jo has let Alice into the maisonette. 'You look a state,' she tells Garth as she enters the kitchen. An observation without apparent expectation of explanation, then her eyes come to rest on Caroline.

Boscombe

Lily realises that they might know nothing of each other: Alice, her dearest friend, and Caz the confuser, a girl she feels genuine affection for and shares stories with that might be better left unsaid. 'This is Caroline,' she tells Alice. 'The girl I met on the beach when I started my ill-fated fitness regime.' She knows she may not have mentioned her at all but Alice's face suggests she is clicking through memories, might think she has failed to log a conversation. Turning to Caroline, she says, 'Alice is my favourite person in the world, apart from them,' and she points at her children. As she waits for them to say something to each other, she tousles Garth's hair. Hasn't a clue where he ranks, odd boyfriend that he is. The washing machine begins to spin and Lily raises her voice: 'Too noisy, let's move to the lounge.'

Alice leads the way and Garth stays in his seat. 'I'll wait it out,' he tells Lily, pointing at the machine. He hasn't complained once about her jogging bottoms and dressing gown, clearly won't be parading them down the catwalk of her hallway.

* * *

They move a little Lego from sofa to floor to create space to sit down. Caroline and Alice seem to hit it off okay. Lily cannot tell if it's just politeness or genuine warmth. She wonders if she has kept Caz a secret for a reason, kept her for herself even, then feels no jealousy in hearing their good-natured exchanges.

The fitness freak is—as she had on first meeting Lily—asking insightful questions about Alice's children. Giving her friend the chance to showcase the delight that she draws from Wendy and Bryony.

'You know so much,' says Alice. 'Are you sure you don't have children yourself?'

Caroline screws up her face at the funny phrase. 'Maybe I should phone a couple of old flames just to check,' she says, and all three girls laugh. Ami laughs too but without a hint of understanding; Jo-jo leaves the room. Lily expects he is going to ask Garth to explain the joke. Who might even manage.

Lily tries to be smart: 'She'll have a baby or two when she develops a better taste in men. Have I got that right, sunshine?' She places a hand on Caroline's bare shoulder, so undone are the upper buttons of her blouse.

Punching a Boy in Sittingbourne

'You wound me, sweetie,' says Caroline. 'My boxer and your Christian are similar: both have a penchant for dressing gowns.'

'Shh,' says Lily laughing. She wishes she hadn't tried to be so personal. It is none of Alice's business. 'I didn't mean anything, I...' Caroline is looking directly into Lily's face; her soft brown eyes hold her. 'Garth's okay,' she whispers. 'Has Clive bothered you again?'

'I've been thinking of him all wrong until now—he's a bad-news boyfriend—dumped forever, truly.'

* * *

Lily and Garth walk towards The Perkin Inn. His black jeans and a checked shirt smelling better than when he does his own laundry. Lily is in her yellow-print dress. Re-enacting their first date in the clifftop pub. Should make a fixture of it, they tell each other. Lily says she will pay the whole bill, a return for his generosity on their first outing here. Garth gently argues against it. His foregoing of lunch today was not a measure of poverty but of self-discipline; he admits a miscalculation in running on an empty stomach. Cleared her out of cheese, used a bit of washing powder, and guzzled an indecent amount of electricity for the tumble dryer.

'Fucking hell, Garth, we sound like two old misers fighting over stale cake!'

He puts an arm around her waist. 'Not fighting Lily, trying to provide for each other. You have a generous soul. Can I say something controversial?'

'If it's in the Bible there is no controversy.'

'Caroline's all right but she's not like us. She lives in money. Her clothes cost as much as the mortgage on my flat. Don't be impressed by the wrong bits of her, Lily.'

They walk on in silence, she enjoys that he is holding her waist more tightly, more confidently. She worried the other night which bits of Caz impressed Garth. She's a dream girl, even Lily loves looking at her so she shouldn't blame him. 'Black, white, rich, poor: shouldn't we all just love each other?'

'Of course we should, Lily, and that Caroline really likes you. Maybe you can see it all better than I do. It's as if we've both latched on to you, competing for your love.'

She turns her face to his, kisses him quickly on the lips. 'Daft bugger. Sorry, you make me swear. Caz and I are buddies; I don't do that sort of love. I'm sorry if...' She tapers off, remembering Tuesday night. She bent his ear something rotten over the girl and now sees that was just the wine skewing her judgement. Caroline is a bit dismissive of her boyfriend. '...you're a good guy. You must have thought you were trapped in a madhouse earlier? My funny friends and me making you wear all my clothes!'

'Ha! I'm over it.'

Everything in his demeanour tells her that he is. She sees that for him humour is all retrospective; excessively worried about where everything is going, he hasn't the confidence that it will end well. The boy's not against having his bubble burst, not prideful.

They arrive at The Perkin Inn to find all the outside tables taken. Indoor seats are available but it's noisy, busy. Children running around. Tired children at the end of a long and sunny day. Their plan was always to have a meal in the beer garden and then go back to the maisonette. Lily wants to relieve Alice of her sitting duties at a decent hour; Garth may stay a short time but will cycle—finally retrieving his bike—to Northbourne at a reasonable hour. This first date since Tuesday's blip has gone well, a warmth between them. They quickly agree not to eat here; Lily knows a chip shop. Garth's eyes enlarge at the prospect of battered fish, he says he can smell the vinegar already.

'Let's go down to the sand first.'

Garth agrees to her suggestion without hesitation. They cross the road onto the cliff top, take the long incline. The waves are lapping up the shore, a couple of fires burning further down the beach but it's an empty tract of sand that lies before them. The warmth has gone out of the day, only a dog walker and two groups of teenagers for a quarter-mile either side of where they stand.

They walk on the sand, each holding their shoes, Garth's with his socks stuffed inside. In the direction of Boscombe, they can make out two or more swimmers but there will have been hundreds just a couple of hours ago. The sea is for die-hards at this time of day.

'We can do it?' she whispers in Garth's ear, pointing at those in the water. 'It was gorgeous with the kids yesterday.'

'I should have brought my trunks,' he says.

'Underwear fella. No wine, no funny business. Let's just swim.' She

Punching a Boy in Sittingbourne

is already lifting her dress over her head.

Garth seems in two minds, he puts an arm around her naked waist, pulls her closer. 'How will we dry ourselves?'

His question puts her in mind of logical Jo-jo, another boy who asks down-to-earth irrelevancies before he can let go. 'We're catching colds, sunshine. One for you and one for me.' As she shakes herself away from the stewardship of his arm, she briefly feels a couple of fingers under the hem of her knickers. Wonders if he was trying to haul her back or pull them down. As her feet meet the shallow water, she giggles to cover the gasp, the cold of sea on her warm skin. Lily runs, jumps over the little waves. Giggles some more. 'Ooh! Cold! Garth!' As she looks over her shoulder, she sees that he has removed, and is now folding, his jeans. He places them neatly on the sand, even picking up her dress, to fold and place carefully while it awaits her return.

He joins her in the water; the sea is not so cold once they are immersed in it. Lily briefly takes Garth's hand until they both lean into a forward crawl. After swimming out forty yards, they stand on a small sand ridge, a half-moon in the sky while the sun waits up in the west-north-west, not yet ready to set on this mid-summer evening. She looks upon his chest, his broad shoulders, wet hair clinging to each side of his head, imagines her own is a state, laden with seawater. Lily laughs, cares for nothing but this moment. Clasping him closer she leans in to kiss him. Do as normal couples do.

'I love you, Lily Stephens,' he says. She looks again into the green of his eyes, her hands around his back slip onto the outside of his underpants. 'Don't push it,' he says. This jolts her from those dreamy thoughts; his prudery no longer annoys her, just another cross to be born. She fears she alone is the sufferer. Marry the fucker, she thinks, and finds herself laughing inwardly at the craziness of the unspoken notion. As she pushes away from him to swim once more, he follows immediately, his hand accidentally or otherwise upon the thin water-saturated fabric that covers the cheeks of her bottom. As they swim in tandem, he tries to simultaneously put an arm around her. Garth is being as spontaneous as he can manage but the move is ungainly, briefly drags her under the water. She takes a little saltwater into her mouth, tosses her head, and spits out what she can. Garth apologises, of course. Shouts to her, 'On your back,' and immediately floats that way himself. It occurs to Lily that he requests this in order see what the water has done to her bra, lace-made and skimpy. She likes the explanation, unsure if she has or hasn't hit the mark. Garth affects to be oblivious to a girl's anatomy; the only boy on Earth so afflicted. She catches him looking her way, then he glances back to shore as though fearing a deputation from his church. Garth Addicks is a creature from the deep ocean, ill-prepared for the shallow waters which an unexpected updraft has marooned him within.

'Come on,' she says standing in the knee-deep wash. He does likewise and she takes his hand in hers, adjusting her clothing with the other. Her knicker-line has sunk a little lower with the weight of the water; she must rectify this for the boy's watching God. 'You're a good sport, Garth. I know that was my choice, not yours.'

'I liked it! Loved it, Lily. Love you. I don't know anyone like you.'

'No but you don't really get grade-one sinners through your church doors.'

They have reached the pile of clothing. Lily shakes herself in the hope that a little water comes off. She has a thin dress that will itself become wet when she puts it back on her damp body, and a light cardigan that she has carried.

'Dry yourself with my shirt,' Garth offers manfully.

'Finally, a decent use for it.' She draws it very gently over her stomach and thighs, not wishing to leave it unwearable for him.

He laughs at her critique of his fashion sense. 'I'd wear anything you wanted me to.'

'Ami and Jo-jo were all for you trying this?' She holds out the yellow-print dress.

He ignores the dress itself while pulling her into an embrace that is barely decent in their dripping underwear. 'Sorry,' he says after finally releasing her from the embrace. Quickly he pulls his trousers over his wet boxer shorts.

Lily turns her back, wonders what he makes of that sight, her bottom scarcely more decent than the view from the front. 'Anytime,' she shouts over her shoulder, as she pulls her dress over her head, repeating and embellishing, 'Anytime, lover boy.'

'And I do love you, Lily Stephens.'

They amble back up the sand and stop on the promenade to put their shoes back on, Garth sitting to fiddle with his socks. 'You missed church for this, I'm afraid, Garth,' says Lily.

'I made a smart choice, didn't I?' She wonders if she has flipped a switch. Not that it is her intention to shake his precious religion from his head. But if it should come a little loose...?

Saturday, 25 June 2016

After a tumultuous week, a phone call from Garth every day, Lily is cycling to Northbourne. In those calls he consoled Lily and swore on the holy Bible—not that she could see his hand on it over the mobile phone—that he did indeed vote Remain in the referendum. His swing from one camp to the other has proven futile: the country will leave the EU; people of a broadminded outlook are meant to zip it.

Today both of her children are to spend the day with Alice and Martin, Wendy and Bryony. Martin was brilliant with Jo-jo twenty minutes ago when she took them around. 'We've got stuff to do, matey,' he said. Jo-jo was super-excited at the prospect. He will be going on the zip-wire. Lily feels guilty that she will not witness this rite of passage, this thrill which her son has long cultivated, having often watched others using the contraption that runs off the end of the pier. She would only worry about him—couldn't watch if she was there with him—but Martin is an old hand, used it himself just to make his own children laugh. She knows Jo-jo is in safe hands.

Lily learnt that Garth told his parents of her existence and role in his life for the first time during a telephone call on Monday. They have—via their son—invited her to eat with them every day since. With or without him present, he told her, although she thinks he is kidding on this point. Today that meeting is to take place. Lily queried why it is so important to Garth. His relationship with both parents seems dysfunctional in her view, if slightly less so than that which she fails to enjoy with the nauseating pair in Sittingbourne.

'We're a traditional family,' he explained. 'Farming stock; we take an interest in each other.'

'But they've never taken an interest in your religion.'

'Oh, they have. They take a very keen interest in it. How to extract me from my church concerns them enormously. I think if I'd gone C of E, they would have been quite forgiving but The Church of the Men of Judea is beyond them. We're not a tradition, we believe it, and they believe in very little now they've stopped growing crops and tending calves. Only ever believed in what was tangible.'

Lily understood that Garth was cross about their outlook when he said it; for herself, belief in only the tangible sounded sensible, mainstream. Not so much wise as child's play. All this dying on the cross so that someone else might be forgiven, so loving the world that God gave up his only son, there is no logic in it that Lily can fathom. Gobbledegook squared is the opinion she struggles to keep to herself. Can manage only so long as she stays off the wine.

* * *

Lily arrives at the strip of shops over which Garth lives. Sixties-built: hairdressers; newsagent; pet shop. One unit sits empty. Lily pushes her bicycle around the back, sees the flight of steps that lead to the flats above. She chains her bike to the railing alongside the lower step. It looks unsightly but she can see nowhere else. Climbs the stone staircase; knocks on the door of number two.

He comes straight out, stands beside her, and closes the door. Not a glimpse inside for Lily. 'My bike is locked up,' he says, taking to the steps which she has just climbed.

'Can't I look inside, Garth. This is the first time I've been here.'

'Not much to see,' he says, turning around, three steps lower than where she stands.

Lily gives a face scrunching smile, a couple of notches below a pout. 'Pretty please?'

He shrugs and then comes back up the steps, repeats his mantra. 'Not much to see.'

Retrieving the key from his pocket, he opens the door he had so hurriedly closed. Garth goes in first and Lily follows, steps through a tiny porch entryway, a couple of pairs of shoes on the floor, a brown windcheater on a hanger. She is in a lounge-come-dining room, a decent size, far bigger than her own. The flooring comprises carpet tiling; Lily stoops to touch it with her fingers. A brush-like texture, a brown chequered pattern. She thinks it's a man's taste, a bit tasteless which is another way of saying the same thing. There's no fireplace in the shoe-box-shaped room: the flats are too modern for that, too postwar hurriedly built. A wall-mounted gas fire hangs where a fireplace might otherwise be situated; to the right of it a monkey-sized Jesus is hanging from a cross, a papier mâché sculpture of no great value, she thinks. Then she adjusts her appraisal. It looks macabre, Garth probably thinks it priceless. The furnishings in the flat are tat. Two dilapidated easy chairs, and another that looks like garden furniture, surround a small television. There is a rickety-looking dining table, three chairs of different manufacture. She steps through an archway into the tiny alcove kitchen. The hob is cleaner than hers, Lily makes a mental note. He is no slob, not a bit of it.

'Can I see the bedroom, Garth?' She tries to say it as casually as those words can be said. Even he shouldn't misconstrue them; she is curious, not on a mission to seduce. More interested in his flat than she is in his parents in truth, not that she says as much.

'Not until we are married, my dear,' says Garth.

Lily feels the timing of a drum beat before they both laugh. Another Garth joke, and a cut above the average, he even sent himself up. She tries the door handle only to see a toilet, the seat of which stands to attention. 'Sorry,' she says, as if this was too great an intrusion, and turns the handle on the neighbouring door. The bedroom is large, twice the size of her own. She walks across the room to his single bed, sits upon the dark blue duvet draped across it, takes in the room from there. She rises to her feet within seconds; it felt presumptuous, Garth standing only on the threshold. A wardrobe dominates the side wall, a large and ancient thing, a family heirloom perhaps, carted here upon a hay-wain from Sixpenny Handley, ornate handles on the doors, a hefty key sticking out of the lock. Bookcases line the back wall; she steps towards them so as to read the titles. Lily loves reading, perhaps it will prove to be a shared interest. She picks a book out at random. 'Peake's Commentary on the Bible,' she says, reading out the title. 'Can't imagine it's a page-turner.'

'I like it,' says Garth.

It dawns upon Lily what an intrusion her visit might be: the disturbance of a monk's cell. Garth has come into the room, he takes the book from her, places it back among others whose titles are equally unappealing. This room has surely never enjoyed female presence during Garth's time here, her fingers on the book will have wrought a change, although not in a manner that she can pin down. She thinks that he fancies the pants off her, there was a bit of evidence back on the beach last weekend. Her presence in his place of meditation, of prayer, might be leaving a distracting trail. She laughs out loud at her own unspoken vanity. 'Let's go and see your folks,' she says, smiling and nodding. Wanting him to feel approval for his strange sanctum. She thinks that she could never live—would struggle to pass a night—in so dismal a slice of Northbourne.

* * *

'You must call me Penny,' says his mother. 'And this is Wilf.'

She sees Garth catch Claire's eye, guesses from the pre-visit briefing that these are not names that either parent is apt to flaunt in front of their children. They may have worn dustcovers for thirty years.

'I'm so pleased to finally meet you, Penny,' says Lily, going to kiss her but then awkwardly settling on a shake of her proffered hand. 'And Wilf,' she says, giving him no choice but the hand. Bloody slipper-wielding swear-merchant, she thinks, as he takes hold of it. Moves his own up and down in a mechanical motion.

For Lily, the meal is one long quiz. Garth's mother—the one she alone may call Penny—bombards her relentlessly. 'You don't attend his church then?' she asks, and 'He told us you met during an accident?' She can answer most of the questions with ease but another always pops up upon completion. When Penny Addicks plumps for, 'What exactly do you see in our Garth?' Lily cannot keep a straight face, tries to hide her laughter with a long draft of table water.

'He's a good swimmer,' she eventually tells the assembled table, after the woman had outstared her, evidently seeing no glimmer of humour in her inane barrage

'Well, he's never won anything,' says Penny.

At this point in the meal and conversation, Claire makes a bigger contribution than any she has managed thus far. Giggles. 'He can keep a secret.' She says it as if she too might be her brother's suitor. The lank brown hair she'd cleared from her face to say it, falls immediately back across her eyes on completion of the cryptic phrase.

Penelope Addicks scrutinises her daughter, perhaps trying to

Punching a Boy in Sittingbourne

calculate the significance of that odd compliment.

Wilfred ignores Claire—he has ignored everything but the roast beef, as far as Lily can tell—chooses this moment to speak to her. 'You live local but you're not local. Have I got you figured out?'

'It's true, Wilf, I grew up in Kent.'

'Are you sure you're not London? That's what I had you down for.'

'No, but I lived there for fifteen years.'

'Oh, you've picked it up.' He gives his wife her first attention of the dinner. 'She started speaking like that from living so long in London. I knew it.'

'Don't mind him, dear,' Penny tells Lily. 'And you do have some cockney in you. I can hear it and I've a much better ear than Wilfred.'

* * *

When Wilfred Addicks has stepped out to smoke a self-rolled cigarette, and his mother is fixing a post-prandial pot of tea, Garth turns to Lily and says, 'Sorry about that.' She shrugs, nothing he had told her of his family had raised hopes of anything more rewarding than this. And her every visit to Sittingbourne is worse. She thinks both Garth and Claire behave as children in thrall to their parents. Too quiet by half, too accepting of these dull-witted know-alls. 'They were incessant, I've never seen them like that, they simply never have visitors.'

'They're fucking crackers,' Claire whispers, then she giggles a little. She has appeared light-headed all meal. It could be vodka or she might have smoked marijuana. Very strange but the rest of the family don't appear bothered by how she is. Lily has yet to get a true sense of this bird-like young woman. Garth has told her how clever and how artful his sister is, she wonders if he knows her at all. Thus far, Lily has felt only the eyes of the village idiot upon her. Now that it is just the three of them, she looks more closely at Claire, free from the verbal assaults of the mother, the occasional foray by the old man. Claire might be the same age as Caroline, looks okay but her skin is blotchy, thin blood vessels show upon her face. Her hair hides it except for the perpetual tick of her hand running across, moving the hair only for it to return. Her exposed arms are pale, red, pink, white but there are also several scratches. They could be the result of accidents but Lily wonders if she self-harms. Garth—the skilled support worker to

Boscombe

troubled children in Baxter's Residential School—has never mentioned this. May not allow such a thought any purchase in his family-loving head. He told Lily about her vodka-laden hip flask, that's the extent of Claire's known sins. 'You know why, don't you?' the strange girl asks Lily.

'Why what, Claire?' She has caught no thread from which this question logically follows.

'Why she didn't ask you about your children.'

Lily nods, not knowing the answer but wishing to hear Claire explain.

'She wants grandchildren, some of her own. Not interested in other peoples. I even think I'm meant to get her with a few—have some—but I'm not gunner.'

Lily looks at Garth, 'You have told them?' she says.

'Yeah, it isn't a secret.'

Garth's mother brings in the pot of tea, she calls out, 'Wilfred' in a sing-song voice, an attempt to sound light-hearted, Lily thinks, although impatience is in there too. Written on her face if not in the words spoken. Lily feels an intense dislike for Penelope Addicks. She runs rings around everyone in this house. It may be that the old fucker was a tyrant in his day—that is what Garth implied when they spoke of his childhood—since her arrival ninety minutes ago he has had three cigarettes and four pisses. Tyranny over, the old git is a spent force; the Penny-woman is the viper.

Lily waits for him, waits until the family is once more assembled. 'Did Garth say that my children are black?' She feels pleased with herself when his mother spits out tea on completion of her comment. Probably worth the alarmed look she sees alight upon Garth's face.

When she has recovered some composure, Penny addresses Lily. 'He explained that they are only one-quarter black.'

She knows it was her choice to stir it all up but Lily feels her own blood boil now that she has done it. Suddenly at war with the Addicks family, Garth too, and that was not what she intended on agreeing to the visit. The feelings coursing through her could turn in any direction.

'Where are they from?' asks the old man, the burnt-out ignoramus.

'Me!' Lily shouts at him, answers him like he's a moron. 'They're from me!' It's exactly what he is. Thick as needs a good shouting at.

'Mum,' says Garth, bumbling into the conversation with an already reddened face. 'I told you that they are dark, a lovely black boy and a little black girl. The percentage of any nationality doesn't matter. I think I said that.'

'They're a hundred percent British,' Lily says over her boyfriend's piffle. Her back in front of the jury boyfriend. 'British like the rest of us. Born in the nation's capital, a British mum and a British dad.'

Claire has leant back in her chair, laughing quietly. Lily had briefly warmed to the crazy girl but it has rapidly cooled. Found the icebox.

* * *

Cycling back to his flat together, they come to the edge of Northbourne and Lily, who is following behind, turns down a promising side street, leaving Garth to cycle on alone. She turns off that one just as quickly, never looks back nor learns if he tries to follow. Lost him in no time. She makes her way across to West Parley, detours to the east of where she needs to be, determined to get home to Boscombe without interception by Garth. She does not wish to talk to or look at him; she cycles down roads he wouldn't think to try. She may resume her relationship with that boy when and if she feels like it. Until the simmering inside her subsides, she cannot stand him. She was never one for comfort hugs or make-up kisses, not from the perpetrator. It can be such misleading shit. She hears her phone ringing, does not pull it from her small rucksack; feeling the light breeze on her cheeks and knees becomes a small pleasure as she pedals the long way home. Without picking over the detail, she laughs about his stupid family: the Threepence Ha'penny yokels. Picks up an off-road route, takes to the river path. A nice sight, the river here is peaceful. No sound of water until she pulls up her bike. Stops. Listens to the silence of early evening and then the river is there, the faint carry of sound as it eddies and ripples over the pebble beds, laps at the tree-trunked edges. Can't stop long, she pushes on and within three hundred yards, she is ringing her bell to pass a few walkers. Strollers, elderly ladies with dogs, even some lovers walking hand in hand along the idyl of the river path. That sort of carry-on is not for everybody. Relationships are a bit marmite at the bottom of it: not for her if turning into thick-headed Wilf and plain-nasty Penny is the most likely outcome. Her own excuse for a father and the insufferable Esme are no better; she really should have figured relationships out before she left stinking Sittingbourne. Steered clear, cycled away long ago.

She passes a swans' nest, sees the angular birds looking cross that people walk and cycle so close to their home. Black eyes atop a long white neck follow the passers-by, stare at them as if daring them to come an inch closer. A disturbance of the nest will draw retribution. Swans are anti-social, generally displeased with the presence of people. She determines that she should sit tight with her children, happy on Cooper Street. She'll peck anybody who has the nerve to intrude. Not Alice, of course, she's always welcome, and she'll hand a free pass to Caroline.

And what of Garth? 'Peck, peck, peck,' says Lily, as she pictures his face, his checked shirt, and his unwavering love of Jesus. 'Peck, peck, peck.'

* * *

When she arrives at the maisonette, Lily stops to get out her key. Pulls out her phone too, she'll dial Alice. Over in ten minutes, she thinks to say. Wants to be with her children. Alice is brilliant with them but this—a small and loving home—is where they belong.

Before the ringtone has buzzed once, she sees a familiar face coming towards her, pushing his bike down Cooper Street. Garth looks completely distraught. 'I'm so, so sorry,' he says, voice loud in the quiet of the street. It's a refrain he has been singing as long as she has known him. The man who loves her but won't make love to her; the fella who plays fantastically, warmly, lovingly with her children, then seems to have some tiny, little—unforgivable—reservation about the colour of their skin.

'What is it?' asks Lily. 'Why are you even here?'

'I was a fool to take you there. I'm blind to how awful they really are. I just saw it through your eyes and I am so, so sorry.' He runs a hand through his hair, tears at it slightly. A mad gesture of his very own. 'Claire's worrying me.'

'Tsch,' she says, not wanting him near, not ready to talk about his treasured sister. Barmy Claire. 'They're terrible, Garth. horrible parents just like mine. I guess that's why we fell for each other but it won't make either of us what the other wants. Can you leave me be, please?' He stands before her, holding his bike. There are no tears on his face, it's like they are lurking in the wings. He might be feeling shitter than she does. 'Call me,' says Lily. It is as much conciliation as she can muster.

Wednesday, 29 June 2016

Caroline is again sitting on Lily's sofa, a break in a jog of many miles, maroon running shorts and top, a good match for her tanned skin. They have turned towards each other, holding eye contact. When the girl first asked her how she was, Lily said, 'A bit down, I'm afraid.' They been talking intensely ever since.

Caroline didn't try to defend Garth, just cautioned her to understand the intentions behind his words. 'That's good, really good,' she purrs. After describing the mealtime with his parents, and her reaction to it, Lily confirms that they've spoken by telephone every day since.

'He's too good for me and not good enough for my children,' states Lily in a louder voice than necessary, enough to bring a child to the lounge door. 'Bed, sweetie,' Lily tells her son.

'I'll tuck you in soon, sweetie,' Caroline adds. Then—when Jo-jo has retreated—she turns back to Lily. 'What have you just said? Really?'

'The truth, he's a good man, stands by the no-sex-before-marriage malarkey...'

'But that isn't what you think at all. Don't give him a nine out of ten for letting you down.'

'I don't. I'm sick of it. It's unnatural. But...' Lily lowers her voice considerably, searches for the apt point to make. '...my kids both love him. What's he got Caroline?'

'You on a fishing line, by the sound of it.' The runner moves up the sofa, puts a hand upon her friend's forearm. 'You need to see him properly, more often. Get him into your bed or out of your system.'

'Oh, that's not happening, he's made that very clear. Unless...' Lily extracts herself from the comforting arm. '...how are you fixed to be a bridesmaid, Caroline?'

The visitor playfully crashes a small cushion on Lily's head. 'Ha!

Like that's any kind of solution.'

'Oh God, I don't know what to do about him, Caz. I'll see him, maybe we can...' Now she becomes flustered by a thought, takes time to gather it together. 'He never quarrels with me; I'm a bit of a bastard with him. I've no idea what he sees in me.'

'He sees a gorgeous girl, the same as I do,' says Caroline.

'But is he bad for me? Bringing out my worst side. Me and Trent never argued, not while we were childless and poor, and not much when we were both so taken with Jo-jo.' Her voice again goes down a register, this is not for her children's ears. 'Ami was loved every minute, me and him but Trent couldn't organise much. We were suddenly a bigger family than he could offer anything more than a little entertainment to. He couldn't take charge; maybe I couldn't either. We couldn't cope in Shoreditch, and that inability annoyed me. We quarrelled then which we'd never done before. Me and Garth, well we've nothing in common except foul mothers. That's not much of a basis for a relationship; we quarrel about what film to watch at the cinema, how much wine I'm glugging. Everything.'

Caroline is silent, Lily is again appraising her, the cheekbones those extra millimetres higher than normal people; her hair is untidy when she jogs, and all the more beautiful for it. Lily knows from their easy chat that she's a natural blond, with a bit of colour thrown in to accentuate the light and dark shades; her eyebrows are a deeper brown which gives her such a captivating look. Fate has granted her the perfect face. 'Oh, it must be tricky for you, sweetie,' Lily continues. 'All this talk of certifiable parents, and your mum and dad so brilliant. Yours are the genuine sort.'

Caroline is laughing at this, a little bit manically. 'Poor me not having a mad mum.' Lily sees tears in her friend's eyes even as she jokes.

'What's the matter? What is it?'

'Daddy is in hospital.' She suddenly squeezes Lily's hand. 'I wish I'd never known Clive, not for a minute. I hate him, Lily, never want to set eyes on him again...'

'What's he done, Caz? How's your dad?'

'It's broken ribs but I think the...'

'How?

Punching a Boy in Sittingbourne

'The psycho was around our house. I was at the gym. Working. He'd lost touch with my hours, my shifts. Daddy went to talk to him, advised Clive that I didn't want to see him, and he suddenly turned. They say it might be the steroids—they cause mood swings, it's why he flipped—but he's the swine who took the steroids, isn't he?' Caroline bows her head; tears flow freely. 'Daddy always said he'd do anything for me. He always has. I owe him everything. He'd get beaten up by a thug to try to stop the guy from seeing me. He would and he did but Daddy's not a fighter at all. He doesn't know how to take a beating. That's Clive's idea of a good time, not Daddy's. I don't know how he's going to get through this. He'll be home but I'm worried it's going to kill him. I don't know if he can get to the other side of this, if he'll ever be himself again.'

Lily puts her friend's head on her shoulder. Hugs her close. She feels for her. It had felt funny when she was comparing the mothers from hell in front of this girl whose parents are centre stage in her dream life. Now she sees the common ground. Lily loves Jo-jo and Ami, cannot tolerate a moment's hurt for them. Her friend, Caz, hates to see her father suffer; taking his money is just an extension of taking his love. The poor man having his ribs broken must make the girl feel mortified. She has strung along a Neanderthal, accidentally set the beast onto her defenceless father. Lily wonders if we are all a bit that way. She went pretty ape in Ferndown, at the Addick's house, started a fire for no greater reason than her dislike of Penny. She's struggled to see anything so primitive in Garth, and on hearing Caroline's story it comes to her that it may be no bad thing. His containment, being boundaried. The young girl is weeping like a baby now. Lily consoles her as she has many times done with Ami, with Jo-jo, comforted them upon this same sofa. Hugs Caroline close to her person, busses the top of her head.

Chapter Four:

A Halo is not a Cooking Pot

Sunday, 17 July 2016

'Can I take you dancing, Lily? There's nothing in this world I'd rather do.' He can picture her sitting on her sofa, surprised perhaps by his suggestion. And pleased, surely. She must be very, very pleased. He hears her give the start of a small laugh, a noise he knows and loves. 'Are Ami and Joey sleeping?' he asks, keen to imagine that this is a most private conversation.

'He's still pottering in his room. Did you want to talk to him?'

'No. I mean, I will if he needs to but it's you that I've phoned, isn't it? I want to be alone with you.' This prospect has loomed very large in his thoughts lately. In less than a week her two children will be away for a fortnight, staying again with their father. He knows that he will feel tempted in that time, he dwells upon what it means in Christian and unchristian terms. Allows himself brief flurries of excitement.

'You should be at church, Garth. It's not like you to skip a service.'

'It was great this morning. You really should come, Lily. I've modernised the music quite a bit. I'm completely on board with Margery now.'

'This morning, this morning. Why aren't you there now? You're a naughty truant.'

Her words draw a gasp from Garth but only because it is exactly how he regards his absence from church. 'I wanted to talk to you, ask you out dancing. It seemed more important. More important to me today.'

'Ha. You are so sweet. I have no choice, do I? This won't be a bloomin' hoe-down in Thre'penny Ha'penny, will it?'

He laughs at her joke, repeats, 'Sixpenny Handley' for the thousandth time. 'It's your choice, Lily. I am a vessel for you to handle carefully.' As he says this, he recalls arguments they have had, wonders if he is making the wrong kind of fool of himself. 'Lindy-hop, salsa: if you want to do it, I'll give it a go. I suspect you should wear industrial boots, a hard hat if there's bobbing and weaving to be done. I'm not skilled but I'll be pretty much dancing with you like a limpet.'

'We're going dancing, Garth. I'm actually okay at it you know. Do you think you'll still be able to resist me when I roll my hips?'

He smiles to himself. Missing the evening service for this kind of talk might disappoint Margery, Garth is treading his own path. 'I can't resist you, Lily Stephens,' he says, a phrase she will have heard from him once or twice already. And the line is silent for a few moments. He has explained that he can, in fact, contain himself; he is a servant of Jesus first and foremost but he would like a wife and he has chosen who. She has not really answered that implicit question, given no sign, other than the odd advance when she's had a few to drink. He thinks it a broad-brush yes but not to all the essential formalities.

'Listen...' Lily breaks the wordfast. '...you're a lucky bugger getting this long, long break.'

'It's the nature of a residential school, long hours, long breaks. The short money is a tough nut for the six weeks I'm off.'

'Short money? I thought you were salaried?'

'Yes and no. It's a retainer; it pays the mortgage but my usual pay includes loads of overtime. August is the hardest, the basic salary is only thirteen.'

'But you won't work at all? Every day on the beach.'

'We have a week of training courses just before the children come back. And I only ever go to the beach with you.'

'I'm going to try it, Garth, work like yours. I think Ami needs to hit secondary before I can. The funny shifts wouldn't suit us yet. It sounds great. Tough and great.'

'You're summing yourself up,' he says without thinking. Immediately regrets it. Tough is a long walk from beautiful.

'I doubt if I'm either, Garth,' replies Lily quietly.

'You're great...'

She cuts him off before he can extrapolate himself from the throwaway line. 'Have I told you about the creep at work, Simon Clarke. He tried to come on to me, and then he had an accident. Broke his neck, or collarbone, cycling in the New Forest. I've heard from

A Halo is not a Cooking Pot

Gillian that he'll be back in work tomorrow.'

'Whoa! You mentioned something but...'

'I thought I had. Married and all that shit, then he phones me up hoping to come around my place on a Saturday night. This was before I'd even met you; he thought it was his right, as my boss or something. Said it could be a date. Cheeky bloody bastard. If you ever feel like hitting someone on my behalf, Garth, he just might be the one.'

'No, go back a bit. I remember the story but not the accident. You never told me about that.'

'It saves you having to punch the bastard, I expect. He's got what he deserved already. Broken collar bone or ribs, I think. An air ambulance jobbie; happened the same day you nobbled me with your bike.'

'I know him, Lily.'

'Really?'

'Well, yes and no. I'm not sure I've ever met him but it must be Cindy Clarke's husband. She's a long-standing church member. On committees and everything.'

'And he goes to your church?'

'Not him, only her.'

'What a turn-up. Oh God, sorry Garth, does me telling you this—that he tried coming on to me—make it your holy duty to tell the wife now. No secrets between Christians or something. I decided it was best to keep my mouth shut but if you must...'

'Lily, this is serious stuff you're saying. Think about it for a moment. About what's right for you. He's a solicitor in your firm, is he?'

'Senior partner since his dad retired. I've only got to put up with him for another six or seven years before I swap careers for Baxter's School.'

'Lily, you're funny but there's a serious point in here.' Garth feels grave concern, unwanted advances from a married man are sinful. 'I'm not sure about the Christian duty, I'd rather work that out with Peter than just say it off the top of my head. Anyway, it's what you want that will guide me. You're my girlfriend, I'll do right by you.'

'What I want...'

He thinks Lily sounds unsure of herself. His knowing Cindy is a coincidence he has sprung upon her, Garth can see that. 'Cindy Clarke might know what her husband is like already but I don't expect she knows that he's harassed you. What it does for their marriage is Simon Clarke's lookout, just his, or him and Cindy's. What about work, Lily? Might he get nasty?'

'I'm tough as old boots, Garth. Remember?'

'I thought different to that as soon as I said it. You're tender even when you hide it away; always affected by everything. Even by me not being all you want.'

'Don't say that, Garth. You're bloody brilliant; we're just different people.' After a pause, Lily adds, 'And I would never go out with someone as ratty as me. I make you put up with a lot of crap. Stuff Simon Clarke, you're taking me dancing!'

'I didn't mean forget it, just think about it. I'll talk to Cindy if you want me to. Just dwell on it for a while first. And Lily...'

'Yes, sweetie.'

'...we'll dance until sun-up.'

Monday, 18 July 2016

The children are excited. Not a surprise to Garth: the final week of every summer term was a heady one back at his own school, and the children at Baxter's have less self-control than most. Little or none. He and Gerry arrived at school early. He cycled from Northbourne to Ringwood—there was not a bus early enough for this irregular shift. They will work until Wednesday afternoon, term's end. The early start is to facilitate a trip to Brownsea Island. They are both going on it, Rihanna and a couple of teachers too. A dozen boys, of course. These trips can be hard work. His endeavours, and those of his colleagues, will make or break it.

He checks that the boys have packed exactly what they need for the day trip. Wonders whether they can ditch the waterproofs. Unnecessary in this reliable summer. He feels a lightness, a giddiness. This three-day shift will be his last time on site for five weeks. He will re-read the Acts of the Apostles, paint the interior of The Church of the Men of Judea and court Lily. They are his goals for the summer holiday. He and Lily still see each other only a couple of times most weeks, although from Saturday she will be unencumbered by

A Halo is not a Cooking Pot

children. He could visit daily if she will allow it.

On the coach to Poole, Garth has to intervene when Declan Keane picks on poor Paul Frost. The perennial victim. Their coach is a full-sized one, two-thirds empty, their party small for it. Garth—backed up by Mr Race who teaches geography—insists both boys sit apart after the fracas. Apart and alone. They must reflect on how they have behaved. Excessive disruption risks the termination of the trip for every child. Garth makes this point quite forcibly to the two boys. To Declan in particular, the instigator. He thinks the teacher—Race—would not have been able to strike the balance. The bargain: the trip's continuance is dependent entirely on their improved behaviour. The boys require certainty, they must be given to understand that a final warning means just that. Any further mayhem will result in an early return to Baxter's School for everyone. Garth would carry it through. Not yet but he makes it clear he has no qualms about it. Race doesn't—he's a ditherer—the kids walk all over him. When Garth assists in Mr Race's classroom, it is always to provide order where there is none. Geography should be an easy subject to teach, it's a nice mix of table exercises, talk and field work. Why Mr Race can't make a better fist of it is a mystery. Rihanna—never short of opinions—says half the teachers come into special education for a quiet life. Garth thinks it risible if it is true. Kids kicking off every five minutes give no one peace; the demand on subject expertise is certainly limited. For most children, learning a few strategies to stave off social exclusion is their principal education. Any exams passed are a bonus and not a greatly tested one. Garth failed more exams than he passed in his own school days, and yet he's a great help in any classroom at Baxter's. His dedication to the study of scripture has turned him into a focussed scholar, however unlikely that seemed during his youth, back when he was just another farm kid with a dunce for a father.

Mostly these boys are simply excited. Perhaps the spat between the two, Declan and Paul, is only an expression of that. After settling the troublemakers and receiving a grateful nod from Rihanna, Garth sits beside Damian Taylor. This was always his plan; his rapport with the boy is the success story of the term. During the previous week, Mr Rogers cited it in Garth's appraisal. 'That boy looked to be beyond us—destined for fifty-two-week care—we've turned him around and you have been the mainstay.' Of course, alongside the work in school, Garth has also prayed for Damian. Prayed quietly in the sleeping-in room at Baxter's School, as well as at his church in Northbourne. Honest young man that he is, he would like to enlighten his manager about the Lord's role in the boy's improved behaviour. Past experience, and his knowledge of Jesus's humility, inhibit such a declaration.

Damian looks relaxed. Any excitement he feels about the visit to an island nature reserve, he keeps to himself. 'Garf,' he says, no better at saying his favourite staff member's name than Jo-jo Kwaku, son of Lily and Trent, 'is it a proper park? With rides.'

'I've explained, Damian. It's a national park, National Trust. The island is a haven, a bird sanctuary. You'll enjoy that, animal lover that you are. It's not very big. And we're going to be doing some geography fieldwork while we're there.'

'The other group 'ave got it better though, 'aven't they, Garf?'

Garth tries to make the case for Brownsea Island over the rock climbing and canoeing which the more reliably behaved boys have scheduled for today.

'It's fair though, Garf,' says Damian, after he has heard out the unconvincing argument, 'I've been a bugger all term, so I don't deserve the canoes.'

Garth raises a finger to his lips, the mildest admonishment for the boy's crudely worded self-assessment. 'You're seeing things more clearly, Damian. And a geography field trip can be fun. It'll help towards your GCSE too.'

Mr Race, who is on the seat behind, pipes up. 'It'll be the UPO's for you, young Damian.'

'Yeah, I know,' says the boy.

Brian Race taps Garth on the shoulder, looks into his face quite intently. It must mean he shouldn't get Damian's hopes up. It has long been a source of frustration to Garth that the school seldom enters its pupils for exams with any currency beyond the world of special education. Damian Taylor has spent most of his recent school days messing about, maybe most of the distant ones too; his learning has improved since his behaviour has settled. Garth shrugs. He's not the teacher, he's not the prescriber of courses. Giving Damian a goal

A Halo is not a Cooking Pot

beyond a qualification none in the country have heard of who don't work in these challenging schools is a positive thing in Garth's book. Who knows how it will all pan out for Damian, for any of these boys. The work of the school—and the prayers Garth says to the One who might help him the most—are meaningful nudges towards a better life. Mr Race's lack of ambition only sums himself up, thinks Garth, as he returns the teacher's stare.

* * *

While the decanted coach party waits at the quayside, a couple of the boys start singing a pop song. Their version includes lyrics Garth presumes to be a long chalk from the original. He has heard it on the radio from time to time but not with these words in it. Nob, cock, fanny, cunt. The staff response is less than united although none are in favour of boys singing obscenities. Race and the other teacher, Miss Spalding, along with Geraldine Hunt—the very Gerry who drives Garth from Ringwood before the start of each shift, back again at the end—are livid with the boys. The French teacher, who has joined the geography field trip for need of a purpose today, scolds the pair as audibly as possible. She lets holidaymakers, day trippers, all those queueing for the boat to Brownsea, know that the boy's loudly crooned homage to male and female genitalia is a disgrace. That Rihanna and Garth are less aeriated is not really a surprise. This is how it is in school. The presence of the public seems only to exaggerate the difference in the respective staff approaches. They would have intervened, of course but the speed with which Jennifer Spalding and Brian Race started on at the boys gave them no room to do so. The difference in their demeanour reflects only strategy and not the purpose behind it. The upset to members of the public is not their primary concern. Garth and Rihanna—through their training—understand that children often behave this way to trigger the very reactions which those staff and some members of the public now display. Outrage can be rewarding to a child who enjoys a spat. Rising to the bait doesn't work. Some staff see it, some don't. Gerry says, 'You can't let them get away with it,' when she and Garth talk about these situations in the car. She can't see Garth's conviction that he doesn't. He is simply more measured. He is grateful to Rihanna for her discipleship in this, it has been a discussion point between them on more than one late evening at Baxter's.

The ferry arrives at the quayside, and a handful of passengers disembark. When the waiting queue is asked to board, a commotion begins. A group of six older people—pensioners, they must be—make a demand of the crew member who has stepped off the boat. Appeal to the captain. 'We're not going if those boys are onboard.' All of them say the same, many times over. Seeking to ensure that the boat's crew, with their hard-to-decipher accents, understand the point.

The captain states—in slow simple English—that they may wait for the next boat if they wish. He cannot deny the boys entry. The large group from Baxter's School have tickets, their visit arranged several weeks ago.

'They should wait. We were in front of them in the queue,' says a white-haired lady in large tortoiseshell sunglasses.

'I'm sorry,' says the captain, a shiny gold-trimmed cap upon his head. English is certainly not his first language, an accent that lends Garth to think him Portuguese. 'They have tickets. You may come on this boat or you may wait.'

The woman is bristling now. A man, most likely a husband, is at her side, nodding vigorously. 'The language those boys used is not befitting of the National Trust.'

Mr Race and Miss Spalding realise they must act. They step forward and begin to argue, admit that some language was choice but say it is now under control. They have tickets, a field trip planned. Race even says that, if denied this sailing, the boys will become restless and may start acting out again.

Rihanna steps forward. 'Guys,' she says, confidently addressing the six complainants, 'we're really sorry. The boys were out of order, shocking words. We stopped it though. Please accept our apologies.' Garth thinks her very smart. Apologies should trump explanations for these old people.

Now Sunglasses' husband speaks; he is the loudest, face about to burst a blood vessel. Looking only at the captain, he says, 'What can you expect when there is someone like that looking after them!' He throws a dismissive hand gesture in the direction of Garth's colleague. Rihanna of Trinidadian parentage.

The two teachers say nothing. Rihanna looks shocked. A switch

A Halo is not a Cooking Pot

flicks over inside Garth's head: he knows what Lily would think. 'You can't say that,' he says, realising as spoken that he has only mumbled, not directed his rebuke at the offenders. He steps up next to his black colleague, looks at the capped crew member. 'Please make these troublemakers wait behind,' he says.

The husband shouts, 'Troublemakers!' into Garth's face. He is livid although it is now fully ten minutes since a couple of boys dropped the c-word alongside one or two other blue ones. The most untoward act since then has been the man's own dismissal of his colleague. There were no words but Garth is certain his gesture—Rihanna's difference—was racist at its core. And done in front of the boys of whom two are also black. He is mentally processing something important, even wondering if the crew member is doing the same. Since the Brexit vote, spurred on by Lily, Garth has talked to Gregor, a Romanian who works in the newsagent below his flat. The name-calling has been getting worse. Snowballing. It seems the country voted to become a nastier place. 'We cannot tolerate having racist comments thrown at our staff, and it is a terrible example for these impressionable children.'

The captain nods his head. He tells the man and his wife they must wait, indicates that the others may board if they are happy to share the boat with whichever passengers follow. That it will include the boys on the school trip.

'This is an outrage,' one of the old ones throws at the captain. It culminates in an agreement that they will go to the kiosk. Receive full refunds. And raise a complaint too. 'Writing to my member of parliament,' says an until-now-silent grey hair. An agreement to disagree.

When the group from Baxter's School is on the boat, seated together, no problems beyond being stared at by other passengers, Race has a quiet word with Garth. 'It went okay but we were getting there. It was over-confrontational, you jumping in like that. Could have gone either way.'

He said it for Garth's ears but Rihanna must have bat-like hearing. 'No, Brian,' she says, 'Garth was brilliant. And look at them.' She waves a hand towards Alex and Pasindu, the non-whites in the cohort of boys. The latter concentrates only on the screen of his mobile phone but Alex Marshall is listening. Gives Garth a thumbs up.

'Sorry, it seemed right,' Garth tells Brian Race.

His brain is looping over the two positives. Their success in boarding this boat despite the boys' foolish swearing, and his spontaneous challenge of the ageing racist. These will have given the group a lift. Race and Spalding are useless. The supposed leaders of this party, then they prove themselves indecisive time after time. Garth realises he has never been so assertive with total strangers before. His strength of mind came from thinking over all Lily has said to him. Her resolve to do right by Jo-jo and Ami.

* * *

The children and staff eat lunch in a small picnicking area at a scout camp on the island. The staff retrieve the food from their backpacks. Children do not carry their own sandwiches. It prevents early consumption, or the losing, selling and stealing of fare in advance of the meal. A little staff control greatly improves the chances of an orderly lunchtime.

Garth watches the children carefully. They had apples and cereal bars before boarding the coach; this is their first proper meal of the school week. He knows that some children, notably Paul Frost and Pasindu Lakshan, seldom eat properly at home. Chaos or poverty—too much of each—disrupting their family's ability to provide. As he thinks this, he recalls Lily's concern when he ran from church to her house without eating anything at lunchtime. She swaddled him in her dressing gown and fed him cheese on toast. The memory is a confusion of love and embarrassment. He turns it over in his mind, the awkwardness all came from his poor organisation. Wrong clothes; ignoring his own hunger; an inability to take a pink dressing gown in his stride. The love was all Lily's. His driven passion for her made him run and run, try to outsmart the dilatory bus service. She has a remarkable capacity to see his needs when he cannot. Clothing, food. Her warmth. And the wisest eye for her children. Garth flinches, fears he is becoming her third child. On that day, a succession of visitors came to the maisonette. Caroline the beautiful, whom he has found an irrational dislike for. All his ardour is for Lily. That was the evening they swam. He held her perfect waist, came closer to her physically than he knows how to ask the Lord's forgiveness for. Hopes He was

A Halo is not a Cooking Pot

looking elsewhere. Alice was there too, not swimming but earlier in the house. He likes her. Lily has described their friendship, and he appreciates the mutuality of it. Alice is a kid too, only a couple of years older than Rihanna, he suspects, although his colleague has not found herself mothering two children...

'Earth calling Addicks,' he hears whispered in his ear.

Garth turns into his colleague's smiling face, drawn so close to his that there is little more than a paper's width from Rihanna's nose to his ear. He knows he would once have flinched at this physical closeness. His tactile relationship with Lily has drawn him over those inhibitions. Taught him not to fear human touch.

'Brian wants them to go through the worksheets, identifying plants and stuff. In this heat, they'll go mental.' Garth has an egg sandwich in his hand as he swivels around to reply. A bit of filling tumbles from the bread and lands on Rihanna's bare leg. She picks it up nimbly between thumb and forefinger, thrusts it towards his face, offering to feed him this finger food. Garth shakes his head, and she pops it into her own mouth. 'What do you think?' she asks as she chews.

'Let's walk them round the island, burn off a bit of energy. Look for the birds and stuff, even if the worksheets are all plants.'

Rihanna nods then grins, puts a hand on the side of Garth's head to pull him close. Whispers quietly in his ear, 'Can't we stage a mutiny? Push Race in the cooking pot and declare the republic of Brownsea.'

He pulls away from her intimacy, worried that the boys will spot it. Think it more indicative of their relationship than is the case. It is not how staff should behave in front of them.

Garth is coughing on his sandwich as Jennifer Spalding shouts across, 'What's the joke, Rihanna? Share.'

She speaks loudly, wishes the boys to hear. 'We're staying here. Garth is vetting the boats across, sending back the racists. It's a perfect island.' She turns to Pasindu. 'Is that all right?'

'Fuckin' hate racists,' he says.

Garth looks at the boy and raises a finger to his lip. A shushing because of the expletive. He realises how much he enjoys being on the right side in this battle. Against no one in particular right now, and an elderly gentleman at the quayside earlier. It is not simple but a fog has lifted. Rihanna, Lily's children, he feels that he was always silently on their side but now—in the rich light of this glorious afternoon on a nature reserve within Poole harbour—he wonders, why the silence? Jesus would never have been mute, not in the face of injustice.

* * *

'Garf!' shouts Damian Taylor. He runs to where the boy is pointing. Declan Keane is again fighting Paul Frost. The latter barely fighting back. With satisfaction, Garth registers that Damian—a friend of Declan's—has put keeping the peace above his allegiance to the perpetrator. Something positive to draw on as he pulls the boys apart.

'Want help,' shouts Rihanna, who has just come around the bend in the track they were walking along.

Garth has wrestled Declan away from his quarry. His hold is not by the book but he feels calm enough. 'No fighting—that's it—no fighting,' he tells the assailant as he pins him to the ground by his arms.

The boy has not calmed. Not a bit of it. He spits in Garth's face, shouts, 'Fuck you!' and with the harshness of his yell, a pair of mallards fly up from the thin undergrowth, just a few yards to the side of where the boy is prostrate beneath Garth.

'I'm letting you go, Declan,' says Garth. 'Don't run, don't go near Paul. You got it?'

'I'm fucking running!' the boy shouts back at him.

Garth releases Declan's arms, rolls away so that he is no longer hovering over the top of him. Does not wish to physically intimidate, that has never been his practice. In a gentle voice, while wiping spittle from his face with the back of his hand, he explains, 'It's an island. Running won't really serve a purpose.' He tries to stop the corners of his mouth from upturning but cannot.

Declan has seen it. The amusement on Garth's face is at his expense, and still, he returns a rueful smile back, the thunderous anger dissipated. 'Fuck off,' he says again, no anger, it is the catchphrase of many a Baxter's boy.

'I'm sorry, Declan. I hope I didn't hurt you. I was just pulling you away from Paul.'

'Yeah,' he says turning away.

Garth glances at Rihanna. These sudden, unpredictable confrontations are hazardous to navigate. He hopes that, from twenty yards behind, she has seen his actions clearly. Worries that Declan is too proud a boy to acknowledge how this arose in his own de-briefing, an event which will occur later today: the school's procedure whenever physical restraint is applied. And Garth has long worried that the fighting—the pecking order between boys, and even staff, regarding their relative strength, their respective capacities to ensure the submission of others—is the lesson that endures, although the message within it is utter nonsense. Might is not right. Garth has no desire to control Declan but until the boy learns to contain himself more fully, the need to do so will periodically recur. 'There will be a consequence,' he tells the boy. Consequence is the neutral terminology used in school which means a punishment will follow. Term's end is so close it may be no more than a stiff word from Mr Rogers, although, in normal times, the boy's withdrawal from an evening leisure activity would be the likely one. The most proportionate.

'Consequence for you,' shouts the boy as he is ambling away, 'when my mates hear about this.'

'Jenny has the first aid kit, Garth,' says Rihanna. 'Would you run please?'

He sees that she has a cloth, possibly her own handkerchief, and she is nestling the other boy's head in her arms. Staunching the flow of a nosebleed. He sets off at a trot, thinking how natural his colleague is. She is not a mother but it is with physical warmth that she helps this boy. The victim today and every day, Paul Frost. He saw her rub the side of his head while holding it close to her breast. Not indecently close but a proximity that could hold a very different meaning for a teenage boy. She loves them, Garth thinks. Gives love to a skinny teenager who can barely read, whose demeanour prompts bigger boys to fight him. Paul calls other boys names as obscene as any heard at Baxter's, gets himself beaten senseless, and then does it all over again. Rihanna has a quality that Garth lacks. She is the natural carer, uses the same qualities with which Lily raises Jo-jo and Ami.

When he reaches her, Miss Spalding is quite flustered by the request. 'Stay and sketch,' she tells the two boys she is supervising, as she comes with Garth. Small rucksack—first aid kit within—clutched tightly in her hands. 'Fighting on Brownsea,' she says with a shake of the head. As if the island's tranquillity should have rid the boys of all testosterone. 'Was the girl involved?'

This question floors Garth. He says a straight, 'No.' He has picked up on this trip that there is no warmth between the two of them. He can think of no reason why she should think Rihanna—the only 'girl' in their party—to be responsible for the fracas. Does Spalding believe boys fight over Rihanna? She might be worth it but she does not cross so many boundaries with these youngsters as to make it probable. She is simply a little more informal than he, the chaste Christian, thinks wise. And he has been rethinking everything over recent weeks and days. 'It was out of the blue,' he tells her. Jennifer Spalding is—in Baxter's hierarchy—far more senior than Garth but he reckons French Grammar is her thing, not tuning into the short-circuiting emotions of Declan Keane and the other boys. 'I was closest, so I pulled him off. Rihanna helped after. Not before or during.'

'On your own? You know you shouldn't physically restrain a child without a minimum of two staff on task, don't you, Garth?' Her training is kicking in, her common sense has gone walkabout.

'I couldn't, there was only me. Poor Paul was being leathered.'

'Wait, Garth. You know what we always say. Wait for back up.'

Garth is silent. Wait is probably the word in the classroom but on the residential wing they care about the kids. Get in there and sort it out in double quick time. And Paul really was having his face mashed in.

* * *

In the evening, back at school, Garth works on Stone unit. A swap of house so that he does not have to work with Declan. The boy has complained about him. Disappointing but not unexpected.

Before she goes off shift, Rihanna says to Garth, 'You've changed, matey.' It is near shift's end, all the boys in their rooms.

He did, over a week ago now, tell her, and Gerry too, that he has a girlfriend. He tried not to make a big deal of it. Suggested they shouldn't tell the boys, and that pact seems to have held. They are residential care workers; they spend hours and hours in each other's company. Although he has kept other secrets from time to time, he feels that sharing this news is the right thing to do. He was never a secret Christian, and he should equally affirm his love for Lily. Bear witness. That is his belief.

'Is she like me? Is your girlfriend—you know—like me?'

Garth thinks his colleague is referring to her skin colour. He starts to shake his head but then corrects himself. Lily's skin is, in this glorious mid-summer, still pretty much the colour of snow, her children are a shade or two lighter than Rihanna but he now knows better than to grade the degree of blackness. 'I think we're all the same Ri-ri,' he says, 'so yes, she's like you on that count.'

Rihanna looks slightly confused by his answer but not displeased. Garth is oddly emboldened. Trying to be casual, he adds, 'And you're both really pretty, of course.'

Rihanna snorts a little laugh, smiles while she does it. It reminds him of Lily's some-time reaction to his sporadic his awkwardness. The girl says, 'Aw,' and gives him a hug. This is a first. Rihanna is usually tactile only with upset young boys. 'Stick with her,' she tells him. 'And don't worry about Keane; I've got your back.' Then she leaves the shift. Garth the sleeper-in on Stone tonight.

Tuesday, 19 July 2016

He is not surprised when Mr Lorimer, the head teacher, calls him into the office the following morning. Nor that Mr Rogers, the deputy head who has lead responsibility for the residential staff, is in the room with him. Declan Keane has complained and there must be a plan to manage it. Investigate the matter and ensure Garth does not work with Declan until it's resolved. That was why he worked on Stone last night; Lorimer and Rogers were both at home but they all know the drill. Today and tomorrow, then the term will be over.

'We're suspending you, I'm sorry to say, Garth.' The head teacher's words shock him. Unprecedented; unjustifiable. The Frost boy was being beaten to a pulp.

'It's without prejudice,' says Barry Rogers. 'After the investigation, you might be in the clear.'

He finds he can barely think. Might be? There really were no witnesses, even Rihanna had a few trees in her sightline. A statement from Paul Frost should back him up. Declan's will be nonsense. Garth doesn't know what Damian will say. 'I couldn't follow the procedure because I was on my own,' he says quietly.

'Yes. There'll be plenty of time to explain that,' says the head teacher.

'I'll be completing the investigation over the summer,' says Mr Rogers, 'once I'm back from France.'

'Don't look so worried,' says Mr Lorimer. 'You won't lose any pay. Not for a month and we should be sorted by then.'

'What has Rihanna said?' he asks. He suspects they haven't spoken to her and she has his back. It's what she said.

'Oh, she thinks you had to do something but she's a little biased after you stuck up for her at the quay. We'll be asking Brian and Jennifer about all that too, not that it's part of the complaint. Not yet. We've to work it out, evaluate what the whole episode says about you. Your ability to do the job. And it's unlike you, Garth, you're usually a stickler for procedure.'

* * *

He goes to see Peter before he phones Lily, needs a Christian perspective on all that has happened. Pops round to his bungalow in the early evening. Peter is supportive in his own way. Says they may pray on the matter but also wishes to talk about his own work. Says that his firm will be employing five new coders and they are to work from home, some will live many hours by car from Bournemouth. Anywhere in the country. He is pondering how best to supervise such remote staff.

Garth doesn't know anything about running a software company; Peter has never set foot in a residential school.

When Garth gets his turn, he explains to Peter how an argument arose before they reached the small island—members of the public involved—and that he intervened on behalf of the verbally abused Rihanna. His friend doesn't agree with Garth about the central issue. 'I think your scallywags started the brouhaha, Garth.' That's how Peter's sees it. Garth explains that Baxter's boys lark about only because they haven't learnt better. Their language was foul but directed at no one. The old people—particularly the husband of the woman wearing the large sunglasses—seemed to think Rihanna unfit for her work only because of her skin colour. 'Old people can be set in their ways, Garth. I think the whole ruckus ruined their day out.'

A Halo is not a Cooking Pot

When he talks about breaking up the fight, Peter looks a little shocked by the task. Offers no criticism of the role Garth played. 'The boy with the bloodied lip is sure to prove a fair witness,' he says. Then Garth says Rihanna will make a statement in his defence, and Peter is less fulsome. 'The girl didn't see much except your devotion to her.' Garth thinks his comment unfair. His devotion is to Lily, not Rihanna. It is through Lily's defence of her mixed-race children that he has learnt to abhor racism. Do it in practice, not simply in principle. All true acts of goodness must take place outside the ruminating mind. 'These boys are a long way from the path,' Peter concludes. 'It must be disheartening trying to put them straight. Lead them where they will not go.' Garth protests. Tries to speak of the progress Damian Taylor has made. Perhaps unwisely, he mentions the UPOs, the exams of limited utility which the boy will sit. Peter only raises his eyebrows. 'You have a good brain for IT, Garth. I could point you to the best courses.' Well-intended counsel which gives him the emptiest feeling. Is Garth really wasting his life trying to help the Baxter's boys?

Even while listening, Garth contemplates how divergent these parts of his life are. He and Peter share a view of scripture, an enthusiasm for the gospels that never dims. Lily, his unchristian girlfriend, is far more interested in his work than in any of that. She roots wholeheartedly for the wayward boys. Her sympathy with the middle finger they raise to the world is not a view he can entirely endorse but she is genuinely concerned, wants better for their unformed futures. He thinks he and she share a perception of what constitutes an act of goodness, although Lily remains a stranger to his church. Has never heard its teaching save the little he has explained. Peter is on board with the general belief—it features in Margery's sermons pretty much every Sunday—but he places little value on the act of helping Baxter's boys, while Lily—and Rihanna too—show an understanding that comes close to his without so much as a nod toward the Gospels.

As he is getting ready to leave, thanking Peter for his time—but not staying for prayer today—his friend raises the subject that is never far from Garth's mind. Lily Stephens. 'When is she finally coming to see us at church? Your girlfriend.'

He looks his friend squarely in the eye. 'I love her,' he states. 'I don't think I've budged her agnosticism an inch.'

'Oh dear, oh dear.'

Garth hears despair in the voice of Peter Carter. He fears that his suspension from work, defence of the richly swearing boys and love of a non-believer have made him its object. His head is swimming.

* * *

Back in his flat, Garth thinks of phoning Pastor Margery. Thinks she will see the injustice of the quayside racism. Wouldn't let age be an excuse. She might see the valour in his pulling apart of Declan Keane and Paul Frost. May understand that the prescribed process—the diktat that physical intervention must only occur when two staff can safely undertake it—fails to cover all bases. Leaves a nose open to pummelling for longer than any of Christ's children should endure.

In the event, it is Lily's number he dials. Margery is excellent at handling the tribulations of chapel life. Her skills in the wider world are largely unknown to him. She is hardly a cheerleader for his befriending of Lily. Peter left him feeling deflated, he could not stomach a second lukewarm supporter. He even finds himself mouthing words that Baxter's children might use. 'Suspension sucks.' Not church language although the boys at youth group have said similar now and then.

'This is a surprise, sunshine,' says Lily. He tells her all that has occurred, the suspension. Why. That it is unjust. 'Jesus, Garth, and you sound like the best one there...' His thoughts drift with her blasphemy but quickly it is forgotten, forgiven. She doesn't seem to notice these things. He gives her a full account of the day, tells her more about Rihanna than he has done in all the six weeks they have been a couple. Omits only her parting hug, and that was a sisterly thing. He and Rihanna have forged a bond of respect, not of love. 'At least I've taught you something,' is Lily's throwaway line on hearing about the quayside. His intervention with the racist.

'Yes, you have.' He has thought about it a great deal since Monday. All she has done in defence of Jo-jo and Ami. Garth is on the nursery slopes. 'Peter seemed to think it was different, because they were old and the youngsters had upset them by using the c-word.' He wonders how Lily's thoughts will match up against that of the puritanical church elder.

A Halo is not a Cooking Pot

'Fuck Peter,' she says.

Garth cannot help smiling. It is an unhelpful turn of phrase but her point is clear.

'You know you can come around if you want a hug. The kids are here, so I can't come to you, I'm sorry.'

Garth thanks her sincerely. Says he feels the hug figuratively but needs to study. He would like a hug, and he is frightened that, in his suspended state, he will be less restrained in the taking of such pleasure. To his very fingertips, he finds hugging Lily an enormous pleasure, like nothing that has gone before. He doesn't voice these many ancillary thoughts.

'What have you got to study, sweetie? asks his girlfriend.

'Galatians currently. I just try to go through everything methodically.'

Lily's tone again turn's serious, as it had when he first told her of his suspension. 'What does it say? Tell me the most important bit.'

'Am I now trying to win the approval of human beings, or of God? If I were still trying to please people, I would not be a servant of Christ. That's the key line for me, Lily. I grapple with this stuff a lot.'

'You do, sweetie. I know you do.'

Garth swallows hard. He has not felt this before but something is heaving within his chest. He fears crying. Thinks he might terminate the call. Lily should not hear his upset, not in the lee of the comfort she brings.

'Tell me, sweetie,' his girlfriend says soothingly, 'in your own words. Why is it that both can't be done? I want to understand.'

He doesn't think he can hold it together. He loves talking to this secular angel, adjudges that she cares for him more deeply than Peter Carter can manage. That man—the IT specialist—cares mostly for a right answer to a known question. Scripture plus logic plus nothing else whatsoever. He doesn't swim in life like Lily Stephens. His Lily. He would like to teach her about Jesus but suspects she understands life itself better than he does. Lives it more fully. 'I think it's about people always having the wrong motivation. Trying to please people will displease God because they want things for themselves. Not for His glory.'

'I don't get what that is, Garth. The His-glory stuff. People are mostly selfish but not always. When we finally want something that is genuinely decent—for the greater good—aren't we okay? Us and God on the same side?'

'If we haven't submitted to His will, how will we know? Sorry, Lily, I'm just saying how we see it in church. Not trying to argue with you.'

'I know that, sweetie. I even think it's more complicated for you. You can be a bit scared of the normal world. Not you personally, Garth, but the lot of you.'

'Ha...' His own laughter catches him by surprise. '...you've just fathomed Peter in one go. It's taken me years.'

'What do you mean?'

Garth doesn't reply for a moment, realises he has tears in his eyes. 'I've got to go,' he says. 'Speak soon.' He hears a plaintive 'Garth' as he presses the red, ends the conversation before he inadvertently cries in her presence. That is not how he wants her to see him, hear him. He will call Lily again when he is composed. Will do it again and again. She understands him better than he does himself.

* * *

Garth spends over an hour in prayer. His thoughts swirl. Images of Brownsea, the quayside. Were the old people more offended by how Rihanna dressed? Dark brown legs, bared shoulders, all visible to young and old alike. Past conversations with Peter turn over in his mind. The feeling of Lily's waist, her flesh, when his arms are around her. These thoughts compete in his mind as he tries to formulate his request to the Lord. Pray. He hears answers to some of his questions but His voice is faint, the meaning of His replies obscure.

Throughout his meditation his hands are atop his Bible. He turns quickly to Galatians, reads a little, smiles at its truth. Studying, querying and interpreting may be beyond him tonight. The words alone are uplifting: "*So again I ask, does God give you His Spirit and work miracles among you by the works of the law, or by your believing what you heard?*" He, Garth Addicks, knows that he believes like Abraham before him. Believes as Paul instructs. He believes without reservation. Jesus is his saviour. His girlfriend's interest in his subject of study gives him raised hope for their future together. That he can lead her to the centre of the chosen flock.

After closing the Holy Book, he picks up his phone. He has received a text.

I'm with you, Garth. Love Lily

Words he will treasure all night long.

Thursday, 21 July 2016

He has a key to the church and takes himself there at seven-thirty in the morning. He had already told Margery he would start painting on this day and did not bring it forward despite the additional free day his suspension from work granted him. He used Wednesday for further Bible study. Spoke only to Lily, did so by telephone, and briefly to his mother, who called him to enquire if he and Lily wish to eat with them again. They arranged no date. He hasn't told Lily of this invite, another meal with the Addicks. It might be hard for her to stomach. He has yet to share his working hiatus, his suspension, the insecurity this is causing him, with Pastor Margery. He didn't trouble his mother with it either. Prayer and the Bible should see him through. That's as he thought in his meditations yesterday. Mr Lorimer should exonerate him. When Garth goes through the facts of the case—and they are never far from his mind—he thinks it the most likely outcome.

When he spoke to Lily last night, she said it more comprehensively than he has let himself think. 'They've no choice, Garth. You've done nothing wrong.'

He enters the church and heads straight for the small utility area by the toilets. The paint is stored there, a wooden stepladder too. Their church is big, would hold three hundred if such a throng was to come and celebrate with them. This could be a long job. It is a modern building. Low ceilinged. Nothing Anglican about The Church of the Men of Judea. He enjoys this type of chore, the opportunity to serve. Makes himself a cup of tea to drink while he works. An early start was always his plan. He expects Pastor Margery will call in during the morning, wants her to see the project taking shape.

Before he begins, Garth goes around the room. Takes down a notice board and several religious-themed pictures. He uses a screwdriver to remove the more firmly secured items. A dampened towel to pull away the dust. Then he starts to paint, puts his brush into the back corner, goes around the frame of the entrance door. The walls are yellowed although it has never been their deliberate colour. This task has lain undone for too long, the magnolia he brushes onto the wall lightens the appearance. Stroke after stroke brightening their hall of spiritual communion.

After an hour or more he recognises how much he is enjoying the task. The fresh and new replacing the old and tired, it is invigorating to behold. Garth sings a few lines of a modern hymn. Enjoying the acoustics of the empty hall, the faintest echo sounding as if the sound might be professionally produced.

Dance, dance, wherever you may be

His voice is true. When the rear wall is completed, he climbs the stepladder to put brush to side wall for the first time this morning. Does it while singing away. Loudly telling all of Northbourne about dancing on a morning when the sky turned black.

It's hard to dance with the devil on your back

To his astonishment he hears his choir sing the line back to him, then they burst into giggles. Garth almost drops his brush.

The girl—Julie Rivington—jogs to the bottom of his steps. She wears white dungarees. Old ones a little blue paint splashed on them already. Not from this job; previously worn for painting, plain as day. 'Hi Garth,' she says. Samantha Smith and the third girl in his tiny choir—the one who's name keeps bubbling away from him—come to her side. These two wear shorts and T-shirts.

'Shouldn't you girls be in school?' he asks from his ladder.

'Holidays,' says the one whose name has yet to register itself with his brain.

'Pastor Margery said you needed help. We're good painters,' says Julie.

Margery never told him but it makes good sense. A collective effort saves time and can be more easily celebrated in church. Theirs is a community of common cause or it is nothing. 'Julie, Samantha, you need brushes, and...' Garth coughs, hopes that this covers up his failure to name the third girl.

'It's Donna, sir,' she tells him. Shows no concern that he cannot name her. Simply helping him over the pause.

'Garth,' he says. 'Schools out and I've never been your teacher.

A Halo is not a Cooking Pot

Please call me Garth.'

The girl, Donna—Donna Wilson as the dormant part of his brain quickly recalls—goes red across her cheeks. 'Garth,' she says, as if it were an instruction and she a reciting infant.

'You'll get paint on your clothes.'

'No, they're old,' says Samantha.

'Julie has dressed wisely,' he says.

'I've a tan,' says Julie. 'I'm not painting over that.' All three girls giggle at her declaration.

They come up with a plan. The girls will go around the lower parts of the hall and Garth will do all the ladder work. Donna Wilson tries to protest, says that he will have too much to do.

'Let's see,' says Garth. 'There is only one stepladder.'

As the painting becomes serious, all four focus themselves well on the task; Garth tries to lighten the mood, surf the spirit of endeavour. He leads the singing of 'When I Survey the Wondrous Cross,' a hymn they have planned for the weekend's service. The girls join in but after a verse the impertinent Julie moves it into the pop song—In the Mood for Magic—which they learnt a month back. Probably known by the teenage girls for a lot longer. It would be churlish to redirect them to his beloved hymn, Garth can see that. He does not own his volunteer painters, his youthful backing singers.

It is a rather cynical song, thinks Garth now that Peter's interpretation has flittered away.

> *If you're in the mood for magic*
> *Magic's what you're gonna see*
> *If your mother loves your father*
> *You're in a minority*

The boys at Baxter's must relate to it easily. He hears no cynicism in Julie Rivington's sweet voice. Hopes Mr and Mrs Rivington have not disappointed her. Garth has met them; they've visited church with their daughter. Not regular attendees. His own, Penelope and Wilfred are inseparable but, in Garth's view, it is resignation and not love which holds their marriage together. From the top of his stepladder, Garth tries to join in, finds he has already forgotten the words he sang those short weeks ago.

Some men search for supermodels
Be it cars or be it girls
I'm looking for a fishwife with a heart of gold
Who's gonna love me all around the world

He had imagined Lily hearing him sing these words with the girls last month. She might have liked how Peter linked them to Christian thought. One evening in Boscombe, he told Lily that she looked like a supermodel. She hooted with laughter at that, granted him that she is thin. Said she shared no other similarities with that strange breed. Now, three happy girls are rolling the tune around the empty church. It sounds good. There is something worthy in that, the joy of singing, whether the girls are thinking of Peter Carter's analysis or the pop video. Their harmonic voices are joyful and endearing. Perhaps his own analysis has too often been the cynical one.

You were in the mood for magic
You got illusion you got sleight of hand
Sadness and happiness are two sides of a coin
When you flip it up it doesn't even land
It never lands

It is complicated to contemplate. Garth decides the Bible is simpler than pop music. Then he hears Julie say, 'Hiya.' Turns around on his ladder to see who the visitor is. Ronnie Clarke has entered the church.

'Are you here to help?' asks Garth.

'Nuh. To talk to Julie.'

He lets them carry on. Teenagers like to talk, not that Garth can get more than three words out of young Ronnie most times they've spoken. All help with the painting is a bonus. He knows better than to be overly demanding of his young assistants. These kids are a million times easier to work with than the ever-swearing Baxter's boys. The newly arrived lad is the son of the solicitor who Lily feels uncharitable towards. And for good reason from what she has told Garth. No action came from their conversation a while back; Lily concluded that Cindy could endure her husband in ignorance. She did not wish any unforeseen repercussion to jeopardise her work, her principal source of income. Simon Clarke's enforced absence from work—awaiting the healing of a broken collar bone—has prompted

A Halo is not a Cooking Pot

him to repent and retract, although Lily disputed Garth's use of the term repent. 'He'll phone another woman same as me, once he's stopped feeling sorry for himself,' she predicted. Garth wonders if her worldliness is correct; Simon Clarke is not a Christian so she probably knows best. Garth queried more than once if Lily wanted him to speak to the wife, his fellow congregant. 'Don't fall out with this Cindy woman on my part, Garth. She's done nothing to me.'

Now he sees Ronnie, their young son, placing hands on pretty young Julie, nothing truly untoward. A little proprietorial. An arm across her shoulders. The girl seems happy enough that he does it. Laughs with him, enjoys posing as if older than her fourteen years.

The two head towards the kitchen, and Garth shouts, 'Get yourself a brush.' The boy answers back that he is to play football shortly. Can't stay.

They are alone for no more than three or four minutes before Julie comes back into the hall alone. She has unclasped the top of her overalls. The front flap hangs loosely down below her waist. She wears a bright yellow vest, her shoulders are bronzed and she reveals a narrow strip of her tanned and skinny stomach.

'Make us tea before you paint, please Julie,' he shouts from his portable steps.

'Okeydokey.'

While she is in the kitchen the other two girls come to Garth and ask about the painting they have done so far. Thick enough, thin enough, does he think the paint is running?

'Great work, girls. Transformational, look how bright the church is now. Just keep it up. 'I think...' He is feeling preoccupied; the conversation with Lily about Ronnie's father still playing over in his mind. '...is Julie dating that boy?' A deputy youth leader needs to be aware of these things.

Donna giggles. 'They're going out. Yeah.'

'I need a word with her.'

Garth enters the kitchen. Julie Rivington is sitting on the worktop waiting for the kettle to boil. She starts to squidge her bottom forward but he indicates she should stay where she is. He leans against the worktop two paces to her left. 'Ronnie is your boyfriend then?'

'Oh Ga-arth,' she says, elongating the sound of his name.

He expects that she is already recalling the discussion at youth group two Fridays back. The Church of the Men of Judea is not so foolish as to discourage boy-girl relationships but there are boundaries that church elders and youth group leaders try to set.

'Is he your age, Julie?'

'Younger.'

Garth gives her a questioning look.

'Four months.'

'Does your mum know you're seeing him?'

'Yeah.'

'And Cindy? Ronnie's mum.'

'We're pals, me and Cindy.'

'I'm pleased to hear that, Julie. Has she counselled you about your relationship?'

The girl laughs nervously. 'Not yet.'

As Garth dwells upon it, he knows Cindy—upright congregant that she is—might be too biased to be objective, too pleased that her unexceptional son has secured the affection of so strikingly pretty a girl. Their liaison is a precocious thing. Years of school ahead for both. 'We've talked about dos and don'ts, Julie. Do you recall that?'

'Yes, Garth, and I don't.'

'I'm sure you don't but I don't really know young Ronnie, does he...' He makes an open-handed gesture, wants Julie to feel able to tell him anything. A good deputy youth group leader is a protector.

'We kiss but no tongues. You said that was all right.'

Garth is surprised by her forthrightness. He has talked more to the boys than to the girls about relationships. They seldom admit to a second's bodily contact. He is sure it happens, knows full well how embarrassing it is to talk about. His role is mostly to remind them that they must do nothing that the girl does not wish to participate in, nor anything involving the parts of the body which polite society prescribes hidden from view. And the sticking out of tongues is impertinent. 'And your feelings for him are not too intense, Julie? You won't let yourself down, will you?'

'Ga-arth.' Again she elongates his name. Crosses and uncrosses her legs repeatedly while they talk.

'I ask because your association began in church, Julie. I think we are collectively responsible, and your well-being is important to us.'

'Thank you,' she says, and Garth notices the girl go to scratch an itch on her thigh. At first, she is rubbing through the fabric of her overalls, the white dungarees she currently wears as loose-fitting trousers, the bib hanging down. Then she says, 'Excuse me,' and slides off the kitchen side. Turns her back to him; puts a hand inside her clothing. As she is doing this, he sees her shoulders move a little involuntarily. She is crying, he is certain of it.

'What is it, Julie?' he says, suddenly alarmed. Fearing something in his counsel has prompted this distress. 'What has Ronnie done to you?'

She turns around, pushing her overalls down a little and he sees her white knickers, a red patch on her bronzed thigh below them. 'My tan's peeling,' she says, inconsolable in the face of this catastrophe.

Friday, 22 July 2016

Garth spends the evening at Lily's, his last opportunity to see the children before their two-week break with Trent. The youth group has broken up for summer.

She finds the tale hilarious. 'Garth, I should be giving those girls the sex education lesson, not you! I'm way more tuned in than you are. And there'll be no groupies for you when you paint my place.'

'You'd be quite good at it but I'm not sure you'd be quite on message,' he says.

'The message that they must deny all knowledge of sex, however much they really know. That one? It doesn't work, sunshine.'

'Just how to keep safe,' argues Garth. 'Physically and spiritually.'

'I knew what I was doing. Twenty-seven when I became pregnant with Jo-jo and I even had fun beforehand.'

He struggles to respond to this. At work he sits in on Health Education classes; the boys pay more attention when learning how to avoid catching a venereal disease than they ever do in maths or English. The school doesn't simply implore abstinence although that is the core of the church's approach. 'When will we have fun?' he asks, and then looks away as Lily gives him a strange look. Garth is the killjoy.

Boscombe

* * *

The children are in their pyjamas for the evening meal. In homage to the first day which he and Lily spent together, Garth has been to the high street, fetched a Chinese takeaway they will share. One or two carefully chosen items that Jo-jo and Ami should enjoy.

Lily has told him that it's important the children feel positive about their Boscombe home while they are with their father: there must be no arguing tonight. She texted Trent news of her boyfriend two weeks ago. When Garth asked what detail it included, she replied, 'Not a shred.' As he collected the food, he thought he was stupid to even tell the anecdote about Julie crying during painting morning. He thinks of himself as a shepherd to the young people at church, those in his Friday evening group. Lily, on the other hand, talks of repressed priests abusing boys, and she says all youngsters have sex on their minds anyway. Thinks it important they try stuff in a safe world with other youngsters. No old creeps. And above all they must know how not to get pregnant. In fairness to her, it is only what they say at Baxter's, give or take a phrase. But Lily doesn't understand that Julie Rivington—pretty little thing that she is—remains a child on any imaginable scale. She only showed Garth her inner thigh because she was distraught about the peeling skin. The innocent young girl had no connected sexual thoughts, he is sure of it. And his own are only of Lily, thoughts he cannot share for fear of how easily she would tempt him with that in her quiver.

Lily serves the food into bowls; they sit around the lounge rather than at the kitchen table. Jo-jo is in his element. Garth tries to stop him from eating a piece of chilli but the boy puts it in his mouth hurriedly. Garth quickly pours him a glass of water. 'No problem, mate,' says Jo-jo, showing Garth his empty mouth. Unaffected by the piquancy of the unlikely fruit; his mother looks on astonished.

After they've eaten, laying sprawled across the chairs and sofa, satisfied, little Ami climbs onto Garth's knee. It reminds him of an old cat back in the farmhouse in Sixpenny Handley. Garth keeps this observation to himself. The child is precious to him too, and he guesses her mother would dislike the feline comparison. Within minutes he notes that Ami is sleeping, and once it is clear how deeply she has slipped into it, Lily rises from the sofa, takes Ami off him to carry away to her bed. 'You've got the knack,' she whispers.

* * *

'It must be nice to have a break,' says Garth, when both children are down the hallway. In bed. 'Two weeks to yourself.'

Lily shakes her head. 'I get lonely as hell. These two children are my life, and our lives are down here now, not in Shoreditch. Not really. I don't even like thinking about them up there. It's not their home either. Trent's good, I suppose, it's just that I can't bear being apart from them.'

'I'm sorry, I can see what they mean to you. I should have thought before speaking. What will you do?'

'Fitness on the beach with Caroline. No running me down this time, matey. I'll be fit in a fortnight. She says so, and she's got a gym.'

'Really? That's the plan?'

'It should keep my mind off them. And Joey will be impressed if I can get my tummy as flat and hard as Caz's.'

'I can...' Garth hesitates, wonders if he might say this all wrong but ploughs on. '...come around a bit. Keep your mind off them.'

'Come anytime, Garth. I actually like having them on my mind. They're all I have. And I know you won't stay over. It would break the rules I broke when I was your little painter's age.'

'Lily...' There must be no argument is his most prominent thought. '...we've a lifetime. Things to work out. You know I want to, and you know I can't. I'm conflicted...'

'...which must be how God likes it,' Lily finishes for him. Garth nods although his planned phrase was going to state that he would figure a way in time. They have talked about it once or twice. About consummation. Quiet conversations, nothing that her children must overhear. 'You know I'm not on the pill or anything,' Lily told him. Garth's concerns were predominantly of marriage; how they stood in the eyes of the Almighty. The hell that awaits the fornicator.

In the silence following Lily's disparaging of God's teasing plan, it comes to Garth that he should go down on single knee. Propose the marriage he has already suggested in the most off-hand way. He fears she would laugh, scream or just say no. And anything less than a heartfelt yes would be unbearable. To date, her reluctance to come near The Church of the Men of Judea is an insurmountable impediment. That a married couple should share a common religion is a certainty in Garth's mind, even though Cindy Clarke gets away with it. He is not at all certain that it works for Cindy, suspects it doesn't. Some marriages are just a dirty compromise. He could not bear for that to be his. The real conundrum is what Garth thinks of Lily. She has no declared faith; blasphemes without noticing she has done so; cannot talk about church without going into a diatribe about paedophile priests. She may have given herself to more men than Garth would wish to hear accounted for by a defined number, and yet he knows her to be entirely saintly. There is a goodness within Lily that might be gentle when she plays with or tends to Ami but might be a rapier when she is righting the wrongs of the world. He recalls how—when he relayed it to her by telephone—Lily disallowed him any glory in his defence of his colleague, Rihanna, from a racist verbal assault on the quayside at Poole. His actions were a duty in her wise book; he was a fool to be so pleased with himself. Saint Paul, in the letter to the Galatians, has told Garth the same. Lily got there instinctively. She understands what is good without Bible or Messiah. He, and most in his church, dream of the days of the first century, when the Holy Spirit was palpable among men of faith. He has come to suspect that Lily's unspoken creed pre-dates even that glorious time. He has gleaned from her that she has led a life of mixed morality. Fornication and shoplifting both pepper her past. He thinks she has done this without feeling undue guilt precisely because the source of her instinctive behaviour, her connatural guidance, pre-dates the fall.

Sunday, 24 July 2016

Garth is again sitting on a garden chair beside Peter Carter in the middle of the pristine lawn to the rear of his smart bungalow. They are beneath a parasol, the heat of the sun quite intense. Peach juice on ice in a glass beside each, his friend has diced small cubes of watermelon into the concoction. It is extraordinary fare. 'Do you ever think about Marie?' he asks, and the question draws Garth up sharply.

'Of course, Peter. We never forget, do we?'

'I hardly knew her,' states Peter. 'I believe you were already together when I joined the church. An item, as I have heard it termed.'

A Halo is not a Cooking Pot

'Oh, I doubt that, Peter,' says Garth. 'We dated very few times...'

'Really? It is confusing, do you not think? Your feelings for a girl in this life and for our Lord. For the wider certainty of heaven beyond. They compete, I can imagine?'

'It is hard to recall my feelings for Marie.' Marie was a congregant of a similar age to Garth. They went out together only briefly, minimal compatibility despite their shared faith. 'It quickly became evident that she wished to be dependent upon me. Or if not wished it, could not help herself from becoming so.'

Peter chuckles quietly. 'Is that not how a husband and wife must be, Garth? I suspect your Lily cannot subjugate herself to your dominion. That might be a bigger stumbling block...'

'Peter...' Garth interrupts him mid-flow, feels a sting in the implication of his words. '...I am not seeking to subjugate her to my...' Garth stops talking briefly. Thinks about his words. '...whatever it is you call it. To the Lords greater guidance, yes, perhaps...' He hesitates again, before completing his thought. '...no, not perhaps. I would like that very much and it is an enormous, possibly an unimaginable leap, for Lily. But I think she will be in church very soon. She will try it. I have extracted half a promise.'

They sit in silence. Garth may have played his trump card, his prediction of her impending dunking of a toe into the waters of The Church of the Men of Judea. Thrown it down far too early, the half-promise is weeks old. Uncashed. 'You've not heard from Marie?' Peter resumes after those reflective moments. His line of enquiry bewilders Garth.

'Five years, Peter. It's five years since she and I went on dates such as they were. I must tell you...' Garth leans forward in his garden chair, takes a sip from the peach juice, a little melon piece within the tumbler lands on his trousers. He brushes it onto the well-kept lawn, hopes this is not disrespectful of his host's hospitality. '...with Lily, I talk freely. We expose each other to personal thoughts, ideas and emotions without judging one and other. Marie was a strange girl. Same age as me, same church, but she was only concerned with how to get closer to the Lord. I believe she shunned His gift of free will.' Peter is again silent, and Garth wonders if he has articulated this correctly. His evenings with Marie were unexciting Bible-quoting affairs. He never learnt what she looked like below the collar line. If it was an affair of the mind, it was without fantasy of anything further. Not that Garth will share with Peter its limited dimensions.

'And Lily is not leading you in a contrary direction? She does not appear very interested in coming to know the Lord.'

'She will be coming to church!' he says more loudly than required. Peter holds his eye. Garth feels he has said something wrong, irreligious, cannot work out what Peter is seeking to elicit. 'She's not quite ready. Her life is more complicated than ours. She has children but she will come. You'll see.' He knows he is arguing like a child.

Peter responds in a slow, measured tone. 'Garth, affairs of the heart can be disturbing. Long ago Elspeth Dunn advised me that Marie—the girl you dated, however briefly—was a member of our congregation from childhood until the two of you broke up. It might be that she had some feelings for you long before you declared a formality to the relationship. These allegiances of love play with young lives, limit where the heartbroken can go. Poor Marie no longer attends church. You are a good man but something in her was lost when you and she could no longer maintain...'

'I didn't drive her away from church, Peter. She simply didn't want to see me...'

'These allegiances, Garth, they may wreak havoc in a young life.'

He shakes his head, disagrees completely. 'No, no, Peter. She did not lose her faith at all. I'm not in touch with her, pretty certain she still lives in Wallisdown. She started attending the Church of England, the one they have in Wallisdown. That was the last I heard.'

'Oh, that is a loss of faith, Garth—not in her own mind perhaps—a diminution surely. The spirit moves more slowly, drifts aimlessly, among the sparsely populated pews of that exhausted denomination. Let us not argue...'

'Next Sunday, Peter, you will meet Lily next Sunday, I know you will, and I think you will see what I see...' They both nod; it might be a fair point he is making. '...if you can open your eyes.' Garth looks away, hopes he has said all he needs to on the matter. Drinks noisily on his peach juice.

Tuesday, 26 July 2016

Garth stands on the kerbside, the handlebars of his bicycle in his hands, as Lily emerges from the offices of Capaldi-Clarke. She smiles, and he feels relief in it. Garth has been a little confused by her reluctance to see him until tonight.

'I thought we were on for eight o'clock,' she says.

'Couldn't wait until then.' The street is becoming busy, offices and shops, comings and goings. 'I love you,' he adds quietly.

'Sweet,' she replies. 'Are you equipped for the beach routine then?'

Garth is unsure what this entails, thinks briefly of their raunchy swim earlier in the summer. He has been on Boscombe beach since with Lily and her children but the conduct then was far less compromising. The presence of youngsters keeping life simple. 'We can go to the beach if you like.'

'Not like,' says Lily cryptically. 'It's not about like.'

'What's the plan?'

'I thought I told you, I'm Caroline's project now. She's pretty much a fitness instructor. And you, Mister Garth, don't get to see me sweat that much unless you join in.'

He suspects this surprise visit may not be the spontaneous joy he hoped for. They had a later meeting time planned but Garth felt restless. Picking up and putting down a crime thriller. The Acts of the Apostles, his planned reading matter, proved overstimulating. Thoughts of Declan Keane, Damian Taylor and, of course, Lily Stephens pinging round in his mind. Gate-crashing Bible study. He has not come here prepared to work out on the beach. And he knows that her friend, Caroline, runs between Boscombe and Christchurch quicker than he can connect the places by bus. He suspects Lily might put him to shame although she decries her own fitness. Occasionally blames him for nobbling her when last she began to do something about it. 'I've not got the right clothing with me.'

'No worries sunshine. You're in shorts and I've got you a change of T-shirt for later.'

'I can't wear yours. You're way slimmer than I am.'

'What's so funny?' asks a man with an arm in a sling, who has emerged from the same door Lily came out of. Capaldi-Clarke's.

Lily is openly laughing at Garth's befuddlement. She wears smart clothes: a black skirt, tights and a white blouse; in contrast, Garth has cycled in torn-off jeans—not proper shorts but a thing he has self-constructed from a longer pair—and a checked shirt, frayed at the collar. Sweat is already upon it from his ride here. Garth has no idea who the man is. The friendly tone tells him only that he is familiar with Lily. 'I'm not wearing her clothes,' he states, hoping to sustain the humour Lily is enjoying.

'Is he bothering you?' the suited man asks Lily.

'She thinks her clothes will fit me,' says Garth.

This makes Lily laugh more, a mildly hysterical laugh but Garth can see that the conversation is a bit funny. Unexpected. 'My boyfriend must wear my clothes. It's the only thing I insist upon.' With that she takes Garth's arm and walks away.

He goes willingly, pushing his bicycle carefully with his free hand, up the crowded pavement. 'I don't get it,' he says when the man is out of earshot.

'That arsehole probably thinks he's missing out on the dirtiest of all possible fun.'

'It was him?'

She confirms it: 'Simon Clarke.'

Garth wonders why he didn't guess. What possessed him to try and joke with a colleague of Lily's who he has never met before. And work is not a comfortable environment for her, she has made that very clear. It is formal, only ever an act for her. 'And I'm not wearing your clothes.'

'Got that, loud and clear, sunshine.'

* * *

Garth enters the maisonette with his girlfriend. It feels daring to be there without her children at home. It reminds him of the day they met, several weeks back, the last time he was in her home while Jo-jo and Ami were in London. At that time his thoughts were of putting right the wrong of Lily's injury. True to recall, she was only lightly clad and his eyes saw more of her than he ever expected to see of a woman at close quarters. A woman to whom he had spoken no marriage vows. It made him giddy with the certainty that the feast for his eyes was part of God's wider plan. His thoughts ran more conservatively then,

A Halo is not a Cooking Pot

trying to understand how the unfortunate accident would unfold in his and Lily's lives. Now he is a boyfriend, one of longstanding in this throwaway society. He hopes to be a welcome presence in her home. Feels excitement in the sharing of it if only for short periods while worrying that this free-and-easy lady might overtempt him. He is a Christian or he is nothing.

'Do you want to stay in here while I get ready for Caz?' she asks.

'Do you think I should come back when you're done?'

'We're a team, Garth, in this together. And I've a change of T-shirt for you, you'll be okay after.'

He feels a degree of trepidation. He may be an embarrassment. He cycles, has never ventured near a gym. And Lily's talk of having clothing for him is strange. It is more than a month since she washed some of his clothes in her machine; he is sure he wore them all later the same day. Left none in her maisonette. She goes into her bedroom but leaves the door open, shouts a conversation to him as she is changing her clothes. Margery's story of Mahatma Gandhi comes to his mind, he tries his best to push it away. Stays resolutely in the lounge while thinking about how she must look disrobed. 'I got a text from Rihanna, the girl at Baxter's,' he calls through the open doors. 'She thinks I should join the union. They'll take up my case retrospectively. Defend me in the disciplinary.'

'Great idea, Garth. Do it.'

'We don't really believe in it though, Lily. The Lord protects us.'

She stomps into the lounge, communicates in her walk exactly how she feels. She wears the black shorts he has seen before, above them only a white bra pinning back her breasts, a black T-shirt in her right hand still to go over her head, cover her up. He can see as much of her flesh as he ever has. White, muscle visible across her abdomen. He's no idea what her heavy footsteps portend. 'For fuck's sake, Garth. Fight for your job, fight for it in this world. Rewards in heaven are a bloody long time coming.'

'But you said I did nothing wrong. Why would I trouble the union? And they might get the managers' backs up. Unions can be very, very strident.'

For the third time in this short visit, Lily is laughing with minimal control. 'Strident! And you're not strident?'

Boscombe

He thinks he can see what she's driving at but then loses it in his bewilderment, his barely concealed wish to gaze upon the flesh of his girlfriend, Lily, whom the Lord has been kind enough to put before him. She says it because she cares but it isn't quite rational. This world is the temporary one, the hereafter of far greater importance. She will see it when she comes to church, hears and accepts the Word of our Lord.

* * *

The three of them run to the beach. Garth feels like he's been tricked into the foreign legion. Caroline is a militant, a sergeant major and then some. The pace exhausts him in no time. He is astonished that his girlfriend is so quick, her stride so confident. He wonders why he—Lily's junior by more than he likes to think about—is the one with a reddened face, a ponderous step. She is bouncing, a little breathier than the young girl but Caroline does this for a job. It is Lily whom he considers amazing. Whose hips he watches go up and down with each stride.

'Cover stretches,' shouts the gang leader. Lily knows what this means. Drops her bottom to the sand and stretches a long leg out before her. He tries to copy, does it with uncertainty. Curling one leg behind himself might look stupid although both girls can pull it off. Caroline has put her forehead onto her left knee as it lays outstretched in front of her on the sand. From this position, she sits back, does it repeatedly. To his side Lily finds it harder, her hair falls across the knee while her forehead is some three inches short.

'Calf all right?' asks the instructor. As Lily breezes a 'yeah-yeah' in reply, Garth wonders if it is a dig at him. The man whose bike did the damage all those weeks ago. 'Right knee,' shouts Caroline. She has instantly swung the other leg out in front of her, tucked the left back in. Lily likewise. He sees that both can touch their forehead upon the straightened knee as they intend. Looks straightforward but it is not. 'Hopeless Garth,' comments the instructor. He turns her way but doesn't hold the eye contact. Caroline can't be touting for business, even Garth knows that insulting punters is a serious mistake in fitness circles.

Another girl has come to sit beside Lily, her eyes are set on their blond instructor. 'Is it for free?' she asks.

A Halo is not a Cooking Pot

'Enjoy,' says Caroline.

They start to do a curious press up in the sand, side on, left hand only, presumably until they change over. Garth tries it, cannot hold the posture for five seconds. The girls all manage twice that. Caroline could do it forever.

The new girl is good at the push ups and leg stretches. She sports a tan as rich as their facilitator, wears only the tiniest all-white bikini. Dressed in not very much at all, string and three tiny swatches of cloth. Garth collapses on the sand and makes a point of looking only at Lily. She is his girlfriend, and he decides that any desire with which he looks upon her is through the prism of slow-burning expectation. He wants her when the time is right. When Pastor Margery has conducted a ceremony of marriage. And it's not so much to ask now he's come frolicking on the sand for her.

* * *

The sun is dipping, mellowing into that deeper orange, setting somewhere beyond Poole. The three now seated on the sand feel a chill as shadow engulfs them. Noticing her goosebumps, Garth puts an arm around Lily's shoulders. She nuzzles into him briefly then shrugs him off. An affectionate gesture, he suspects she does not want to be canoodling in front of Caroline. The younger girl— perspiring mildly, a damp patch in the centre of her purple-coloured top—looks serene. Exercise on the beach is her religion.

The interloper has gone. When the erstwhile instructor asked her what her name was, she replied, 'Doesn't matter.' Caroline now observes this to have been a strange reply indeed.

'She was shy like me,' says Garth.

'About right,' says Lily. 'You really are.'

'I was too.' They both look surprised that a perfect specimen like Caroline Yorke should have ever suffered this affliction. Garth can't really believe it, nor is he going to argue with her.

'Hey,' says Lily, 'what's the daftest thing you've ever done? Most embarrassing, that area.'

Garth leans forward and holds his bare toes. He is not keen to answer. At thirty he remains shy.

'When I was fifteen,' Caroline begins, 'in fact it started before that, when I was thirteen or so...' She pauses, as if it might be too mortifying to share. '...I was a right one for those pizza restaurants. Not so much the mains—my parents liked to tuck into them—I went for the ice cream fountain. I would go up and down from the table, bowl after bowl. Daddy—my crazy Daddy—bought me an ice cream fountain for my fifteenth birthday. Girlfriends would come around. I was the toast of Christchurch. Then I started to wink at boys, you know what I mean, Lily. That was when I realised that I was eating too much of the sweet stuff. It all came to a head when I invited a boy from school to supper. It was only a few months after Daddy had bought it but my view of the contraption had changed. Mummy rigged up the ice cream fountain, the boy said, "No thanks," and I ran upstairs crying. Shouting at my parents that I hated the thing. Hated them for buying it.'

Lily laughs. 'The lad wasn't rejecting you, Caz, he just didn't like ice cream.'

'I was a bit fat back then. I really think I was. It was a dig at me, Lily. I gave up ice cream altogether on the back of that.'

The three look over each other without speaking for a moment. 'I bet they cost a bit,' says Garth. 'Ice cream fountains.'

Caroline ignores his comment and the three of them sit hugging their knees on the sand, the younger girl says, 'Garth?' He hunches his head over his knees. 'What was your most embarrassing thing?'

When he continues to avoid eye contact, Lily says, 'Come on, Garth, just give us one of your top ten.' He raises his eyes to meet hers, and she adds, 'And not one with me in it.'

'I'm too easily caught off guard, embarrassed,' he says, hesitating before he finally goes on. 'A year or two back I was out of milk so I put some ready-made custard—from a carton I had open in the fridge—into my tea instead. It just floated, awful globules. It looked rank. Tasted even worse.'

For a moment neither girl says anything. Then Lily turns herself his way. 'Who were you sharing tea with, Garth, the Queen?'

'No.'

'Who then?'

'I was alone.'

Now both girls splutter hysterically. 'You should have kept quiet, Garth,' says Lily. 'It didn't embarrass you once until today. Not until you opened your big mouth.'

The boy doesn't argue, sees that his tale is ridiculous to these girls but also thinks they are wrong. We are never alone. What we do is known, understood, and appraised by the Almighty. God may have chuckled a little at his misuse of custard, may even rib Garth about it come the fateful day. He's not anticipating any problems in the main exam. The judgement.

Again, they all hug their knees against the evening breeze. Caroline runs sand through her fingers. 'You're go,' she says to Lily. 'You wanted to hear what we had.'

'Mine was more along the lines of shagging a lad on Whitstable quay and getting caught at it by his mum. Not a story for the tender ears of you two sweety-pies.'

Caroline rolls over on to Lily, straddles her stomach and places a hand over her mouth. 'Not in front of Garth!' she admonishes and both girls begin to giggle uncontrollably. The boy tries to laugh along while finding himself puzzled about his wayward girlfriend. Has she made this up? He hopes so. Perhaps she really was like a Baxter's boy all those years ago in Sittingbourne. A Christian girlfriend would be an easier thing for him to comprehend; it was not to be and the Lord has chosen to open up his—Garth Addicks'—eyes by setting this exceptional lady before him. He feels he is getting a comprehensive understanding of Paul's message, his missives which implore the inclusion of the Gentiles, the uncircumcised. He loves a non-believer and thinks he is uncovering a more intense meaning to his life in the doing of it. It can be heavy going.

* * *

'Put vinegar on it, olive oil.'

Garth is a plain lettuce man. His mother buys salad cream but he never uses it. 'The salad will be better dressed than you girls on the beach,' he says.

'Not me or Caz, sunshine,' says Lily. 'You must have been watching the girl in the thong.'

'It wasn't that bad,' he protests, 'and I wasn't.' He feels a bit ambushed on this; she insisted he should accompany her to the beach, of course there is flesh on display, it's high summer. 'I only have eyes for you.'

Boscombe

'Sweet.'

'And this is great,' Garth interjects, pinching the red and white hooped T-shirt he is wearing. 'You shouldn't have.'

'You say that now. Really, you were petrified that you'd have to wear one of mine. Cross-dressing is old hat. Clothes are just to cover your bits up anyway.'

'Don't buy me anything else. We're neither of us rich.'

When Lily passed Garth this brand-new garment to wear, after he had showered on returning from the beach, once again sweaty and smelly from the exercise which the two girls squeezed out of him, she said, 'I was going to wrap it up for your birthday but this is way too early. I'll find something better.' He did not reply any more than a mumbled, thank you. Felt surprised that Lily was planning their relationship that far ahead. It is six weeks before he turns thirty-one, nearly as long as they have known each other. He thinks it is another token of the love she speaks only through symbols, and one deeply appreciated text. The one she sent him on the day of his suspension.

She places the plates of food on the small dining table. 'Better than chips,' she states. The initial plan was another takeaway but Lily has explained to him that she is trying to eat carefully this fortnight. 'Caroline's been a lifesaver,' she says. 'Exercises, meal planning.'

'I'm quite partial to chips,' he tries to quip.

'But if we're not going to marry for a hundred years, until you've finally converted me to the Men of Judea, do you want a fat old fishwife, or still-slim Lily?'

He thinks to answer, chips, to keep going for funny. Doesn't because her casual reference to marriage throws him. The hundred-year wait is almost a lifeline. 'Come to church on Sunday. I think you'll get something from it.'

She places a small piece of chicken in her mouth, chews it carefully. 'Definitely maybe but probably not.'

* * *

Garth is confusing himself by how amorous he has become on the sofa. He thinks Lily has looked like a film star all evening. On the beach, in shorts and T-shirt, he realised how much fitter than he, she is. He couldn't hack Caroline's military routines, he knows he must jog and cycle more, go faster. Practise weights if he can find something

A Halo is not a Cooking Pot

heavy in his flat to lift. He needs to match her, mustn't be a weakling with so strong and energetic a girlfriend.

Before they left the beach, Caroline insisted on feeling Lily's tummy. 'Coming on well, sweetie,' she said. He wondered if it should have been him touching Lily in so intimate a place. The cheeky upstart then put a hand on his stomach. 'Work to be done here, boy.' She was smiling, good-humoured but he never invited her to paw him. Nor to broadcast the flabbiness she felt. Decided he too must take getting fitter seriously.

Now—post-shower—Lily is in a summer dress he hasn't seen before. Red with large white circles upon it, almost white wheels with spokes but more abstract shapes, not a replication of any real object. When she is standing, the dress covers her knees, and then sitting on the sofa, it has ridden up. He likes this, they have been seeing each other long enough. He is much older than Julie Rivington; a mature man with sufficient self-control. He hopes.

After the meal, they played cards. Garth taught Lily how to play Honeymoon Whist and she made lightly suggestive jokes about his intentions in introducing such a game. He tried to make a joke himself, rehashing one he had read before in his book of card games—that this game was not the best thing to get up to on a honeymoon—but then he could not recall the punchline, the name of another card game for two that is reputedly superior.

'Very funny,' she told him, although mirth seemed further from her then than it has been for most of the evening.

Now they kiss again, Lily lets her hand linger on his thigh. Garth contemplates reciprocating but does not trust himself. Hers is bare, and it is all more than he allows the teenagers he counsels at church. It is late, turned eleven, Lily has to work in the morning but seems at ease about his continued presence. Her hand rubbing his leg, she asks him, 'Have you noticed?'

'I see everything,' he says, wondering what he might have missed. 'You look gorgeous, Lily.'

'It's more comfortable in summer,' she says. 'Only at home, of course.' He nods although he has no idea what she is talking about. 'It doesn't mean anything unless you want it to but underwear and hot nights don't mix well.'

Garth instinctively lifts his hands. Not that he dislikes where they lingered but fears what they might come into contact with. He struggles with his fight-or-flight mechanism. Flight is simpler, it has been his instruction to young Julie, to boys and girls alike in youth group. He really should not be sharing a sofa with Lily while she has no underwear on. It is not an actual commandment but only because it's too obvious. He puts a hand on the outside of her dress, around her waist, confirming scientifically, and as decently as he can, the truth of her declaration. The absence of knickers. The result shocks him.

'I think you know what it means to me, I mustn't break the laws of Noah.' She puts her hand back on his thigh but casually, this comfort between them has taken a long time. He suspects that she knows she has crossed a line; secretly, he feels excited that she even wished to. 'And I hope you know how I feel about you, Lily.' She turns her face, receives his kiss. 'Come to church on Sunday, sweet girl,' he says, the quid pro quo of the farmer's son still at work in his mind.

* * *

When he is cycling home, having left the maisonette no more than five minutes after the most seductive conversation of his life—and it might not have made Lily's top hundred—he passes a large group of young people near the university campus. It is approaching midnight, they have doubtless been drinking, and he notices a young girl lying prostrate on the ground. A student Garth presumes.

He brakes sharply. The gathered throng, six he thinks—both genders—do not look threatening. A little bewildered but no more than that.

'Is she all right?' he asks.

'Sick,' replies one and Garth realises he cannot interpret this: it might mean many types of sick. Might even mean that she is fine.

'From drinking?' He is off-work, Baxter's School closed for summer, Garth Addicks suspended until Mr Lorimer comes to his senses. This might be his only chance to complete an act of goodness for quite a while.

'We've all been doing that,' scoffs a boy.

'But she's vomited?' He can try and take control, show these supposed undergraduates the maturity they will need to pick up during the rite of passage of their student years.

A girl, tall and quite confident, black-rimmed glasses and braces on her teeth, steps towards Garth. 'Thanks, but don't worry. She's sick of her parents and one or two boys as well. We'll watch out for her.'

He is standing by his bike, alongside the sensible girl. 'She doesn't need an ambulance?' asks Garth.

'I think hers are psychological problems, not a red-light job.'

'Does she see the student counsellor?'

'We're not students. We work at MacDonald's. We need to get her home and she always plays dead two or three times along the way. We'll always see her home, we're her friends.'

'Okay,' he says, preparing to get back on the bike. 'What's her name?' He likes to have markers and signposts with which to recall what he has seen. Know the names of those for whom he is to pray.

'Lily,' says the sensible girl. 'Lily Fraser.'

'Take care of Lily,' says Garth, thinking it plausible that his own girlfriend of the same name once lay drunk on a street in Sittingbourne. Sick of boys and parents and the unsteadiness arising from being without a God to guide her. 'God bless you for taking good care of Lily.'

Sunday, 31 July 2016

'Come to me, please,' she tells him across the skies, the connection of their mobile telephones.

'But Lily...'

'I just can't.'

Garth feels frustrated, Lily was to cycle over in time for the eleven o'clock service and now—at nine-thirty—she's bailing out on him. 'Don't speak, don't sing, just listen to us.'

'It's not for me, Garth. Deep down, I think it's all bollocks.'

From any other lips, this would be bait, make him quote an apt rebuke from the New Testament. Invoke the journey of the soul beyond this bodily segment. With Lily he is playing a waiting game, testing his own forbearance. His soul can endure this wait, even the impatience of his own transitory body. 'Shall I cycle to you then?' he submits.

'Bring a change of clothing for the beach,' she instructs.

'No, not that again. I'll miss the evening service if you skip the exercises with Caroline, please? Let's take the train into Bournemouth and have a proper day out.'

They agree on the change to Lily's plans. She promises to text her non-participation to Caroline. 'She'll make me do double tomorrow, bend over until my head pops up the other side.'

'It's all voluntary, Lily—she can't make you do anything—I don't even try half the stuff.'

'You should feel my washboard...' Garth thinks he knows what that odd term means. '...but not until we're married, of course.' His girlfriend's laughter at her own joke comes through the phone's distorted pitch, and he contemplates how far away it seems—marriage—alongside the certainty that he would like to feel the parts she names. Every inch of her holds an interest. He has been unable to usher her into his church even once. Peter and Margery remain unknown to her. He is the only Christian she mixes with, and he is unsure whether he is at his best or at his worst in her company. Pleasure confuses: sins wrapped up in gift paper.

* * *

The girls sing softly and gently, the congregation try to do likewise. They are all celebrating that this is the tone and manner of Jesus' calling to them. He is calling them home, forgiving all. Garth never recognised how much he likes this hymn before today. Hasn't previously thought about the home it promises. Lily will be there, at home with the Lord, and Garth too. The deliverance of all God's bounty will come to pass in the fullness of time.

Pastor Margery takes her lesson from Galatians; Garth sees the hand of Jesus in the coincidence. She is covering the same ground as his recent reading. While he broadly agrees with her interpretation, he thinks that she has missed a significant point. Margery does not emphasise the openness of Christ to those for whom the Jewish faith which pre-dated Him seemed closed. The profound difference between the Judaism that Jesus was born to and the wider fulfilment of His ministry. He has imagined going through this very text with his girlfriend. Saint Paul calling Lily, he wants to say, thinks she may feel overwhelmed by all he has familiarised himself with, the higher truth of this epistle. Her sticking point—that it all sounds like bollocks—leads him to conclude it remains too early in their relationship to go for the conversion. Not full throttle. Some things cannot be rushed.

When the service is over, he chats with the girls, his choir. He is wary of speaking to the Pastor or to his mentor, Peter, having advised both that Lily was to finally present herself amongst them. He feels her absence as a personal failure. Fears that they are marking him down for associating so closely, so enthusiastically, with one not on the path of righteousness. Julie is telling Garth about a coffee shop date she undertook yesterday with her young beau, Ronnie. His mother drove them and then picked the couple up again ninety minutes later. He finds the idea of the two teenagers spending that length of time nursing a cappuccino and failing to connect—true intimacy must be beyond them at the tender age of fourteen—to be quite a sweet notion. He puzzles over the lift. Cindy Clarke driving eight hundred yards or thereabouts from his house or her house, into Northbourne, and then doing the same again to collect them. It's pathetic, they should have walked. Or is Cindy keeping an eye on her son, worried that he's a chip off the old block? The father of roving eye and indecent proposition. 'Shouldn't you have walked up there? You neither live far from the Wimborne Road.'

'Ga-arth,' replies Julie, elongating his name with a hint of disdain on this occasion. 'He can't really walk with a broken leg, can he? Were you listening to our prayers, or not?'

'Indeed,' he says with a Christian nod. Indeed, he was not listening, he realises. He hopes his knowing nod has disguised the fact. Garth will pray for the boy tonight; he must think of Lily less. Not a lot less, and nor must he let thoughts of her drown out all that is important in the present. He suspects he was praying for her to finally come to church while neglecting to attend to whatever prayer Margery offered for young Ronnie.

He feels a hand upon his elbow. Julie immediately tells Pastor Margery that she loved the service. It is a platitude but a nice one to hear from a teenager in church.

'A word,' she says to him, points her Zimmer-frame once more at the front door of the church. As they start to step away, she turns her head and says, with a rare note of formality, a deepening of her voice, 'Wonderful girls, wonderful painting of our place of worship.' Garth did the lion's share but wants no praise. It was a duty, and the lick of magnolia has made it look fresher, sharper. Garth knows their church is wonderful only in the hearts of those who worship within it. The renovated nursery will appear plain—unremarkable—to those who cannot sense its purpose. The stepping stone that it is between this life and the new creation.

'I am disappointed,' says Pastor Margery when they are out on the street.

Garth does not argue, the disappointment is his also. Still his love for Lily puts it in the shade. He tries to explain Lily's decision to his pastor. 'She is a girl with more than a touch of Jesus within her but she says religion is all poppycock. Her experience to date has led her to think this.'

'There is a strong vein of support for that view out in the world. Many think it, and doing so allows them to give in to temptation. Indulgences we willingly forego. Are you sure it is not her world you are in love with, Garth? I worry that she is one of many young single mothers for whom good old reliable Garth may represent a most attractive catch.'

Garth thinks how his mother—although ill-disposed to the colour of her children—still asks fondly about Lily. She might think the girl will lure him away from the derided church. For Margery it works the other way round. The possibility of his loss from this communion unthinkable. Friday youth group, guitar and choir: he is a linchpin.

'Margery, I do appreciate your counsel. I have to add, Lily means more to me in the world than anything except Jesus. It is not He or she. There is no trade-off to be done.'

'And He would be content with how you conduct yourself with your lady-friend? With Lily?'

Garth reddens. 'Yes, content. And Jesus wouldn't bug me about it.'

* * *

When they are sitting on the train, she takes his hand and says, 'Sorry, fella, I just couldn't do it.' He knows she means her attendance at church, and he has prised her away from Caroline for the day. It is a small measure of compensation, Garth not an entirely impotent man.

A Halo is not a Cooking Pot

On his arrival at her maisonette, he agreed to her request to give Bournemouth a miss. Lily had a flier for the art fair in New Milton, told him that it looked fun. He likes to do as she requests, create goodwill. One day it will give her little choice but to reciprocate, come and try The Church of the Men of Judea. If it takes a year, it will be an agreeable year of pleasing Lily.

The carriage is quite full, the only seats free when they boarded in Pokesdown were across the aisle from each other, Garth diagonally forward a seat. No full pair was available; holidaymakers returning from the coast. It is noisy, many drink from tins of beer. As he tells Lily a little about the morning service, omitting his inattention but relating the news that poor Ronnie Clarke has a broken leg, a cycle accident to mirror his father's, she appears to go inside herself. 'Poor kid,' she says. He thinks her mind is no more on the Clarke boy than his own had been during whichever prayer had earlier asked for the Lord's intercession on the matter.

'Something's on your mind,' he tells her.

Lily looks around, points at a child, a curly-haired little black girl, nothing like her Ami but for their similar ages. 'I'm missing them, Garth. I hug Ami for so long every day. Joey too.' She turns away, looks across the gentleman in the seat beside her. 'Joey too.'

Garth takes her hand but she does not turn back towards him and before he is able offer words of comfort, a man carrying two coffees passes down the aisle, requiring cessation of the hand-hold.

'Lily,' says Garth.

'Give me a moment.'

The man sitting beside her leans forward to peer around Lily and take a long stare at Garth. His look is accusatory, and it crosses Garth's mind that Lily is probably crying. He wonders if this has been so all morning. She has told him before that this two-week summer trip to London is the longest that the children are away from her all year. She said she didn't know how she would survive it. He didn't take her point seriously. Thinks he relished too fully the possibility of having her to himself. He was selfish, didn't think deeply about how difficult the children's absence is for her. He leans across the aisle and says, 'Oh Lily,' close to her ear. The man leans forward once again, Garth ignores him. The nosy man should see that he is not the cause of her upset.

Boscombe

She leans back in her seat and finally turns towards him; her tears flow freely, a smile of sorts on her face. 'I love them, Garth.'

He nods, wonders what in his life might give him so intense a feeling of loss. 'Six days,' he tells her. She used this phrase at the beginning of the day, during the phone call in which she told him she could not attend his church.

'They'll be back in six days, Garth. I can't be myself until then.'

* * *

At the station, they ask for directions to the art fair. Initially, no one can tell them, not as promising as the flier implied. The short walk to town finds more knowledgeable inhabitants. An old man tells Lily how to reach the venue, the rugby club. The couple joke about it as they walk, rugby and art make a curious mix.

A large marquee, a few smaller tents, and a couple of roped-off areas where dance displays are taking place make up the fair. 'Tinpot,' is the word Lily uses to describe it. Garth has no depth of knowledge about art, no expectations beyond seeing some nice paintings. A little craft.

'Even I can dance like that,' he tells her, as they pause to watch a troop of forty pensioners treadmilling their way through a soporific line dance. It's not a boast on his part, just a simple calculation.

Inside the big tent, several displays make positive impressions upon the couple. A seascape artist has confused the expected colours, deep purples and greens create a dazzling storm. 'I'd love that in my lounge,' says Lily.

Garth argues that the picture is excellent—imaginative—but it would disturb one's inner peace if it were hanging in a living room. 'Would you really want a storm forever in your line of sight?'

'I think that's the difference between me and you,' observes Lily. 'You look for tranquillity, try to bring it, and I've been surfing the knot in my stomach ever since my mother first told me off. When I was aged about nothing.'

Garth feels shocked by this analysis, puts an arm around her. 'You bring me peace, Lily.'

'I do not! We're pushing and pulling each other where we oughtn't to go. Animal attraction for you, and you didn't even know you had any before you met me.'

A Halo is not a Cooking Pot

'I don't push you, do I?'

'In the direction of God, matey. You think He's the magnet but I'm like the south pole.'

* * *

At seven o'clock, they are in the Methodist church hall. Garth tells Lily it is madness that any religion should allow the cancellation of evensong for an art fair. He queries if Latin American dancing even constitutes art. 'You said you'd take me dancing,' says Lily, and she gets no argument from him. He is simply surprised that the itinerary of a small-town art fair has ensnared him into making good on his fortnight-old promise.

The class leaders look like a husband and wife, no Latin blood between them, he guesses, while knowing that voicing such a stipulation would make a fool of him. We are all of one blood, Lily has taught him that much. Garth guesses that the wife is younger than his girlfriend, she's equally slim, and as they demonstrate the very first moves, rolls her hips in a way he finds mesmerising. Garth tries not to look too hard.

He sees that many of the dancers have dressed for the part, the men wear shoes that are more expensive than any he owns. His trainers are plain daft. Dancing gracefully in his knee-length trousers is not going to happen. Lily looks the part, again she wears the red dress with white circles upon it. He has reassured himself—by way of an affectionate hug—that she has remembered to put on her essentials.

When they try the first of the moves, Lily giggles, whispers to him how tricky it is to follow. She is excusing his own clumsiness. She can salsa her hips just like the dance teacher. Rhythm comes as easily to her as it does awkwardly to him.

The class is a taster, the salsa teachers might hope to drum up attendance at a more regular convening. They skip on to merengue. The beat is hesitant to Garth; Lily shrugs, tells him to roll with it, not that it is a choice his coordination allows. The teacher, the male, cuts in. Tells Lily she has promise. She smiles at Garth while this man, probably of her own age, is holding her hand, another on the small of her back, leading her smooth performance of the learned moves. They look a graceful couple.

The wife—the young wife—comes to Garth. 'Let me show you,' she says.

'I'm not cut out for it,' he tells her, and she moves on to help a more elderly gentleman. Not a superior dancer to Garth but one keener to place his hands upon this young blonde's hips.

Garth watches Lily dance.

* * *

When the dancing is over, they return to the railway station. And then to Pokesdown for Boscombe, to her maisonette.

'Come in a while,' she says. 'You were good to your word.'

He agrees without being sure that he really was. 'The dancing?' He held her on a dancefloor but feels he has let her down. Flat-footed when he should have swept her away.

They start to talk about it and Lily laughs. 'You out-danced Trent simply by being there.'

Faint praise but he will take it. 'Lily, you could do them all...'

'I've barely danced in a dozen years,' she says. 'Loved it when I was younger, when I was childless. It's like riding a bike.' He smiles, she is in a good mood, although the day has been up and down. She beams back, something cheeky in her look. 'Like sex too, I expect.'

A provocative afterthought. Garth knows that he has let her believe he has some experience in this matter from his pre-Christian days. His long-ago fumbles fell short of the act itself. He has determined that it is only Lily he should share such joy with, and only when this can occur without concurrent guilt. Without jettisoning his profoundly held beliefs. 'Lily?' he asks, 'can we do something for me, only not quite what...'

She cuts him off. 'I shouldn't tease you like that. You've been lovely, Garth. I've a mean streak.'

'I know it's important to you. I feel like I'm letting you down but may let Jesus down if I go with my feelings.'

Lily takes his hand. She hasn't sipped a drop of wine all day. 'You need to work it out. I'm here, I'm not really so demanding. I just tease too much.'

Garth worries that his adherence to the laws of Moses makes him a child in her eyes; she sees his obedience but hasn't begun to understand his faith. 'I'd like you to pray with me,' he says. 'You wouldn't come earlier today, and I know being in church can feel very public. Much simpler here, in this room.' Lily assents, slips off the sofa to kneel on her carpeted floor. Hands clasped together. Garth begins to copy but knows the posture is unnecessary and will prove discomforting if they are to pray properly. For a meditative duration. He puts an arm around her, beneath her far armpit, guides her back onto the sofa. As they sit side by side once more, he says, 'A bowing of the head is sufficient, really. The point is to be thinking beyond this plane of mortality. It is through thought that we transcend this world. Kneeling isn't really needed; it was a medieval-monk thing.'

'All right,' says Lily, and she turns her face to him, they are only inches apart.

Garth bows his head, makes a point of bringing his arm back, keeps it exclusively in his own orbit. 'Lord,' he says, 'I am going to sit quietly and think about all I am thankful for. Please help Lily to achieve inner peace with which to embark on her own reflection.'

He is quiet, Lily mirrors his posture. He finds his thoughts winding down paths familiar and unfamiliar. He is grateful for the gift of Lily, confused that the Lord gave her twelve stitches in the bargain. He has long been reconciled to the notion that He needed to do something to stall them. Give them long enough to find each other. Aloud, he praises God for the gifts of Alice and Caroline, the two friends of Lily's whom he has met properly. Gifts for her he declares, not stating his personal feelings for them either way. For the latter he holds a little tug of dislike, bringing her to mind breaks the meditative mood he'd found. She's a nice but spoilt girl; the snag is being over-indulged can keep anyone from a more righteous path. He sometimes thinks Lily puts too much store in the young narcissist. 'Give me wisdom, Lord,' he suddenly says in breach of another silence. 'I love Lily, as I know many others do. Lord, I pray that Jo-jo and Ami grow in Your light and in the warmth of their mother's love. Closer and stronger, every day. I thank You for their loving father, Trent.' He stops talking. Silence prevails once more, and he glances sideways at Lily, head still bowed. She looks back, mouths a 'Thank you' although he feels he has said nothing insightful yet. Prayer often brings him into a clearing, makes the lay of his life certain and explicable. He worries that Lily's presence is distracting him, tries to corral his thoughts. He wanted her to pray with him, pleased she agreed. His meditation starts to gain shape, purpose. It's been quite a day. Lily's tears on the train were an education. Her earlier call, refusing once more to visit his church told him of the roadblock, makes him now ponder if it is him more than her. If there is something more tangible that he must give for her to find trust in him and confidence in the future he can offer her. That art fair really was a tinpot affair, he muses, thanks the Lord for the joy it effortlessly brought to the good people of New Milton, and maybe the odd scallywag in the bargain, that's just the way it works. Jesus spreads His bounty generously. If the Lord had blessed Garth with dancing feet his learning would not be as great, his passage through this life too smooth. He thinks about how he felt when the older man, the teacher, was holding Lily. He knows there was some jealousy in there but he's wise enough to direct it neither at the dance teacher—a good man practicing his craft—nor at his girlfriend. Dance-starved Lily deserves the simple physical pleasure she derives from moving to music. Deserves far more if he can only lift her from the tribulation that her life oftentimes seems to entail. The day has shown him something which he needs to meditate upon further. Is the dance a metaphor? The choreography of their romance equally awkward. She likes his work; respects his religion in their most serious conversations but she has no feeling for it. He adores her simple goodness; she is the most fantastic mother. She is thirty-six years young, her outlook refreshing even after navigating a most complicated adult life for some twenty years.

'God,' he hears her say, 'God, look after Garth. I can barely look after myself. Doing all I can for those two little ones does for me. Look after Garth.'

He keeps his head bowed; her words have jumped the needle on his thoughts. In his mind, he hears her spoken prayer again and again but cannot be sure what she was thinking. The message sounded like she was bailing, leaving him to God alone. And yet she prayed, she tried. He knows how hard it is at first. All the youngsters at church say the same. 'Jesus, Your wisdom will show us how to love one and other without fear or hurt, without pain or misstep,' he intones. 'I look to You—Your teaching, Your guidance—to produce in me the acts that shall give You the most pleasure, satisfy You that I am righteous in Your eyes. Jesus, keep Lily with me on this journey. Bring her to You,

A Halo is not a Cooking Pot

and I shall never drop the hand I know You intend to have in Your circle.' He opens his eyes as Lily looks up at him. Garth nods. Amen is for larger congregations than this. They gaze into each other's eyes for a few moments longer. Garth says, 'I should cycle,' and Lily immediately gives him a kiss on the lips. As they stand, he puts his arms around her back, pulling her chest into his own. They kiss again, very quickly, as if a watching presence may disapprove, and then he steps through the kitchen, into her courtyard, collects his bike and leaves through the side gate. The pedal back to Northbourne.

Boscombe

Chapter Five:

The Changing Room

Monday, 1 August 2016

Lily barely trusts her own observation: Gillian Garrett—who sits across the office from her—is being exceptionally pleasant today. She is not warming to her—Lily isn't one to forgive in a hurry—it's a nice turnaround, nevertheless. Gillian has suggested that she may go home early. And this is all part of a strange day for Lily. She is missing her children, recalls that this—the start of their second consecutive week with Trent—was when she had an emotional meltdown at work last year. Crying in the toilet. Not that she let anyone observe her, learn how much their absence was hurting. She doesn't cry, has never been seen doing it at work. Alone in the toilet doesn't count. At the very least, she thinks it highly improbable that Gillian is aware of her previous upset. Has kept it quiet for a year if she is. Lily thinks it more plausible that Garrett is sick of the sight of her. That this explains the offer of an early finish. Lily goes home at three o'clock every day most weeks of the year. That's the contract, she has kids to collect. Only when they are with Trent does she work until five. A few extra hours, extra pounds.

All day Lily has felt distracted. Having kids away from home too long must do that to any mother. And if Gillian Garrett noticed, it wasn't an inability to do her work that drew the attention. Lily has got through plenty of it: audio tapes, type, type, type on her word processor. She feels like the last of a breed, a monkey trained in the nineteen fifties. Ami is her biggest distraction. That girl should be in her arms, not in Shoreditch. A Boscombe kid now, it's all she knows. The boy on the date last night, Garth Best-Mates-With-Jesus Addicks, remains one weird kid. The dancing she can tolerate, even the treading on toes, although if they try it again, she might take up his suggestion. Steel toe caps: health and safety is no joke. Prayer! She gave it her best shot but Garth Talks-to-Dead-People Addicks was the only one listening. Unless Mrs Coombe in the flat upstairs put her ear to a glass and held it against the floor. Lily's ceiling. She will have had a good laugh at the expense of the pair of them if she was doing that. The two of them on a date, and then there they were talking to someone who lives in a book. And not any book, one written so long ago that no one alive can truly say if it was only ever a wind-up—a book of tall tales—and it keeps women oppressed to this day. Still stifling free thinking after all these years. The Bible holds no interest for Lily. Garth's enthusiasm, his appeal to obedience, to its stultifying tenets—no sex please, we're Christians—only goes to confirm her contrary position. God is the dullest houseguest, and she will never champion the prejudices of a bygone age. She expects to find no common ground with her boyfriend on this. He's in it head over heels, smitten with Jesus, and it gets in the way of everything else. She won't be going to his church, she's decided that. Period. When he talks about his pastor—Margery said this, or Margery explained that—Lily feels like slapping her. And the poor woman walks with a frame.

Two days ago, Lily promised Alice that she would go to see her after work today; they will meet on the beach with Wendy and Bryony. Alice texted earlier this afternoon to say that she and the children are there already. Martin has bought the family a beach hut. Lily even feels a tiny pang of envy. Alice is just a kid, ten years her junior, and now she has a beach hut. Just like Caroline, who is another kid with everything she wants except a boyfriend worth a damn. And Garth is a bit of a kid too, she knows she shouldn't think of him that way, not while she still harbours some floating hopes of a proper relationship. Just as soon as the good Lord retreats back inside His dust-covered book. Leaves the poor boy alone to figure out what he really wants without all the finger-wagging. She knows that she could—in theory—do what he, Garth Addicks most wants. She won't because she's too headstrong by about a thousand miles, but she could. She has the self-control to pretend, go to church and pray. She could—at a bloody big pinch—tolerate the Christian friends he has still not dared introduce her to. He would marry her in the blink of an eye, then they could have a proper love life, a sex life, find out if they really are suited to be with each other or not. That's the back-to-front way

The Changing Room

round the Christians go. She hopes he proves better at making love than his dancing suggested, but Trent couldn't dance either and for a long time they were physically in tune. The rhythm of sex is not the merengue. It's a bike gone rusty in the shed to Lily's current thinking. And if she did all that, married the bugger just so he could finally pass first base despite Jesus watching his every move, her ascetic residential support worker wouldn't buy her a beach hut. Can't do any better than his depressing flat which sits too far away from the sea. She's not materialistic—not a bit of it—but if you can't afford a garden, then at the very least live near a beach. Lily figured that pearl around the time she left Shoreditch. Boscombe's the place to be.

'It's kind of you,' she tells Gillian. Smiles gratefully at her before heading out the door. On the short walk to her maisonette, she contemplates if the office manager's unexpected cordiality is in any way linked to Simon Clarke. She can't quite muster how it might be, yet Lily noted that Gillian Garrett was very abrupt with him on two occasions today. The first was just telling him he couldn't use the meeting room because Des Capaldi had booked it. She said it like she was dressing down a schoolboy. The other time was telling him that Lily would come to his audio tape in good time, there was more pressing work to be done in advance of his. Gillian certainly pierced his impatience. If the frosty old sow turns out to be on her side, Lily will be genuinely grateful. For now, it is only a hypothesis. A lot more evidence is required for Lily Stephen's to start shouting miracle.

At home, she runs herself a glass of water, takes the bottle of orange squash from the cupboard, then puts it back unopened. She's imbibing to Caroline's orders, cutting out the sugar. Sitting at the kitchen table, she puts her head in her hands. She loves seeing Alice, little Wendy and Bryony are cute but the thought of it brings back what she's missing. Five more days, she tells herself as she glugs down the water before going into her bedroom, getting out of her working clothes.

* * *

Lily, in her ubiquitous black shorts and a T-shirt which Jo-jo chose for her last birthday, pulled on over her bikini top, runs slowly down to the beach. Towel, underwear, an optimistically included novel, bounce around inside the small rucksack on her back. The beach, when she gets there, is heaving; young and old are sunning themselves. Families, couples, the odd singleton. This is a balmy summer. She looks around at the beach huts while unravelling her towel to extract her phone and call Alice. Unsure which hut is hers. Before she has scrolled the contacts, she sees a familiar figure waving. Her friend is up on the second row, a tier back. Beach hut raised far above the promenade. A changing room with a view. The children sit on wooden decking to the front of it. Lily slides the phone back into her bag and jogs up to her friend.

'Look at you.' says Alice, and it is true, Lily in beach attire looks fitter, she is becoming toned. Caroline both drill sergeant and sculptor.

'Any sunblock?' Lily asks. Alice has tiny children, many tubes of sunscreen. She passes one to Lily who immediately rubs a little into the back of her left calf. 'I'm getting really self-conscious of this ruddy scar,' she says, putting a hand to her mouth when she sees Wendy turn her head at the almost-expletive.

Alice smiles. 'Garth did it, and he gets to see the rest of you which is...' Lily narrows her eyes, wryly amused that her friend doesn't spot the flaw in her supposition. '...untarnished.'

As she rubs a little more cream over her white skin, she laughs. 'I'm tarnished all over, sunshine. I think I've been tarnished inside and out. But...' She looks at the children as she says this, checks they are not listening; Wendy holds a small children's book and little Bryony is simply clinging onto her mother's leg, it could be the mast of a ship in a storm. '...Garth doesn't seem so interested in tarnishing me anyhow.' Alice shakes her head at the state of things. Lily leans into her, cheek to cheek. In a whisper, she says, 'Late night prayer. He insisted on it. Whatever spirit moves me, it's not holy at all. I don't even know what most of his religious gobbledegook means.'

Alice giggles now. 'He just believes in all that, he doesn't fancy you less, petal.'

'He can't convert me; I can't convert him. What's the opposite of a cold war?'

'A hot war?'

'No, the other way round. Me and Garth have a cold romance.'

'Aw, Lily, don't say that. I think he's sweet.' When Lily keeps staring at her, she adds, 'In his own way.'

Wendy is keen to swim although Bryony is sleepy. Lily says she will take her in the water. She laughs when Alice tries to stop her from inflating the arm bands. As Wendy's mother, she thinks it's her job, and then only Lily can blow them up with ease. She has completed one while her younger friend perspires with the other orange float limp on her lips. Failing to grow in size. She takes over and then Lily takes the girl by the hand, walks her down the steps across the promenade and over the sand. Little Wendy no longer asks where her friend, Ami, has gone. Sings a song—happily—not a glance at Lily as she chunners it out.

London Bridge is falling down, falling down

* * *

When Lily and Wendy return from the water, it is to Martin who has joined his family. He gives his older daughter a home-from-work hug. Lily jokes with him about his beach clothing: he wears pin-striped trousers, a loosened tie. The matching jacket lies across a plastic chair on the hut's veranda.

'I shall be transformed,' he declares, stepping into the wooden cabin and pulling the door closed behind him. A second later he pokes his head out, Lily thinks she sees an unclothed shoulder. 'No peeping,' he says, winking at Bryony who giggles.

Alice explains that the children don't appreciate barbecues yet. They have quiche, tomatoes, a pasta salad she has prepared. She asks Lily if this will be okay.

'Oh God, I should've brought something.'

'No, you were working,' soothes Alice. 'You're our guest.'

Martin emerges in only a pair of swimming shorts, bright blue and bedecked with a pattern of yellow pineapples, he also sports star-shaped sunglasses. Pushes them onto his nose, then swipes them off again every fifteen seconds.

'The city stiff has fled,' Lily tells him.

'He was never here; it was just Pineapple Pete put the wrong clothes on this morning.'

Wendy giggles. 'Pineapple Pete,' she says to her sister.

Lily asks him about work but Martin is keener to tickle his children, be the man in the bright shorts. He and Alice have both described Martin's job to her, she remains unsure exactly what it is he does. Very good with IT is as much as she's grasped. And it pays well, beach huts cost a ridiculous amount of money.

They have a table made from hard plastic on which Alice has laid out the fare. The chairs they sit on are not a set. The two children share an old-fashioned deckchair. They giggle and squeal, enjoy sitting together but then both cry when a bumping of elbows makes them drop their sandwiches to the sandy decking. Martin stands in his funny shorts, acts a clown letting his own quiche fall too, and standing on it with a bare foot. Both girls laugh at him, arrest their own tears in an instant. Pineapple Pete is the funniest man. Lily laughs with them. If he's clever it doesn't stop him acting the fool. Might start a food fight for the silliness of it. She also thinks they replace wasted food one way or another. Martin and Alice might have a late-night takeaway, their waistlines attest to it. Freer with money than Lily, eat what they like, when they like.

* * *

Caroline arrives on the promenade around seven in the evening. The family are wondering whether to go or stay. She has a massive smile on her face when she tells them attendance is compulsory. 'Running, jumping, stretching. Summer is for somersaults.'

'Me! Me! Me!' says Wendy. Little Bryony hops from foot to foot, equally excited by the instruction.

'Of course, you will,' Caroline tells the tiny ones. 'You guys are much more bendy than us old ones.'

Martin laughs, he is up for it. Lily suspects men will always do whatever lithesome Caroline Yorke asks of them. Except for her Garth, of course. Odd man out. Alice looks wary. She and Lily have sauntered miles up and down this coast but gyms and jogging are not on her compass.

The party troops onto the beach. 'You know the drill,' the sergeant major tells Lily, and she drops to the sand, legs in front, bending her head close to the knee. She can touch her forehead to it with a bit of a heave. Caroline can hold the pose; Pineapple Pete sits on the sand and flops about a bit; the little ones are terrific, made of rubber.

'It gets easier the more often you do it,' Lily advises Alice. The latter

The Changing Room

shrugs, puts a hand on her T-shirt covered stomach. The bulge.

Caroline is astute, she changes the routine from the usual medium-level torture to a series of running and jumping games. The little girls are in love with their new gym teacher. 'Handstands,' she shouts, and when Wendy throws herself at the task too enthusiastically, Caroline catches her ankles before she falls on her back. Holds her up in position for half a minute; tells her when boys are upside down, they turn into girls, and when girls are upside down, they turn into boys.

When the little girl is back to her accustomed gender she says, 'You do it.' Caroline—as Lily has grown to expect—holds her handstand unaided for thirty seconds or more, T-shirt tumbling down, tanned stomach visible and taut, legs waving at Boscombe's evening revellers.

As she rights herself, Wendy wraps her arms around the girl's right thigh. 'You're not a boy now. You're not.' She looks over her shoulder. 'She's not a boy, is she Mummy?' shouts Wendy.

'Definitely a girl,' says Martin.

The fitness regime turns to playing in the sand. The girls are burying Caroline when Alice suggests they scale it down. Bedtime is nearing.

'I've got to put Lily through some paces,' says the partially buried one. Lily nods her agreement.

'You can both change in the beach hut. Lily, you could drop the key off tomorrow lunchtime.'

Lily thanks Alice for the offer, glances at Caroline.

'Nothing to change into. I just run home.'

Lily agrees—the swim was ages ago—she is dry, she is decent.

* * *

When the family have left, Caroline is punishing. Lily surprises herself by the pleasure she can extract from the many stretches and hops demanded.

The younger one does her share—usually more—she is astonishingly fit. 'How are you feeling?' she asks Lily when they finally sit down. Plenty of sweat upon even the younger girl's back.

'Good. Really good.'

'Run with me, up the coast a way.'

Lily looks a little hesitant.

'Stop at the Perkin,' says Caroline. 'Refuel.'

Boscombe

Lily thinks to say no, she hardly feels suitably dressed to visit a pub but then she catches herself. She is not stiff like poor Garth. If Caroline can visit a pub in shorts, a sweat-laden T-shirt, why can't she?

They run at a pace—a hell of a pace, Lily thinks—she hadn't guessed the jog to be still more of the military training. The benefit of running fast is getting there quickly. In no time at all, one mildly flushed girl and one gasping and panting woman are at the bar. Banana-shaped grins on their faces. Lily feels pleased with herself, her improving fitness. The accident on the promenade is long behind her. She tries to insist on paying for the drinks, Caroline is the winner even at this minor contest. As Lily picks up her chilled wine, she stares for a moment at Caroline's pint of cider.

'I burn it off, sweetie. Never include alcohol in your calorie count.'

'How do you do it, Caz?'

'Do what?'

'Jo-jo's the same with you as Wendy tonight. You have the little ones eating out of your hand.'

'I love your boy, Lily, love them all. It's us grown-ups who make life too complicated.'

Lily nods in agreement.

They move away from the bar, find spare seats at a table already occupied by two men. They look a couple of decades older than Lily, comfortable behind sturdy pints. As they slide down onto their chairs, one of the men pinches the side of Lily's sweat-dampened T-shirt between two fingers. 'What's this?' he says.

She looks at it, the T-shirt her son gave her one birthday ago. A cartoon mum on the front—a most unflattering cartoon mum—a fiendish glint in her eye as she cradles an ugly baby. 'We came off the beach, not really dressed up, I know.' She flashes the man a smile, it should suffice.

'Nuh,' he says, 'you both stink quite a bit. What have you been up to?' He turns to his friend, winks suggestively at him. 'What do you reckon this pair have been up to, Tom?'

'Fuck off,' says Caroline, waving a dismissive hand and then pulling her chair closer to Lily, her shoulder turned away from their impertinent table companions. She leans her head into her. 'How's it going with Garth?'

The Changing Room

'Don't swear at me,' Lily hears. Caroline does not so much as look up.

Lily tells her friend it might be a dead-end relationship. She is reluctant to expand upon this sombre summary.

Tom, the man who has not yet spoken, stands and cuts across the girls. 'We're going to sit over there because you two smell awful.' He looks accusingly at the younger girl as he says it. Then both men turn their backs, step away.

'Our strategy worked, sweetie,' says Caroline at volume. 'We got rid of the silly old gits.'

Lily places a hand on top of Caroline's. 'I'm common, not you. Don't swear, please.'

The girl just winks at her. 'Tell me about Garth.'

In a quiet voice, Lily says she is finding Garth's religion the equivalent of having a maiden aunt forever in the room.

'Is he normal?' asks Caroline.

'He seems to be,' giggles Lily. 'I try to check it's working when he snuggles up to me; I think he'd do the lot if Auntie would just leave the room.'

'What are your options?'

'I'd do it in front of Auntie but Garth is a stickler.'

'No,' says Caroline, 'he can't be normal at all. I think you look amazing and I'm a girl. Or have I done too many handstands? Flipped over.'

'Thanks,' says Lily, 'but Caz, what happened with your dad? Is awful Clive on a charge?' She hopes she has pitched her question right; this subject has upset Caroline a time or two.

'Yeah, Daddy's still feeling bruised, he's on the mend anyhow. I know he meant well but it wasn't smart poking his nose into my business. Not really. Poor old Dad.'

'He's out of hospital?'

'Yeah, yeah. Wasn't in long at all. Taking it easy but on the mend.'

'And Clive? Has he been charged?'

'None of us want to put me through all that. My parents would die if they had to hear about my sex life in court.'

Lily ponders this. Poor old dad got himself some broken ribs in the bargain. Caroline is everybody's princess, and even as she takes her old man for granted once more, Lily wants to hug her. Won't be pointing out her defects. 'You're not still seeing him are you, not after what...'

'No, I will not! We're never getting back together. Never ever. Whatever it was I saw in him had nothing to do with his brainbox. He doesn't actually talk like he's dumb as an ox, then deep down, it turns out he is. I've quit him for good. No more of him. Not ever. Did I say, we used a picture of Clive and I for the gym promotion two years ago? We belonged in the picture. Looked good in it. Not in the living, breathing world: in this one we were always a disaster. I've dumped Clive twelve times, Lily. I'm not completely stupid, won't be giving him a thirteenth chance.'

Wednesday, 3 August 2016

'One more week and you'll know?'

'Should do,' Garth replies.

'Only one outcome, fella. I've said so all along.' As she tells him this, assures her boyfriend that no ill can come of the incident with Declan Keane, she finds herself crossing the fingers in which she holds her mobile phone. Lily isn't superstitious and nor does she think he has done any wrong. Her worry is that the school may treat him unfairly. The world is full of just that kind of crap, injustice everywhere you look. Always has been. She wants him to know that she trusts his reasoning, the motivation behind his restraint of a child. Her doubts are not about his innocence but their suitability as a couple, ill-matched and centred differently as they are. Garth is the opposite of a child abuser: he obsesses on the right and wrong of every footstep he takes. He stopped the other kid from getting his nose broken, that's a good thing every way up.

'We should do a day out Friday,' says Garth.

'I've told you, I'm cleaning.'

'You took a day off work to clean?'

'Garth, you know I collect them Saturday. Those two come home to a clean house. It's just the way I am.'

'All right. I'll come and clean too. We can finish by noon, and then out we go.'

The Changing Room

'Bring your swimming things. Fitness with Caroline at six.'

'Cancel her, I'm not being class dummy again. I'll find another place where we can go dancing.'

'Text me when you do, and I'll relieve you of the army training corps.' She laughs as she says it but Lily sees competition developing between the two. Her boyfriend and this young girl. It is even playing out in her mind: in Garth there is some hope of a bright future but it seems to rest on her having an unlikely Damascene turn. She must first see the Lord in all his glory, and on the back of it spot that the Men-of-Judea church is the rightful destiny of all who have understood the Word of improbable God. She wonders if she likes much more than the novelty of again having a boyfriend; the safety of Garth is not itself an appealing thing. Who opts for raincoats and big insurance premiums? He is the first man she has been close to since leaving Trent. She could write a book—The Pros and Cons of a Having Celibate Boyfriend—unlikely to sell well, the victorious negative case jumping out of the title as it does. Her relationship with Caroline is actually the more exciting. She—well-spoken and elegant when not underdressed and perspiring—is edgier in every way. And when they were in the bar on Monday, Lily felt the eyes of all the men upon her, even if she was the object of only their second glances.

* * *

'Did you work out yesterday?'

'I did. Running and stretches. You've got me hooked, Caroline, perversely hooked.'

The routines are the same as on Monday. This evening the instructor is, in the absence of Alice and her children, far more severe. They are stretching their thighs out on the sand. Over and over. Again, a random girl joins them, seems to think it is a club. Then they do jumps of a demanding variety. The new girl struggles to keep up and, after a short time she jogs away. When Lily is red-faced, exhausted, and Caroline glowing radiantly, the pair of them sit on the sand to talk.

'If I can get as fit as you, I might snag a better boyfriend than Garth. What do you reckon, Caz?'

Caroline splutters with laughter. 'You're almost there and you already could, sweetie. Then again, I'm no judge of any of that, am I?'

'I think you know a thing or two...'

'Is he not everything you're after?'

'I think you know what he is and isn't. Nice fella. Really good in lots of ways.' Lily sits up and slaps Caroline's knee. 'Nothing dirty in that is there?' Caroline shakes her head, smiling, not in disagreement, just looking at her friend closely. 'More's the bloody pity.'

They both start to laugh again. Caroline taps her quite playfully. 'He can be a bit disgusting that boyfriend of yours. The custard-in-tea thing: yuk!'

Friday, 5 August 2016

Lily has, with vigour and plastic gloves, been cleaning sinks and baths since seven this morning. She has vacuumed and dusted and sifted through some toy drawers, making sure that hairs and traces of what once was food are no longer in them. Garth does not know it—she won't scold him because these are her chores and not his—but he is late to the happening. The cleaning of Ami and Jo-jo's home. It is nine forty-five when he arrives, rings the bell, kisses his girl, and enters the maisonette.

'Where shall I start?'

'Washing up,' she suggests. She has stacked her modest stock of crockery upon the kitchen side. This is not tidying, it is ritual. No corner will be left unclean; if it moves, they will wash it. A clean home is her children's welcome after every stay with Trent. Presents of high value are not in their mother's gift. Some bedding is hanging on the line in the small backyard. Lily goes out again to feel it, finds it is not quite dry. They were in the machine before seven, two hours on the line already. She always leaves the bedsheets until the final day. Wants them to smell their freshest for Ami and Jo-jo.

When he has toiled for ten minutes, soaked many but not all, of the predetermined pots, she puts a hand on his arm. Stops him mid-sponging. Clicks the kettle on for a cup of tea. 'You're very good at duty' she says.

'It's my duty.'

'Or is it mine you're stealing?'

'Oh Lily,' he says, 'I want to steal nothing from you, or if I do, it is

The Changing Room

everything. I want to borrow you from your life to mine. Or maybe the vice-a-versa.'

'You're riddling today, Garth Addicks. What's got into you?'

'I've picked up a little of your own elevated mood, Lily darling. Is that allowed, or will you be needing it all?'

They jabber on, and she puts teabags into two mugs and pours on the boiling water. There is a point at which he says, 'Last adult swim before the kids come back,' and she feels a conflict of emotions. She plants a kiss on the lips of her Christian man-child. An adult swim was what he couldn't really manage, she recalls, and he is clutching at the opportunity for the couple to be alone. For Lily, deep down—or maybe right at the surface—she wants her children more than she ever will Garth. They are the better part of her.

'You really did cancel the Caroline experience, didn't you?' he asks her while drinking tea.

Lily laughs but thinks it a cruel affliction, his irrational fear of the pretty girl. Everyone loves Caz, except Garth. He was born ill at ease, and that girl multiplies the feeling for him. 'You'd stretch and jump if Pastor Margery asked you to, Garth. What is it about my Caroline that gets your goat?'

'She's a kid, Lily, and you let her run you like a greyhound.'

This has her cracking up, time spent with Caz is always a pleasure. She kisses Garth on the lips, leaning across the kitchen table; he tells her that he loves her. 'Maybe, sunshine. Maybe you do.'

* * *

They finish their beakers of tea and get back to cleaning. The project is taking shape, the maisonette very close to spotless. A car honks loudly in the road out front. Initially Lily ignores it but the prolonged hoot sounds again and she rises from her seat. 'That's an Alice-like toot, isn't it?'

'Kind of her to entertain us with a car horn,' says Garth.

Lily goes to the front door, and out into the road. Alice has the window rolled down, pointing at two excited children in the back of the car. Little Wendy is making extraordinary faces at Lily, a tongue lolling out, her hands going over the top of her head as if she has a million fleas.

'Just dropping the key,' says Alice.

Boscombe

Lily takes it from her hand, leans in through the open window and pushes her cheek against her friend's. An almost-kiss. 'You are so good to me,' she says.

'And me!' shouts the oddly behaving Wendy.

'We're off to the monkey zoo,' says Alice. 'If they keep this up, I'm leaving them there.'

Little Bryony offers a guttural, 'Ooh, ooh.'.

Lily blows a kiss to each of Alice's children. Her own are a day away, it is getting easier. Garth has come outside by this time. He looks at Lily as the car pulls away. She guesses he missed the key exchange; it can be her secret. 'Just dropping by,' she tells him. 'Couldn't stop.'

* * *

Back inside the maisonette, one hour later, beds made up with the freshly laundered sheets, Lily admits that the flat is clean. The sun foretells another scorching day. 'I'm putting on my running gear,' she says. 'We can jog it to the beach.'

'You're turning into Caroline.' There is good humour in his tone.

Lily remembers that she was wearing the black shorts when they met. He seemed to like them. She is only in her room a couple of minutes. She has on those same shorts, a white T-shirt covering her rich-red bikini top, and she puts a summer dress in her small rucksack to wear later. 'Where's your swimming gear?' she asks. He points at his waist. He is not a man to take his clothes off more frequently than is strictly necessary. Lily prepares a sandwich in the kitchen, wraps it in foil, adds it to the contents of the bag she will wear on her back. He steps out beside her, and as she pulls the door to and lolls into her stride, she says to him, 'Let's see what you can do.' Her pace is quick but today he matches it. Keeps up and can even speak clearly as he runs.

'I like running a lot more than the funny stretches.'

She looks at Garth through narrowed eyes as he runs beside her. 'Have you been practicing?'

* * *

'I think you want to see down there,' she tells him.

Garth reddens a little. It is oddly private inside the closed beach hut, contrasting the hundreds upon hundreds of people milling

The Changing Room

around in the sunlight outside. Lily took off only the T-shirt, bikini top already haltered around her. Garth—having carefully removed his shorts—stands self-consciously in tight navy-blue swimming trunks.

'I just thought...'

'I swim in the shorts. Always have.' She leans into him and kisses him on the lips, draws back quickly. She knows he finds this stuff a bit tricky. Especially with the door closed. 'Let's swim,' she says.

They lock up the beach hut, walk down onto the sand carrying two towels and a bottle of sunscreen. As they walk, Garth is rubbing a little of the product onto his shoulders, and then carefully dabbing some cream onto the bones of his cheeks. The beach is heaving, and they have to take themselves quite near the water to find a space where they can put their towels down. It is baking hot; the air is still; the intense sunlight wobbles visibly in the sticky air. English Channel calm as bathwater.

'Rub some into my back, Garth.'

The boy does the task as she sits on the towel with her knees drawn up in front of her. Lily likes the feel of his hands upon her skin. She rolls onto her stomach, lays across her towel. 'And the backs of my legs, please.'

'Can't you manage that yourself, Lily? I did my own.'

She thinks about his screwy religion, his fear of all things sensual. Everything she knows about the creed followed in The Church of the Men of Judea alienates her from Garth. Thinking about it can make her feel prejudiced, narrow-minded, the very things she tells herself not to be. The basic tenets, the no-sex-before-marriage nonsense, are the same in every church she's ever heard of but his crowd take it seriously. Taser themselves at every step that could lead to that unforgivably sinful place. Don't really trust themselves an inch. Lily has enjoyed good times doing what they avoid—real pleasure—she recalls no lightning strikes from his wrathful God. She sits up and rubs cream on her legs quite vigorously. 'It's a practical thing, Garth, not a sexual thing.' She says it loudly. A man and woman sitting on deckchairs turn their heads.

Garth looks momentarily down, and then back at his girlfriend. 'Yeah. I should have done it.'

In a quieter tone she says, 'See what your missing,' and pushes her creamed fingers under her shorts to the top of her left thigh. He looks away; she has overstepped the mark; forgotten once more that God is a prude. Her thoughts start to vegetate in the heat of the sun. She realises their water bottle is back in the beach hut; Lily has not brought so much as a book to read down onto the sand. 'Swimming,' she suggests.

'For sure.' They stand, and as they step towards the water, he takes her hand. She realises there is no bitterness within him. Garth accepts his eunuch status stoically. As the waves ripple over their ankles and calves he starts talking. 'We never did this, Lily, never. I learnt to swim in primary school but it was what I did in swimming lessons, not outside of them. When Claire learnt, I took her to the public pool once or twice but it was an hour by bike to Blandford. We seldom went. We liked the water but didn't really learn to show off, to be...'

Lily pulls on his hand, draws him close, they embrace, momentarily tumble into the water but she is laughing, says 'Sorry,' as they climb back onto their feet. She wonders what prompted him to tell this childhood tale of trivial despair. He cannot seriously wish for pity, the quality we'd all be better off without. 'Did you not take holidays?' Garth shakes his head. 'Did Wilfred never go lobster red on a Spanish beach?'

'He goes that colour talking about the tax on diesel, Lily. No sun required.'

Lily laughs, takes Garth's hand in hers, holds it close to her breast. 'We're okay. Different.' She puts his fingers to her lips, kisses them. It feels as if she is the man in their relationship—their Victorian courtship—Garth the frightened young thing sticking rigidly to a code he hopes will keep him far to the east of life's beastliness. They are thigh deep in the water, she drops his hand and leans into a forward crawl. Garth follows her immediately. They swim out from the beach, heads down, forty or fifty yards further out and they can stand on a ridge far from the shore. Head and shoulders, the top of Garth's chest, comfortably above the waterline. 'What's the connection, sunshine. I've never figured it.' She finds herself breathing more heavily, the effort of swimming and the chill of the water. Big breaths which heat up her insides.

'I don't know. Between what?'

The Changing Room

'You hated Thre'penny Ha'penny, you adore the little church in Northbourne. Aren't they just two small worlds?'

'Lily, Sixpenny Handley is probably great. Is great. The countryside is God's gift. It could be boring, and my parents made sure it was that in spades inside our farmhouse. I didn't hate the place.'

'Really? You'd go back? Me and you, my kids, in a cottage in a thre'pence ha'penny village?'

'Why not? And my church isn't a small world at all. It's the whole world.'

'Is it? They sound okay, I'm sure your pastor's a good soul but the choir's only three girls. It's...'

'...building Christ's kingdom, Lily. That's what we're doing.'

'Tell me, what would be so wrong if you threw in your lot with the others? The Methodists or the Mormons?'

Garth grins at her suggestion. 'Lily, the Mormons are crackers, and the Methodists have started letting their churches out for salsa dancing...'

'Yours does playgroups for money, is it any different?'

'It's an act of goodness—the charge only covers costs—and all who use it are encouraged to come back on a Sunday. Some do, some don't. We would never compromise the sabbath for a tuppence ha'penny arts fair. Not for anything.'

'Tuppence ha'penny: I thought you liked it?' Lily's voice is rising only because of the time standing, breathing a fresh lungful of air to hold against each wash of a wave. This is a debate, she thinks, not a row, although the subject matter criss-crosses contentious ground.

'It's what you called it. And I loved it, love being with you. Lily...?'

'What is it, sweetie?' She holds him closer; finds that the chill of the water numbs their touch.

'If I was just a twitcher—you know, a birdwatcher—or a model railway enthusiast, I think you'd put up with me more easily. What's wrong with me being what I am?'

'Nothing, Garth...' She stops in mid-thought. '...talk on the beach.' Lily flashes him a big smile, uncertain in her mind if it is heartfelt. 'Carry me on your shoulders.'

Garth is half a head taller than Lily; she scrambles onto his broad shoulders, and sits astride them, imagines him to be more the caveman than he has ever let slip. As the water trickles off her, the warmth of the sun soothes her as his underwater embraces could not. She whoops a little, seriousness abandoned. High time they let themselves go. As the water gets shallower and Lily's long white legs simply drape over Garth's shoulders, she in the sunshine, he only knee deep in sea water, she hears him grunt. 'Hey, buster, I'm not so heavy.'

'No, not at all.' Truly, Lily is slim, light for a girl of her height. 'There are stones under my feet.' He attempts to kneel in the low surf, needs a place to set her down.

She taps him on the shoulder, tries to make a cowboy's yelp but it is half-hearted. Garth doesn't seem to know it but he is not a playful man. She tumbles off his stooped head and shoulders and catches herself with her hands. 'Oh bugger,' she shouts, picking herself up, seeing that a stone has cut the palm of her right hand. Garth offers her sympathy; it is an accident. Lily notes that she tends to be the bloodier of the two in all their physical encounters. They arrive at the towels which they left on the sand, the small bag containing the beach hut key.

'Is there a plaster in the hut, a first aid box?' he asks.

'It's in an awkward place.' She gestures her wounded palm. Licking off the blood. 'Sit.' Lily is the first down. Her bottom, her shorts, land half on the towel and half in the sand. She raises her cut right hand into the air above her head; a sure way to staunch the flow of blood. 'I've a sandy bum now,' she says as Garth plummets beside her.

He looks round the back of her, it is clinging to her wet shorts, her make-do swimming bottoms. 'You can brush it off.'

'I'm not getting sand in this cut.'

'I'm sorry I dropped you. I've got to learn to lark about better.'

It sets Lily off laughing. 'It's true: you're no good at being good for nothing.' The boy smiles back, there is no tension. Not over a little cut to the palm of her hand. 'Back there in the water, you said about being a birdwatcher, the difference because it's the Men-of-Judea thing that really—you know—floats your boat. Is it you or me?' Garth looks blankly back at her, probably not tuned into her thinking yet. 'I think the difference is huge.' He furrows his brow, says nothing. 'If you just watched birds through binoculars early in the morning, you probably wouldn't care whether I came along or not. You and a flask of coffee, that would suit you fine. And I'd come if the kids were at Trent's. I like birds, they're real. I like the pretty ones. There you have it: I'd know what I was looking for. But, Garth, you pray to God, and there's nobody home in my book. And for you, my not attending church is like I don't love you properly, not how you love me. Well...'

'I think that you love me, Lily,' he says.

Lily finds a little bemused smile coming to her face; she wonders if Garth is misinterpreting this too. 'You use the word love like a Christian. Me and you...' She pokes him quite teasingly in the ribs. '...we've not so much as watched the birds on the marsh in the early hours.'

He takes hold of her poking hand, her right hand, sees the blood upon the palm and lets it go, takes up her left. Kisses the fingers, then looks into her blue eyes. 'We're not so different, I want all that you want. I guess my club has a few funny ground rules. I think that's how you see it?'

'But Garth, I don't want to dismiss it. I know it's more than a club to you. That's where we seem to be at loggerheads. You're in, I'm out.'

He puts an arm around her waist, feels her flesh, touches the side of her bikini top, pushing a finger under the strap. It is a gesture Lily cannot interpret. Might be the unconscious roving of his hands; all his focus seems to be on the conversation. 'Where do you want to go? What are you saying here, Lily?'

'Oh, Garth. I'd go where the music takes me. I've told you; I haven't dated in years. Not with the kids being pretty much the whole of my life. Couldn't get off the starting blocks. Now...'

'Lily, I think you could come on Sunday. If not this week, then next. I could mind the children for you. I'm not trying to show you off to my friends, you know. Not at all. I think I want to show Jesus off to you. That's what it is... Don't smile like that, Lily, I'm deadly serious. Everything about you... I think God has touched you already in so many ways. Your wisdom; your love for your children. That's more than a human thing...Lily!'

'I'm sorry, Garth...' She cannot stifle her laughter. '...you make me sound like a Martian. "More than human," you say but humans are all I know. All I want to know. Whatever you see in the way I love my children is just the same as every normal mum feels. I know that I'm no better than most. Alice is a wonderful mum. Off to the monkey zoo just to make the kids laugh. She'd do anything for them. Look at Caroline, no children but she's beautiful with my two, was terrific with little Wendy the other evening. It's how women are. Not all but most.'

Garth is sitting upright, attending her words like a sermon. 'Men made up God,' she says, 'because they didn't love their children enough. Pouring love into some abstract power when you should love the powerless, the needy, the helpless...'

'No. You're wrong. It's through loving Jesus that we learn to love most purely.'

'This is what I'm saying. You try it out in pretend. Love yourself but call it God, and then allow that duty means you should give your family the scraps.'

The boy has pulled his arm away, his knees are up and he has his head in his hands. 'It's not like that. Or if it is, then it's only so in the Church of England. Or the Catholics. The ones that have stopped thinking. In The Church of the Men of Judea we're down to earth, totally down to earth. It's a community of hope, of faith. Not of ritual. My choir of schoolgirls isn't there to chant mass, it's just to ensure there's some kind of tune when we worship Him in song. Margery interprets scripture but we do more than listen, we grapple with it. We don't revere her every word. She's not infallible; she doesn't think she's that, not even close. We're all sharing, trying our best to understand the most important information ever handed down to man. I think you're judging us from afar, Lily. You'd not like others to judge you that way, you say so. The horrid looks people give you just because your children have dark skin...'

'Garth, you might have some point here. I don't mean to judge, it's just...well, I can't imagine ever thinking all the stuff you think about Jesus. That He is here. That you have...' She does the two-fingered gesture, makes inverted commas in the air around the keyword. '...a "relationship" with Him...'

'But I do, Lily.'

'At the expense of one with me, it seems.'

'No. There's no prohibition...'

'There is. I prohibit it, Garth. You're two-timing on me with Him. Or no-timing, I don't know how it works.' Then Lily puts a hand on

The Changing Room

his shoulder, raises it to his cheek which she caresses. 'Forget I said that, sweetie. I didn't mean it. Hot sun. Let's just...' She draws up her own knees, puts her arms around them and hangs her head forward. 'I'm sorry, Garth. I'm not myself today.'

They murmur civilities, words which fail to unsay what has already been said. Lily thanks Garth again for the cleaning he did in the maisonette. He is a dutiful boy, a willing helper. His contribution was sincere.

In time, they rise and start to walk back to the beach hut. 'Is your hand okay?' he asks her.

She throws it around his waist. 'I'm making a bloody imprint, Mr Addicks. I hope it's not an unwelcome exchange of bodily fluid.'

When they are still only halfway up the beach, he pauses, kisses the top of her head. As they turn into each other he touches her eyes, the closed lids, kisses her lips gently. Lily responds, she does not know what to think. Imagined her unplanned anti-religious rant was presaging a breakup just a few short minutes ago. Thinks it would be the simplest course of action, while retaining good feelings for this loyal puppy dog whose own motive for loving her sits within a realm she cannot grasp. Apart from his untapped lust of course. She enjoys it when she catches him eyeing her, his glance traversing her legs, her Caroline-tautened waist. He only stares when he thinks she won't notice. She has not had attention like it for a few years, and his discretion, the subtlety with which he expresses his caged desire is a secret pleasure. Lily is a skilled Garth-watcher.

They pass a queue at an ice cream vendor on the promenade and Garth asks her if she would like one. 'I'll pay you back,' he says. Acknowledgement that the only purse to hand is Lily's; he has money in his shorts, back in the beach hut.

'Not today, ice cream's mostly a kids' thing really.' As she says it, she hears both her error and truth. Ice cream is nice enough, adults eat tub-loads of the stuff; however, Garth is a man-child in her eyes. He rows like an earnest sixth former in a school debating society; wells up about Jesus in the land of Narnia; thinks an ice cream might rekindle a romance. The remedies she would apply if Jo-jo and Ami came to blows. 'Money's here if you want one.'

He shakes his head.

Boscombe

Perhaps he has briefly tuned into her wavelength. 'It'll be all right, sweetie.' She gives him a peck on the cheek. He looks doleful and she wonders what she should have done differently. Keeping her trap shut has never been Lily's way. She fishes the key from her bag, starts unlocking the beach hut door. 'I need to get out of these wet things, just look the other way. We're grown-ups.' They enter the hut together and Garth pulls the door closed. From bright sunlight to total darkness. Lily stretches her hand back toward the doorframe, hoping to find the light switch. Before she has found it, her arm crosses Garth's sun-warmed flesh. He takes a hold of her shoulders and pulls her into the closest embrace of the day, squashing her breasts, the still-damp bikini top, into his chest. They kiss with a passion that is confusing to Lily. She wonders if Garth might have arrived a bit late to this particular party. Her head is still awash with the quasi-row they had on the beach. Her hand flicks the switch and there is illumination. A large white globe of a lampshade hangs so low that Lily's head will touch it. Only Alice's children need not duck beneath this ill-chosen fitting. As she sees Garth's face pulling away from the kiss, his mournful demeanour is unabated. She could give him what he wants but he is not the boy to take it.

'Lily,' he says plaintively. She waits for his thought to form. 'I love you, Lily Stephens.' There is nothing new in this declaration.

'I know,' she answers.

Lily turns her back, faces the small kitchen area, fridge and hob along the back wall of Alice and Martin's tiny waterside pad. 'I'm changing now. Don't look but hand me that dress from the back of the chair, please?' She has a towel in one hand and as she begins to tug down her shorts with the injured right one, Garth's hand is upon hers, his other hand on her left hip. 'Ooh Garth,' she says, the pleasure in her voice expressing feelings she can only parody. Perhaps this contact is a start, although it hardly feels like the right time. It doesn't dispel the argument which has bubbled between them since arriving on the beach. To her utter surprise, he pushes the black shorts to the ground, she instinctively steps out of them, feels only shock when his hand cups her unshaven pubic mound. He mutters something she cannot make out. It might have been the word birdwatching. 'Garth!' she snaps sharply when she feels him—the most unlikely part of him—poking around behind her. With two hands on her back, he pushes her down, bends her forwards. Tests the flexibility that Caroline has wrought in Lily. Her waist is at ninety degrees, she could touch her toes. There is a cold sensation of shock, no familiarity, no pleasure, as he pushes himself inside her. 'Garth!' She has lost her bearings. They both have. 'Fuck!' she shouts when his unasked-for thrust causes her head to strike the corner of the kitchen side. 'Fuck, Garth.' There is genuine anger in her voice now. A gripping pain on her temple. She caught the angle of the hardwood on her hairline. As she stretches out a hand to prevent herself from falling, something clatters to the floor. Items plummet from kitchen side. Garth coughs, pulls himself out from inside her. The light goes out. Lily feels dazed; the bash on the head was vicious. Hurts like hell. She stumbles and falls onto the floor of the kitchenette, catching her cheek on a low cupboard handle as she does so. It could be a power cut; she's not fainted, she's still in the room. Lily raises a hand to her scalp, returns it to her nose. Smells blood upon her fingers. He's a fucking brute. She can scarcely believe what has taken place; the man in the beach hut with her is a stranger in these unexpected moments. Lily is crying.

'I've got to go,' says Garth, spoken at the same volume as he might a solemn amen. Light streaks into the beach hut from the open door. She is naked on the floor at the back of the cabin, the strip of red bikini top around her waist now. He pushed it down from its place, ran his hands across her breasts as he never did before. Everything in the encounter was odd. Unpleasant. Like finding herself with an unknown man. The door closes, and he has gone. The hut back in darkness.

Lily sits herself up, dizzy from the strike on her head. 'Fucking animal,' she mutters to no one. It is with unfamiliar feelings, a pain emanating from her bumped head and a discomfort deep inside her, that she stands and stretches again for the light switch, as she had done no more than two minutes earlier. Two terrible minutes which she thinks may already have disappeared from history. They do not belong in her life; if they belong in his, he is not the man she'd thought him to be. With a flick of the switch, the light is back, no outage: off-on, off-on. It was Garth playing tricks on her. That stupid, stupid boy. He could have talked to her, talked about what he really wanted. Sex is a need in grown-ups; Lily thinks it's true. It doesn't turn her into his blow-up doll. She runs her hand down herself, feels those other lips into which he has trespassed. Frothy white liquid, Garth has done what she thought he never would. As she surveys the room, she sees blood on the kitchen side, on her towel, and on a towel of Alice's too. A yellow towel, now red-stained, draped over a chair. She must have put her hand on it. The kettle is on the floor, a now-broken plate down there too. She didn't register what it was that fell when it happened, heard only the metallic ring of his no-longer-buoyant halo. The untimely shattering of his Christian vows. She starts worrying that she cannot fix the hut to be again as Alice had left it. Feeling faint, she slides once more to the floor. 'Garth!' she shouts as loudly as she is able. She knows she might just as well call out for Jesus. As she thinks the apt blasphemy, there is a rap on the door.

'Miss, are you all right in there, miss?' The voice of an old man—she can hear a quaver within it—not anybody she knows. There is not a squeak of Garth Addick's sanctimonious delivery in the call. The no-good Samaritan has buggered off, failed to live up to the standards he set on bicycle-clattering day.

The door opens two inches. 'No! I'm all right,' she shouts. A weak shout, not the assertive Lily of old; she really does not want a stranger to see her in this state. Nude.

'Are you sure?' asks the disembodied voice. 'I heard you shout.'

'Talking in my sleep. I do that.'

The door opens more, a thin grey-haired head, narrow features, poking around the door.

Lily, still sitting on the floor, pulls her knees up, hopes she has covered all she must. 'Get out!' she squeals. The door starts to close. 'Pervert! Peeping Tom!' She hears the click of the handle, the door closing. Lily starts to cry inconsolably. The man only wanted to help; she could use a bit of that. She stretches an arm out for her bag, the one she took to the beach, digs within for her phone. Dials a contact. 'Please pick up, please pick up,' she says like a mantra but the phone goes to answering service. She waits for the pre-recorded blurb to finish, tears still streaming down her cheeks. 'Alice, I've had an accident at the beach hut. I've broken stuff.' She sobs a bit before clicking red, thinks her message must sound horrific. Why didn't

The Changing Room

Alice pick up? She always picks up.

She tries again, a different number.

'Hi Lily, fitness session back on after all?'

She cannot speak, cannot bring down this chirpy, loveable friend.

'Lily, are you there?'

She tries to compose herself. Cannot.

'Are you crying? What's wrong, sweetie?'

'Are you working?' blubs Lily across the airwaves.

'Where are you?'

'Alice's beach hut...'

'I'll be there in twenty minutes. Don't go anywhere.'

* * *

Lily manages to dress, begins to pick up the broken pieces of crockery, kettle back on its pod. It is in a trance, a state of disbelief, that she does this. Garth had no need to leave, or maybe every need. She cannot understand who he is anymore. Who she is come to that. Feeling a little dizzy she puts herself, once more, onto the floor of the beach hut, the changing room. Sits down, red and white dress on the wooden floor. When the knock comes upon the door and she hears Caroline's voice ask, 'Are you in there, Lily?' she senses that her friend is a visitor from an unchanged world. The one beyond the beach hut, a parallel place to where she has dwelt this last half hour. She hugs her knees, wonders if Caroline can bring her back.

To her faint reply of 'Yes', the door opens.

'Oh God, Lily, you're caked in blood.' Caroline picks up a beach towel, looks around quickly, and then runs it under the cold-water tap. Very gently, she puts it up to her friend's scalp, the headwound from the counter-corner.

'Tell me if it's hurting, sweetie,' she says, pressing the cold wet towel onto the wound.

'They'll be back tomorrow, Joey, Ami. I can't be like this.' Lily starts to cry.

'I'll see you're all right.'

Lily cries freely, trusts that Caroline will do as she says.

'We can get you through this, sweetie. It's a right nasty cut you have.'

'I messed up,' she says as Caroline brushes Lily's black hair away from her face. 'Me and Garth messed up.'

'Do you want to tell me what happened here?' Caroline speaks slowly. With concern.

'Oh, Caz...' She pulls on her friend's hand, tears briefly abated. 'Never have sex in a beach hut.'

'What? This isn't funny, Lily. You're hurt. Should I be calling the police?'

'No, it's got nothing to do with the police.' She says it hurriedly, her tears back, clogging up her throat. 'This is between me and Garth. I shouldn't have called you.'

'No police then, Lily. I'm here to help you, and it's what I'll do. Your face looks bruised.' Lily turns into Caroline, hugs her closely, blood smearing onto the younger girl's bright T-shirt, even a handprint of it on her jogging bottoms. 'Lily, I'm taking you to hospital. No ifs or buts. It's what I'm trained to do. You know I'm a serious gym bunny, right? Procedures to follow.'

Lily smiles at her through her filmy eyes. 'Wait,' she says, rising from the floor of the hut. 'I've got to clean up first.' Caroline shakes her head firmly. Lily clutches her bag to her chest, sees her phone on the side, and puts it in. Feels her hips. At least she remembered to put her knickers on. 'How do I look?'

Caroline points to the stains across her dress, some of the white wheels in the pattern upon it appear misshapen by the blood which has soaked into it. 'Not at your best today, sweetie but I'll get you right. I can.'

As they open the door, the afternoon sunlight dazzles Lily. She takes a step back inside. 'No,' she says to Caroline who is proffering her a hand to hold.

The younger girl closes the door keeping hold of the handle, narrows her eyes as she looks into Lily's. 'What did he do?'

Lily dips her eyes down.

'Did he punch your face? What the hell did he do?'

Lily raises her head, tears staunched. 'I fell. Take me to hospital, please?'

'For sure.'

As they walk along the promenade, Caroline in her gym clothes — a little blood-stained from comforting Lily — rich brown headband holding her golden hair back, Lily wonders about the stares they are getting. Caroline links her arm; Lily feels that she is being hauled away. A person unclean. Perhaps the sounds of sex were audible in all the huts close by, although she can remember making none, hearing none from untethered Garth. No sound but for crockery breaking, rulebook no longer centre place when he did what he did. The old man who poked his nose in may have told all the beachgoers about the ill-tempered naked woman he found on the floor of the hut. Or perhaps they are not looking at her at all, it's just feelings of shame which she cannot explain.

A five-minute walk to the parked car, the efficient Caroline has a bottle of water with her, insists that Lily drink. When they get into the vehicle, Caroline starts the ignition. 'Tell me?' she says quietly.

'Did you skip work for me?'

'It's okay. Tell me? What was it with Garth?'

She says nothing as Caroline manoeuvres the vehicle out of its parking space, begins to purr up the hill. Heads for the hospital. Lily buries her head in her hands momentarily, then lifts it up quickly. 'I don't deserve you.'

The driver shakes her head. They glide through the traffic in silence for a couple of minutes.

'I was too much for him, Caz. I can be my own worst enemy sometimes. All men are animals—you know that; you must—and I just forgot.' Once more tears flow. She cannot describe what she does not understand. She invested only a small amount in Garth Addicks—so she thought—but he came looking for her soul. Pillaged everything she has. As Caroline drives, not speaking, attuned, Lily tells herself that she is a survivor, not a mental case. Manages it without moving her lips, no giving of contrary evidence. She even stops crying.

When they are stuck fast in the town traffic, Caroline begins to speak: 'Even I thought Garth was different, sweetie. He seemed kind of...' She can't finish the phrase.

'...kind of virginal?'

'Perhaps, Lily. But what did he do?'

'It's okay. He did what all men do if you let them. I banged my head is all. Bloody hurts though.'

'But where is Garth?'

Boscombe

'Gone to seek forgiveness, I expect.' Caroline turns her head while driving, looks momentarily into her face. 'He won't be getting any from me.' A few more tears splutter out with the conclusive sentiment.

* * *

In the casualty department they learn that the wait is to be long. The numbers of Bournemouth's newly sick, and accident-prone, swelled by the misfortunes of a small proportion of its many holiday makers. Caroline talks fitness, family, a little about her brother, George—nine years older, and living in Amsterdam—who she has not mentioned before, Lily is sure of it. She tells Caroline of Gary, her own brother. Younger, not much cop. 'At least he's not in prison,' says Caroline. This confuses Lily, she does not recall speaking of him before but Caroline says that she has. It's a bit of a blur. Nothing has been as clear as it should be today. Didn't plan to break up with Garth. Doubts if he had a plan either. A blur it is.

Lily, when finally seen, is surprised to find herself attended to by the same young doctor who stitched her leg wound several weeks ago. That she recognises him is unremarkable, his greeting of 'Welcome back' an astonishment. Gives her pause to believe for a second that Garth is following a pattern. The doctor insists on looking briefly at the back of her left calf. 'Not bad,' he says of his stitch craft. 'Narrow. It'll fade more come the winter.' He asks her how the latest came to take place. Bashing her head on a corner of a cabinet in a darkened beach hut is as much as she admits. Caroline looks at her through narrowed eyes. Lily mentions no accomplice in the forging of this injury. Then the doctor examines her head wound from every which way, holds up fingers for her to count. Looks worried when she tries to explain that she felt faint. 'How do you know you never actually fainted? he asks. When she tells him that she just does, he replies, 'The blood loss goes hand in hand with that feeling.' Lily is confused by his musings, alternately wondering if she is wasting his time or sicker than she imagines. 'You don't seem concussed right now but is there someone to keep an eye on you?' he asks.

Caroline points at her own chest, nods to the doctor.

'The nick on your cheek is nothing. Right on the bone so the bruise looks bad—discoloured—but it will heal. However, the wound there...' He points at her scalp. '...is much nastier. It'll take four stitches

The Changing Room

to put right. It's going to hurt a little, the hairline's an awkward place but I'll put a spray on...'

'Won't it heal without?'

'Heal, yes, look good, no. I advise strongly...'

'She's having the stitches,' says Caroline. She turns to Lily. 'I'll hold your hand.'

'Whatever she says.' Lily has half a smile on her face. She likes this girl a lot, and her own looks were important two or three hours ago.

The doctor completes the procedure in minutes. Caroline is good to her word; Lily squeezed her hand tightly as the stitches went in. Driving back to Boscombe, she asks, as she had done on coming here from the beach, 'Are you sure you shouldn't have been examined...?' Caroline points towards Lily's crotch.

'None of his business.'

'And you can't be pregnant?'

'I'm okay,' replies Lily. Inwardly she worries that her assertion may not be true. She no longer feels able to report—even to herself—exactly what did happen back in the beach hut. The fucking man of Judea certainly used no protection. Right now, she couldn't stand a mini-Garth, hates the thought of seeing him—the big one—and she has wondered to herself many times in the last three months if she might love the curious boy. That Geiger counter is currently registering absolute zero. If he had stayed, cleaned her wound, taken her again to hospital, then who knows? She can imagine there are relationships out there which began with worse sex. 'Cowards can't impregnate,' she tells Caroline. The comment receives the look of concern that it deserves.

* * *

Caroline tells Lily that she is going to stay the night. She's promised the doctor, and she would never break such an oath.

Lily is starting to wonder if she has imagined most of what has gone on, fantasised a more ebullient Garth than could possibly stalk this Earth. Deep down she knows exactly what he did, she has the stitches, further proof of his unasked-for encroachment. Normality is creeping back into her life. Distance gathering from that strange trauma. She has seldom thought of Muzzle these last twenty years: stains can be covered over. No need to recall those grim two minutes, the stifling, head-spinning warmth within that beach hut. 'I'm funny,' she tells her friend. 'I spent the morning preparing for Joey and Ami coming home. Cleaning. I've made their beds up freshly, and I'm not keen for anyone else to sleep in them. I'm sorry.'

'I'll sleep in yours. It's you I've to keep an eye on, remember?'

* * *

Later that evening, when Alice phones, Lily's mood swings from the relief that Caroline's kindness had brought her, back to guilt. Crying in no time. 'I've made a bloody mess in your lovely beach hut,' she confesses. Offers recompense.

Alice refuses. 'You sounded so upset in the phone message.'

Caroline proprietorially removes the phone from Lily, speaks to Alice with her back to her friend. Lily hears her say, 'A thing with Garth; a bad thing.' Then Caroline steps up the corridor towards Lily's front door, seems to listen to Alice. Lily can't make out a word they are saying, starts feeling vexed.

In no time, the phone is handed back to her, Alice's voice still emitting from it. 'Lily,' says the disembodied voice.

'Uh-huh.'

'I'm coming around. Don't worry about the ruddy hut, petal.'

* * *

When the three girls are sitting in Lily's lounge, Caroline jumps up and says, 'I'll fix a snack. Tea?'

Lily looks at Alice and says, 'Wine,' but Caroline shakes her head.

Alice nods at Caroline, and the latter goes into the maisonette's kitchen. 'She's looking after you,' she says when they are alone.

'I've made a right bloody mess at your place, Alice. You're going to hate me.'

'Lily, it was Garth, wasn't it? Caroline's worried. Do you think I should get the police out? Is it a crime scene?'

Lily drops her face into her hands. Shaking her head but without conviction. She has told too much to Caroline—first Muzzle and now this—too much. Needs to disabuse both her friends of any certainty they have inferred. She puzzles over whether she has any reliable recall about those brief minutes in the beach hut. Did she encourage or discourage? He was an animal, which in better circumstances is pretty much the point. 'It was a misunderstanding,' she finally tells Alice.

The younger girl reddens a little as she contradicts her friend. 'Sex is always all right or all wrong. And you needed stitches. Are you sure it was an accident?'

'No police, Alice. Sex is always wrong in Garth's stupid fucking Bible. I think that's why the big shit fucked off...' Alice puts an arm around the sobbing girl. '...you've not seen it. I've ruined your beach hut. I'm so sorry.'

Alice hugs her tighter.

Saturday, 6 August 2016

As they awake on Saturday morning, Caroline is again full of concern for her friend. 'Are you up to it?' she asks. 'If you give me the address in London, I could collect them.'

'Jo-jo's already in love with you, Caz. He'll up and leave me if you give him a reason.'

In the event, they share a leisurely breakfast. In response to her friend's questioning, Lily repeatedly confirms that she feels okay, better, not dizzy. Pretty much believes it herself. Then Caroline drives Lily to the railway station, offers to drive all the way to London but Lily thinks it would be madness. She bought the rail tickets long in advance, can't be wasting that sort of money.

The ten-past-ten is more crowded than even her last such journey to collect her children. Back when the stupid Christian was still an undated enigma. She has a novel in her small rucksack, and a drink and sandwich which Caroline prepared. The book spends the journey cover closed. She sinks into her own thoughts, goes over the conversation she shared in the middle of the night. The small hours. Her double bed again accommodating two, and neither a child.

'Will you see him again?' Caroline asked.

Lily doesn't know the answer to that question, obvious as it seems most of the time. Replied only vaguely. At one point she asked Caroline, 'What would you do?'

'I went back to Clive until the bastard hospitalised my dad,' Caroline reminded her. 'Don't take my advice, or only my new, wise-after-the-event advice. A clean break, Lily. You deserve better than Garth. What I don't know—can't guess or feel—is if that sounds like the right thing to you.'

'I'm not sure what I've seen in him, Caz. He didn't look like another bastard to me. He just turned.'

'I don't know, Lily...' The girl ran her palm down Lily's forearm beneath the bed covers. 'He gave you stitches twice. I didn't see too much happiness in the middle, sweetie.'

'He tried. He seemed to try, up until yesterday.'

'I think he mistreated you more than you're letting on,' she said.

'It was a misunderstanding.' Lily repeated the formulation she had earlier told Alice. 'Wires crossed. I thought I wanted to give myself to him but he was just a closed book. It all went wrong when...' And as she is thinking about the night-time conversation in the train, she realises that the account she gave Caroline—not an account of the sex of which there was insufficient to be worth the mention—of the encounter, was not an accurate one. Lily wonders what part she really played. She had been surprised Garth even entered the wooden chalet. That felt like a first. She'd thought it was a sign that he was becoming normal, trusting himself, not that he was about to flip over into some horny Neanderthal overdrive. He became a different person. If she had understood, she could have stopped him, calmed him, made it all happen differently. In the bed which she shared last night with Caroline, perhaps. And now the whole Christian-atheist rapprochement seems to be in the past. The wheelie bin. Nothing there to rekindle. She has learnt only that she never knew him.

She removes her phone from her small rucksack, scrolls through the contacts to G. The composition of the short text takes her many repeated and deleted efforts.

We need to talk

She signs it off with a sad face. Wonders why she cannot say more, deleted ten times as many words as the four remaining. And she never uses the emoji nonsense in normal times; it just seems right. The face is better than words. With those, Lily would only start swearing, get angry. That's been lurking close to the surface ever since the beach hut. The emoji used is better, truer. The sad look: he has done that to her quite directly, removed a lot of hope from her life. She presses

The Changing Room

send, holds the phone waiting for a reply. Holds it, looks at it. Thinks about Alice, who has texted twice already this morning. Nice messages, a valued friend. It comes to her now to offer to clean the hut, to pay for professional cleaning. Whatever it takes.

Sorry about the mess, how can I repay you?

In the time it takes thumbs to move nine times she hears notification of a reply. Looks at the screen.

Shut up

If Alice can answer promptly why the hell can't Garth Addicks?

A moment later she pulls her phone from the rucksack pocket, four musical notes signifying another incoming text. Word from Garth, she imagines.

Hut was easy to clean. It is what he has done to you that worries me. Love Alice

Lily stares at her phone, at the absence of a reply from the unforgiven Christian.

After both had showered yesterday evening, Caroline borrowed one of Lily's dresses, light blue, the shortest she has. Lily washed away more than the salt and sand of the beach but silently cried while doing so. Scrubbing herself where Garth had done his best, and she was starting finally to fear a pregnancy although she feels no sign within her. The knotted stomach, she is sure, is only anxiety, anger's more resigned sister. Keeping that fear to herself, the two girls chatted in the lounge. It was a warm night and her friend's presence helped her to relax. The clothing Caroline chose was too big across the shoulders but the waist was just right. Her tanned legs crossed before her, or lounging aimlessly on the sofa, Caroline's summer style contrasted with the thick flannel pyjamas which Lily wore.

'It's wrong, isn't it?' said Caroline. Lily didn't pick up a meaning at all, gave her the question-mark face. 'Did you wear this dress with Garth?'

'Once. I tried to dress to please him but I don't think I ever figured what did and what didn't.'

'But...' Caroline thought a little, twiddled with a shoulder strap before making her point. '...we enjoy dressing up, even being a bit

263

immodest, don't you think? Clive—he was shit in bed, actually, Flash Gordon, if you know what I mean—it was his idea that if we met, we should probably give it a go. If I showed an inch too much boob or bum it was unavoidable. We like the attention but not necessarily the consequence.'

'Garth was nothing like that. Jesus was everywhere, and Jesus is one hell of a cold shower. Then Alice—whose fault it is not—buys the only beach hut, only eight square metres of planet Earth, in which the good Lord, the good-if-you-like-that-sort-of-thing Lord, has no jurisdiction. That was my bad luck, it could have been good luck if I'd figured it out earlier, played the hand better.' And even as she said it then, her hand was reaching up to her new stitches, tears flowing down her cheeks.

Caroline was patient, heard her, didn't press her. A better friend than Garth has ever been, and yet on the train now, she stares again at the phone. Waiting for him to emerge from this meaningless silence. She sends another message to the man who ran away.

???

Once sent, she sits looking out of the window as the outer suburbs of London run to and recede from the windows of the train.

* * *

At the flat in Shoreditch, Trent looks shocked when he comes to the door. 'Lily, look at you. Did someone hit you?'

She denies it. Says that she slipped in a beach hut.

Trent knows little about her life in Boscombe. 'Beach hut? I thought you lived in a proper flat there.'

She tries to explain the arrangement, how great a thing a beach hut is. She could never afford one but her friend does.

'And Alice helped you when you fell?' Lily hears the old protectiveness in Trent's voice. 'This Gart' fella, he wasn't there?'

Trent's speech pattern mispronounces the name, and Lily misrepresents the truth. 'Another friend was with me and she helped. And it's nothing, Trent, a scratch on the cheek.' The only visible bruise is the one on her cheekbone. Lily is—following Caroline's wise fashion tip—wearing an accessorised headband that covers all trace of the four stitches. Keeps her scalp line from the viewing public. She

The Changing Room

worries it could seep blood but so far, so good.

Lily agrees to go upstairs into his flat. Drinks tea with Trent, both children looking on. Ami runs between each parent, clutching first the knee of one and then the knee of the other. Jo-jo is more circumspect. Even asks if Garth will be at home—visiting them—this evening. 'Not tonight, Joey,' she answers. Never again, might be the more honest reply. There has been no returned text. She checked before ringing the doorbell. None of that is for Trent's ears, for Joey's ears. Not so much as a hint.

* * *

Trent is good to her, pleasant but not pushy. His concern dissipates with her casual explanation for the cheek mark, the benign story of slipping on soap in a beach hut. Before her arrival, she had determined that this is what her children need to hear. During the train ride home, Jo-jo asks again about Garth. How often Lily has seen him, and when it is next going to happen.

'I don't know, Joey, Garth and I are a bit chalk and cheese.' The boy doesn't understand her phrase, takes an interest when Lily explains what she means. Points out the chasm between herself and Garth.

'Go to church then,' he instructs. A solution that takes account of only the very limited information she has shared.

'I think it's wrong to pretend you believe in something that you really don't,' says Lily.

'You tell Ami to be good for Santa Claus, Mummy. Why not do it for Garth?'

Lily glances at her daughter. Ami's ears pricked up at the reference to her and Santa, the little girl is laughing. Lily suspects she is already a yuletide agnostic, a new development since this time last year.

* * *

Throughout the train ride, Lily continuously checks her texts; one comes in from Alice asking what time she will be back at Pokesdown.

From Garth Addicks there is not a character of response.

* * *

As Lily and the children emerge from the station, Alice is standing waving from beside her parked car. She drives them to the maisonette, saving them all the one-mile walk.

'I spoke to Caroline,' she tells Lily. 'She was really worried. Wished she had gone with you. I didn't know the doctor said you were concussed.'

'The doctor didn't say I was concussed.' Inwardly she is surprised, had not known her two friends had phone numbers for each other. This must have arisen at some point the day before. She hopes Alice gets the pretty face image when the girl texts her, wants the three to stay fast.

'You might not remember quite what the doctor said if you've been bashed on the head,' Alice plays over her reassurance. 'I'm sure that Caroline did. She's looking out for you, just like me, petal.'

Lily nods her head, eyes frowning. Her children think she slipped on a bar of soap.

Alice comes into the maisonette with her; the children are delighted to find it so tidy. Lily feels herself welling up, takes deep breaths. This is not what happens on homecoming. She is strong. Always very, very strong. Ami hugs her and then picks up the light-blue dress which Caroline wore; it has been left draped over the top of the single lounge chair. Lily cannot recall whether it was she or Caroline who left it there, thinks she went to bed before her friend. Can't be certain. Ami unfolds the garment; Lily recalls that her daughter has always liked it.

'You wore that for Garf,' says her shrewd and mistaken son.

Alice give's Lily a puzzled look, says nothing.

* * *

No Christian of any denomination texts Lily this evening. From one specific member of The Church of the Men of Judea the absence of correspondence is a jellyfish's sting. A burning sensation that denies her needed sleep.

Sunday, 7 August 2016

Soon after rising Lily receives a sweet text from Caroline.

> ***Stretches, jumps and running to and on the beach have been cancelled for today. To be resumed when you are once more in sand-pummelling good health***

She sends her an instant reply.

Tricky anyway with the kids back but I am committed!

Mid-morning, Jo-jo and Ami are watching a cartoon; Lily enters her bedroom and makes a telephone call to Garth's mobile. He doesn't pick up as she knew he wouldn't. When the answering service kicks in, she talks anyway. 'Garth, I've been cross with you, angry actually. But that's not how I feel now. I don't like to be left with silence...in fact, I hate it. You shouldn't give me the cold shoulder, it's not right. You owe me some kind of explanation, I think. No, I know you do. An explanation. You owe me that much. The thing is, Garth, we've been close for quite a while. Closer than I've been to a man for a hell of a while. If we've not really been in step, it's been both of us who... I wonder if you went a bit crazy when you left the beach hut. I even wonder what the bloody hell you were wearing but that's your lookout. You shouldn't have gone like that. Caroline...Caroline's been great, she took me to the hospital when I needed stitches...' The rest of the message includes sobs as Lily cries saying: '...all you've bloody given me is stitches... and worry. Are you worried? I think you bloody should be. You weren't normal, Garth. You became someone else. Maybe it's who you always were, and your God is just a fucking bromide. I'm not sorry I said that; you've treated me worse, and its true...' She presses the red button hurriedly when she realises Jo-jo has entered the room. He comes to the bed and starts to tug at his mother. Climbs up and puts his eight-year-old arms around her. His crying mother. 'I don't think we will be seeing any more of Garth Addicks,' she tells her son.

He nods sagely, holds her tighter still. 'That's all right,' says Jo-jo.

Monday, 8 August 2016

Lily works only a three-hour morning on Monday. She'd known Capaldi-Clarke to be a more family-friendly firm than most when she signed up over two years ago. She talks briefly with Mr Clarke—the young one, Simon—it is a chance event, they are making coffee at the same time. 'I heard that your son broke his leg. I hope it's getting better.'

'That, yes. It's been a hell of a summer one way or the other. He's on the mend, thank you.' The father still wears a sling, the boy in plaster, apparently. When he says, 'Your hairband looks nice'—it is a red tartan that sets off her jet-black hair—Lily turns away, feels affronted. 'I'm sorry. I didn't mean anything by it.' She turns back to meet his gaze, puts her head to one side. Decides to accept the comment without trusting him an iota more.

* * *

She collects her children from the childminder, Lily sees six children including her own. Just one adult. Far more children there than she expected. Mrs Lyons—a mother of grown-ups—copes with them alone. If cope she does.

'These three were dropped off early,' she says, indicating a sibling group. 'It's more than I'm meant to have, it's just that summer gets tricky for everyone doesn't it?'

It certainly does, thinks Lily. Hard to navigate. We can all stumble into situations we might later regret.

* * *

She walks her children the short distance to the maisonette. They change clothes and then, because he will spend the afternoon at a friend's house, she walks Jo-jo across Boscombe, Ami in tow. After dropping him off, she and her little girl walk down to the cliff top. The view is breath-taking, the sea a flat blue that the sun is trying to turn green. The dry air brings Purbeck and the island to their fullest clarity. Lily points out landmarks to her daughter. The Needles; Old Harry Rocks. Ami seems underwhelmed, points more enthusiastically at a dog-walker's groomed pooch. And even Lily is feigning her enthusiasm, keeps glancing at her phone.

For three days now, she has received no calls or texts from the twat Garth Addicks.

Tuesday, 9 August 2016

After work Lily takes Jo-jo and Ami to the beach hut, the first time her children have been to it. She has a queasy feeling as she is walking them along the promenade. Pictures Friday last as if it were a horror movie, and Garth the villain in grainy black and white.

'What's the matter, Mummy,' asks her thoughtful boy, and it comes to her that nothing is truly wrong. Not today. She is cracking up over nothing. Banged her head is all. Worse happened to her on too many occasions when she was young. Six or eight years older than her son's current age. She oftentimes drank too much vodka to remember exactly what transpired. Who had done what to her. Garth a pussycat compared to the bastard, Muzzle. A daft Christian tomcat: a timid thing, fled at the sound of a kettle's clatter.

Alice is attentive, it is just her and the children. They all play together on the sand, paddle. Alice minds Ami while Lily takes Jo-jo in deeper, he swims well. Then she swims in the shallows with her little one, Jo-jo splashing Bryony kindly. Playing carefully with her.

When the children are back on the sand together—Wendy impersonating Caroline, leading a handstand contest, telling Bryony she is getting better through her practice—Alice asks Lily a little more about the fateful day. 'How did it end like it did, Lily? I didn't have Garth down as one to run away.'

'Nor me, Alice. I was wrong about him.'

'I don't understand. It seems like you and him... finally... and that's when he calls it off. And that boy really couldn't do better. You know that, don't you?'

'Can we talk about it another time, Alice? I feel like I let you down but it was complicated. He violated... we violated your beach hut...'

'Don't be daft. Martin and I did that first. And we managed without any cuts and bruises.' Lily gives Alice an appreciative smile. 'I just want to understand, Lily-petal. You were in pieces. Caroline said so. Whatever happened, it's not what making love should be.'

'No, Alice, it really wasn't.'

Alice has asked Lily a time or two if she has heard from Garth. Once more, on the Boscombe sands, she confirms that the answer is no. Not hearing from Garth has become a monotonous state.

Wednesday, 10 August 2016

After just a bit of cajoling, Lily is on the beach at six o'clock with her two little ones and Caroline. The intensity of square bashing has eased off. Caroline tells Ami that she cartwheels better than anyone she's ever seen. Jo-jo asks her to swim with him and Lily is surprised to hear her agree; Caroline has not gone in the water during all their previous visits to the beach. It takes her a couple of minutes with a towel around her to get the swimsuit on. Lily observes Jo-jo watching Caroline undress. When the fitness instructor and her son go out into the water, Lily stays back with Ami. She does not see much of the pair together but after ten minutes they are back. Caroline is a picture in an all-white one-piece, Lily's son holds her around the waist. Lily worries what ideas are getting into Jo-jo's head, raises the matter a little later in a quietly spoken conversation.

'He's eight!' laughs Caroline.

'If he finds a girl as nice as you in ten years, Caz, I'll be made up.'

* * *

By seven-thirty it has cooled off. The light is good but the temperature has plummeted. Caroline comes back to the maisonette. She offers to put the children to bed, sings to them while she does it. Lily—in the next room—hears that her friend sings off-key. She smiles to herself, won't mention it. Lily listens closely; Caz's singing is truly awful.

When they sit together, kids possibly sleeping but probably not, Lily again asks Caroline if she's managed to put terrible Clive out of her mind. 'Not really,' she replies. 'It's like I have a dungeon in my brain. He's in there and I can hear him faintly. But I've thrown away the key. He'll not be getting to the parts of me he'd like. I loved him once but not like I love my dad.' Lily likes hearing this. She has only met Caroline's parents the once, still she can picture them. Agrees with the girl's choice. Lily's parents have been the let-down; she thinks it is familial love which has anchored Caroline. Lily hopes to be as reliable for Ami and Jo-jo.

When the flat is quiet, after Lily has checked and found the children fast asleep—lungs full of sea air, little Ami in the tail end of brother Joey's bed—they again talk quietly together.

'When I stayed over, Lily, you were talking in your sleep. Shouting out loud while you were fast asleep.'

'Is this going to be embarrassing?'

'I think...' Caroline leans in and cups a hand to Lily's ear. '...that "fuck off, Garth," was the central message.'

'A fine message it is too. I keep texting him to ring me, Caz.

The Changing Room

Unfinished business.'

'What's left for you to say, sweetie?'

Lily snorts a laugh. 'I never got to say fuck off properly. My head was hurting, I was shocked he finally...' She doesn't find the words to finish the thought, steels herself to hold back tears. '...I hope he dreams that I'm telling him to fuck off. That would be fairest, Caz.' She is not the teenage-Lily any more, the hardening fails to set and she finds herself crying again.

Caroline holds her, hugs her like a child. 'I'm sorry, sweetie, I shouldn't have brought it up.'

'It's not you, you're a life saver. I thought I might be alone before, thought it almost every day in Boscombe.' The tears are only tracks upon her face now—eyes red—she can talk through this. 'I think I was proud, not needing a fella. They're mostly no bloody use anyway. Then I get Garth. He got me really, a shit cyclist, bowled me over before I saw his face.'

'That's a story, sweetie.'

'I think his church is like a tourniquet around whatever limb the soul sits on the end of. It cuts off the oxygen supply and all the easily-led of the world think that they've found the window into their souls when it's really only a numbness that they're feeling.'

Caroline looks at Lily, nonplussed. 'I don't know anything about souls. Heart rate, blood pressure, we've got it in a can but souls...?'

'None of us know it. We just try, we imagine being in love is a special feeling, and perhaps it is. Might believe it changes us, and it sometimes might. We feel a connection when we read a story, a news story about the parents of a missing child, that sort; we can't fathom if we're at our most selfless or our most selfish. The bite of it, the thing that has us in its grip is just our being here; this is our time, what we experience. And Caroline, I have to tell you, being with Garth for just a month or two taught me that the God Squad have a whole different approach. Or Garth's crowd do, at least. They're not here. They're in the land of Jesus. In their minds, they're all wearing Roman-time togas. That crap. They visualise the miracles Jesus did—let themselves think they've seen them happen—although it's all Lord of the Rings nonsense, don't you think? Of course, you can visualise what's in a book. I do it all the time—love reading—but I know it's made up, I'm

271

not stupid. The Men-of-Judea lot think that once everyone does it, acts like it's all true, the thinking of it will transport us back there—the first century A.D.—and that's when Jesus will finally show up again. The great big second coming that they bang on about. When Garth...' She glances across at young Caroline, her friend listening intently. '...could follow his commandments no longer, when I'd loosened his tourniquet, got it so loose the damned thing slipped off, the rush of blood sent him right over the edge, Caz. He doesn't live in a world of navigating temptations, he lives in a computer game, destroying them on sight. I think he only ran me over with his bike to put me out of the game before I could lure him off his ruddy pedestal. He should never have come to the hospital, spent hours in my company when I was only half-dressed. A big mistake.' Lily leans forward on the sofa, puts her head in her hands. From this penitent posture—without looking directly at Caroline—she continues with more Kentish gravel returning to her voice than usually shows itself. 'I think I hate him, Caz. Or maybe I love him and hate that he won't call me. I wanted what he took, just not the way he took it. He wanted me to go to his stupid church, meet his pretend God, and learn the wonders of never having to think for myself ever again. What did I do to him? I turned his world upside down. Should I have let mine go the same way, joined his Men-of-Judea cult? They don't top themselves or anything, they just deny themselves any fun. Any fun at all, full-stop.'

'I'm not religious,' says Caroline. 'Years ago, Mum had me confirmed in the Church of England. Dad was always sceptical; it's my mother who's that way inclined. Confirmation lessons were a chore—as dull as you say Garth's crowd are—but prayer was all right...'

'You pray?'

'No. Age fourteen, fifteen, probably sixteen, I did...'

Lily leans forward, takes hold of her friend's arm. 'They were answered in your case, Caz.'

Caroline is a little flustered. 'No,' she retorts. 'Maybe yes. I know I seem to lead the life of Riley but it's not all...'

'Sorry, Caz. I'm probably jealous of your looks. We all have crap to deal with. Did you think praying helped?'

'I did. It was the meditating on yourself, trying not to be all, me, me, me, when you're doing it: that was the good bit. God? I've no idea.

He wasn't in the programme, not so far as I could tell.'

'And what made you stop, Caroline?'

'I felt a bit of a dick, I expect.'

Friday, 12 August 2016

Early evening, Lily is at Alice's house. She has her children with her. They are all playing together under Martin's supervision. She waits by the door of the lounge; her friend is upstairs, changing her clothes, putting on make-up. The two girls are to have an evening out.

Jo-jo reads a picture book to the youngest, to Bryony; Martin comes and stands next to Lily, says quietly, 'He's a fine young man.'

Lily smiles at him; Jo-jo's dyslexia can frustrate him terribly and here he is playing teacher. She picks hold of Martin's fingers. 'Alice has been brilliant to me. She deserves you.'

He smiles back into Lily's serious face. 'A fine young man,' he repeats.

* * *

Later, the girls are walking down the promenade to Bournemouth, and Alice says, 'Do you remember when we met those cyclists?'

Lily stops in her tracks. 'There's only one thing worse than bicycles...' Demonstratively, she strokes her left calf. After a suitable pause, she completes her idiom. '...the ruddy men who ride them.' Alice protests, and Lily concedes that Martin is a good one. She tells her friend that her next date will be when Ami is eighteen, screws her face up in feigned calculation. 'When I'm sixty-five, with no teeth and titanium knees.'

Alice laughs but tells her that this is why she's got to find her a fella tonight. 'While you're still gorgeous,' she says, and the phrase sticks with Lily although she is sure Alice meant no foreboding. Then Lily decides she doesn't wish to enter the crowded bar. She recalls going into it with Garth, making up after some row or other, such was their time together. The girls keep walking further along the beach, and at Durley Chine they climb the hill a short way. Sit on a bench overlooking the bay. Lily tells her friend the story of Muzzle, the boy whose jaw she deservedly broke all those years ago. When Alice says, 'You pick the funny ones,' Lily wonders if she's really listened. She picked Garth, that's the truth. Had plenty of chances to send him packing before it all went wrong. Before he buggered off of his own volition, jaw still inexplicably intact.

'I think my life's been simpler than yours,' Alice states.

Lily wonders how that can be true. Thinks these are probably words of sympathy however indirect their construction. We look out through the slot of whatever little letterbox we're trapped inside. See what we see, feel what we feel. Nothing can be easier or harder than being oneself, she thinks. It just is, until it is no more.

By the time they have returned to the house, all four children are asleep. Ami is top-to-tail with Wendy, and Martin has prepared a blow-up bed in the lounge which Jo-jo sleeps on. 'No point in disturbing them,' says Martin.

Alice runs Lily home in her car to pick up an overnight bag, nightie, dressing gown. She is sleeping on the Mulhouse's sofa tonight. She would never sleep alone in her maisonette with her children just a few roads—three-quarters of a mile—away. This is her time, these children the beating heart of it.

Sunday, 14 August 2016

After four rings, it is answered. 'Garth here.' His voice is in real time, she is not hearing a recorded message. 'Garth, it's Lily...' and then the phone goes dead. This happens at ten o'clock on Sunday morning. He's getting in the frame of mind for his fucking church, and he clicks the off-button at the sound of her voice. Is that a trick Jesus taught him? Is all this send-your-friends-to-Coventry crap in the Bible? Lily wishes her anger didn't erupt as it does. She should leave God out of it. Garth is the arse here, Garth Addicks and no one else.

Tuesday, 16 August 2016

From the time of his hanging up on Sunday through all of Tuesday, Lily telephones Garth on no occasions at all. Sends him a number of texts totalling precisely zero. Doesn't so much as enter the ward of Redhill and Northbourne. Writes no letters to her very-ex boyfriend. Emails, Facebook posts, WhatsApp messages: these are barely in her ambit. None of the above does she dispatch in the direction of Garth.

Lily has thought of the boy incessantly. It is annoying beyond toleration that her thoughts should stray upon him time after ruddy time. He has no hold over her; this is self-flagellation and she has no time for it in so many ways.

Wednesday, 17 August 2016

At six-thirty, a slither of morning sunshine is scheming its way through her tightly closed curtains. She is barely awake but has been in this amorphous state for a time, ideas and images rummaging around her early-morning brain. Phone in hand.

Thinking of you

As she sends the message to his mobile, she knows that she certainly was. It is the most conciliatory message she has sent him. By a country mile, it is. Even Lily doesn't know if she means it. Doesn't disclose in her three-word text exactly what she thinks about him. There is more than a little residual anger lurking. Didn't say it but there is. A bucketload at most times of day. Nothing to do but wait, and experience tells her it will be fruitless. Endless. Lily is on a treadmill she cannot leave.

She is reading the book she bought earlier in the summer, a novel about missionaries in Africa, a compelling book about sisters made strange by their mad-preacher father. She loves it, her thoughts spark off in all directions. It is not Garth within its pages—nothing to do with Garth, Peter, Margery or little Julie—the book is about some other nutters. She devours some twenty pages before hearing noises from her children's rooms. Time to rise.

Breakfast is fun; Ami is cute today, insists on eating a whole banana, she would normally share one with brother Joey. Yesterday was her birthday, a small party held: she is big now. She repeatedly tells her mother this important truth. 'Six,' Lily confirms. 'Very, very big.' When she is packing their bags for the childminder, she notices how Ami is waiting, not impatiently and not rushing back to her room to play. She is taking the business of being six very seriously. As they step out of the door, Jo-jo carrying a child's rucksack and Lily another, plus a large handbag, little Ami insists that she can carry her own. 'All the way?' asks Lily. They have a half-mile walk ahead of them.

'All the way,' says her daughter.

It is only eight twenty-five, and already the sun is warm. As they walk, her gorgeous girl-child leans into Lily's legs, twiddles her fingers on the yellow-print dress the mother wears. 'Tired already?' asks Lily in a kindly tone.

'No,' says Ami, pulling herself up.

* * *

'Are we the first,' Lily asks Mrs Lyons, the childminder, on their arrival.

'I've only these two today,' she answers. 'If you'll sign for it, I can take them to the beach.'

Lily wasn't prepared for this, feels a little flustered. She hasn't brought their beach things; thought she might take them there herself in the afternoon. Doesn't like Jo-jo to swim unaccompanied: he's good but he's a child, too little to enter the water alone.

'I've left their swim things—costumes and towels—at home,' she tells the lady.

'No. We'll just be watching on the prom. I get myself a coffee there,' explains Mrs Lyons. 'It's too much of a faff going down on beach, getting sand everywhere. I don't do that.'

'They might like the walk,' Lily acknowledges. Then she kisses the children, tells them to be good for Mrs Lyons. She—their loving mother—will take them paddling, swimming, rolling in the messy sand, later in the day when her morning shift is over. Tells them as much with a wink.

'Will Caroline come too?' asks her son.

Lily eyes him with mock suspicion. 'I'm your mummy, sunshine,' she says scrunching up his wiry black hair.

* * *

Mrs Garrett gives Lily a string of tasks to do. The quantity is fine with her, keeps her occupied. She thinks her office manager's tone of voice is pleasanter than usual, more grateful. She wonders if the shorter hours she works now her children are back home is prompting this, making her value more noticeable by her regular absence.

'There's a new solicitor starting next week,' Garrett tells her during a break, both drinking coffees.

The Changing Room

Lily asks the name—takes an interest—wants to hear how the balance might be shifting in their staid offices.

'His name is Pringle, Charles Pringle, and he said we're to call him Charlie. A nice young man, your age probably.' Then Gillian Garrett lowers her voice to a whisper. 'Best not to get any idea's though, Lily. I heard from Simon that Charles Pringle lives in Poole with another man.' She nods her head knowingly, holding Lily's gaze for a moment. 'No ideas at all, I'm afraid, Lily.'

Such is their relationship that Lily nods back, as if thanking Mrs Garret for the information. Then she picks up her coffee and turns to her own desk, her computer screen.

'Are you all right?' asks Gillian Garrett. 'Have I upset you?'

Lily's shoulders are heaving with laughter, there are tears in her eyes. Good, funny tears. 'I come to work to type audio,' is all the reply she can manage.

The office manager looks a little affronted. 'It's not a laughing matter. You and I will have to treat Mr Pringle like it's all perfectly normal.'

Lily says, 'Yes, like normal,' but still it is through laughter. Garrett is a hopeless case.

* * *

In the late afternoon, she arrives on the beach with her children. A text has confirmed that Caroline will be here in less than an hour.

Her newly matured daughter insists that she can watch from the sand as mother and son swim deeper than Ami yet dares to. Lily has a word with another young mum who sits close to them, who agrees to keep an eye on her. Needed reassurance before Lily will venture out with Jo-jo.

When they are all back on the beach, Lily asks her children about their morning? How Mrs Lyons looked after them.

'She's a bit old,' says Jo-jo. 'Me and Ami can look after ourselves.'

Lily worries over what her son has said. Fears she has plumped for the wrong childminder. 'What happened this morning?'

'We just sat, Tom and Jake were with us. She talks with a friend at the café.'

Lily doesn't know who these boys are, learns that both are in school with them. Tom is in her son's class. They were present accompanying

Mrs Lyons's friend, another childminder. 'Is that all you did?' It sounds too boring; she contemplates cancelling work the next day. Wonders how that would pan out.

'She's a bit of a shirker,' says Jo-jo.

Ami giggles and says, 'Ice cream.' This prompts Jo-jo to shake his head. To try to shush her but it is too late.

Now Lily laughs with Ami. 'She bribes you with ice cream?'

Ami nods. 'Bribe with ice cream,' she says. Lily doubts if she has fully understood the word with which they describe Mrs Lyons's motivation for the purchase.

Caroline arrives while they are talking. She's dressed for exercise, for working out. Lily isn't, not today. She wears a red swimsuit. 'Looking sexy, Miss Stephens,' says Caroline. Lily has not worn her black shorts in almost a fortnight. Washed and stashed away. Ami does handstands, her mother's friend prompts this response in the girl through her presence alone. Caroline alternates between sitting beside Lily and jumping up to hold the little one's ankles. Praising the straightness of her back. When Lily shares her childminding dilemma with her friend, Caroline says, 'Leave it to me.'

Lily objects. 'What about the gym?' This was not her intention.

'I'm on shift at the weekend, so no gym for the next two days.'

'You can't be serious,' says Lily. Caroline will not be dissuaded. 'If I pay you what you're worth, Caz, you'll bankrupt me.'

* * *

Later in the evening, Lily and Caroline share the cost of a takeaway pizza, bring it back to the maisonette. The kids love it, they laugh and play with both adults. It's a hilarious time, and once or twice Lily notes that Garth is off her mind. The problems, the distractions of the day, have helped her. All after a six-thirty-in-the-morning wobble. Sending that stupid text.

When Caroline is leaving, Lily already showered and dressed in jeans and T-shirt, both children in bed—although Jo-jo is playing a game in there, electronic noises coming from his room that she has no wish to restrict today, he has been a gem—she thinks about the new childminder: Caz. She still looks like the gym instructor, wears all the gear, although it has been an evening of child's-play plus pizza. She is to run back to Christchurch. The girl runs like Lily ties a shoelace. Effortless: her legs eat the miles.

'Eight-thirty,' the girl tells Lily, 'I'll bring the car and we can all go out, when you're back from the office.' Lily even wonders what Caroline sees in her, why she gives herself so lovingly to Lily, to her family. She decides to think about it less, enjoy it more. Caz is a character.

Sunday, 21 August 2016

The following Sunday, Alice has agreed to look after Jo-jo and Ami for the morning but—little white lie that it is—believes she is doing so because Lily is to use the free time to go running, to keep up the regime which Caroline instigated during the fortnight her children were absent. Alice pulled her fitness-face, or her anti-fitness-face as Lily calls it, when she explained the reason. Agreed to help out, always will. Lily pushed her bicycle round to Alice's house, children by her side. Even they believe she is cycling back to meet Caroline, who they have not seen since Friday. Who both children know to be the world's greatest childminder, although she can fulfil the role no longer because of her paying job.

After kissing her children goodbye, Lily rides away in the direction of Northbourne. Rides very singularly on that course, quickly finding she is making better time than needed. May arrive far too early for the prospect she has in mind. She locks her bike outside a coffee shop in Winton, orders a cappuccino and picks out a sugary muffin—likes the idea that it might fortify her, sweeten her sour—puts it back when the cashier registers the two pounds and twenty-five pence it is to cost. She slips a paper of brown sugar into the coffee instead, then regrets it, the taste much sweeter than she likes to drink it. Wonders to herself what she's doing here, her children back at Alice's? Well, it's happening, she is doing what she's doing. She has resolved to think no further than that.

She spends exactly twenty minutes in the coffee shop and then returns to her bike, cycles the last mile and a half more slowly. At three minutes to eleven, bicycle chained to a railing outside a high street supermarket, her heart pounding to an uncertain beat, she steps through the entrance into The Church of the Men of Judea. It is gloomy coming from the sunny morning outside, only the shape of the building's interior is clear to her. Low-ceilinged, bland, school chairs in wide rows. She takes a seat three-quarters of the way back. Further from the pulpit than any other congregant. Quite right. If the little lectern out front can be called a pulpit. Pathetic bit of plywood. As her eyes adjust to the light, she takes in the lady facing the gathered throng, and guesses it must be Margery Cox. She, Garth's often-spoken-of Pastor, gestures that Lily may come closer. She acknowledges this with a smile, budges not an inch. It is at this point that she sees the man with the guitar, sees him clearly. He sits with his adoring little choir. She can tell at a glance which is Julie Rivington. The only one Garth spoke about. Meanwhile, he is looking down, looking at his feet, or little Julie's feet. Doing so with a certainty that tells Lily he has briefly looked up and will not be doing so again. Or he might try but who knows what contortions such effort will wreak upon his face. Lily mouths some words. She doesn't think that he is looking; silently mouths them anyway. 'I am in your stupid church.' There are other words coming into her mind, words she forbade herself to think during the ride here. Words which would shock the flock if spoken out loud. She tries again to rinse them from her mind. She told herself to try the religion—give it a go—the first-century babble of The Church of the Men of Judea. There might be something in it: she enjoys kicking a football with Jo-jo, hated soccer as a kid. If she bumps into Garth Addicks while she is here, then such an event was meant to be. The Lord must have fixed it. Kidding herself like a Christian, she doesn't expect to get used to it. Telling lies to Alice about going running, the same to her own kids. Lies to herself about why she has come here. Lies about the second ruddy coming. Everybody's at it.

Then the sound of the guitar being strummed fills the hall, and the girls are singing. They begin with a verse about turning water into wine, Lily grins to herself, imagines that she approves of this miracle more than most in a church full of killjoys. Then the whole congregation, the flock—the lambs awaiting their inevitable slaughter—are piping up in unison.

Our God is greater, our God is stronger

They belt it out with an intensity of feeling Lily cannot locate in her own emotional range. She thinks wryly to herself how possessive they sound. Do these cults not share? Has God really given them exclusivity, signed a single denomination deal, and with such a paltry-looking outfit as this? Garth-like haircuts on every man; frumpily dressed women except for the cute little choir. When the singing ceases, Lily watches Margery make her way gingerly to the small dais. As she does, she spies Garth, who spent the song with his eyes transfixed on his singers. Little Julie, most likely. She really is a pretty thing. Now he glances between his pastor and the frets of his guitar, the instrument lying dormant across his lap. For all she knows, this is normal church conduct for him. She feels the avoidance of his gaze like a frosting.

'Let us pray,' the disabled lady intones. Everyone sitting in this make-believe church with its emulsion-finished ceiling, opaque double-glazed windows—no stained glass for ascetics—has their head bowed in anticipation. Lily too; she can fake it. Give us your best prayer, Madge! Then, to her surprise, she finds the woman's words resonate within her. Lily tries to mentally dissect them as they pierce her consciousness. 'Please God, keep us open-minded and help us to listen to you as we search for whatever it is that we have come to seek.' Open-mindedness is Lily's own mantra. She has off days—it's a big ask—but she values it highly. She thinks that the hobbling God-botherer has rumbled who she is. Garth always confided in her; he told Lily as much. She must stand out in here; she doubts if they've seen a new face since the choir popped out of the womb. 'Give us hope, Lord but steer us from false hope. Give us strength Lord and help us to direct it at what should most usefully support ourselves, and support you, our Master in all decisions.' No. This is utter nonsense, thinks Lily. Always thought it would be. She has no master. Trent was smart enough to know that. Garth is the dunce; he believes every lie they were peddling in the year dot. 'Lord, we are every day stunned by the goodness in you, the forgiveness you found in your heart for a populace, a world, that watched on as you were crucified. Show us, O Lord, how we might be so humble, so meek, so forgiving, in the aftermath of the small and insignificant trials that beset us.' As she listens to these few words, Lily feels wretched. Feels her cynicism is a crime. She was uncertain on arrival if she was here to embarrass or reconcile with the wilfully blind guitarist. Now she wonders why she has chosen this place to confront him; she is not here to puncture the balloon of these timid people's faith. She wonders if her whole mission—to deflate Garth's religious hogwash, to render him normal like her—was one of cruelty. She wanted him to compartmentalise his belief, pay less regard—none at all, ideally—to the drivel which mesmerises all the scaredy-cat Christians. Certainties engulf her, giving doubt to her mission. They, the sheep of this flock, are managing their humdrum lives the only way they can. And Garth is just another one of them. She puts her head in her hands, knows that any eyes upon her will think she is praying. Overcome. And perhaps she is; the conflict that love and hate curdle in the stomach. She wants her children here. Wants them, the only people in this world who arouse anything good in her wayward soul.

Pastor Margery continues to stand before her congregation. Good of her; Lily can see from her face that there is pain even in standing. She reads an extract from the Book of John. Lily listens intently, less disdainfully. She doesn't know what the Bible says but it is old. Meant something to a lot of people in its day. The passage Margery reads tells of a miracle: helping the lame to walk. This strikes Lily as a bold statement from the arthritic pastor. Lily is not one to wish pain on another person. Margery, Lily thought of fondly, when Garth first described life at this church, when they were forging bonds over what they do not have in common. Before it all began to frustrate her. Then her fable comes to the punchline, the sting in the tail. Jesus tells the healed cripple to sin no more, that worse may happen if he does. Lily wonders if Margery chose this passage, this message, expressly for her. It seems improbable—Lily gave her only three minutes' notice to come up with it—yet the content speaks. She finds herself wanting to debate with Margery Cox what the nature of sin really is. Let this woman judge if it is she or Garth who should face banishment. Lily has no wish to join their silly church, none beyond the notion that doing so might right a wrong. A wrong which no person in this room, except her and Garth, will have the slightest inkling about. The choir are back on their feet, Garth strums; they are praising the spirit in creation. The sound swells in the hall, within it she hears Garth's voice. Audible, strong. Her presence has not silenced him, not done as she both hoped and feared. It comes into her mind that he has processed her presence, figured out how to meet with her when the service is over. What to say. And Lily hasn't a clue. It will come out if it wants to, that is the way with thoughts and feelings. She again wonders if she is here to take him down a peg, or for some kind of reconciliation. This is the place for the latter but Garth has not been the boy for it. Lily doesn't know this hymn, doesn't care for it. Bows her head and mouths again, 'I am here in your stupid church.' Does Garth know why she's here? Can he sense it? He may have a clearer notion than she, her reasoning has been confused from first to last. He never phoned, picked up or texted. Hasn't given her a clue. She hates his silence, has no firm notion of what he feels toward her. What he ever felt. When they meet, she could kiss him or, more likely by far, spit in his face. She cannot see that far into the future—a couple of minutes—never ever has gone in for prophesy. Margery is speaking once more, going over the week ahead, praising some fund-raising effort or other, then there are more prayers—ritual prayers, Lily thinks but it is a guess—the woman's style is as informal as Garth occasionally moaned about. As heads come up, Pastor Margery asks everyone to greet in Christ those beside them.

Two elderly women who sit three rows in front of Lily turn around. One speaks to her in a well-projected voice. 'I am Edith, and in Jesus's name I greet you, my friend, and I welcome you to our church, for I have never seen you here before.'

The second lady says similar, more quietly but Lily can hear. Her name is Dorothy. 'We hope you find peace and happiness amongst us.'

'I am Lily, very pleased to meet you,' she answers. Edith mouths something to her, Lily gets it. 'In Jesus's name,' she adds. She had thought to avoid this nonsense—tell people she was an observer not a believer—now that she is speaking with them, she finds no wish to belittle these two ladies.

A man has stalked down her row of seats, he too greets her in Jesus's name, states his own. 'Peter.'

Lily nods. 'I am Lily,' and when Edith mouths the Jesus word again, she ignores it. Peter Carter is a man she has greater wish to lace into, holds herself back only because she first needs to discover if he really is the odious toad that she has inferred.

He seems to have nodded away the ladies—deployed some Christian semaphore or other—just the two of them within talking distance now. The followers of Margery's creed are breaking up, going through a back door or out the front. 'We are pleased to see a new face amongst us,' Peter says, and Lily immediately thinks he is playing to type. 'Am I correct to surmise that you are already familiar with our guitarist? With Garth.'

Familiar, she thinks, is that a biblical term for had sex with, been shagged by, fallen pregnant to. Thankfully, the last in the list she has ticked off as a negative. Proof to the contrary arrived almost one week ago. 'Yes, I know Garth Addicks.' As she says it, she looks toward him. Sees that the choir has disbanded, guitar and its strummer no longer in plain sight.

'I learnt there became some differences between you,' he says quietly.

'He told you that?'

'No, no. Garth has not sought my counsel on these matters, I understand that Margery has had a heart to heart, supported the poor boy. She joined up the dots for me, let me know the bare bones. Pastor Margery,' he adds, gesturing in front of him. The lady is now standing in the aisle a short distance away, she clutches the rim of her walking aid and smiles benignly to the newcomer they have rumbled.

'Oh God,' Lily mutters, 'this is between me and him.' She turns away, starts shuffling past the chairs. Wants to find Garth.

Peter puts a hand upon her shoulder. Gently. There is no evident malice in his touch. 'Garth departed church promptly. Please don't take it personally but I think he is fearful of the feelings you arouse in him.'

She wants to scream at this pontificating creep, who has not spoken to Garth but knows the whole story by osmosis. 'Why should he fear me for Christ's sake,' she says, her blue eyes flitting angrily at Peter Carter and over his shoulder at the woman on the Zimmer.

Before the man can react, Margery starts talking. 'Come,' she says, gesturing for Lily to walk with her. 'Come, friend.' For lack of an alternative, she follows the pastor. Through a side door into a small room at the back of the church. Peter follows them and Margery asks him to unstack two chairs. They are in a storeroom—a large one—lit only by a naked light bulb. Shelves of toys, children's books; no natural light.

'Three chairs?' queries Peter, when two are out.

'Leave us girls alone please, Peter,' says Margery.

When it is just the two of them, Lily asks, 'What do you want with me?' She hears the accusation within her own voice. Thinks it entirely justified.

'We wish you to come and meet the Lord, and this is the place for it. I am uncertain if that is truly why you have come.' Margery takes a hold of Lily's hand, clasps it with both of her own. 'My, my,' she purrs, 'I can see what it is that Garth saw in you.'

'Where has he gone?' She is sharp in tone, warmed to the pastor when she was preaching but this is cod psychology. The same flattering nonsense Lily used when selling dresses to women who thought a change of clothes could improve their sullen personalities.

'I think you and Garth are on different paths, however close you once were. And I believe it was once a more intense relationship than Garth knew how to conduct himself within.'

He's told you the fucking lot, she thinks, and he strums away beside the Julie-girl with your eternal blessing. Your Jesus-inspired forgiveness. 'I don't put barriers between myself and others, Margery,' says Lily. 'Garth and I should figure everything out between ourselves...'

'I appreciate that many people would but he feels he needs to rely upon us now. We are his church.'

'Isn't that just cowardly? Not facing up to...'

'What is past is past. He has no wish to stray from Christ's teaching and so he shall not...'

'Teaching! We're not children, Margery. He doesn't have to live by rules if...'

'Laws, Lily. Laws, covenants, the verification of sins. And we may all stray occasionally. It is wise to understand and seek to prevent it. To fail to codify right from wrong is to allow ourselves free rein. This life is too short to waste on denying ourselves redemption in the next one.'

Lily cannot think, cannot argue. She is worried she may just shout, that's bullshit and you know it, at this patronising pastor. Take to the low ground which she was so determined to avoid when she set out this morning. 'Why will he not see me really?' She wonders why she has let herself be led into a cupboard.

'He told me that you had the deepest insight into your relationship. You saw that he could not find it in himself to satisfactorily love you and Jesus both. I am so sorry, Lily, and your insight is a testament to you. The Lord is waiting...'

Lily stands and turns, emits a snort of laughter as she opens the storeroom door and walks out. Leaves the pastor to bask in her make-believe righteousness. The church hall has become empty while they were in there. Lily walks to the back door through which she had seen some of the congregants leaving earlier. There is a small rear courtyard—an olive tree in a bucket—a dozen or more still out there. No sign of Garth Addicks. He strums and runs, what a fucking loser. Lily strides towards the pretty girl, Julie of the choir.

'Hello, welcome to our church.' The little girl's smile is pure innocence.

'Hi,' says Lily. 'You know Simon Clarke's boy, right?'

'Ronnie?' Her eyes look briefly down. 'I'm his...' She doesn't complete the phrase just nods while Lily's eyes narrow angrily at her.

'Well, I hope Ronnie's all right, never met him. His dad came on to me a few weeks back. You know what I mean? Asking if he could come around to mine at night, despite having a wife and kids at home. That kind of come on. Angling for...well, I think you know what he was angling for. I hope Ronnie's...' The young girl's face has turned scarlet; Lily wonders why she has chosen this irrelevance with which to turn over the tables in the temple. 'I don't think your all-strumming Garth Addicks is any better. That's what I think. Sorry Julie but it needed saying. Garth is a Christian nob, actually. That's exactly what he is.' For no reason Lily can think of, the teenage stick insect has started to cry. Lily turns and walks back into the church. Margery is coming into the courtyard as she does. She can clean up the mess. Speaking to little Julie might have been an error. Down the long aisle to the front door and out into the road. That's that. Lily takes the key from her jeans pocket. Starts to fiddle with the lock on her bike. Snorts another laugh as she does it—a bitter one—but at least there are no tears this time. She had to handle crap that was a million times worse than anything she has dished out. More than a million. Had to cope alone when she was Julie's age. No Jesus Christ bobbing along beside her. No izzy-whizzy-let's-get-busy magic protection when Lily was a kid. Never had it, doesn't want it.

Boscombe

Chapter Six:

Thrice Crowed the Cockerel

Friday, 5 August 2016

The day is too hot for him, and he finds the conversation impossible. She seems to be raving mad at everything. Has no focus. It was sticky cycling over and then she made him join in the manic cleaning of her maisonette. He gets it, she really loves her kids but it's hugs they want and need. Far too young to fuss about hoovering and pot washing. The swim was better but then he went and dropped her while she was horsing around. She likes that stuff too much for a woman in her thirties. He has always thought her the sort to choose her words carefully and then she goes and says this. Says that his religion 'floats his boat.' Silly words, just plain silly. Disrespectful too. Loving Lily does not get easier. Perhaps it never will. She goes on and on. Her hare-brained theories are pretty insulting if you think about them. Take them seriously at all. It's a cross which Garth continues to bear, and from which he can glean no pleasure. When she does the gesture, sarcastic inverted commas—makes out that his relationship with Jesus is the joke—he feels physically sick. He might need days to work out what to do about this. Garth has no chance in this heat. She teases and tempts him, of course. That is another cross, a Christian's life. He wonders if he has taken more pleasure from it than he should have. Nor does Lily offer him the commonality he has foolishly guessed was to arrive. The possibility that their minds might meet. She listens to her own grandiose flow, intelligent sounding but it turns out to be only a regurgitation of the present noise. She toys with social issues with a good heart and then transcends nothing. She's not listened to him at all, that is the most disappointing thing. She is dismissive of what she doesn't already know and opposes Christian thinking as a point of principle. He's explained a lot of important ideas to her but she doesn't dwell on them as she should. He's tried to help her to see what matters. Very carefully he has contrasted the meaninglessness of high church ritual with the determined acts of goodness which set The Church of the Men of Judea apart from all others. She never gives it proper consideration at all. Her mind is made up. She resents our Lord, and that's not the kind of open-minded place from which one can begin to receive biblical truth. No one would ever let in the Holy Spirit if we all thought that way. If she listened to him properly it would turn her miserable life around. Then she won't so much as try. He cannot set a candle before her—hope, prayer, prospect—without her blowing it out. It's like a reflex to Lily. It might be the devil breathing through her.

As they trudge back to her friend's show-off beach hut, he is once more walking behind her, looking through the hot sun's haze and upon those same black shorts she always wears. Got uppity with him earlier when he asked if she had proper swimming briefs on underneath. He remembers, weeks back, on the beach with her younger friend, doing the exercises when a stranger joined them, a girl wearing a thong—that's what Lily called the girl's lower bikini—she admonished him for looking but she keeps herself wrapped up there. Always in the same black shorts even when she swims. It's not modesty, he thinks, not in one with two children. She says herself that he...

Garth arrests his thoughts, stops to kiss her on the beach, tries to feel what there is in his heart as he does it. The heat is intense, and he feels mostly just sweaty. He asks his girlfriend if she wants an ice cream. She doesn't even agree on that. They move on up the promenade to Alice's beach hut. Lily unlocks it, then inside they are plunged into darkness, and she finally kisses him. Passionately it seems. The mood has changed.

Then he thinks it's him.

He wants to lead her down the path to salvation. She won't have it, and here he can give her what she wants. Could, can.

He feels her, down where he has pushed away her black shorts. He is in the grip of an uncontrollable passion. Or a need. A desire.

It is her religion that has seized him.

She says it, says it in the crudest way: 'Fuck!' He can't resist this.

He should but...

...he hasn't.

He thinks that the heat of the sun has addled something in his brain. He can't stay; there is shame in what he's done even if Lily Stephens can do it without such a feeling. Without shame. It's her thing, she long ago made that clear. Called it birdwatching earlier today. Makes out it's a frivolous thing when it isn't. It's wrong when you're not married.

He wonders how she ended up on the floor. She seems to have knocked some of her friend's kitchen stuff over in her passion. He heard a plate smash, thinks something else—a kettle—fell down with it. With her. He has long known that she is in thrall to her lust, never saw before how close to the surface that devil lay. As he quickly pulls up his swimming trunks and grabs the little bag he brought—rushes from the scene of the shaming—he sees blood on his forearm. Lily cut her hand back on the beach; he presumes it's from that. It is unpleasant to think he might have menstrual blood upon him although his religion doesn't fear it. They're not superstitious, plenty of depth to their beliefs. He hopes he didn't do it wrong. If he did—he has no experience of debauchery, it's not his thing—then maybe it all has been a less heinous act than he fears but he thinks he was in the right place. Briefly. He didn't sin for very long. He's unsure what difference it would make, it's still a sin even if it went in the wrong hole. Peter would know the difference. It's in Deuteronomy somewhere. He expects she enjoyed it as he could not. The devil gripped him for those few moments, he feels his soul may be forever stained. He goes quickly into the beachside toilets. The smell is rank. He doesn't think he can change in here, not with urine on the floor. He goes back out to the promenade, takes his shorts from his bag, and puts them over his wet trunks. It feels as if people are watching—perhaps they do, perhaps they don't—they are of no concern to him. It's the Lord's vigilant eye which he fears. He hopes that He diverted His eyes within the beach hut. Surely, He must have; being all-knowing is not to be a peeping Tom. Seen or unseen, Garth cannot deny what he's just done, knows better than to try. He hopes that the Lord agrees with his reckoning: Lily was partly to blame, a fifty-fifty. Slightly more her, in fact. She's the one who talked time and again about doing exactly what they've done. Assuming he was in the right place, she never mentioned the other. He—Garth Addicks—will shoulder his proportion of responsibility. Thirty percent, probably. Makes no difference really, he has let Jesus down. She let only herself down; it's a path she has trodden many times. He quickly slips a T-shirt over his head. He wants away from this place, from the beach of sin. Gomorrah. From the lure of Lily Stephens. He can run to her house quicker than she does now; he's been practising. Lily's good, good at running; he had to practice but the Creator bestowed the physical advantages on his gender. A fit young man will always outpace a fit young woman. It crosses his mind that such prowess has always aided men in flight, running as he is now. He can't think why God made it so. There must be some utility for which men require this skill. Hunting most probably, superfluous in this day and age. He can draw no pride from running away. It just needs doing. He thinks she has dirtied him, tries to re-think it, understand his own role. At Baxter's School, they teach the boys that they are responsible for their actions. The problem is, her actions all preceded his. They might share the guilt, but he guesses that she feels only that she's won. He went where he shouldn't, and she never set foot in his church. It wasn't much, she tempted him, and he succumbed. What it adds up to is beyond his overheated brain. It wasn't worth it, that's as much as goes through his mind. Over and over. He runs. Very fast. A good stride. Runs like Lucifer is in hot pursuit. One pace behind. At Lily's house he goes to the back gate. It's six feet high. He is agile enough, leaps and grabs the top, gets elbows over. As he hoists his legs up, he feels a little scratch on a knee. He has scraped it across a splinter of wood. She cut her hand, he a leg: they are even. Once he has clambered down—inside her back yard—he hoists his bike up into the air, rests it on top of the gate. He tries to climb back up, stepping first on the adjacent dwarf wall but the bicycle slips from his grip. Drops over the other side with a loud clatter. When he's scrambled back, eased himself down carefully beside his fallen bicycle, he finds that it's okay. The saddle has twisted around but he rights that easily enough. He'll cycle home; no dancing tonight. He agreed to it for all the wrong reasons. He has nothing more to say to Lily. If she makes the first move, acknowledges what she's done, he might have another think. The problem he foresees is that he will still have nothing to say. She'll want to do it again and he's done with it. All the lurid sex stuff. Once was too much. Unforgivably too much. She said it was her or Jesus and still he's gone and done this. He feels ashamed in the knowledge that the Saviour watches over his actions, the acts of goodness and foul-ups like this, too. The Lord may have felt rejection, might reject Garth in turn. Tit for tat. This thought is a knot in his stomach. As he cycles there is wind in Garth's face. His eyes water, these are not crying tears but it probably looks the same. He wonders if Jesus will indeed forsake him, as he did Jesus for a couple of minutes back there. He never imagined that he would need forgiveness, not for a deadly sin. A big one. He thought he was just the man to handle a seductive girlfriend. Garth was only ever half-interested in that side of it—sex, physical relations—didn't expect to be much good at it. Probably wasn't.

When he arrives at his flat, bike locked up under the shelter behind, inside, in his own sanctuary, he quickly feels worse. Cycling gave him purpose, putting miles between himself and the girl who outwitted him. He just feels hollow now. An emptiness. Christ suffers on the cross above the redundant gas fire, His face turned away. Garth can look upon the figure no more; it shames him to think of Jesus's suffering, his body stirred yet by his and Lily's wanton debauchery. He moves into the small bathroom, removes his clothes, showers although the water is only lukewarm. Does so for a long time. He thinks he put it in the right place—his penis—maybe not. And all places are wrong when you get to the bottom of it. He wants to stop thinking about it entirely, hopes he can but it was a new experience. He feels a changed person. Different. Inferior to the one he thought himself to be. He starts mumbling a prayer but repeating, I'm so sorry, to his God seems neither well formulated or clear about what he would like done for him. He has no idea how to rectify the situation. He banged into Lily again, he realises. Didn't really see what was in front of him until it was too late to avoid. Praying in the shower, unclothed, feels completely wrong. Everything is as it shouldn't be today. What he did in the beach hut tops that shameful hit parade, and now he cannot stop thinking about it. Who knows, he may dwell upon it, and feel the concurrent shame every minute of every remaining day in his life. This—his interminable re-living, as if on a video loop, of that unforgiveable minute—is purgatory. The real thing.

Dressed decently, long trousers, he picks a piece of dry bread from the package on the kitchen side, takes it with him as he leaves the flat. His first thought is to walk to Peter's house but then he thinks Peter will gloat. And he will be at work anyway. Working, gloating. He will not go to Peter's house. He cannot speak to Margery; well, he can—often enjoys their lively chatter—not about this. Cannot speak to a woman about what he's done. She wouldn't understand him. Nor would Peter, he's not interested in girls. Garth is alone. He has lately spoken to Lily about his concerns—the suspension from work—but that has been his ruin. She won him over for her own purposes.

* * *

He walks and walks. It is hot, brings out the pungency of the tarmac road. Just walking, feeling the firmness of paving beneath his feet, sweat upon his brow although his pace is unexceptional, he crosses the borough line into Poole. Stays far from the sea, far from the beach. The unclad. Wants no part of any crowd. Walking. Aimlessly walking. Thoughts form in his head, not ones he really wants in there. Prefers to walk without an idea surfacing. An hour and a half from Northbourne, footsore—one training shoe a little dilapidated—he stoops to tie a lace. Looks around. He is on an estate of sixties housing. He doesn't know where he is, so far from home has he wandered. A large church looms in front of him. Laces tied, he steps towards it. Our Lady of the Sacred Heart, he reads on the sign. No need to check the denomination of this one.

He goes inside and sits on a pew at the back, then slips down onto his knees to pray. Can think of little to say to Jesus who used to love him. 'I'm so sorry.' That sums it up. He feels he is at God's mercy, wants prayers said for him, not by him. He stands and walks around the inside of the church. Strange hues of diverse colours filter into the church through the stained glass. Garth sees designs of Christ's Earthly mother, a holy personage he gives little thought to. This is an alien church. Garth thinks he will be banished from his own if they learn how he has behaved. It would not be unjust. Parallel with the pulpit but against the other wall, are two adjacent cabins. Two halves of a little wooden Victoriana, beautiful and pompous. Garth is ignorant of this faith, momentarily he thinks them to be toilets. Then he recalls how Catholics use confessional booths. He wonders to himself if his initial thought was disrespectful. Probably. He has spent too much time with Lily. She lampooned all things religious at pretty much every turn. He laughed along when it wasn't The Church of the Men of Judea she was ridiculing. He sees now that this was a weakness in him. One that may never be exorcised from Lily. She always wants to hurt those she envies, those who have seen the light she cannot.

He looks into the small enclosed space, coughs, hears a shout of 'All right' from somewhere in the church. He steps back outside the cubicle. A priest is coming down the aisle, waving him back inside. 'I'm coming, I'm coming,' says the man in black. It was not intended but Garth can feel only grateful: a man of God has sensed the urgency in the situation.

He goes back into the confessional. Hears a door closing in the neighbouring half of this odd box. The old priest is in position. Garth doesn't know how it works; he even wonders if confessing his sin to one of a contrary faith will put him in double jeopardy. Seeking the agency of God through a misaligned channel, it could compound whatever sin arose during the episode in the beach hut. That thing. And yet the man wants to help. The overweight priest. Garth is in a most confusing situation. Gerry, the colleague whose car he shares from Ringwood to Baxter's School, is a Roman Catholic. She's spoken of it once or twice during their morning commute. Wished to imply it gave her solidarity with him but she is barely even a Christian. Only goes to mass at Easter and Christmas. Remembers her more frequent attendance some years back with fondness and then hasn't the will to rekindle it. Catholics don't lapse—except for the angry ones—mostly they just lose interest. Occasional Christians, idling believers. No denial of Christ's love or divinity, nor the stomach to let it change their lives. Lily is a lapsed everything. Unnecessarily angry at this world, disbelieving of the better one beyond. Chooses to keep far from heaven, wouldn't let him foist a ticket on her. When she spoke about racism it was quite instructive, but all her thoughts are of Mammon. All about the corporeal. She needs to see further. It comes to him now that her children will grow up, leave home, and she will become a fornicator once again. She's already started.

'What are you wanting to confess now?' says the priest from behind the curtain, his Irish accent quickly apparent as he speaks more than the earlier two-word shout.

'Can we just talk? I'm at a low point.'

'Aye, we can but we needn't be in the confessional for that. And I've a hunch in me that you've confessions to unburden. Am I right, young man?'

'I guess but I don't know how this works.'

'Ha, I get you. You're not a left-footer then. We can talk but it's not my forgiveness you're needing but the Almighty's.'

'I know that, sir; I'm wondering how the land lies.'

'Ha-ha. I'm Father, Father Sullivan. You'll not knight me, please? Now what's on it?'

'I'm sorry.' Garth cannot follow this man's flight of conversation.

'What's on your mind?'

'I... is it true you mustn't tell this anyone?'

'Tell me your name, son. I'm sure you know the answer to that last one. You know what my cloth means, surely you do.'

'I'm Garth. I lost my girlfriend today. And I sinned terribly.'

'Well, I'm sorry to hear that Gart' on both counts. By lost, I hope you don't mean to tell me she died? That's the most dreadful thing if you do...'

'No, she didn't die.' As he states this simple fact, he thinks it is a more complicated situation still. Something died inside him. He saw her more clearly and, for the first time, he did not like what he saw. And it was after seeing this that something snapped within him, led him to commit a most grievous sin. He feels driven to confess it all to Father Sullivan although how he has even brought himself inside a church of this denomination is bewildering to Garth. The action of a man he does not know. He tells the teenagers at youth group, Julie, Donna, even Ronnie Clarke if he's there, that God is all light, that there is little mystery at the heart of it. It is people who stupefy themselves with their own misconceptions, their inability to accept what He sets before them. Is it God who has led him to this place or did he arrive by his own aimless meanderings? His flight from righteousness or his route back. He always thought they were in it together, him and Jesus, guided by the special relationship Garth has forged with Him. He does not doubt that he must take the rap for the

Thrice Crowed the Cockerel

beach hut debacle. Can't blame it all on Lily. How will it work here? Catholics assess sin with a slide rule. Genuflect and hail Mary their way back from the brink. He is a member of an action church. His path is to bear witness, undertake acts of goodness. Earn one's way into the warmth of Jesus's love. He shouldn't really be needing a priest but circumstances—his unparalleled shame—have brought him here and this gentleman has been thoughtful enough so far. The final obstacle to absolution seems to be the doctrinal errors of Catholicism; Garth believes himself to hold no prejudice against anyone. Lily never believed any of it. Took umbrage to the interest he tried to take in her children's lineage. At least Rihanna sees he is without prejudice. She is the more trusting. He feels this confession may be an act of sincere kinship across the divide that his church has maintained with this strange and puffed-up place of worship. Or it might be pure folly. It is what it is. 'I had relations with a girl, and I should not have.'

'Oh dear, oh dear. Well, you're not the first, Gart', and it explains how you lost your girlfriend. Girls don't stand for that kind of shenanigans.'

Garth takes a moment to realise that Sullivan has got the wrong end of the stick. 'It was my girlfriend who I defiled,' he explains, 'and myself, I fear. I don't think she minded but really it is not who I am.'

'You say the girl didn't mind; is she a Cat'lic?'

'No father. She's not anything.'

'That sounds a bit disrespectful, Gart'. You'll know God loves all his children. For sure, you do. And now, have the two of you said you'll part for good, or simply fallen out over what you did to her? It happens all the time you know. The key is to put it behind you. God forgives but you've got to learn from it, amend your ways.'

'I learnt too much,' Garth tells the priest.

'You did? I hope you didn't learn you are better than the girl, not thinking yourself down that way. What if the Good Lord has blessed the poor mite with a child? Do you think that might happen?'

'No, it was all too quick.'

He thinks he hears the priest laugh. 'I don't think it works like that, Gart'.'

The boy is blindsided by this most obvious observation. He falls to his knees and starts to pray aloud. He praises God, and the priest stays silent as the Garth recites his well-worn lines.

'You're an evangelical,' says the priest when he has become silent for some moments.

'We don't really call it that.'

'The we, of which you speak, is a church near here?'

'I attend. Yes.'

'I see. I think what you've done, and with your girlfriend, mind, you're feeling some shame, Gart'. You're not up to speaking with your like-minded ones, am I right?'

Garth mutters but his words are unintelligible, his thoughts unclear. He is surprised at how insightful this priest proves himself to be.

'I think the elders in your church will prove to be much like I am, Gart'. You might worry that they'll think a little less of you after this but they'll understand how it is. There can be a devil working away in all of us, and their concern will be to help you overcome it. Judging really isn't what we're here for, and you sound to have strong views about the errors of your ways anyhow. We're all pretty much on the same side in this. We're all Christians. I think that's why you've come in here.'

He mutters, 'Thank you.' There is a comfort in finding the unexpected warmth this man has for Garth's own unnamed church. His certainty in their common aims. 'But can you hear my confession.'

'Have I not done that already? You're not of the Cat'lic faith, Gart'. You can tell me anything, and I'll pray for you, I will. The penance, well, that won't be for you. You've meditated upon it already. You have. You're a good man. You've sinned, it's true, and for that you're wanting forgiveness but you're a good man.'

'Father, I pursued a girl, a woman. My...' The young man gathers his thoughts, pictures the priest's face, his blotchy skin and half-rimmed glasses, as he saw when the man was striding down the aisle of the church before dropping into the strange voice chamber. '...my girlfriend—the girl I was dating—she was an older lady with two children already. Children she bore in London, outside of wedlock. I knew this but still pursued her, Father. I asked her to my church, hoped to save her soul. I failed to see that this was not in my gift. She was indifferent. I, ha-ha... I...' The young man stutters, an almost-laugh before he expands. '...you see, I don't know what she saw in me. An opportunity to corrupt, perhaps. When we talked, I mistakenly thought her wise. She considers the world with some care but has no moral code to which she adheres. Picks up a good cause and then puts it down again. It is a whim. She lives by the sea, always took me swimming. Body worship, I call it. Her and her younger friend, fitness fanatics, wished me to join in their proclivities. I made it very clear to her that our relationship was strictly platonic. I thought we might one day be as one—physically—never wanted it while she denied the presence of our Lord. Just today she cut me, almost shredded everything I hold dear, perhaps that is what she's done. Jesus, she said, was the interloper in our relationship, the unwelcome presence keeping us apart. Father, I am a believer, I knew as she said it that our friendship—my courtship—was over. Our Lord is my saviour. Still, I followed her into the changing room, a beach hut, and there she offered herself to me and I sinned most egregiously. Strayed to where I should not. I always believed I could contain myself. Have done so all my adult life, and now I have been found wanting, Father.' Garth's voice breaks as he finishes speaking, cracks in tone. There are no tears. He is dry, hoarse.

'Gart', it's an old, old story. There's probably no harm with your lady friend, not as you've said. Just between you and your God. That's the relationship you've to repair now. I'm not giving you the penances. You'll have heard of it, hail Marys and what have you. You're not a Cat'lic, so there's really no point to it. I think you must pray for your lady friend. She's maybe in a tizz too, even a break-up is an upsetting thing, you know? And you're right, Gart', you cannot keep seeing her. I've had people in the box where you're sat now who can't stop doing the same sin, time and again, and it's generally the one that you've happened upon. I want to say a prayer for you, Gart'. Will that be all right?'

'Yes, Father. Thank you, Father.'

'Lord, we beseech You. Gart' here before You, has confessed his sins. Needs the comfort of Your forgiveness, if forgive him You can. We know that You gave Your life so our sins will be forgiven, and this is a young man who tries to do the right thing. Tried and failed but he is in earnest to try again, Lord. I'm certain he is. And we pray also,

Lord, that the boy's lady-friend can find her way to You, that You might teach her to change her ways and be at one with You and all Your teachings. I think Gart'll be speaking to You from his own church in a day or two but we're all pals, Lord, all seeking the same closeness to You. He's done the right thing looking You up here today. In the name of the Father, the Son and the Holy Ghost, Amen. God's blessing upon you, Gart'.'

The young man slides again to his knees. His mouth moves quickly, invoking Jesus in words more familiar to him. Then he says, 'Thank you, Father,' speaking more loudly than he has at any time inside this church. He rises from his penitent posture, says, 'Goodbye,' with a heartiness that comes more from its finality than any improvement in his inner composure. He strides down the aisle, re-enters the world. Steps away from the Roman church that he feels both grateful and conflicted towards. Speaking the words, confessing his actions is an unburdening, and the priest a good soul. At least, he probably is. Garth's own judgement has been all over the place today. Pals, the man said. Believes that their churches are pals. That is a novel construction, the informality that he is learning to admire in Margery Cox. Said in a Catholic confession box it sounded like silly talk. Or is it simply that he—Garth Addicks—is too pernickety? As for Jesus's forgiveness, he feels he has asked for it half-heartedly. Done so in the wrong church, the faith of smoke and mirrors. Lily was right when she declared his Saviour to be coming between them. He went around Jesus, betrayed his greatest Friend, just to feel the inside of a woman. Coming here has removed his shame. Father Sullivan has simply confirmed for him that his sin has been committed by others countless times before. Garth is a common fool.

It is with dejection for a sackcloth that he trudges back in the direction of Northbourne. As he walks, he wonders what is left for him, held in conflict as he is between the certainty of God's love and his expectation that it will be denied him. He has torn up his own life. It was a course he set himself upon with that act of unconscious deliberation: bicycling into the rear of the runner in the black shorts. From that moment until today he has just kept going, thinking he was doing right. Hoping that he was doing something worthy. Hospital, friendship, dating an unbeliever whom he aspired to convert. Perhaps it was the initial sight of Lily's backside which transfixed him, set him on this deviant course. Divergent from the Lord. He cannot recall making the choice he knows he has made. The devil has been and gone.

Saturday, 6 August 2016

It is a subdued Garth who spends the following afternoon at his parents' bungalow in Ferndown. Not a loud lad at the best of times but the difference—his heightened reservation—is picked up, ingested even, by Claire, his sister. She speaks to him with concern. As much of it as she can muster.

On arrival at their house, he and his mother drank cups of tea in the lounge. She enquired after Lily, only to be met with silence. Ratcheted up the questioning. 'Do you think you'll marry the girl?'

'We're cooling things down for a bit,' he replied. Dissembled.

After studying his face, Penelope Addicks called out, 'Claire, come and listen to this,' and his sister emerged from the bedroom in which she spends an inordinate proportion of her time. 'Garth and Lily are no longer seeing one and other. What do you think about that?'

'I'm sorry, Garth. She was nice.'

Garth remained unmoved, both facially and emotionally. He never confirmed the break-up as starkly as his mother interpreted his words. Nor did he dispute her formulation. After a time, he nodded at Claire. 'Maybe, but she's not right for me.'

Claire made sympathetic noises, the 'aw's and 'aah's and pulling of a screwed-up face that he had noted Lily to make in the giving of sympathy. Her girlfriends too and even Rihanna Williams at Baxter's School. It is not prayer, and it fixes nothing. Garth chose not to point this out. 'Come and see me later,' said Claire, returning to her own small room.

And now he is there, in the gloom of his sister's bedroom. Curtains forever drawn. His mother had asked random and unrelated questions: what they'd fought about; does he like how Lily looks; has she suddenly come into a lot of money. He could not really answer them, simply said a few words. Placated his mother. His father was happy to keep his head in the local paper. He has no time for relationships, not with Jesus, not those maintained by Garth and Claire, not even for the one he has enjoyed or endured with Penny, his wife of thirty-seven years.

'I think you're going to miss her,' Claire tells Garth as he sits cross-legged on her bedroom floor. She is holding the same posture on the counterpane of her single bed.

'I think I will. I thought she'd be in my life forever but it shouldn't even have been fleeting.'

'Tell me, Garth, tell me what went wrong. You'd do the same for me, I know you would.'

'I think I'm too religious.'

'Did she say that?' probes Claire.

'Not in so many words but it was...What are you smiling at?'

'There weren't really any words there, Garth. You went out for months, she must have said something about your religion.'

'I think she couldn't stand it. Never came to church. Not once. She kept promising that she would, then always backed out. In the end, I saw how much she dislikes the idea that there is a God, that Jesus could help her.'

'Jesus-phobic. She's like me.'

'You're not Jesus-phobic, you just can't stand arguing with Mum and Dad about my church.'

'No. I am phobic, Garth. I tried your church and it set me out in hives.'

Garth puts his head in his hand. He is not in the mood for Claire's strange jokes, her irreverence. He tries not to talk faith in this house although alone with his sister he has always felt more acceptance. 'Do you remember when I used to take you swimming? From Sixpenny Handley. You were still in primary school.' Claire turns her head back to him, stares at her brother. 'Mum would never have let you cycle there alone but I wanted to help you to learn. Took you quite a few times. I think I paid your entry money to the pool.'

'I don't remember if you paid. I remember you dragged me hours away on my little bike so that you could look at the girls in their cossies. My hair was wet cycling back. Gosh it was cold on those country lanes.'

'But you could barely swim, and I taught you how. Showed you how to do the leg moves.'

'Perhaps you did but what's it got to do with your girlfriend and her little black kiddies?'

'Not so much, Claire, but I could do that for you. Lily is accomplished, I could do nothing for her but show her the way to the Kingdom of Heaven and that was of no interest...'

'It's probably not a turn-on, Garth.'

'...I think it should be. It's just that...'

'...and she couldn't turn you on?'

No answer comes from the brother.

'Or is that what she did? I can see it might be a problem.'

Garth tries to shake his head but the colour invading his cheeks has already told his sister that she has struck oil. The boy wonders whether it was a blind guess or if she really knows him that well.

'It's all right, you know. Pretty odd for a fella to split up with his girlfriend because she wants too much sex. I've got myself dumped once or twice for being the other way around. And not because I was saying a flat no.'

Garth doesn't like to hear this. His sister's sex life is not something he can let himself imagine. 'I never knew what Lily really wanted. I kind of took over because I'd knocked her to the ground with my bike. She probably wanted me to go away but teased me in the saying of it.'

'She probably wanted a father for her little black children, Garth.'

'A father figure, it makes sense. But Claire, the kids were terrific. I never had an argument with them. I think they'd have come to church gladly if Lily had let them.'

'But you'd stand right out, wouldn't you? Two white ones with little black children.'

'We stood out without them. My faith, Lily's lack of it. That was the mixed marriage, the odd-couple thing. Colour is only skin deep, faith goes right through into the soul.'

Claire throws a pillow at Garth. 'Says you! You should have taken what you could get. Might've enjoyed doing it!'

He thinks she is uncomfortable with talk of the soul, of heaven. Claire is far from the path he once guided her towards. On another day he will try again to help her back to Jesus but the route is no longer as clear to him as it was just a little over a day ago. Perhaps the disorientation he now feels will turn him into a confused soak. Akin to his sister.

Sunday, 7 August 2016

He has been receiving texts and phone calls from Lily. He screens them, doesn't pick up. Earlier this morning—the time he would have been at church if he had felt at peace with the Lord—she left a long and confused rant on his answerphone. He could barely listen; it was offensive. She even claimed that it was the superficial girl, Caroline, Lily's body-worshiping encourager, who took her to the hospital. He did that—Garth Addicks—not the rich girl. Paid the taxi from his meagre wages. Did that for her because he knocked her over; she stepped into his path though. Probably should have paid half. And the young show-off wasn't there when the accident occurred. That's actually what it was: an accident. Garth got it wrong about the Lord. They actually happen quite a lot. He's been thinking about it overnight and God probably keeps out of it: people just bump into each other, crash planes now and then, all sorts of accidents. In the message she left, Lily just went off on another anti-religious rant. She has it in her to be quite horrible. He pressed delete before the message came to an end. It was that bad. He wonders if Lily needs psychological help, doubts if it would go down well were he to text back this sound advice. He fears his actions have set this off within her. How disturbing sex turns out to be; he has been wise to avoid it.

* * *

Just before one o'clock his phone rings again, the screen shows the caller to be Margery. He thinks twice and then presses the talk button.

'There you are Garth,' she says, 'I pray that you are all right.'

'Yes.'

'Your guitar playing was missed. Sweet Samantha tried her best, and we are grateful to her but you are the more accomplished musician.'

There is a short silence.

'Samantha's coming on,' he says.

'Indeed. But that is not what you and I must speak of Garth. Were you once more with your Lily, in preference to our church service? We were unaware that a substitute musician might be needed until time to sing.'

'Yes... No. I was not with her. I'm here.'

'Where is here, Garth? Your telephone goes wheresoever you go. That is my experience of these times.'

'I'm at my flat.'

'And Lily is with you?' Garth fails to answer immediately, and she adds, 'Unaccompanied?'

Garth is shaking his head, the side of which has his phone clasped to it. He is unsure how much of all that has transpired he wishes to tell Margery Cox. He said it all to the Irishman, the Catholic priest. He's not ready to hear her dismal condolence for his fallen state. He has talked to Jesus several times since Friday. Prayed to Him but He is not replying. It is a new development since Friday last, Garth has felt nothing while praying. Nothing but the rejection he deserves. He is in a quandary—the state of purgatory perhaps—although he still hopes all is temporary. Hopes to navigate his way through this confusion. Feel the Lord's forgiveness if He will extend it. He has known other men get over break-ups, and perhaps their circumstances too included matters requiring God's intercession. 'I've not seen her,' he finally says. 'I'm not seeing Lily.'

'I don't understand you yet, Garth. Not seen her today or have you stopped seeing her altogether?'

'Altogether.'

'Well, that is a surprise. I expect you are feeling rather muddled about it all.'

'That's it, Margery, anyway, I've got to go now, something's burning.' His thumb goes for the red button.

'Garth,' he hears, in a tinny shrill from his handset before the screen goes blank. Nothing is burning in the flat. Nothing except his trammelled soul.

* * *

During the afternoon, further calls from Peter and Lily trouble his phone. Garth has concluded that their concerns are not ones he can currently shoulder. Lily, he thinks of now as a physical presence. Absent but present. She looms too large in his thoughts. When he recalls the conversation on the beach, the words no longer arouse the anger which he felt on Friday. Wordplay is a game to Lily, never with any serious weight or lasting conviction. He was hot-headed to take offence. He finds himself dwelling upon the touch of her hips, the feeling of taking himself within her. He's convinced he got it right. That he's done it. These are thoughts he must but cannot, banish. How she has tempted him is her sin. Far greater than her many blasphemies. She has left him with nothing but shame.

He puts his phone into the kitchen drawer and goes out for a walk. Jonah fled from God, only to be returned by the strangest transportation. He—Garth—wishes to flee only from his own mind. The thoughts it keeps having. Let down by it, that's how he feels. If God cares to give him a sign, sweep him back to his flat or his church by tornado or tsunami it would be most welcome.

He goes in the direction of the river, finds the river path. Ambling beside the flowing water is usually soothing. Today it does nothing for him. The absence of rain has rendered it tranquil, his blood, in contrast, thumps in his temples. He could be a runner waiting for the starting gun. The priest was right. He and Margery would be fine pals, larking about in the light our Lord casts. Muddled, she called his thoughts. She doesn't know what she is saying. Margery counselled him as she might Julie Rivington if she and Ronnie Clarke were to part company. Does Margery understand the intensity of sexual desire? Perhaps that devil has never touched her. Probably not, Garth even wonders if it is an exclusively male cross to bear. But that does not explain Lily Stephens at all. Her coquettish presence, her insatiable need for that which he finally succumbed to.

* * *

In the late afternoon he feels a hunger that should not surprise him. Garth has walked for miles, followed the river when he could, drifted away from it when the path veered thus. At the latest outcrop of houses, he asks a man coming along the road what town he is in. The old fellow laughs: it is an extraordinary question. 'Wimborne,' the simple answer.

He takes himself into the centre. The shops have already closed but the young man enters a corner shop—the open-all-hours variety— finds a small area of upright refrigeration in which a few unsold sandwiches remain. They are inexpensive, he deserves nothing grander. Picks an egg and cress, paying the shopkeeper with a twenty-pound note.

'I've cashed up.'

'I've nothing smaller. I'm so sorry.'

'What have you got?'

Garth had been fingering coins in his purse before brandishing the large note. He pokes into its corners once more, fishes out eighty-six pence, shows it to him in the flat of his palm, 'Not close. I'm sorry.' The young shopkeeper gestures for him to pass it. It is an egg and cress sandwich. He is reducing the price by over fifty percent but perhaps the man is lucky to get anything at this time of the day. 'Thank you,' says Garth, the man to whom he has offered this gratitude waves it away. 'I'll pay in full when I'm next in Wimborne.'

'When you're next in Wimborne,' he hears echoed back as he is stepping out onto the street.

There was sarcasm in the tone, he is sure of it, and he believes his assertion was sincere. Garth is a man of his word. Then he qualifies the thought. True up until two short days ago. Broke his duck on Friday. The shopkeeper's doubt is insightful.

* * *

He eats the food on a bench outside the large parish church. Garth knows that it is his sin which has again attracted him to another formal—and in his mind, soulless—church. The Church of England: the Catholics who dare not speak their name; muddle themselves up with protestant theology while wearing the frocks and baubles of the Roman church and its Orthodox cousins. As he dwells upon this, he feels unnecessarily cynical. It is a quality he despises, attributes its presence within him to the girl he no longer loves. He will enter the church precisely because Lily would not. As he steps up the path, he momentarily fears it is a trick, his every judgement gone awry. That once more he must dance the salsa. He recalls how he could not do the task while Lily relished it. She is a natural in the frivolous world. He thinks he has spent three months gawping at her, as Ronnie Clarke does Julie Rivington. He wonders how he—dedicated to Christ—mistook love for a roll of the hips. The sight of a slender white leg.

Inside, the gloom is pervasive, an antidote to the undeserved heat of the day in which he tramped from Northbourne to this place. There is a smell of old damp wood which he initially associates with the finely carved pews that line the large church. As he slides into one of them, he picks up a Bible from the wooden ledge that is in front of him. The church is full of them, one for every seat. Not the pocket-sized New Testaments of his own church. Serious, doorstop-sized Bibles. He raises the Book to his nose. It smells beautiful. He hears an organist practicing. Not a distinct tune, a roving mass of chords. He expects an evening service is to begin but he wears no watch, carries no mobile telephone with him. No certainty of the time, nor any familiarity with this church's schedule. He has foregone the services in The Church of the Men of Judea both morning and evening today. Samantha must strum once more. He is hours away from Northbourne, feels too fatigued to walk it back. Egg and cress are not high-octane food. He thinks it might be more than chance that he is sitting here. The service of a contrary denomination might give him some solace. It is Margery Cox and Peter Carter he is avoiding. Not Jesus, not God. From Them he would love to hear.

Away from the eye of the sun, Garth puts his head on his knees. Thinks again of Friday last. Silently prays for some forgiveness. He implores the Lord for a sign that there is a way back. He sees that, as well as an organist bleating and belching away—roving through chords for no more reason than to ensure he has unclogged each pipe before the service proper—there are four or five other people at prayer. It is an unusual feeling for Garth, to be in church with strangers, so predictable is the attendance in Northbourne. He glances across the aisle, a woman sits alone, elegantly attired. Dressed for the evening service with a flourish that few in his own congregation ever think to concede. She is not old. Perhaps Lily's age. When he sees that she has lifted her head, is praying no more, Garth coughs. The lady looks at him. She smiles a greeting his way, a small gesture. He stands, walks towards the welcoming face. Seats himself by the lady. 'Is this your church?'

'It is,' she answers, quickly looking him up and down. Assessing, guesses Garth, if he is a nutter. Even The Church of the Men of Judea has attracted one or two.

'I hope I haven't disturbed your prayer.'

'I am at peace,' she says.

Garth introduces himself, tells the lady he has walked further than is usual for him so will miss the service in Northbourne. He mentions nothing of putting the phone down on Margery. Neglecting guitar duties.

The Church of Englander tells him her name. 'Rosemary. Please call me Rosie.' She has been a congregant at this church for three years. She tells him that she never felt the presence of the Lord until her husband of ten years passed away, was taken following a difficult cancer. A brain tumour.

He expresses sympathy but Rosie waves it away. Years are passing. She tells him that she always prays alone before evensong, feels that she has a connection with Peter this way. With her late husband, Maurice. It comes to Garth that this may also confine her within her own grief; he has heard of this in church discussion groups. The lone survivor of a marriage or the parent of a deceased child allowing ritual to keep a false presence, when in truth the loved one is away. In heaven, not to be found in this or that church. Her late husband has surely left Wimborne for good although Garth has no desire to break this news to her. Wouldn't wish to bring upset to Rosie, however helpful it might be in the long run. 'Whose presence do you feel?' he asks, not censuring her practice but nudging Rosemary toward the truth she seeks. His is a religion of action, and it feels good to have put aside self-obsession.

'Sometimes Maurice, sometimes Jesus, sometimes plain Rosie Welch.'

'The middle one,' says Garth, 'He watches over us.'

'Thank you,' she says, looking bemused at his certainty. Glancing over her shoulder as if the Lord, of whom he spoke, might be entering the church.

'Are you Church of England?' she asks.

He inadvertently pulls a sniffy face. His mouth makes a pained circle, as his head wags a denial. He quickly stops himself, recognises this could be offensive. 'I don't know what I am anymore.' He looks upon Rosie's dress. It bears a floral pattern, cream but with reds and blues across it. The sleeves are short, the colours pleasing. Cut to a more conservative style than any which the skin-flaunting Lily

Stephens would wear. 'I...' Garth is a little lost for words, feels uncomfortable sharing biographical details in a church. He thinks that he is supporting the grieving woman, not weighing up their prospects as a couple but that was how he thought of Lily when he took her to hospital. That act of goodness took a very unexpected course. '...have you children, Rosie? Were you and Peter blessed with issue?' As he says it, he realises his trite phrase is meant to disguise his prying. Talking as he imagines her vicar might, and it feels deceitful in so fallen a Christian.

She sighs. Garth wonders if she is thinking him forward. 'They neither like to come to church, and I'm not minded to make them. My late husband's parents still love having them around, they spend much of Sunday with them. They need that bond.'

'Yes, yes,' he says hurriedly. 'I'm sorry, I didn't mean to intrude, to be so nosy...'

A wrinkled hand rests gently on the shoulder of the lady as she listens to Garth. Another congregant has arrived. Garth glances around. There are now over twenty people in church; the service must be due to commence. Rosemary stands and talks with the old gentleman who has greeted her. There is familiarity in their respective demeanours. Eye contact held. She places a hand on the gentleman's sleeve momentarily. Garth realises that he misses The Church of the Men of Judea. Wonders if he has set himself adrift from it forever with this aimless Sunday tantrum. These are other people, not his people, other ideas of how to communicate with the Lord. Not ones in keeping with his own. Their dress, their clothing, is special. Everyone in their Sunday best. In his church all is ordinary. Sunday is for church; every day is for worshipping Jesus. A vicar walks down the aisle, if vicar is his title. Not a bishop, Garth is sure of that for he wears no hat, but the man could be a deacon or a canon. The dress code within this church's hierarchy sits outside his knowledge. The man goes to the steps which lead up to the precipice of this grand church's pulpit. Takes a seat beside them. Garth looks above him, the podium from which the servant of an angry God might sneer down on the sinning masses below. Garth looks upon the smiling gentleman—the probable vicar—white silk flapping from the neck of his black high-necked top. A tweed jacket weighing him down with unnecessary layers in the summer heat. Garth guesses that the smiling man will do no hectoring of his flock today, has no inkling of the sins which Garth has done. And as he looks from the vicar back to the pretty and upright widow whom he has quizzed for reasons he cannot entirely fathom, he wonders if he is the sort of man who will repeat his sins. Lily, Rosie, mothers of two. He feels a little physical sickness rising within himself. He nods a thank you in the direction of Rosemary Welch. She returns it with a smile. Probably thinks he is going back to the pew from which he came, instead Garth Addicks makes for the main door. Walks out even as a small throng, a dozen men and women, are coming in. This is not his church and his motivation for talking to Rosie was all wrong. He has more atoning to do. A trudge back to Northbourne on no more than an egg and cress sandwich is only the start of it. He murmurs a prayerful apology to the Lord, should never have tried the back door.

Wednesday, 10 August 2016

The buses to Lyndhurst are infrequent, Garth alights in the tiny New Forest town an hour earlier than he would otherwise need to. He will undertake the walk out to Baxter's School shortly but there is no hurry. There may be no one on-site if he turns up too far in advance of the planned meeting. The bus has dropped him close to the visitor centre and, although it has started to rain, Lyndhurst is vibrant with young and old. Pensioners carrying bespoke plastic bags laden with souvenirs; teenagers clutching ordinance survey maps. A car hoots, its passage blocked by the thronging holiday makers, day trippers. Garth steps back to the pavement, gestures to the driver. He is one of many and he cannot control this crowd, torn between their planned walks and the rain-free coffee shops.

A girl stands before him, says, 'Hello Garth.' He peers into a tightly pulled cagoule hood, recognises the dampened face.

'Hello...' He says it tentatively, knows who he is talking to but requires a moment to bring the name to mind. '...hello, Donna.' It is the girl from his choir. 'Are you with Julie?'

'We don't hang out.'

He feels a bit foolish, asking after young Julie when he has no greater association with her than with this plainer, pastier chorister.

'Are you out walking?' Donna asks him.

'A meeting at work.' He doesn't offer what it is about, nor does she request further insight.

'I've got to stay near Miss.' She starts to go up the street, turns and gives Garth a little wave, which he returns. She joins a loose crocodile of similarly waterproofed girls. He sees two or three adults any of whom may answer to the title, Miss. Guide leaders, he guesses the recipient of that title to be. Donna Wilson out walking in the rain. It's a more suitable pastime than idling away the hours in a coffee shop with Ronnie Clarke.

* * *

He arrives at Baxter's School soaking wet. A light jacket on him but it was no match for the sudden downpour. Caught him good and proper on his short trek out to the school's forest setting. He's surprised to see so many cars parked up. Speculates that he might have found a lift if he'd tried harder. Tried at all. He turned down the offer that Mr Lorimer made to collect him from the bus stop. An offer made two days ago, on their Monday telephone call with which the head teacher fixed the time for this important meeting. Garth is independently minded, more dogged than resourceful but generally satisfied with his own endeavours. He is here.

When he enters the hall there is no receptionist. No boys either, this is mid-holiday. The smell of paint is everywhere. He sits in a soft chair in the waiting area.

In due course, Mr Lorimer's office door opens. 'Garth,' says the head teacher, then a look of surprise overtakes him. 'You're soaking wet.'

'Only water,' he says, holding Mr Lorimer's concerned gaze. 'It's only water.'

'Better come in, lad. Can I fix you a hot drink?'

Garth shakes his head. This is a formal meeting, and he wants the bones of it. Not sympathy for walking from Lyndhurst through driving rain. As he enters the head teacher's study, a woman he has never seen before greets him. It is another whom he speculates to be Lily's age, give or take. She even has similarly styled black hair, although this lady—in a short sleeve blouse and skirt—has richly tanned skin, not white as Lily always was. Is: he knows she still lives, deletes her texts on a twice daily basis. This one wears a red skirt, short enough to display her bronzed knees as she swivels her chair around for the greeting. He was expecting Mr Rogers, would have preferred to have seen him. A known entity. At the present time, Garth feels conflicted in the presence of attractive women.

'Ellie Rawlins, Garth Addicks,' announces Mr Lorimer, by way of introduction. 'Ellie is replacing Barry. Started in post on Monday last.'

Garth looks back blankly. 'Barry said nothing.'

'No. We couldn't share it with staff until the plan firmed up. Barry is off to Carrington, up at Swindon. He's doing senior management a grand turn, helping them out up there. Ellie is new to the company, and...' Mr Lorimer turns to his new deputy. '...you'll find Garth an asset, don't let the topic of your first meeting with the lad make the wrong impression.'

Garth's head swims a little. He assures himself that the positive words must mean they will not sack him. Having a new boss who bears a physical resemblance to Lily is unwelcome. He searches her face, her physique, wants to draw out the distinctions. Her eye-colour is quite different. She tans and she has brown eyes; he hasn't inadvertently had sexual relations with her.

'Now Garth, I hope you don't mind Ellie sitting in on this, and nor is it a choice. She needs to come up to speed on all matters concerning the residential side of things.'

'We're all here to support you, Garth,' she says, 'to get the best out of you.'

He hears a London accent. Not very dissimilar from Lily's Kent. A small divergence but disarmingly close. 'Thank you,' he says, grateful for nothing in particular. It seems wise to be polite.

Mr Lorimer brandishes a written report, the one prepared by Barry Rogers. Completed before his transfer to Swindon, Garth presumes. The head teacher goes over the incident in detail, mostly for Ellie Rawlins's benefit. He tells Garth that the nature of the complaint against him required consideration of his suitability for the work and any support needs arising were he to continue in it. He also rattles off the sources Mr Rogers has explored. Statements from both boys, victim and perpetrator. Another by Rihanna Williams, residential support worker; and one by Jennifer Spalding, the French teacher.

Plus Garth's own version of events. Barry conducted the interview with him over the telephone during the final week of school. Garth thinks he might have done the entire report then. Wonders why he has been made to wait so long. Did typing the report and drawing a conclusion truly require the best part of three more weeks? He has been to hell and back. He knows better than to blame the suspension for all that has happened but it definitely knocked him off kilter. Played a part. In going over what each contributor has relayed, Mr Lorimer raises Rihanna Williams possible bias. 'Garth had intervened on her behalf earlier in the day. Challenged a member of the public who was being a bit racialist.'

'Oh, I like that,' says Ellie Rawlins, 'very proactive.'

Mr Lorimer looks at his new deputy over the top of his glasses. 'Rihanna was very concerned that Paul Frost was being injured in the fight. She thought his actions—stepping in quickly—justified his unorthodox hold. The way he grabbed hold of Declan Keane. We hope it is an unbiased view. Rihanna saw the boy's injuries. Frost's nose was bleeding before Garth pulled Declan off him.' Ellie Rawlins nods her head, listening intently. 'A complicated business. We have strict procedures to help us avoid this sort of thing. It's not good at all to have boys complaining about how staff treat them when they kick off. If it's all done by the book, they can have no grounds.'

Miss Rawlins takes the folder of evidence from Mr Lorimer, peruses it for a few seconds. 'Jennifer Spalding's account backs up Rihanna's,' she observes. 'The boy was badly bloodied, Garth did right, stopping it quickly.'

'Would you like to add anything further for us to consider, Garth?' asks Mr Lorimer.

He shakes his head. 'I've said it.'

They ask him to step outside, and again Garth feels a little cheated. Thinks Lorimer is enjoying dangling him on the thread of his suspension. Nothing he has heard today—except for the misrepresentation of events within Declan Keane's sparse statement—suggests anything but exoneration.

When he goes back into the room, Miss Rawlins leads the meeting. 'Garth, I know this is not the best way to start your relationship with me, your new manager. However, I have been impressed that you took it upon yourself to help young Paul when another worker might have seen an excuse to wait for backup. It was a tough decision, a lot of risk. I want us to talk about managing risk in supervision. In unit meetings too. The support you were to our Rihanna before you reached the island was music to my ears. You were an example to all the boys that we don't tolerate racism. Ever. I don't think it made Rihanna biased. You made her see a white face which wasn't dismissive of her. Well done.'

Garth glances across at Mr Lorimer; he is moving papers across his desk. Garth suspects they haven't agreed on this point but Miss Rawlins seems to be running the show.

'I've asked for you to be put forward for special physical intervention training, Garth. It should come up soon in the new term. I hope there is no similar need arising any time soon but the fact that Declan was hurt by your improvised restraint is not good...' She looks at Garth who is squirming in his seat. He could challenge Declan's assertion. The boy needed no medical treatment for whatever injury he claims Garth inflicted. No words come; he isn't being sacked. '...and this could have reflected badly on the school were his injuries more serious. On the basis that this was a needed intervention, we are not proposing any censure at all. This is a disciplinary hearing but you have not been disciplined.'

Garth manages a smile. He always believed this would be the outcome, believed it back when Lily said as much. Back when he was still trusting her. The measure of relief, relaxation of tension, that he feels is seismic. He wonders fleetingly if the effect of this stress unbalanced him Friday last, at the beach hut. He tries to push the thought from his mind. Those musings have no role to play in this meeting, his conversation with this Lily-lookalike.

'And Garth,' she adds, 'Mr Rogers ran this incident past both the police and Hampshire Child Protection. Submitted a brief report to the latter. They're not making any independent enquiries. The sergeant said it could not be deemed an assault. You used reasonable force. That's allowed under common law. We must always use the minimum but using reasonable force to get a needed job done comes with the territory now and then. Well done, Garth, I'm looking forward to working with you.'

Friday, 12 August 2016

Garth continues to screen Lily's calls. He has nothing to say to her despite, two days ago, composing a short text telling her the outcome of his disciplinary meeting. He quickly thought better of it. Deleted it unsent. He even retched once more over his kitchen sink at the thought of what occurred in that beach hut. How she caused him to betray the very God he loves above all Earthly things. Later in the evening he accepted a call from Margery, spoke only briefly to her but agreed that she might visit him this morning. Come to his flat. He realised only after he'd come off the telephone that she has never been here before. She knows where it is, of course—lives only a couple of roads away herself—now he wonders if she can manage the steps. It's raining again. The steps are not unduly slippery but his pastor is— unspoken topic that it is—disabled. He considers calling her back, suggesting he might go to her house but knows that she doesn't like a fuss. He has cleaned and tidied, spent much of yesterday on the task. Not with the fetishism Lily applied in preparing for Jo-jo and Ami's return from their summer stay with their father, but a greater effort than he musters in a normal week. It brings to his mind Lily's one and only visit here, something he did no cleaning for at all so unintended was the event. They were Ferndown bound and she smuggled in a detour. 'Just checking your bed really is single,' she said. So should hers be, he thinks now. He seldom found funny retorts at the time, nor did he really grasp what Lily might find funny. Their talk was forever at cross purposes. He hopes he doesn't blabber this nonsense to Margery Cox.

* * *

Garth sees her little Smart car pull up. Takes himself down the steps to greet her, to ensure she can come up without mishap. 'You've no coat,' she tells him. He fears this might be a harbinger, the first of many veiled or unveiled assaults upon his judgement. He finds that he agrees with her imagined perspective. I told you so. That would sum it up.

Garth shows her the steps she's to climb, asks if she will be all right. She looks at the challenge and clarifies that Garth's front door is the first one at the top of the external flight. 'Pop my frame back into the car for me, Garth. I can use the handrail, it's what they're for.'

He does as she asks, and Margery takes the steps ahead of him. He catches up with her before the top step, opens the door and they step inside, away from the drizzling rain. Garth has already boiled an expectant kettle. Margery asks for coffee.

'I only have powdered.'

'Lovely. Two teaspoons, please.'

He puts a few biscuits on a plate. Plain biscuits, theirs is never an extravagant church.

'How have you been?' she enquires when they are both seated.

He looks at her, she's a trustworthy soul; it is Garth who has been unnecessarily critical of her innovations. 'Confused,' he says.

She doesn't respond for a moment. A fat finger scratches her nose. 'Man confused by woman: that's quite an old story, Garth.' He sees that she has caught him smiling at this. He is not the completely hopeless case he thought himself to be. There is laughter after Lily even if it is at his own expense.

He tells her more than he has previously done about the relationship he briefly enjoyed. About his now ex-girlfriend. 'She's a really splendid mother. Admirable.' Margery nods, accepts the truth of his observation. 'I was determined to remain chaste.' She lets him know that she never doubted it. 'Lily drank a little more than I would ever advise. Alcohol that is.'

His pastor does not cast a response to this, not directly. 'I wish I had met her, Garth. I fear you wanted her away from church lest we judge, and that is not my style, you know. Nor your friend Peter's, I'm sure.'

'I wanted her to come to church. Wanted it more than anything.' He feels as though he might be pleading a misunderstood case. 'I thought I'd managed. She would say yes on a Monday and no on a Friday. On a Sunday morning one time.'

'And you had frightened her with tales of the stern Margery Cox?'

'I did not. Do you know, we talked about religion quite often? She took an interest at first, wanted to hear what our beliefs were, wanted to know me, but...' Garth looks around his small flat, glances up at Christ on the cross that dominates one wall. '...in our final argument, she told me it was her or Jesus. She was jealous of my love for our Lord.'

Pastor Margery turns the coffee cup around in her hands. 'Is that so surprising?'

Garth is taken aback by the comment. Lily's demand rankles with him even after the precise wording has slipped from his mind. 'It was never an either-or, Margery. I met someone whose company I enjoyed...' His voice softens. '...who I loved. I wanted only to open her eyes to Christ before allowing the relationship to become more than the friendship it was.'

'Look at me, Garth...' Margery has found her stride. '...on Fridays, I think you tell our youngsters that if they choose to date, to begin to forge boy-girl relationships, it is essential that they do so exclusively with boys or girls from church. People who share their outlook...'

'I do, Margery but they are children. Look at the wider congregation. Cindy Clarke is married to a man whom I suspect is not Christian at all.'

She raises her eyes at this attestation. Her look suggests to Garth that Margery is not surprised by the content of his comment, only that he too should know so much about Cindy's partner. 'Never mind,' she continues, 'imagine you were to go on a date with a lady from a double-glazing company. She was everything you were looking for in a girl and she was clear that she wanted to spend the rest of her life with you...' Margery raises her voice a fraction for the punchline. '...once you'd purchased a new set of windows. A front and back door too.'

Garth laughs. He loves to debate. 'It's not the same, Margery. Nothing like that. We're not engaging in minor modifications to people's homes: we're saving souls. You are, and I aspire to the same.'

'Not from your Lily's viewpoint, we're not. She just sees a man trying to mold her. People find God in their own time. We share our beliefs, Garth, bear witness. We don't take hostages.'

He puts his head briefly in his hands, rubs his chin where an hour ago was stubble. 'Are you right?'

'I hope so, Garth. I've been round the block and back again. My analysis is not directly from the Bible and if it's not in the Good Book it's only guesswork. The form guide is on my side. I've met men and women who thought they were in love but did not share a faith, many, many times. I always root for them, Garth. I love to read a good

Thrice Crowed the Cockerel

romance novel, hoping for the continued happiness of others is the most natural thing. It seldom works out though, not between a believer and a cynic. I do wish Cindy and her husband well, by the way, as I did you and Lily. I prayed that your girlfriend would indeed come to church. Would see the glorious world within that captivates you. That simply never happened, did it? She never came.'

'Margery...' Garth's hand starts to tremble as he speaks now, '...can I confess something to you.'

'You may tell me anything, young man but I am your friend, not your confessor. We are not Catholics.'

'I know, I...' He glances again at the hanging Jesus. The most meaningful of all sculptures and still Lily called it 'frightening'. The only solace in our world, and it was far beyond that awkward and beautiful girl's comprehension. '...after our argument, I...' His face is distraught, the words are choking in his throat. '...it is shameful, Pastor Margery, I let down the Lord.' She remains unmoved, looks levelly at her honest congregant. 'I took what she offered me, Margery. I committed sin with...' Tears are streaking his face. '...I'm so, so sorry.'

'Garth,' she says, her voice gentle as she responds, 'this was wrong, it was a temptation too far. You might think yourself to be a young man, although, in truth, you are not so young as all that. Lily has had experiences. Children indeed. We hope to navigate this conflicted world without such recourse but I know some who would argue that it is for the best that you have got it out of your system. The lady concerned will cope, no doubt. She has done so before, and so must you...'

'Margery, I think Lily cannot cope. She texts, she phones. She wants me back, I fear.'

'Garth, you are prized both in our church and in the wider world. Peter has advised me that your employer's enquiry has exonerated you. You spread love wherever you go. Lily is clearly grateful for the love you have shown her, and that is why she is unwilling to let it go. That is understandable and it is for you to show resolve.'

As she tries to explain, soothe, put a worldly perspective to his unfortunate situation, Garth sits, head in hand. Cheeks salted by his tears. The weight of his sin has rendered him disconsolate. 'Is it not more damning?' he says, 'I thought I could remain chaste despite her temptation. Have I ruined her?'

'Garth, you are an honourable man to think this way. Even taking advantage of those who offer themselves does them the gravest disservice. Ruined? Well, that is unlikely, I hope...' Pastor Margery pauses, a thought has gripped her. '...well, you know what you have done and any risks that arise from it. Please pray about this matter on Sunday. Pray for Lily but it is not for us to speak of again. It is past. We both live in the certainty that Jesus forgives.'

Sunday, 14 August 2016

He has his guitar in hand, strumming chord progressions in the key of D. Trying two contrasting fingerings for the major seventh chord the song requires. His phone rings and Garth walks across his flat, guitar strap across his shoulder. He picks the mobile device off the dining table where it lies, answers it in a single flip. 'Garth here,' he states.

Instantly he hears her voice. 'Garth, it's Lily...' He presses the button, the red. An emergency brake—garlic to the vampire—with that simple action he aborts the telephone call. Breathes deeply, twice, thrice. The guitar in place all along, strap hung across his neck. His fingers move from the major seventh chord to the C and G sevenths, he sings quietly but insistently. A Johnson Ronson song from long ago. He learnt it in his teens, often practices the intricate fingerstyle while seldom troubling himself with the heartless lyric.

> *You have your town and I have my town, girl*
> *I've heard there is a bus*
> *but you ain't worth the fare*

Garth has nothing to say to her. Why he didn't look at the screen before picking up is beyond him. He cannot keep letting his guard down.

* * *

On arrival at church, he anticipates an inquisition. Instead, it is smiles and a couple of handshakes which are the order of the day. He missed a week, only Margery knows what troubled him, waylaid him. Even had him knocking on the door of an Anglican church, a Roman

Thrice Crowed the Cockerel

Catholic one too. Their mistaken cousins.

Peter insists on sitting alongside Garth and the choir. His presence makes the young man feel more self-conscious about his return than if he was alone with the three youngsters at the front of the church. He knows that Peter only mouths the words, cannot carry a tune. As he glances at his small choir, he recalls hearing Julie Rivington at youth group many weeks ago referring to his friend as 'creepy Peter.' Garth was searching the storeroom for spare ping-pong balls, replacements. On the other side of the door behind which he rummaged, the girl regaled her friends with this odd and offensive name for the youngest church elder. Told them how 'freaked out' her boyfriend, Ronnie Clarke, felt whenever Peter spoke to him. 'Closeted gays are the worst.' This speculation explained his perceived creepiness in her mind. Her juvenile outlook.

Garth has viewed Peter differently since hearing this, only to resolutely treat him the same. Peter may or may not be gay. Garth has no radar for such a turn within a person; it is mentioned in the Bible, not a new phenomenon. The point—the important fact in this matter—is that Peter is chaste. If he has the inclination to commit a particular and heinous sin, he needs no forgiveness for he does not act upon it. He is the better person. Garth understands this implicitly. Peter might be anything under the sun; through his action and inaction he is, simply and purely, a good man. He feels momentarily proud that he never shared Julie's insight, true or false, with Lily. Never gave her that brickbat with which to further abuse his good friend.

* * *

When the service begins, Garth perceives in himself a paternal warmth for his young choir, a feeling he thinks richer than any he has previously allowed. They sing in fine harmony. Julie and Samantha have each made a comment about his absence last week that indicated neither judgement about nor insight into his absence. Donna spoke only of how wet she and her Guide group became in the Forest on Wednesday. He adjudges that Julie's view of Peter Carter reflects only her immaturity. He will, in time, teach her to be open-minded. Hate the sin and not the sinner: withdraw her petty condemnation of Peter, love him as our Lord surely does.

Boscombe

Margery Cox prays, and Garth tries to sense the presence of Jesus. He wants to confess his sin silently to the Saviour but the Eternal Light, the certainty of His presence, does not envelop him today. He feels jolted from his parallel introspection when the pastor prays for that most familiar name. 'Oh Lord, please show the path of righteousness to Lily Stephens; we are grateful to you for your forgiveness of her, and for your all-encompassing love which also absolves each of us here today of our sins.' Glancing to his side, Garth sees Julie Rivington, his fair-haired choir girl, looking back at him. Taking in his attention to the words. Surely, she does not know that his is the sin that the pastor is confirming Jesus has now wiped from the slate. He feels his cheeks colour under the young girl's visual examination while speculating inwardly that the Lord has a second ledger. That the forgiveness which God doubtless grants him for his atrocious behaviour does not mean that He has forgotten the offence. Forgive and forget sound alike but they swim in different ponds. Further explanation may still be needed down the line, on the day of judgement. He still did it.

As Margery crunches through the gears from prayer to sermon, Garth hangs his head down, he has turned from her words to prayers of his own. Lips busily mouth the words his breath will not give voice to. 'Almighty Jesus,' a lip reader would infer if he or she were able to look up from Garth's knees, see the earnest face upon his contritely hung head, 'forgive me, for I have sinned. I know that you have forgiven Lily Stephens. She is one of your flock—a stray—she does not know or respect your law. When You reveal Yourself to her, she shall be transformed. I am foolish, Lord. Wished to do Your work. Felt that You had put Lily before me, crossed our respective paths, to give me that purpose. I now see it how You intended. You tested me Lord and I have failed You, failed to keep Your law in a manner that shames me. I am a lapsed Christian asking You, Lord, for readmittance to this communion. It is a fate I do not deserve. My love for You is boundless and still I sought that other kind of love. Filthy and wrong. It is my heartfelt wish, Lord, to try again. Amen.'

Garth turns his attention back to his pastor. She is telling the congregants that the Lord will be bringing order where there is chaos. Paul's letter to the Thessalonians confirms it. *'And then the lawless one will be revealed, whom the Lord Jesus will overthrow with the breath of His mouth and destroy by the splendour of His coming.'* She expounds upon this citation. Gives heart to the faithful in her certainty of Jesus's splendour. Garth lowers his head once more. Jesus gave no sign while he prayed a moment ago and there is no other explanation for how things have turned but that the lawless one ran a-mock within his soul nine short days ago. He fears his journey back will be a long haul.

* * *

The girls sing the tune well. Many of the congregants add to the musical swell.

> *I danced for the scribe and the pharisee*
> *But they would not dance, and they wouldn't follow*
> *me*

Everybody in this church knows this one, a more vigorous tune than most. Unusually, Garth loses the rhythm. Twice in this single verse he has mistimed his chord change. Has to stop and count simply to get back on course. Julie Rivington casts him another funny look but Donna, the plain girl, keeps her head facing forward. Sings the words truly, correctly, in syncopated time.

As the hymn comes to an end and Pastor Margery has the hall again bowing their heads to pray, it comes to him to thank the Lord for Donna. For girls and boys like Donna. Then he looks around the church, head held high as all others stoop theirs in prayer. Julie Rivington has high hopes for herself. She wears too much of the pride that presages nothing. Donna Wilson—barely comfortable inside her own skin, awkward in company—will be the truer. He, Garth, is a Donna. It is his happy fate to help others without the expectation of reciprocation. He is well suited to acts of goodness. Recently he thought himself more like the Rivington girl. Thought that walking arm in arm with Lily Stephens made him a creature worthy of greater human attention. He even believed that Lily was somehow important. That the love she showered upon her children was a demonstration of how she could change the world if she would just clamber onto the chariot of the Lord. He was drunk on her looks. In church today, he has not heard the voice of the Lord but he has stumbled across a piece in the puzzle. Come to understand the extent of his folly.

Wednesday, 17 August 2016

He has praised the Lord almost hourly for His miraculous intervention. Still to feel His presence as he used to, he knows that his actions have temporarily estranged him from God. He made a very poor choice while navigating an uncomfortable three-way relationship. He is better out of it. He has a fleeting sense that he has chosen the Lord over Lily but that was not a serious dilemma. Never a contest. One offers salvation, the other only that sordid pleasure that he did not enjoy. Even without feeling His presence, Garth sees His hand at work in the recent development, the cessation of Lily's texting. This has held true for three days. This morning he wakes to a text from the temptress, and it reminds him of the hold she has recently had upon him.

Thinking of you

That is as much as she has said. Left him to speculate on the nature of the thoughts she is having. Whether she thinks of him kindly, misses his conversation and friendship or simply wishes to feel that ungodly part of him inside her once more. In fact, his prowess as a lover is probably not it. He was quick but he understands it is not a valued skill. And a kitchen appliance fell to the floor, a plate broken upon it also. Not de rigueur, he is sure of it. They were mostly good company before she led him to do what he did. He saw verve within her darting blue eyes when she was thinking, debating, and expanding upon a subject. He momentarily likes to picture her thinking of him but sees too many pitfalls, the bear traps—the beach hut—which such ill-disciplined ruminations may lead him towards.

He should not really expect Jesus to stop Lily from texting him although he had assumed it was His intervention during that three-day hiatus. This whole episode, from the misfortune that gave her twelve stitches on the back of her left calf to the still greater one with which he lost both his virginity and the trust which he believes the Lord had previously staked in him, is but a test. Garth knows that the right thing to do about Lily Stephens is precisely nothing. There is no action that can improve matters. He will plug his ears from her Siren call. If he had run his bike into a girl of no attraction, he would have done his duty. Attended the hospital, seen her home, and then moved on. His life on his own tracks, hers on whatever course it had previously been upon. That is how he and Lily are now. None of it would have occurred had she worn suitable clothing on that fateful bank holiday.

* * *

In the evening he visits Peter. For the longest time neither speak of Lily. His friend mixes another of his expensive fruit juices. Pink grapefruit with carbonated mineral water. He tells Garth that it is better than champagne—which is a stretch—Peter is strictly abstemious and may believe his reassuring fiction. Garth has drunk champagne but too long ago to recall the taste beyond the excessive perpetuity of its fizz. A quality Peter's concoction fails to replicate. In his spotless sitting room, they celebrate the restoration of Garth's employment status. That his suspension from Baxter's has ended happily. 'It was never in doubt, Garth. You are an asset to any troubled child. They finally saw it.'

He thanks his friend for his support. They chink glasses of grapefruit for the second time.

'And is the other matter behind you, Garth?' asks Peter, when the fourth or fifth prolonged silence has again made awkward their conversation. It is with a deepened voice that his friend asks this. A shadow across the fortnight past.

The other matter of which Peter speaks is Lily Stephens, Garth infers, then momentarily doubts this insight. It could just as aptly refer to his feelings of infatuation, the uncontrollable lust for women which he had contained for his first decade of church membership but failed to extinguish entirely. 'I think so, Peter,' his meek reply.

'It's for the best, my friend. I think you may still feel the need to talk of the matter, and I am your willing counsel.'

'It's hard to talk about. I took a wrong turn.'

'Before this bother, this souring between the two of you—Lily, I recall her name—Margery and I raised a smile at the manner of your meeting. You are so righteous, Garth, you could never put a woman in hospital without wanting to atone through deeds.'

'I don't walk away but I outstayed the need I could help her with.'

'Yes, you imagined you could help her in more ways than there are for a man like you to aid a woman like Lily. And that was always my fear.'

'Peter, you have lived alone for longer than me. Never married. No courtship that I'm aware of. Have you always felt content to live this way?'

'I have many things, and if a wife is not one of them, then that must be how the Lord intends it.'

'I saw a sign when Lily Stephens' life collided with my own. Was it so wrong to think it possible? And might there have been signs—true signs, truer than that which I foolishly let direct me—which you may have mistakenly disregarded?'

'You were not wrong at all, Garth. Your optimism was touching. A testimony to your character. I could never blame you for hoping—trying vainly—to rescue a lost soul.'

'Peter, I venerated a woman for no better reason than my infatuation with her appearance. I drew her into my heart alongside Jesus Christ, without ever knowing who she was. What she was.'

Peter folds himself back into his comfy chair. 'Is there room in our hearts?' he asks, not of Garth, of no one. It is a rumination, a Peter Carter soliloquy. 'No room at the inn. The Lord has need of all the straw and all the water. The cheer our hearts might offer can only truly be for those who are already making the same sacrifices that we do. Necessary sacrifices in the service of our very demanding God. We are not part-timers, Garth. You and I are leading those who will follow into the light. What is a wife but a distraction from what we really seek? A cover to make the world believe us more normal than is our true nature.'

Sunday, 21 August 2016

Garth has dwelt upon his conversation with Peter Carter. It held some answers but he fears he is closer to regular people, shares more in common with the sinners than his friend does. He is less able to be the beacon of rectitude he once thought himself. He worries that the presence of the Lord is eluding him, that for his deplorable sin he has been banished, if only to the world in which he was already living. His purchase within the normal, everyday world of sinning, non-believing, commonplace people, feels stronger than it used to, and this is not how a man dedicated only to his arrival in heaven should find it to be.

He confounded himself on Friday. Telephoned Rihanna Williams, let her know the outcome of the disciplinary hearing. He knows that he has felt closer to her since the incident at Poolequay, and there was always an intensity in their late-evening talks on the unit. Mutual respect. They are, in their working styles, the opposites which attract. Each is equally dedicated to their task even if she is natural and carefree and he studied and cautious. Now, the unfamiliar post-Lily Garth finds himself dwelling more and more upon this other girl. The dark-skinned, smiley Rihanna. She is no Christian; his eyes are open to this. He is pursuing a closer, less-guarded friendship. He liked the company of Lily, a woman who was at ease with him but she came to dislike his love of Jesus. He has learnt something from this, if only belatedly. On the telephone to Rihanna, he asked, 'Would you like to meet up before school restarts?' It was an innocent question. They have arranged to meet next Thursday, in the daytime, the date-word did not cross his lips. He fears she might have laughed had it done so. Garth will travel to Winchester, the girl's hometown. Rihanna still lives with her parents. He wonders if he is insuring himself against becoming Peter Carter.

He heads for church as he used to do. He must pick up his old life, see past Lily Stephens by recapturing all that he had before he knew her. At church he chats, and runs through the playlist with his young choir. They love it when he uses these terms. Calls a service a gig. Margery has praised him for it. Says the words used are less important than the reaction they draw. He is unsure about that but has grown to like watching how Donna Wilson laughs if he says anything close to humorous. Cindy Clarke speaks to him. She wishes to know if he and the girls can sing something uplifting for ten minutes during next Saturday's coffee morning. Garth has already anticipated the request. They are free, they will sing Lord of the Dance, and a couple of other vibrant hymns. She asks him if they could reproduce the song which went down well in church some weeks before. In the Mood for Magic. The pop song they sang before Peter analysed it in his sermon.

Boscombe

'It's not a hymn,' he says with a shake of the head. It really isn't, and a church coffee morning is not a discothèque.

The hall quietens and Garth goes to sit with his choir. Margery Cox is shuffling forward, preparing to lead them in worship. Garth glances up and sees a familiar figure at the back of the church heading towards him. He looks down, back up, down again. She has slipped into a row of seats far away, at the rear of the church. It is Lily: she has come to church. Arrived too late. Far too late. He studies the plectrum in his fingers, tries to picture Rihanna—a sideways glance at Julie Rivington—any image is welcome in his mind except for the girl at the back of the church. The scarlet woman.

He feels a gentle kick on his ankle, Julie is silently questioning him. She must have seen something change in his demeanour. Everything changed, he suspects. His throat has gone dry. He is uncertain if this young girl registered the entry of his ex-girlfriend into church. A girlfriend which he believes his choir to be unaware he ever had. Already Margery is gesturing to her, to Lily. It is a welcome of sorts, for they are a church. Garth would rather be, like Gandhi, in bed with a few nubile young women than in this church at this moment. There he would have half a chance. His urge is not to fornicate, it is to scream. This morning may break him.

His head swims as Margery leads the service. She does it as though nothing untoward is occurring. The pastor has some nerve. He hears her prayers, asking God to aid those congregants most in need. Within her commentary, he hears Margery speak clearly but indirectly to Lily. To caution her, lower her expectations of so rash an act as coming to his church in search of further mutual defilement. She tells her that Jesus is the master in all His personal relationships. Garth wonders if Lily can really hear this. He made the divinity of the Lord very clear to her many times. She didn't laugh out loud but she wore a silly grin most times he explained it. Never paid it the mind required if one is serious about not going to hell. Garth finds that he can listen to Margery and simultaneously pray, head bowed, as she reads and discusses verses from the Book of John. He quickly realises where her talk will lead. Jesus works his miracles for those who sin no more. His pastor has only a passing interest in the stranger in their midst. Her knockout blow is exclusively for him, for Garth Addicks.

Thrice Crowed the Cockerel

Lily never really sinned in the beach hut; she has never lived an inch above such abominations. For her it was not sin but lifestyle; it is Garth for whom the Lord has recently acquired these vexing reservations. This explains the radio silence he has experienced from his Saviour. He wonders if Margery is a conduit of hope or banishment.

The choir sings Praise the Spirit in Creation. They determined they would play this one a week ago but Garth finds it fitting in ways he would not have dreamed possible. He sings louder than the girls, not showing off but wanting the Lord to know that he is sincere in his fulsome praise. He wants to be heard, wants the Lord to open again His door to him. Returning to his seat, Garth waits, prays for guidance from the Lord. It comes to him that this is a further test. He must pass the re-sit. He can see Lily in church, talk to her in this hall where he has passed so many hours in humble worship. There is strictly no sexual intercourse here, it's a church, it goes without saying. What words might he exchange with her? Perhaps Jesus is reaching out to her now, perhaps she wishes to become the Christian she must if they are to rekindle so much as a nodding acquaintance. This is the trap, he thinks. She is again giving me hope when it is not only my decision but the counsel of Margery, and Peter also, that there is no hope. He continues to pray. Wishes Jesus would pick up. Once more Garth leaves a message on the machine.

Julie Rivington nudges him, she is taking a greater interest in his dissembling behaviour than he thinks she should. He counselled her about the way she should conduct herself with Ronnie, learnt she is yet to kiss with her tongue. Long may it continue. He glances round, people are standing. He has not really been paying attention. 'I greet you in the name of Jesus Christ,' says Julie. A little smirk crosses her face with the words.

'Could you put my guitar in the storeroom please?' It's not the orthodox response, it is all he can manage. He goes straight to the back door. There is a gate from courtyard to side street. Garth will spring the devil's trap.

Wednesday, 14 September 2016

In the second week of term, Ellie Rawlins calls her first team meeting. Garth is beginning to see his manager as a person in her own right, not simply a visual approximation of Lily. He likes her. She has praised his practice, and her boundaries are clear. He and she have personal respect, not personal chemistry. It is exactly what he would have wished for. At the meeting he sits next to Rihanna. They have cemented their bond of friendship. She has agreed to come to Bournemouth next weekend, a visit to the cinema. He read the film review most carefully before proposing such a course of action. They have also agreed not to share this information—the actuality of their first date—across the school site. It might not work out. They each need an escape hatch.

'I don't think he's right for this school,' Ryan is complaining. The current discussion is about a boy who joined the school only eight working days ago. Was unknown to this staff group until then. 'Barry knew he wasn't going to have to deal with him when he accepted the little tyke. It's not your fault, Ellie. You should be with us.'

His assertion, the 'us' that implies the staff group all agree with him, seems to be too much for Rihanna. 'Ryan, we're still getting to know Dean. Figuring what makes him tick. We shouldn't give up on a lad just because he's different. He's not interested in the other boys, and that's like his social report says. Calls him autistic...'

'... and there's special schools for them, isn't there?' Ryan is quite certain Dean is in the wrong place.

'...I was going to say but he's not properly autistic, is he? Eye contact, listening. He's good at all that but incredibly wilful. Won't go to certain classrooms because he hasn't made a good association with them. Hates the art room. Wherever he lives, that is what they'll have to help him overcome, so it might as well be us, here, who sort him out. Kids seldom really need another move, do they? What they need is a bit of understanding.'

Garth finds himself thinking, whether she knows it or not, that Rihanna has a Christian soul. He has gleaned from her that she attends church with her mother now and then; that was a complete surprise to him. She has distinctly never said that she believes in God. Back when they used to spar, disagree, as a kind of intellectual sport, she said it was important that the school professed no religion. 'If we did, we'd be excluding boys who disagreed,' she argued. He thinks her to be very smart indeed, separating her motivation from the detail of the task. Baxter's School is not an evangelical mission. He always agreed with that general assertion and then bored everyone by banging on about his own motivation. He recalls how he spoke to the boys last year about opting for celibacy as a positive choice. He was a fool. He's never going to speak to them about failing to live up to his own expectations. Their lives are on such contrary trajectories to his, it never had meaning beyond giving them a line to tease him with.

When he saw Rihanna in the coffee shop in Winchester—their not-quite-a-date meet-up during the holidays—she told him that the assembly in which he spoke about celibacy had made a lasting impression upon her. She thinks many staff try too hard to impress the boys, counts herself in the number who may have done this. She said that he—Garth—has a message for the boys. He never deviates from it, and for this reason alone it must get through to them. She called it neuro-linguistic programming but he doesn't think that was correct, thinks she over-reached her current knowledge when she deployed that term. He chose to keep silent about her choice of words. No wish to sound critical of her. 'Hey,' she had added, 'your calmness when they kick off is the best. Beats bragging about not shagging. It was ludicrous that Lorimer put you on a disciplinary for the Keane thing. You're Mr Non-Aggression.'

'Thanks,' he replied, and in the spirit of keeping an even relationship with this new friend, being less preachy and irritating than Margery has told him he might have been to Lily, he added, 'I've given up the boasting-about-not-shagging schtick. The kids never bought it anyway.'

'Don't stop on my account,' said Rihanna. And that ambiguous phrase has stuck with Garth. He is trying to forge a closer friendship with her, neither a race to convert her nor to undertake sexual congress. The future cannot be hurried.

'Thank you, Rihanna,' says Ellie, making it clear which side of the debate she is on. 'It is for us to make a strategy to help the boy. If the first one fails, we'll make a second and then a third. It is not in my make-up to give up on children, and I need you all to ride along with me. Do this for Dean.'

Garth's almost-girlfriend is beaming, and he believes that Ellie Rawlins has already figured that he is not one to give up on boys either. He thinks this term is going to be a real advance. Mr Rogers who now works in Wiltshire and Mr Lorimer, the head teacher, are deadweights like Ryan. They, the head and the former deputy, talk a good shop, deep down they occupy important positions with minimal ambition. Ellie is a revolutionary, doing all she can to effect needed change, doing it under Lorimer's nose.

* * *

Later, after the working day has finished, he is alone in the sleeping-in room, reflecting on the evening shift. He and Gerry had to hold a boy. The new boy, Dean. He'd gone crazy when there was a last-minute change to the available evening meal. In fact, it wasn't last minute at all. None of the staff had noticed that the list pinned to the notice board was from the wrong week; the Wednesday choice from week one of the menu plan.

Before they held the boy, he'd turned over a table in the dining room and it had landed on poor Paul Frost's ankle. As the two of them intervened—before Garth had even started the calming words, preparing for release—Gerry did the daftest thing. She whispered to Garth, 'Or should we just defrost a pizza and be done with it.' He'd shushed her and she said no more but it was the most stupid thing to say. Surely Geraldine Hunt, with over ten-years of experience, knows that autistic children can hear every bit as well as non-autistic children. Following strategies is what residential workers do. The hold was unpleasant, restraint always is but it was working. Garth thought that Dean had begun to calm down although Gerry's unhelpful intervention made him start grunting all over again. This is going to be a good term if the staff could all be more like Ellie and Rihanna.

Jesus is still not returning his calls, and Garth is coming to believe that it is the acts of goodness in themselves that are the point to his life. Perhaps uncertainty about which realm beyond awaits us is God's cleverest strategy. It ensures that even the pious relate to other people without condescension. Offer them the love that Jesus intended.

Insecurity is a most humbling state.

Sunday, 25 September 2016

For the second weekend in a row Garth has a date with Rihanna Williams. Peter and Margery have still to learn of the girl's role in his expanding life but they will approve whenever he goes public. Rihanna's mother attends The New Light Church in Winchester, and Rihanna has been there quite a few times. She sits on the fence and doesn't yet profess herself to be a Christian. With Garth and her mother both pushing, she can only fall one way. That she had previously fooled him into believing she was an atheist just shows how skilfully she has avoided mixing the personal and the professional. She is younger than he is by several years. She has told him that her past boyfriends were 'not serious.' He wonders if this means he is the more sexually experienced. If it is so, it is by the smallest degree. The most shameful two minutes of his life.

He is not seeing her until three in the afternoon. On Friday he suggested meeting at this time so that she might still go to her mother's church in the morning. 'Maybe,' she said. He didn't press. May invite her to his own church but not yet. Not for a while. His own decision to excuse himself from today's services, to falsely claim family conflict when advising both Margery and Samantha—she will strum guitar in his stead—is based upon two factors. He feels conflicted when singing in church of a love of Jesus while his mind is focussing itself on a more corporeal soul. He and Jesus need a cooling-off period. He has been the staff member who lectured wayward boys on the wonders of celibacy. For his efforts, Jesus gave him temptations and tests beyond his capacity to resist. He didn't come out of it clean. It may all fall back into place in time but he is through with just thinking on his own. Ambiguous signs have him stuck at a crossroads.

He has chosen to cycle into Bournemouth. He will meet Rihanna at the train station. The weather is good, and they will spend time together, walk along the promenade before sharing an evening meal. He has read about a Caribbean restaurant in town, it seems like the right place. He set off far earlier than required, has chosen to ride a circuitous route, to head for Tuckton, and then cycle along the miles and miles of promenade, east to west until he reaches the central pier. Today is a fine day for it. He likes to cycle along the seafront for no greater reason than the absence of gradient, and the stunning views. Garth feels fitter now than he has ever done. He is cycling to and from work regularly, has done so since Ellie changed his shift pattern. His schedule and Gerry's no longer dovetail. The bus fares are outrageous, so the bike it is. He has learnt to enjoy feeling the power his strengthened limbs give him.

When he is in the vicinity of Southbourne—cycling on the flat promenade, walkers and runners spread thinly, his ride unhampered—he decides to stop and drink in the sight. The blue-green sea; the coastline from Purbeck back to Hengistbury. The Isle of Wight stares back at him, crystal clear in the late-summer sun. He finds a free half-bench, leans his bike against it, and sits a few feet along from a solitary older man. As he turns and examines the pathway behind him, the slope and steps that go up the cliffside, he thinks he has stumbled upon the bottom end of the way up to the Perkin Inn. He and Lily entered the sea here—the first time they ever did so, a little paddling aside—both wearing only underwear. Revealing far more of their physical selves to each other than should occur between an uncommitted couple. If it is a censorious judgement, it is still true. Their behaviour was lewd: just look at where it led them. He hopes in time, and in better circumstances, to share similar intimacies with Rihanna. Commitment first. Marriage! Order in all things. This is not the right place for him to rest, he thinks, the view is fine but the memories are disturbing. He takes his bike back from where it leans. If he arrives in Bournemouth earlier than the girl on whom he has now set his heart, he has the funds to buy himself a coffee. Pass the time there. Garth pedals on.

He recognises the exact features clearly as he approaches Boscombe pier. Sees the area of sand on which Caroline and Lily practiced stretches and press-ups; activities of which, when asked, Rihanna giggled and said, 'I can't be bothered with that.' She is right for him, as Lily never was. He glances across the beach; they are not there. Why should they be? He cycles on. Beyond Boscombe pier. The final leg before Bournemouth.

The promenade is getting busier at this point; lots of day trippers who park in the town centre and walk a mile out either way. He has been on the walkway when it was so crowded, cycling was a hazard. May bank holiday. It isn't that bad today, quite a few but not heaving. There may not be another weekend this sunny for months. A jogger is running ahead of him and he recognises her instantly. She—those same black shorts atop the familiar white legs, bounce of long hair in a single ponytail and a children's rucksack bobbing on her back—won't have seen Garth who is coming up behind her. He is very unsure if he should engage with her. Avoiding her completely has worked thus far. His very determined strategy since his Lily-enticed fall from grace. Then he thinks how wrong it is to be uncivil. He has moved on. He has no desire to tell his ex-girlfriend about Rihanna—to rub her nose in it—but he can conduct himself with Christian courtesy. He should not stop practicing it just because he failed the test the first time. Lily is running a little in front of him. He speeds up his cycling, has determined that he shall speak to her. As he approaches, he thinks suddenly that it would be mortifying to make any kind of accidental physical contact. Injure her as he did when first they met; this simply must not happen. He swings out wide, gives her the widest berth the promenade will accommodate. She is jogging alone and as he passes, he jingles his bell. Ten yards in front of her, he brakes sharply, swings his leg over the crossbar and stands looking towards her. Hands on his handlebars, face set in half a smile. She sees him. He is sure that she sees him, and yet her head goes straight down facing only her shoes. Observing her own running feet. In a couple of seconds, she will be alongside him but he has felt her cold shoulder. She tried to contact him for weeks after he broke it off, she even came looking for him in church. At the time he felt vindicated in his approach. Lily was not in her right mind. Taunted young Julie Rivington, and made her cry. Since that day she has ceased in her pursuit of him; it got something out of her system. He wants to forgive her. It would be the right way to end their association.

'Lily!' he says loudly, brandishing the most conciliatory smile he can muster. She raises her head in a quick movement, directs her running exactly at him, as if she might topple him over. Then, as she swerves past him, her left arm, the nearest, swings a clenched fist into his jaw. He never saw it coming; she punches like a man. He thinks he hears her laugh, a snorted laugh, the type he never liked. And then she has gone, jogging on to Bournemouth. A lady close by on the promenade looks enquiringly at him. Garth waves a hand. 'I know her,' he says, and the woman turns away—walks on—satisfied that this happenstance must justify such an assault. He feels his jaw, nothing broken but he can taste blood in his mouth. And he fears a bruise that will be difficult to explain to Rihanna.

It is juvenile but he can see why she has done it. Punched him as hard as she could. He has not shown her one jot of rapprochement. Ignored her calls, even fled from his own church when she finally came to it. No contact at all since the unfortunate incident in the beach hut. He has been cold. That he has been thinking less harshly towards her, that his thoughts of Rihanna have crowded out some of the more unwelcome recollections—the feelings of lasciviousness certain memories incited—has helped him a lot. That will have been of no use to her. Not seeing as the thoughts were all in his mind. When she was heading his way, the notion came to him that she might still be cross. He never anticipated violence. That was every bit as surprising as their initial collision must have been to her, when his front wheel-nut tore into the back of her calf. He injured her by accident, pure and simple. Lily's fist was more than intentional. She even laughed. He stopped thinking she was abundant with goodness on the day she ensnared him, drew from him the intercourse he will forever regret. He is surprised that her reserves are this low. He finds that he still likes the way she looks while seeing that it is her character he should have understood and rejected before he became so foolishly attached. She is childish, bares grudges. It is a new insight for him that she is this way. He hopes it is not his doing, that this is not a change in her personality that his romantic encounter with her has brought about. Does she fear she may be losing her sensual power? His rejection of her coming so swiftly after her successful seduction. In the very same moment. This idea doesn't quite fly in his mind. It wasn't really like that. It wasn't really like anything that should have happened. He swallowed a sweet without taking a moment to savour it; ran away from whom it was stolen. No word of thanks passed his lips. Forbidden fruit are quite unpleasant, that is all that he has learnt. He never thanked her because he was ashamed, not grateful. With her

Thrice Crowed the Cockerel

experience, she really should have figured that out. His jaw is sore to the back teeth; she packs a mean punch for a skinny one. It crosses his mind that this is term time, and here she is, out running on a Saturday. If Jo-jo and Ami are home alone in front of the television, it would suggest that Lily is losing it completely. No longer the doting mother he has cracked her up to be. All he can do now is pray for her. He will do exactly that this evening, after his date with Rihanna, when he is back home in Northbourne. For the sake of Lily's immortal soul, he will go through those motions. As he dwells on it, his past certainty appears as a child's sandcastle. Insubstantial, his faith made of mist not iron. He knows everything about Jesus, reads the Bible with unwavering regularity, and yet he has come to feel doubt like a thundercloud. His prayers are not being listened to. Perhaps the Lord is giving preference to the communication of others.

Acts of goodness might see him over the line—secure his entry into the kingdom of heaven when this life is no longer his—unless he has fallen short of the mark. He and Lily both banished from that place all for a moment of pointless sin. The misuse of her friend's beach hut.

Freewill is a burden, the consequences of our choices sit beyond our comprehension. It is one long waiting game.

Printed in Great Britain
by Amazon